D1246275

What the critics are saying...

෨

Full Ride

5 Roses "Full Ride is one of the hottest stories that I have ever read... Full Ride is not for the faint of heart, but the connoisseur of domination and submission" ~ *A Romance Review*

"Poignantly soul-wrenching story with masterfully written twists and turns..." ~ *eCataRomance Reviews*

5 Angels "The sex scenes in this are very steamy and amazing." ~ *Fallen Angel Reviews*

"Ms Faulkner's talents are evident when it comes to the erotic scenes of their D/S relationship. Every detail is scintillating." ~*The Romance Readers Connection*

"I so rarely find a book that places its characters in such intimate and vulnerable scenes with grace and believability." ~ *I Just Finished Reading*

Slip Knot

Recommended Read "Gail Faulkner weaves her stories with fascinating plots, wonderfully complicated characters and satisfying sex scenes…Slip Knot is a fascinating erotic thriller…" ~ *Fallen Angel Reviews*

5 *Coffee Cups* "Ms Faulkner immediately pulls you into the story, both with eroticism and suspense." ~ *Coffee Time Romance*

5 *Roses* "Gail Faulkner reins as one of the hottest writers I have had the pleasure to read. Not only do her stores have steam, but also they have an intricately webbed plot." ~ *A Romance Review*

GAIL FAULKNER

ELLORA'S CAVE
ROMANTICA PUBLISHING

An Ellora's Cave Romantica Publication

www.ellorascave.com

Knot Tonight

ISBN 141995489X
ALL RIGHTS RESERVED.
Full Ride Copyright © 2005 Gail Faulkner
Slip Knot Copyright© 2005 Gail Faulkner
Edited by Mary Moran
Cover art by Syneca

Trade paperback Publication October 2006

Excerpt from *Jamies Cherub* Copyright © Gail Faulkner, 2005

Excerpt from *Blackwind: Sean and Bronwyn* Copyright © Charlotte Boyett-Compo, 2005

With the exception of quotes used in reviews, this book may not be reproduced or used in whole or in part by any means existing without written permission from the publisher, Ellora's Cave Publishing, Inc.® 1056 Home Avenue, Akron OH 44310-3502.

This book is a work of fiction and any resemblance to persons, living or dead, or places, events or locales is purely coincidental. The characters are productions of the authors' imagination and used fictitiously.

Warning:

The following material contains graphic sexual content meant for mature readers. This story has been rated E–rotic by a minimum of three independent reviewers.

Ellora's Cave Publishing offers three levels of Romantica™ reading entertainment: S (S-ensuous), E (E-rotic), and X (X-treme).

S-*ensuous* love scenes are explicit and leave nothing to the imagination.

E-*rotic* love scenes are explicit, leave nothing to the imagination, and are high in volume per the overall word count. In addition, some E-rated titles might contain fantasy material that some readers find objectionable, such as bondage, submission, same sex encounters, forced seductions, and so forth. E-rated titles are the most graphic titles we carry; it is common, for instance, for an author to use words such as "fucking", "cock", "pussy", and such within their work of literature.

X-*treme* titles differ from E-rated titles only in plot premise and storyline execution. Unlike E-rated titles, stories designated with the letter X tend to contain controversial subject matter not for the faint of heart.

Contents

Also by Gail Faulkner

Romeo

Jamie's Cherub

Darius

About the Author

∞

Hello everyone. If you're reading this, I hope it means you've enjoyed reading one of my books. If you have some other opinion of them, feel free to lie to me anyway. I hereby absolve you from all possible guilt and consequences for flagrant, adjective, saturated lying to the author.

I'm a chronic fantasizer. Every good romance novel ended too soon. After a while, I started making up stories when I had a few minutes to while away. So now, instead of sitting around with a blank look on my face, I've taken to writing them down.

Because of my father's job, we moved every three years in my early life. My first memories are of Bermuda, and then we were in several African countries. It was a wonderful childhood. I gained a rich cultural background in the world community, but never learned to spell. As an adult, I avoided writing at all costs, embarrassed over my limitations.

But the writer will not stay silent forever. She broke out, and insisted on learning the mystical world of grammar and spelling. Haven't mastered all of it yet, but they let me write for you anyway. Bless every editor on the planet. They give dreamers a place to send fantasies and save us the embarrassment of owning our shortcomings.

Gail welcomes comments from readers. You can find her website and email address on her author bio page at www.ellorascave.com.

FULL RIDE

ॐ

Dedication

℘

Warm gratitude and thanks to Allen, Char and Patti.
Mary, you believed, thank you.

Trademarks Acknowledgement

The author acknowledges the trademarked status and trademark owners of the following wordmarks mentioned in this work of fiction:

Mercedes E Class: Daimler-Benz Aktiengesellschaft Corporation

Jell-O: Kraft Foods Holdings, Inc.

Chapter One

ഌ

Prin almost staggered in shock as she stepped into the room and saw the man who faced her. This was not what she'd expected! That familiar visage was one she knew well, yet not at all. His aura of power and domination overwhelmed her, just as it always did in her dreams. Logic insisted this could not be the dark warrior from her nightly journeys into submission. Every other sense insisted that it was.

He stalked silently across the plush carpet to circle behind her. Cool eyes inspected her, as she stood in the required stance, naked. After Prin removed her only garment, a coat, she stood before him with her legs spread wide, elbows behind her back clutched together, her chin lifted, eyes lowered submissively. Coldly, his eyes moved down her back, to the slope of her flanks, slowly they traveled over lightly muscled legs to slender ankles above elegantly arched feet in five-inch heels.

A mirrored wall allowed her to see his hand swing back. It cracked loudly on her bare backside before she had time to brace herself.

"Present yourself, bitch. Bend over. Grab your knees and spread wider," his deep voice barked at her. Commands came in swift succession as she staggered inelegantly.

"More! Arch your back. I want cunt and ass on display." He stepped back as she adjusted herself, steely eyes locked on private flesh.

That smack fired right through her like a bullet. It pitched her headlong from panicky and shocked to intense arousal. His demands effectively focused her entire attention onto the shameful submission he required.

With an arrogant grunt, the dark stranger turned and walked back to the bar. She heard ice tinkle into a glass then a soft splash as liquid flowed over it. Bent this way, Prin could no longer watch him in the mirror. Still, she felt him return to her like an aggressive force of nature. His breathing was deep and even as he came to a stop behind her. Time dragged while he examined her fully exposed rear end. It was a leisurely scrutiny of everything normally hidden from the world.

Feverish heat swept up her body while she waited. Her utter vulnerability to him in this stance intensified with every moment on display. Her flesh prickled in humiliation while this stranger stared at her. The naughty thrill of being looked at like this vibrated down her body.

The shapely globes of her bottom stretched wide to showcase that innocently clenched hole between them. Her cunt, pulled open by the extreme arch of her back, was swollen in obvious excitement. His gaze tracked up the damp folds and he could see the protrusion of her clit as it begged for his attention. Luscious breasts were clearly visible between her legs, mounds of soft temptation that rocked gently with her every pant. She made a perfectly lovely, carnal picture.

Prin's legs trembled as sweat bloomed across her entire body. It wasn't all fear, but most of it was. Moisture began to trickle down her exposed inner thighs in shameful testimony to her excitement. The stranger, what he made her feel, the strain of presenting for him, it all came together in a decadent mix of fear, wicked anticipation and humiliation. It created a smoldering concoction of emotions too long absent from her life. Evidently, one could not get over the need for this.

Time hadn't dimmed the wicked cravings. She wasn't sure anything could.

She'd tried. Oh, how she'd tried. After Kurt's death, Prin was convinced she could shut the door on that portion of her life. Be a "normal" person. Ha! Four long years of wanting, denying, refusing to face it brought her to this place. Naked.

Perched on high heels, bent over and spread as wide as possible for a stranger.

* * * * *

Prin had been somewhat overwhelmed ever since Dave handed her the key-card in the car after casually telling her they were going to the Grand Hotel. Her Dom was waiting for her in the Presidential Suite on the top floor.

Automatically taking the key-card she questioned, "Are you sure about this?"

Dave chuckled and glanced at her. "Oh, yeah. Our boy does it right, babe. I wouldn't let you near a loser, Prin."

"But the Grand is the most expensive place in town!" she exclaimed, her tone turned suspicious. "You didn't tell him to take me here, did you, Dave?"

Dave laughed outright at that. "No, it was all his idea. I got my instructions just like you did." He chuckled again then took pity on her. "He's in town on business, Prin. It's where he regularly stays. Don't worry about it. He didn't put himself out."

When Prin stepped into the Presidential Suite, she froze. It was *her dream Dom*. How could it be him? Shock slammed into her and shattered all the giddy anticipation that enabled her to actually go through with this.

He leaned against the bar across the room, obviously waiting and somewhat irritated. Gleaming brass and mahogany framed the grim warrior who'd haunted her dreams for the last twenty-four months. She stared at him blankly and absorbed the crash of reality doing a head-on collision with fantasy. Her mind whirred feverishly trying to explain this. Nada. Nothing. Total shutdown loomed when the reason she'd come there flashed back to her. Frantic to deny the fantasy part of this, she snapped out of the shock.

To cover her bewilderment, Prin swiftly followed the contract's instructions for entrance into his domain. He couldn't possibly be the man from her dreams! That was even crazier than agreeing to this hedonistic night in the first place.

The man before her stood at least six-foot-four. His intense face was not "pretty boy" good-looking. More like "Oh, damn, I'm wet!" good-looking. A compelling face you wanted to keep looking at but didn't because he might catch you staring.

His glossy black hair was a little too long. His silver-blue eyes were much too intimidating and disturbingly cool in their intensity. They were startling against his dark coloring. His cheekbones were prominent, as was his nose. The sculpted lips were neither too thick nor too thin. His height made him just a bit frightening. A heavy layer of muscle and the obvious confidence were just overkill as far as Prin was concerned. All those features put together told her of the fierce Native Americans who resided within his family tree. They made up a face dipped in sin and washed by the sun.

Her current situation was rudely brought back into focus as he slid the ice-cold glass down her spine. It glided between the globes of her ass until he held it upright, pressed against her tight rear entrance.

"You're aware I'll use every hole." It wasn't a question. The deep rumble of his voice was calm, almost musing. "The agreement you signed clearly stated that. I want to be sure you understand. There are no safe words. You have given me ownership of this body, and I will control it until the agreed end-time. I know what I am doing. I know what you can take. I'll know if it's too much."

The glass moved away from her quivering flesh as he took a drink then set it down. Remaining silent, Prin stared down at the thick carpet. It was part of the agreement. As soon as she stepped through that double door, she became his to command. No talking without permission, no nothing without permission.

One long masculine finger snaked out to hook a swollen cunt lip. That rough digit held damp flesh exposed a drawn-out moment. Moving around to her side, he clamped a forefinger and thumb onto her distended nipple in a hard grip. Firm fingers manipulated her breast simply to watch soft flesh jiggle lewdly. The large hand opened abruptly to engulf her breast as he enjoyed how it overflowed his big paw, how it pressed out between dark fingers as he squeezed roughly.

Her nervous panting was the only sound in the room while he handled her like a piece of meat. This examination made her feel as if she were standing on an auction block for public viewing. In a way she was. He could reject her at any time. That was also part of the contract. If she displeased him in any way, he could send her away. No questions, no explanations, no arguments.

Feeling scrutinized like an item up for sale was new for Prin. Was it intentional? Did he know how this affected her?

* * * * *

It was *Her*! Shock overwhelmed him as she'd stepped into the room. This living, breathing woman was *His Dream Angel*. Lounging against the bar as she entered saved him the humiliation of sinking to his knees in stunned disbelief.

As ordered, she'd arrived exactly on time in a trench coat and heels. Looking up at him, her lovely face seemed to be all big brown eyes. Behind her, masses of rippling strawberry-blonde hair streamed down her back. The two of them had stared at each other for almost a full minute after the door clicked shut behind her. Neither moved until she stripped off the coat and laid it over the back of a chair. Just as he'd mandated in the contract, she wore nothing under that coat.

Dream Angel was five-foot-seven, with a familiar oval face. Her large eyes were slightly tilted and the color of warm chocolate. The luminous skin was pale cream that looked like silk. Her nose was slender and straight. Those lips were full and softly expressive. Damn! She wasn't what he'd expected. This exquisite woman had been made for sin.

It was a good thing she'd snapped out of their mutual stare first and followed her instructions. He'd been too astonished to move. Then that delectable body went on display and he'd been unable to stand still. His struggle for composure became monumental as he now moved around her. This inspection of the curvy body that trembled and gushed at his every touch stretched his self-control to torturous limits.

Anxious to think of a way to regroup after the shock of seeing her, he returned to the bar as soon as possible. Getting a drink was an attempt to calm down. He was desperate for a chance to look at something other than her spectacular body.

Breathe, idiot! his brain hissed at him. *Just take deep breaths and think of baseball.* Squeezing his eyes shut the moment his back was to her didn't help. That sensuous body was burned into his eyelids. He could barely remember what baseball was. Every glorious inch of her trembled and glowed like a vision that wouldn't fade.

He'd dreamed of this woman for what seemed like his entire life. Each feature, right down to the delicate facial bone structure was made for his pleasure. She embodied the perfect figment of the male imagination that showed up for every jack-off session since the age of twelve. Most guys used any number of visuals but he'd only used one. His entire life there had been only one face in his mind. This was HIS woman!

Recently, twenty-four months ago to be exact, she'd become so much more. Exploring her in his mind kept him sane like nothing else could. Defining their relationship in intimate detail was his only escape from the endless, grinding pain. Dream Angel became more real than the utter hell he'd endured. She made it possible to drift away when reality wasn't worth living anymore.

Dream Walking is a handy talent when you're locked up in the armpit of the world. The practice of Dream Walking among The Nations was a loosely held secret. Most people believe Peyote rituals are required to walk with spirits. That mistaken conviction shields numerous unexplainable events. Grandfather once told him Dream Walking would save his life. He'd not thought about the gloomy statement. Not until he needed his Dream Angel to survive.

His last mission went "bad" in a big way. He'd acquired the hostage. However, in doing so had stumbled into a meeting of two terrorist organizations. It wasn't just the local yahoos, but highly trained guerrilla forces present when he went in. He'd delivered the hostage to the extraction point, but for the rescue to succeed he'd remained to lay down cover fire. Hence, some really pissed off psychopaths acquired him.

His life then became the source of fierce competition between the two terrorist leaders. They passed him back and forth each month. Several high-stakes bets rode on which faction would break him first. These were very creative individuals when it came to torture. His death would lose the bet for whoever caused it, so they'd been careful not to kill him. The big mistake was assuming that since he was captured alone and the government wasn't actively negotiating, nobody was coming.

At one point during a Dream Walk, he'd decided to remain in his Dream Angel's arms. He planned to just stay with her until there was nothing more. She wouldn't let him, and gently breathed life back into him with her words. She fed her spirit into an almost dead will to survive. Dream Angel demanded he believe in hope. As it turned out, rescue came a week later.

It required a clenched jaw and gritted teeth to keep from sucking wind at the astonishing sight of his Dream Angel in the flesh. Years of concentrated endurance training kept his facial muscles immobile as she moved to her required position. Mostly the hours of torture endurance did it for him. Nothing else even came close to the self-control required to dominate her as she needed right now.

That brought him smack up against his most pressing problem. How was he going to alter the deal? Now this venue restricted him. Now that it was *her*. This wasn't how he wanted to start with her. For her, he was perfectly willing to fall on his knees and beg her to teach him. Teach him her touch, her smell, her essence. Teach him the ways to make her smile, how to know when she was sad. Show him the things he needed to know to memorize her soul. A steady stream of expletives spiraled in his head. Damn that airtight contract he'd both written and signed.

How was he supposed to comply with that contract when the other half of his soul had just walked through the door? Not some stranger! The contract gave him this one night. Only this night, governed by the rules they'd both agreed to. Then it ripped her away from him. There was no margin for error. No time to move cautiously into a relationship. He had to find a way to reach into her and touch her from the inside out. Show her she was already the air he breathed. Well, hell. How he'd get around it wasn't clear right now. Nonetheless, the ability to alter a plan in a fluid situation kept him and his kind alive a long time. Another talent passed down from a people who had refused to be cornered or contained.

He needed to wrap his mind around the reality of this woman immediately. The fact that he'd stumbled onto the only lover who could complete him was hard to believe. He'd never dreamed that she could be alive in his time. For about two seconds he contemplated asking her to trash the contract and start over. The problem was, doing so released her to walk out the door, if she wanted to. No. No. Wait. This could work. The contract restricted him, but it also controlled her. He could do this! His first priority had to be binding her to him. The Dom/sub relationship was actually a pretty effective way to demonstrate how completely they belonged together. Besides, just looking at her sucked the air from his lungs, he knew in that moment that he could not, would not, let her go.

Her breasts were large enough to rest on her slender rib cage when she stood tall and proud. Tipped with rosebud nipples blushed a deep pink. Dream Angel's waist nipped in above a gently rounded tummy. Enchanting hips flared out to perfectly balance those magnificent breasts. Her cunt was smooth and naked. It glowed damply with silky moisture.

He'd never seen anything so perfectly beautiful and yet sinful. His stomach cramped as he examined her. How could this woman possibly be unclaimed? Was every damned man in the upper Midwest blind and stupid?? Evidently, thank God. One thing was certain. She was claimed now! She just didn't know it yet.

Right now, he'd like to know why the hell Dave hadn't introduced them in a "normal" situation. Good old Dave, who talked him into this, was due for a long chat.

Well aware of the base beast awakened within him, he already knew it was a possessive, obsessive snarling monster with only one mate. He'd found her. Every male molecule in his body rose up and demanded that he take her, NOW!!

It had started so casually. Dave brought up a familiar subject during a friendly game of golf. Dave knew his preferences where women were concerned having been his college roommate. However, the conversation came with a twist and a request. He'd said "No", to begin with. Then, "Hell, no!"

It was about spending one night with a submissive woman Dave knew. It was risky. The Dom/sub relationship was too involved for just one night. He wasn't looking to "test drive a used car". However, a brand new one was usually disappointing. Besides, he wasn't looking, period. Dave nodded sagely at this bit of "male speak", understanding completely.

Dave then continued with his argument and insisted she really was a sub, one who knew the life. Not some rookie experimenting. Good old Dave ignored the whole "test drive" portion of the decline. Dave described her as gorgeous. She was a widow whose husband, her Dom, had died. She wasn't looking for a relationship. All she wanted was one night of submission. She wanted no expectations from either of them beyond that one night together. No names. No commitments.

She didn't know who he was. She didn't want him to know her name. No other information but vital stats. Everything sounded great at the time. When Dave told him her measurements, he hadn't believed them. In fact, he decided that if half of what Dave said about her was accurate, she was too good to be true.

Oh, hell, yes! his internal beast bellowed. This woman was everything promised and more. Being in excellent shape was a safety measure when you looked at her. It made one wonder what her husband died from. On second thought, it was a good thing that guy was gone. The situation could have gotten ugly abruptly if he'd met her on the arm of another man. All right, that was something not to be thought about again. Ever! Intense, irrational rage flash-flooded his system at the thought of her belonging to another man. Rage was not a useful emotion. It made a man do stupid things.

Right now, coherent thought eluded him though. It could be a question of which head was in control. *Okay, down boy. She's here.* She'd never done this before according to Dave. She sure wasn't going to do it again. Not with someone else, that is.

Get a grip, man! Damn good idea his beast agreed.

His hand stroked down past her blushing ass cheek. Two fingers traced through the liquid hunger that graced her inner thighs. He drew in a deep breath and her scent went straight to his dick. The magnificent body before him quivered as his fingers bypassed the soft, swollen petals of her cunt this time. More liquid slid out of her as he watched her cunt contract and release in excitement.

Her responsiveness was as overwhelming as was everything about her. He struggled to maintain the cold, aloof Dom she'd asked for. It hadn't been a problem before tonight. Being a Dom was the natural expression of his aggressive, protective, assertive personality. He'd never even considered another way to express himself sexually. However, this woman made him a man who wanted *her* more than he wanted to dominate her. The unfamiliar ground he now stood on was about like walking across a minefield. One wrong step and he'd lose her.

This woman's need and hunger leapt at him off the questionnaire he'd insisted she fill out. On paper, she was open, a little shy, but seemed honest. He'd studied between the lines carefully. Her response on paper could have been a deal breaker. If he'd sensed, just one time, that she was not being straight with him, it would have been over before any meeting occurred.

What he'd seen on paper actually made him hard. She'd even mentioned dreams briefly. It was in her response to the question about why she needed this. When he saw her answer, the hair on the back of his neck stood up. Really. That answer alone had brought him here.

I have a repeated dream that I must escape. He is a dark Dom who I feel will not leave me until I have lived what he wants me to feel, she wrote. That cloudy statement with its murky meaning hooked him, at the same time it chilled him.

The questionnaire didn't included questions about dreams. How often were they? Had she ever Dream Walked before? He needed answers to all those things, but those answers would wait. Having her in front of him right now took up all the space in his blood-starved brain.

He picked up the tube of lubricant from the coffee table as he walked around behind her. Reaching down, he pulled her ass cheeks apart rudely and inserted the tube in her tiny rear hole. Insistent fingers squeezed the cold slippery invader into that constricted orifice. She jerked at the rough handling, but steadied herself quickly. Easing the tube out of her, he rapidly applied a line of lubricant down his two middle fingers and tossed the tube on the floor in front of her. Taking hold of her hip firmly and using his thumb to pull her ass back open, he pressed one large finger against her tight opening.

"Now breathe deeply. Relax and push back." His finger pressed in and she tightened around it.

"If you don't relax, it will hurt more, pet. Either way the plug is going in." He barely managed the harsh tone while watching his finger sink into her ass down to the first knuckle. A streak of lightning zipped up his balls as he attended to the wicked invasion.

He paused and permitted her to catch her breath. When she'd relaxed enough to be unsuspecting, he sharply pressed all the way in. Her tight, hot ass squeezed down on that invader as it forced untouched tissue to separate and admit him. More cream slid down her leg as her vagina clenched in desperate spasms. That physical reaction told him all he needed to know. She wanted this.

Prin gasped loudly at the intrusion as the dangerous stranger behind her chuckled. Panting hard and trembling from head to toe, Prin tried to relax while his finger worked its way slowly out then back in again with a hard push. She gulped air harshly when he repeated the motions more swiftly this time.

He was glad she couldn't see his face as he pressed that digit into her. The grimace would have frightened her as he struggled to control the powerful impulse to take what was his.

Her ass was on fire! It was a fire burned through with secret pleasure. She knew it was depraved to enjoy a man doing this to her. Somewhere in her foggy brain, a stuffy puritan screamed at her. She couldn't focus on that right now. Well, she couldn't focus on anything right now. All normal functions ceased as this new, potent brew of sensations and emotions ripped through her being.

When her knees started to buckle, his other arm snaked around her hips.

"Oh, no, you don't," he crooned, and dragged her staggering body backwards against him into the bedroom. His finger remained rammed in to the hilt as he shoved her up onto the bed.

The bedroom was palatial. It easily housed the California king-sized bed that was draped in a burgundy spread. All she could see of the room was that spread as he deposited her on it.

"Kneel. Head down," he commanded in staccato instructions. She quickly struggled to obey without dislodging the finger up her ass.

Her knees spread wide as she perched on the edge of the bed. Calves and feet dangled out into space while her face was buried in the spread. Clutching the bedding, Prin braced for his demanding use of her body.

Moving between her knees, he firmly gripped the rounded flesh presented to him and added another finger slicing into her. He plunged in steadily. Twisting the fingers as he withdrew, he never crossed the line into pure pain. Almost methodically, he administered the finger-fucking to her ass. Undeniably ensuring her submission by increasing the intensity as swiftly as she could take it.

The carnal insistence of his movements stated ownership. This was preparation. Her, for his use. He wouldn't damage her, but he would use her as he pleased. This complete domination fed every shameful, secret desire buried deep within her. He dragged the nasty whore up from her shadowy hiding place with each thrust of those appalling fingers. His total control was her guilty pleasure. It immersed her soul in this consuming, shattering experience that imposed submission in every way.

Burning pain overlaid with unimaginable excitement held her in its clutches. How she needed this! Shock, coupled with carnal fire affected her like a drug to enhance the pleasure into a spinning mass of mind-altering sensations. Her world narrowed to just her body, deliriously soaking up every decadent reaction. This ominous, demanding stranger allowed her to revel in the whore he made of her. Her cunt now felt empty and hungry. Without thought, the needy whore strained her back painfully, trying to present it to him.

Gasps and moans escaped her mouth every time he plunged those two fingers into her sizzling ass. Suddenly three fingers slid into her, stretching her. The words just fell out of her mouth as her body absorbed this new assault.

"Oh, please, please. I can't take it! You're killing me! Please…" she shrieked as his other hand landed sharply on her bottom and a new fire exploded up her spine. The fingers inside her paused and then ruthlessly spread out as wide as possible to stretch her. Never had she felt more possessed, more dominated, more owned than at this moment with this man.

Her entire world was swiftly, expertly, ripped away from her. Her total self subjugated in a way that allowed no memories of past lovers. He permitted no thoughts outside his complete control of her. He'd intentionally focused every shred of her consciousness on his possession of her. There could be nothing but him. Nothing but what he demanded she feel. He'd spread her out and taken what he wanted with no preliminaries. Straight to her deepest fear, her most shameful fantasy, he owned it.

Fear rocked her, but it wasn't fear of him, it was her own horrifying reactions to him. Submission was supposed to be something she enjoyed but could give up. This one night she intended to be her last venture into that world. She'd agreed to this because of the dreams, because of her need to escape. She'd deluded herself into thinking this would be a night of a little naughtiness, but mostly just entertainment.

Regardless of all the posturing on paper prior to this encounter, who would have believed that the personification of male Domination lived in one man? He didn't ask. He took everything. There would be no warming up to his desires. He expected her to take him when he wanted it, and how he wanted it. His abrupt intrusion into her virgin ass had decisively driven all prior experiences from her mind. It was a statement and a test. He stated his ownership while testing her willingness to comply.

Her cunt oozed its silky essence. Engorged and flushed, it quivered with intense excitement and proclaimed her body's need of him. His expression turned feral as he surveyed her swollen clit and wet cunt.

"Calm down, Baby Girl. That's it," his voice soothed while she regained composure. His unwavering gaze enjoyed the picture she made, spread before him with three fingers jammed up her newly deflowered back hole. Her whole body quaked with fine tremors that she couldn't control. God, she was beautiful.

If there'd been any hint that she didn't want this, wasn't eating it up, he would have gathered her up into his arms and just held her the rest of the night. His pleasure would be the gentle worship of her body. To that end, he'd lick every inch of it reverently, and suck on the tender bits until she literally floated on a cloud of ecstasy.

Dream Angel's naked little cunt was swollen and slathered with her excitement. Her impaled ass was shyly pushing back onto his fingers. He could feel her press into each nasty invasion. He smiled darkly. Baby Girl liked the razor-edge of pain with her pleasure. It wasn't such a bad thing that they started out here. Sexually, it put all the cards on the table.

Her surrender of dignity and control stroked his inner beast. Deep down, in a place she probably didn't even know existed, she knew she was safe with him. He'd intentionally gone right to the one thing she'd never done. It was necessary to get her absolute surrender fast. If she could do this, she would soon be totally immersed in what they were together. Her focus on his possession of her, his complete control of her pleasure was the only plan he'd come up with to tie her to him immediately.

"Now, then," he murmured quietly when he knew she could hear him. "That was quite a fit. Don't think we won't address it later, my lovely little whore. For right now you have one job, don't move. Do you understand your instruction?" he demanded when she didn't respond immediately.

She swallowed loudly and nodded. Speaking again seemed unwise. Prin's eyes closed tightly, she waited for whatever was next. Oh, God, what had she done? What did "addressing it later" mean? The possibilities loomed large as the fire from that one spank still ate at her ass. The terms of the agreement flickered in her mind. Its ironclad demands for total submission could not have been made any clearer, including speaking only when given permission.

Chapter Two

∞

It started when her best friend Marisa suggested a solution to Prin's sleeping problem.

No, it started with those damn dreams! Whenever it started, she didn't have the time or desire to find a Dom. It was just too much trouble, and way too risky. There were so many "wannabes" out there. Besides, no one could replace Kurt. She couldn't even imagine finding that again.

Kurt hadn't been so much a true Dom, as he was an inventive, loving playmate. He enjoyed the Domination/submission sessions, but it wasn't their lifestyle. Her submission was an addictive, exciting game they played often, but he never pushed her like he could have. Perhaps he didn't even know how much more she wanted. It was too late now.

Now she woke up trembling and crying every night. It wasn't the sharp pain of losing your lover anymore. No. Utter sexual frustration was the cunt-cramping pain that now tormented her nights.

About two years after Kurt died, she started having dreams about a dark lover. His face was cloaked in shadows — only pale, piercing eyes watching her were always clearly visible. They looked into her soul and demanded her submission as he took her repeatedly. He was so large, so wicked and *so dominant*.

In her dreams, he'd taken her in ways Kurt never had. The mysterious Dom made her feel things that should have been new. His demands on her body should have been wrong, too much, but they weren't. She'd wanted every minute of his domination. Her body would be bathed in sweat as her dripping cunt pulsed in empty desperation when she awakened.

Her dreams were vivid, so wrenchingly real that she started to avoid sleep. If she got tired enough, perhaps he wouldn't come to her. She wanted to get over it, or him, or whatever the hell he represented in her twisted subconscious.

He kept coming for her. Sometimes he just held her, but he was still there. When he was gentle like that, it affected Prin even more. Making her long for someone who didn't even exist. He drove her to question her grip on reality. *How could you want a dream lover to the exclusion of everyone else?* People were put away for this sort of thing.

Her best friend noticed her frazzled condition and demanded to know why. Marisa would not be stopped when she got her teeth into something. She badgered and hounded an already exhausted Prin until Prin told all.

Marisa told her husband Dave about Prin's dreams and how she couldn't escape them. They reasoned a safe encounter with someone who could be trusted might help. Dave suggested a Dom he knew.

Prin immediately said, "Hell, no! Not in this lifetime."

Two months later Marisa insisted on telling Prin all about this guy Dave knew. He was the image of the dream lover Prin had described. He wasn't looking for a relationship. He wouldn't want anything else from her. Dave had known him for years and he was safe, not a whacko. Besides, Prin had started to look like week-old shit.

In an attempt to put Marisa off, Prin came up with a long list of rules for any hypothetical encounter. No names, no personal info, no contact before or after the one night at a hotel. He couldn't live locally. There had to be no possibility that they'd ever meet again socially. He must allow her to leave first, and he could not be someone Kurt had known.

Prin was sure no sensible Dom would accept that from a sub. Not for just one night, sight unseen. Prin stopped worrying about it, reasonably secure in a forthcoming negative response.

Three months after she'd sent him off with her list of requirements, Dave handed her a written contract. A very detailed questionnaire accompanied the contract. Prin was instructed to answer it and return it to Dave, who would return it to the Dom. Apparently Marisa and Dave were working together, Prin registered with disgust. They worried about her total lack of interest in men since her husband died. However, with a dream lover like hers, who had the time?

This "wonder" Dom of theirs had signed one contract and she was supposed to sign the other one. Dave would retain both signed contracts so neither party got a peek at the other's name.

The long document listed his requirements as well as hers. It explained how to prepare herself in intimate detail. She blushed wildly and became incredibly wet as she read those instructions. The contract told her how to be clothed for him, what to do when she entered the hotel room, etc.

Several arguments compelled her into this trek down the yellow brick road. One was her extremely high safety level. Her best friends knew where she would be and with whom. The insidious temptation grew with each supposed safeguard. Just one more taste of the wicked pleasure submission brought her. Perhaps the dreams were her subconscious demanding just a little bit more of the fire and pleasure. Maybe if she could take her need to submit and fulfill it completely, then it would fade.

Dave was to drop her off and pick her up. She would not have agreed to this without someone being there directly after the night. It discouraged unwanted physical abuse. The possibility of just one night with a reasonable substitute of her dream lover became too seductive to pass up. At the very least, she would end up with a bit of relief from the relentless ache between her legs. Add to that the possibility of a good night's sleep afterwards, and the idea was downright irresistible.

Her present situation could not claim even a speaking acquaintance with safe. This dangerous man inflamed her lusts in ways that only one other had before. His intoxicating domination flowed over her like a tidal wave of depraved pleasures. Oh, God! Could her dream lover be real? NO! Slamming the door on that intensely disturbing thought, Prin struggled to focus on her instructions.

His fingers closed and carefully withdrew from her tender opening. Immediately, her ass was stretched open over a hard object. He slowly pressed the plug in. Panic filled her as she felt it spread her to new limits. He just kept pushing it in. She couldn't hold back a startled yelp as the wide base was forced past her tight ring of muscle. Her protesting bottom closed around the object and locked it into place.

Her back arched uncontrollably as she strangled on her moans while wave after wave of pleasure and pain radiated from her stressed rear. Nothing prepared her for this. Her body writhed helplessly through the intense sensations.

The visible end of the modified plug had a valve on its flat head with a hose and squeeze bladder attached. He immediately pumped the air bladder, which inflated the dildo inside her. His heavy hand on the small of her back held her down as she arched and thrashed on the object that impaled her. He'd given her no time to assimilate its intrusion before increasing its size. She felt it expand inside her. Filling her. The rude intrusion shot a haze of agonized lust up her spine like liquid lightning.

"This plug expands about two inches around, and is nine inches long. Not quite me, but close enough. We're not going to inflate it fully right now. We'll do it a bit at a time through the night until I feel you're ready," he explained in a decisive, cold voice.

She barely heard his quiet comments as he adjusted the plug. Prin squeezed her eyes shut and panted through the burn, frantically trying to calm down. The evil thing got bigger?? When she regained a shaky control of her limbs he moved back, leaving the tail of the little hose and bladder hanging down between her legs.

To see her like this pleased the beast in him that demanded dominance over its mate. He took a deep breath and allowed the sight to blaze into his memory. Her complete surrender had driven him into a white-hot fever of need. Every inch of him ached. His balls were drawn up tight against his cock and were probably blue already. Time to get some relief for the length of pig iron that used to be his cock.

"All right, pet. Stand up and turn around," he instructed softly.

She gingerly backed off the bed and turned around. Shakily she assumed the first position of standing with legs spread and hands clasped behind her back, head up and eyes down.

The bedroom vibrated with waves of sensuality that rippled off both of them. Decorated in burgundy, black and gold, their surroundings soaked up the ragged energy and wrapped it back around them in a velvet cloak of dark desire.

Before he could take her, he needed her to see *him*. Why he needed this was way too complicated to figure out right now. It had to do with her acceptance and total surrender freely given. With letting her know he was willing to give up the same dignity to her that he demanded from her. It wasn't a one-way deal between them. He wanted her to know that what he took from her would be returned tenfold. He only took what she required him to, what she needed to feel safe in his care. Well, whatever it was, it rode him hard. It forced him to take the time now and show her what was going to have her. Even if what she saw disgusted her, he knew he'd take her anyway.

"Look at me, pet." His voice was gravelly and rough with need.

Glazed eyes swept slowly up his body to meet those white-hot pale eyes.

His smile seemed more of a grimace as his hands went to the buttons of the crisp cotton shirt.

"Watch me," he murmured. Baby Girl was *so* far past the point of no return with him, but could she step through this door? For some damn reason he needed to know right now. Fucking irrational, really.

Buttons slipped loose and the shirt fell to reveal an endless expanse of chest and abdomen. The temptation to run her hands across that steely width was tough to resist. A light cover of silky dark hair swept across his upper chest and trailed—like the road to ruin—in a tempting arrow down into his low-riding jeans. It only partly concealed the numerous jagged scars slashed into his corded flesh.

Prin gasped. What happened to him?

As she took in the muscled pecs and washboard abs, his hands swiftly went to the snap on his jeans. Lowering the zipper with caution over steel-hard flesh that was pressed so impatiently against it, he bent to shuck his pants. He took off his socks and shoes in the same movement. Rising slowly, he stood naked before her. Hard. Waiting.

Her eyes traveled over every visible inch of him, and there was a lot. His torso held scars and marks that were still pale and shiny, declaring their newness, as well as old ones that were faded. In places, the flesh was twisted and bumpy, others looked like rippled burn marks. Some of those wicked scars wrapped around his torso. She suspected there were more down his back.

Along his upper thighs, in that crease of tender flesh between each hip and leg was a row of small round burn marks, about the size of a cigar butt. Air sucked in between her teeth as realization struck her.

The package between his legs was as fierce as the rest of him. His erection was long and thick. The fat head flared out, the eye in the middle seeped a drop of pre-cum for her. His testicles, which hung heavily behind his cock, were in proportion to the rest of his overwhelming size. Everything about this man was large.

Her eyes flashed up to his as he stood there before her and watched her look at him. He waited, his face immobile, those intense eyes tracked her every expression.

Prin blinked rapidly. Each scar, a story of pain and torture written clearly across his bronze body, stabbed at her. Biting her lip, she searched his eyes. What did he want? What was he waiting for? It was clear from his command to "look at him" and then undressing that he expected something from her.

The rules forbade her from reaching for him. Her body trembled with the desire to rush to him and explore each mark with her tongue, lips and hands. She needed the emotional relief of soothing, petting and holding him. That need was a primal scream in her brain. Why this man moved her on this level mystified her. It wasn't just that he personified "magnificent" in the physical sense. Something about him reached right into her heart and mind.

The large inflexible warrior took a deep, ragged breath, and then reached for a leather slave hood on the dresser. Made to fit over a sub's head, it covered the eyes, yet left the mouth and chin free, and snapped around the neck.

"Now that you've seen the monster, you won't have to look anymore, baby," he murmured as he raised the hood to slip it over her head.

Her hands flashed out to stop him.

"Please, Master. Permission to speak." Her eyes locked with his as a muscle ticked along his jaw. One eyebrow rose, which informed her that he'd noted both her hands stopping him and the talking without permission.

"I am not your Master. Call me Sir. Speak."

"If you wish to use the hood to increase your pleasure, Sir, please do. But I beg of you, don't use it to keep me from looking at you." She took a deep breath and jerked her hands away from his wrists, just noticing that she still held them.

"Sir, I am sorry if I offend you by taking pleasure in looking at your body. Seeing you is overwhelming. I have never been with any man but my husband, and he was not as you are." Her eyes dropped to the floor and her hands returned to the small of her back. She subsided and licked her lips, which were suddenly dry.

"I told you to look at me!" he bit out. Her eyes again glided slowly up his body. He sucked in a breath as she caressed him with them. She conveyed desire, hunger and passion in glazed pools of chocolate that finally dragged up to blink at him.

"You want to see this?" A flick of his wrist indicated his chest. "This twisted mass of mutilated flesh turns you on?" he asked incredulously.

"No! Oh, no, Sir. Not mutilated, beautiful. You are the most beautiful man I've ever seen."

Her rebellious little hands were suddenly on his chest, smoothing lightly down his pecs and across his clenching stomach. Gliding up his sides and back down, to trail over the burn marks reverently until they reached the throbbing shaft of his erection. With a whisper touch, they explored the vein-roped staff of his cock. They glided fleetingly under his balls, cupping them gently. Her eyes never left his as she stepped a little closer and pressed her perfect breasts to his chest. Her hands still gently stroked his cock while her head tilted back and she pleaded.

"Please, Sir, let me taste you. Let me please you."

His eyes narrowed as he gazed down at her lips. His hands clenched at his sides while she rubbed herself against him. He frowned and shook his head to clear it, grabbed her upper arms and forcefully set her away from him.

Still staring narrowly into her eyes, the dark stranger asked harshly, "Why didn't you mention you have a thing for the grotesque? I would have thought that was relevant, wouldn't you?"

Now her eyebrows rose. "Grotesque? You think I have a fetish for ugly?"

Her brow crinkled in puzzlement that soon morphed into anger. Before she could think about it, her hands landed on her hips and her stance stiffened to challenge. Prin leaned forward from the waist to put her little nose directly in his face. Well, as close as she could come to it from that far down, and proceeded to tell him what she thought about that.

"If that were true, I don't have much reason to stick around," she hissed. "The only guy here is a Greek God. That wouldn't interest me much, now would it?"

He stepped back a pace from her fierce outburst. She followed him punctuating each statement with a finger jab into the pelt on his chest. Those chocolate eyes flashed and sparked hotly. "I like this body. I want this body. If you don't like it, tough, but don't you tell me it's ugly again. You can do whatever you like with me, we agreed to that…" She gulped and paused a second as she realized what she was doing again. Then her spine stiffened. Well, how much more trouble could she be in? In for a penny, in for a pound, as it were. Her palm flattened out on his chest to caress the masculine heat beneath it.

"Sir. What I mean is, please don't make assumptions about what I do and don't want to see. Use the hood for your pleasure. But not because you think I want it, Sir." Her voice trailed off but her eyes never broke contact with his. She very deliberately stepped back to assume the required stance again, not breaking eye contact as she looked up at him.

Astonished at her own reaction, Prin realized how distinctly territorial she'd become. A desert wind of anger had rushed through her at his obvious anticipation of rejection. He actually thought the badges of honor written across his body were too ugly to look at. Whatever happened to him was horrific, but her need to accept him was immediate and unconditional once she saw those scars.

He was hers in every way, strange though that might be — consciously not thinking about the dreams here — and she could not allow him to think those scars were anything but a testimony of principle. Purposely not worried about how she knew he'd earned each one in service, or for the service. Really, really serious about not thinking about the dreams now.

He backed up another pace and sank into the leather writing desk chair behind him. He sat there like any man would, with legs spread wide, his erection lay against his abdomen as he leaned back and contemplated the spitting little kitten that stood in front of him.

What the hell just happened? His hand absently drifted down to stroke his dick as his brain whirled. Her eyes dropped to watch the lazy strokes and he realized what he was doing. He watched her prickly attitude fade into a light pant as her eyes were drawn to the hand on his erection. He grinned. She tried to look away, but she couldn't seem to manage it.

The thing between them involved so much more than just sex. He'd known it would as soon as she stepped through that door this evening. It appeared to go both ways. Baby Girl was right there with him in the deep water, whether she knew it or not. However, with both of them naked and turned on, it was damn difficult to concentrate on anything that required higher brain functions for long. He smiled now as he watched her want him. His primary objective to tie her to him looked hopeful. Her reaction to his body was baffling, but possessive as hell.

His twisted flesh made her gasp. He'd expected that. Nevertheless, she hadn't backed away from him. Her face hadn't turned white then flushed with disgust. In fact, she'd marched right into his personal space when he moved away from her. Baby Girl became downright fierce in her denial of any revulsion over his scars. Now that sweet little warrior woman wanted to play again, in the worst way.

"You want this, pet?" he questioned her softly. The large cock jerked in his hand as he leaned it out toward her. Another pearl-drop of pre-cum seeped out of the tip as she stared at it avidly. She nodded her agreement with her gaze locked on him. Her little pink tongue flashed out to dampen her lower lip.

"Come, kneel," his deep voice commanded. She dropped to her knees between his outstretched limbs, her mouth open, eyes glued to the swollen head of his dick. He scooted his ass to the edge of the chair, while he held the base of his cock with one hand—his other large hand grabbed the hair at the back of her head tightly. A firm grip let her know he would control the movement of her head.

He slowly bent her head to his cock. Her lips formed that perfect "O" of every man's dreams. Decadent satisfaction slithered down his body as he watched the flared purple head disappear into her hot little mouth. He kept pressing her head down until he felt his cock hit the back of her throat. Her velvet-soft mouth was stretched wide to envelop all she could of his hard male length.

Her sweet mouth surrounded him like a warm honey wrap. Her succulent lips sealed tightly to his thick flesh. Her eyes blinked rapidly while she fought the gag reflex and sucked hard in her effort to gain control. He held her head steady until she breathed through it. Only about a third of his cock fit in her. His fist marked how far she could manage.

As she regained control, she realized he hadn't moved. Prin avidly sucked on the forceful, stiff cock that overflowed her mouth—she stroked her tongue up and down, and drew on him deeply. As she swallowed, he could feel her throat compress around the head. A low rumble rolled up from his chest as he pulled up on her hair gently to indicate the rhythm he wanted.

She followed his direction eagerly and slid her hot, damp mouth up and down. Her tongue curled around the head on each upstroke and fluttered down the sensitive under side with each downstroke.

His body clenched rock-hard from scalp to toes, and jerked with each flicker of her tongue on the vein-roped steel she serviced. Lust had never been so intense. He was so consumed by this pleasure that it blanked his mind, wiping it clean of every painful memory, and removed the violence required by his former life. Shimmering and unreal, tangible and tactile, she was every wish and fantasy he had ever imagined.

He watched her suck on that length of pulsing masculine demand. The erotic sight of this perfect beauty with her lips wrapped around his cock while his large hand ensured her compliance blazed through his mind. She wasn't shy about the sounds her avidly suckling mouth made on him. Little moans were interspersed with the damp sucking noises as she slurped him up in apparent bliss. Her eyes remained closed in total concentration on the big shaft in her mouth.

The sight of her like this sent him to the ragged edge. He could feel civilization quickly becoming a distant memory. His every response came from the primitive male animal that was shrugging off four thousand years of progress like yesterday's garbage. This guy was in charge now, gazing down at the submissive woman who knelt between his legs.

"Take all of it, yeah…just like that," he breathed. "Suck it, baby, let me see you take it."

Her sweet mouth pulled harder on his straining cock and he increased the speed of her head in his lap.

His lips curled back in a snarl as her velvet-soft mouth worked him while he pushed her head down over his penis. Lightning flashed from his balls up his spine and his head fell back against the chair. He roared in release as the orgasm thundered over him. This was like nothing he'd ever experienced before. Cum jetted out of his cock in endless spurts as his hips jerked up helplessly to thrust into her sweet mouth. She swallowed convulsively, frantically, sucking down every drop.

Slowly the maelstrom subsided, he jerked faintly each time her tongue swept over the sensitive broad head of his cock. She hadn't stopped sucking, searching for more of his salty-sweet passion. Her tongue lapped up and down his pulsing flesh relentlessly, she poked into the slit to swirl around and clean every drop. His fist, still clenched in her hair, held her to the task. His hand eventually relaxed, the large palm petted her lazily as she cleaned him.

Gently, he pulled her head away from him and watched his semi-hard cock emerge from her mouth with a little pop. She sat back on her heels and gazed up at him as he stroked her cheek gently while he studied that sweet face. What he saw in those big eyes melted a hole all the way through his inner beast's heart.

Her lips were swollen and puffy from hard use. Her face was flushed and her scalp had to ache. Yet there she sat, looking up at him hungrily. An eager whore who'd just gotten her face fucked and hoped that wasn't the end of the fucking. The primitive woman within her was alive and well. He smiled into her eyes.

"Come, pet. Sit up here with me." He lifted her up, and arranged her so she straddled his lap. The chair had no arms so her smooth thighs settled over his easily. He gathered her into his arms and drew her face up to his mouth with a knuckle under her chin.

Bending his head to her slowly, his lips drifted in feather strokes across her cheek to the bruised evidence of his possession. Tender, gentle licks soothed pillowy lips. His first taste of her precious mouth contained his essence on her, in her, just as it should. It wasn't possible to remain gentle and soothing he discovered. Something about this woman reached into his soul and stripped away all his resistance. She expanded his understanding of reality, she decompressed the civilized man, freed him from all restraint. With an animal groan of surrender to her primitive power over him, he pressed her open and plunged his tongue deep. He swept over every surface of that intoxicating mouth, drinking her in deeply.

Her breasts flattened against his chest, those hard nipples stabbed him. She distracted him almost completely as she leaned into the kiss. He drew her arms from behind her back where she had been clutching them desperately, to place them around his neck. Her fingers sank immediately into his thick hair, while her body began to shift and rub against him.

His hands drifted down her back. He lazily caressed the cheeks of her curvy ass as she moaned into his mouth. One of his hands snaked down to grab the bladder hanging there so temptingly. He gave it two swift squeezes and felt her thighs clench to lift her up off his lap as the dildo inside her increased in size. He chuckled into her mouth. Prin moaned. His other hand gripped her hip to hold her still while he squeezed again.

The need to dominate her demanded that she accept this as he directed her. She trembled but remained where he wanted her this time. He never broke the kiss while he manipulated her ass plug.

His fingers rimmed her back entrance, tracing the fat head of the plug teasingly, before moving further under her to find her dripping cunt begging for attention. His forearm forced the thick plug tightly into her as his fingers explored her slick folds. She eagerly pressed down onto his hand.

With his thumb buried in her tight little pussy, the four fingers above it spread out to push her outer lips open. Two of his fingers captured her fat little clit between them and began a sawing motion, squeezing as he toyed with her. Instantly, her hips rocked on his hand as moisture flowed down his thumb into his palm.

Excitement hummed through her as her hands no longer petted, but tightly clutched him. Her lower body undulated, riding his fingers as she ate his mouth. Now it was her tongue that plunged deeply into his mouth as she moaned. Fire licked up her every nerve ending. At last, he'd touched her where she needed it. Prin trembled again. His plucking, rubbing fingers drove her wild as he thrust his thick thumb up her engorged, needy cunt. Every action leading up to this insistent finger-fucking had readied her to a peak of unbearable sensitivity. Coupled with his masterful kiss, Prin willingly lost all control. The rise to orgasm was swift and intense.

Abruptly the fingers that strummed her silky folds stopped. A large hand at her hip locked her in place, restraining her firmly while her body demanded she ride those tantalizing fingers. His mouth pulled away from her lips and she groaned harshly, dropping her forehead to his chest and gulping air noisily, quivering from the near release.

His hand slid out from between her legs and trailed up to the small of her back. Breathing deeply, he smoothed both hands up her sides to drag her upper body off his chest. Sitting her up straight and a little further back on his lap, he gazed down at her. Enjoying the fact that with her thighs draped open over his spread legs she was forced to give him a lovely view of her swollen pussy. He dipped his head to look into her downcast eyes.

"Look at me, pet." The deep rumble of his command brought her gaze to his eyes. She panted in frustration and struggled to focus on him. A little half-smile ticked his mouth up and crinkled around his eyes as he watched her get it together.

"Now seems like a good time to talk about naughty little girls who don't do as they're told, who talk out of turn and stop the Dom from doing as he pleases, don't you think?"

Her eyes widened and lost all their fogginess. She sat there, literally hanging between his hands as he gripped her gently under her armpits. Swallowing nervously, her head nodded in consent. Licking suddenly dry lips, she regarded him silently.

"Since you have so much trouble controlling yourself, pet, you force me to teach you control in the little time we have here. Lucky for you, I am prepared to do that. Not having an orgasm just now doesn't even come close to what you've earned, now does it?"

His face lost all humor as he regarded her repentant diminutive self. She shook her head negatively, not attempting to explain or defend herself.

Chapter Three

ဆ

Rising easily to his feet, he stood her in front of him.

"Take the spread off the bed, fold it and put it on the chest," he directed.

She hurriedly turned to comply. The beautiful raw-silk spread slipped easily into her arms. That's when she saw the black leather straps hidden under it.

There were three of them. Glossy black leather about four inches wide, snaking up from the floor. Two longer ones came up from the legs of the headboard on either side. A shorter one appeared in the middle of the bed from between the mattress and headboard. They lay there like silent threats against the white sheets.

Nervously, Prin placed the now folded spread on the ornate chest at the foot of the bed. Then assumed her original stance and waited for his instruction. The dildo bladder that hung from her ass bumped against the back of her thighs with each movement. He made her stand there until the bladder stopped swaying.

"Get on the bed, pet, in the middle, face up." His instructions were clipped but the cold tone had warmed from frigid to merely chilly.

She scrambled up onto the huge bed, grace given up for speed in hopes of appeasing him just a little. Actually, she was filled with curious anticipation over those sinful straps. Grateful her only job was to get on the bed, anything more was beyond her. Her body sank into the plush pillows and obscenely expensive sheets, her large eyes riveted on him again as she awaited his bidding.

"Good girl. Now put your hands above your head and cross your wrists. That's it," he murmured in approval as the bed dipped with his added weight. He knelt beside her to secure her wrists to the center strap.

Her head turned toward him and she found his dick was lined up with her mouth. Prin stared at it hungrily as he leaned over her securing her hands. Glancing down at her, he grinned and arched his hips so the head of his semi-hard cock rubbed against her lips. She opened her mouth immediately to take him in.

He only meant to tease her when he noticed her fascination. Yet, as her lips engulfed the bulb of his cock, he knew he was lost. No thought of teasing remained as he looked down at the sight. He swung a leg over her head to straddle her face. Large hands gripped the headboard above her as powerful thighs pumped his inflamed shaft into that hot, willing mouth.

She'd no option but to close her lips tightly around him and suck the heavy cock that was jammed into her mouth. His balls slapped her chin as he grunted over her. Greedy eyes drank in the sight of her face fucked into the pillow while her arms were restrained above her. This position created a "cage" where she could neither turn aside nor pull back from him. He didn't try to make her take the whole thing as his thighs powered the engorged cock into her mouth. The inner aggressive creature found almost uncontrollable pleasure in this forceful face-fuck. Its complete dominance of the one woman on the planet who was wholly his was like a drug. The primal need to impress upon her that he alone owned her ass was an unquenchable hunger. He came quickly, shooting searing ropes of cum down her throat as his legs trembled from the fierce release.

He pulled out of her mouth after she'd swallowed every drop and cleaned his shaft again. The beast wasn't satisfied yet. He leaned further forward and rested his balls on her lips. She again opened her mouth dutifully and began licking and sucking them, lapping up the sweat and musk of his most private flesh. His wet, semi-hard cock lay across her forehead as she ministered to his large balls. She licked around them, over them and sucked each one into her mouth for as long as he presented them. Unblinking eyes watched her.

The raw visual was intensely gratifying. His woman would take him however he pleased. All remnants of the civilized man he'd pretended to be seemed to have fled the room some time ago. The beast that remained was appeased by her actions. It wasn't so much what she did as it was her unhesitating willingness to do it. He'd never been so basely demanding of a woman. This need to demonstrate dominance in all things was the beast's response to time constraints. His desperate craving for her submission and acceptance of his unconditional right to all of her. The civilized man he'd once been, who'd apparently retreated to the hallway, shook his head in dazed amazement at what the beast demanded of his mate.

Pulling away from her, he sank down on the bed beside her. One arm rested across his tightly closed eyes, hiding them as he sucked in a deep breath and tried to regain some small measure of control. He needed to take care of her better than this. Not exactly sorry for what had transpired so far, but still, she was small and delicate. She had to trust in his care of her as well. It took several minutes before he could turn onto his side and gaze at her seriously.

Her lips were puffy and swollen from taking him twice orally, and now her nose was red from being pressed into his crotch. Her body vibrated with arousal as it flowed like glowing cream down the bed beside him. However, her thighs were pressed tightly together.

"Do you need the bathroom?" he murmured quietly.

She glanced at him, blushing furiously and nodded.

He reached up and released her hands with a flick of his wrist. Sitting up, he gently pulled her arms down, rubbing lightly to get the circulation going. Taking her by the hand, they rolled off the bed and padded across the room to another set of double doors. He led her into the massive bathroom.

It was done in black marble tile with burgundy accents. The towels hanging from heated brass racks were thick, Turkish burgundy. Across the room, raised by two steps, was a huge tub. In the corner, a glassed-in shower with impressive fittings gleamed warmly. The main wall housed a long vanity with three sinks and mirrors that reached the ten-foot ceiling. Against the opposite wall sat a toilet, urinal beside it and finally a bidet. Her hand still in his, he led her to the toilet.

"Here we go, pet. Don't forget to grab your *tail* so it doesn't get wet." He grinned at her and stepped over to the urinal.

She stood there in shock and watched him adjust to that wide masculine stance as he took care of business.

He looked at her. "Come on, babe. If I get done first, you'll lose your chance. Hop to it."

Blinking twice, she realized he wasn't going to leave her alone to take care of this most private chore. Nor did he expect her to be bothered by his bodily function either. Quickly, she reached back and grabbed the hose, and sat down. Nothing happened.

Her face flushed as she glanced up at him. He wouldn't even give her the privacy of looking away. He was watching her. No smile or smirk crossed his face as he calmly finished and flushed. Turning to the vanity, he went to the middle sink. At last, with his back to her, she gained the release of fluid she needed so desperately. Prin purposely refused to think about the huge mirrors that still afforded him a clear view of the entire room.

Quickly wiping, she joined him at the sinks to wash her hands.

While washing he took a soapy hand and sluiced it down his cock, sliding over the head several times then leaned forward rinsing both hands and cock in the sink. Swiftly drying off he turned toward her and spread his towel out on the counter between them.

Once she'd dried her hands, he lifted her by the waist and deposited her on the towel. Lifting each of her legs, he placed the heels wide apart on the countertop. This bent leg position showcased her cunt for him as he snagged a washcloth and ran warm water over it.

"Lean back on your hands, Baby Girl," he directed as he added a little soap to the washcloth. She leaned back obediently while he gently ran the soapy cloth down her thigh. Reaching down with one hand, two fingers deftly held her cunt open as he carefully pressed the cloth into the soft furrows of her sex. Each sensitive fold carefully cleaned, he then rinsed the cloth and brought it back to her, thoroughly rinsing off the soap.

It wasn't exactly clinically done, but there was a casual economy to his actions that conveyed the impression of a man performing a duty he loved. The gentle cleaning rattled her. The intimate nature of the chore denied any possibility of it being called polite. There was nothing polite about his attention to the details of her body. It was raw, primal ownership. Was this how he treated every woman? Somehow, she didn't think so.

Once patted dry, he cupped her private flesh with his whole hand and gave it a little squeeze. His action conveyed praise. As if her acceptance of his care was somehow noteworthy. He lifted her off the counter and grabbed her hand again to stroll out of the bathroom.

By the closet, they drew to a halt and he gave a little tug so she faced him. He framed her face with his hands and dropped a kiss on her nose.

"I bet you're thirsty, too, maybe a bit hungry?" The smile on his sinfully handsome face could only be called tender as he looked down at her. She nodded again.

"Supper will be here soon," he assured her, and opened the closet to draw out one of his dress shirts.

"Here, put this on. It should cover everything." He grinned at her and helped her into it. The shirt came to her knees and she had to roll up the sleeves repeatedly to get her hands out. He buttoned it up with single-minded concentration.

"I don't want the poor bastard delivering supper to have heart failure," he joked gently. Then continued more intensely while he shrugged into a robe from the closet.

"Besides, I never share. Anything. What's mine is only mine." His deep voice vibrated with something she didn't understand. "What happens between us is private in every way, Baby Girl. You never have to worry about me sharing. I never learned how and I don't plan to."

Her brow wrinkled adorably as she listened. He sighed deeply at the perplexed expression. Here he was talking about "always" and she was still at "only tonight". That beautiful face turned up to him did not know it looked into the soul of a man who'd never be alone again. She was about to figure it out though.

"We have a lot to talk about. First, why don't you tell me what you need? Water? There is champagne in the other room if you would like?"

"I need to come. Failing that, I guess water would do," Prin calmly answered.

He'd turned to head toward the sitting room as she replied, but her words whipped him around. First surprise, then something much darker flashed across his face.

"Hmmm, you think you deserve an orgasm, do you, Baby Girl?" His tone was all Dom now as he surveyed her.

"You asked me what I needed. I need that. Anything else is just a want…Sir." Prin responded quietly.

"I see," he mused. "So you think to instruct me in the difference between needs and wants?" His disturbing expression left her in no doubt as to his opinion of that. She jerked her head negatively but didn't speak.

"Perhaps it's a good time to help you understand what your needs really are, Baby Girl." The deep tones of his voice were cold and clipped.

He stalked back over to her. Wrapping a large palm securely around her upper arm, he firmly led her to the bed. On the way, he grabbed a large dildo from the dresser. He sat down on the side of the bed, dropping the wicked thing beside him.

"Over my knees, pet! You know the position," he barked in a harsh voice.

She gulped but complied as quickly as she could. This was not what she'd meant! Her heart pounded in alarm as she draped herself over his legs. Real fear swamped her as his hard hand clasped the back of her neck and with a steady pressure he pushed it down so her body slid across his lap until she was bent fully at the hip. The tops of her thighs rested on the tops of his, her legs dangled awkwardly straight out behind her. Only her hands, braced over her head to the floor steadied her. The big hand left her neck to grab the dildo on the bed beside him. His other hand seized her thigh, gripping it high and on the inside, he jerked it against his abdomen. Her shirt was shoved up to the small of her back.

"Spread that leg out, pet." Coolly he watched her shift the free leg to balance on his knee. Again, cunt and ass were on display. He grabbed the plug bladder and gave it a swift squeeze. Prin gasped through the burn as her plug inflated.

Two hard fingers rudely pushed open her outer cunt lips. The other hand positioned the large, wickedly ribbed dildo at its entrance. He started working it in while he held her open. It wasn't easy. The dildo in her ass pressed her cunt walls in, limiting the available room for entry. She was barely wet after the cleaning in the bathroom. He grunted, as he had to twist the fat head to work it in her straining orifice.

He didn't attempt to excite her clit, caress her or ease the crude entrance in any way. Just twisted the dildo as he pressed it into her opening, forcing the invasion with enough pressure to be uncomfortable, but not tear her delicate membranes. He ignored her gasping cries and steadily worked it into her. When it was inserted a little over halfway, he stopped and left it there.

He'd made sure her ass felt full and uncomfortable by inflating the plug even more. Now her cunt burned and strained around the enormous phallus. Prin's body helplessly jerked causing the protruding end to bounce lewdly. Those two instruments jammed into her focused Prin's entire attention on cunt and ass. She knew somewhere in her dazed mind that she should be screaming her head off. Why wasn't she telling him what a damn asshole he was?

"Now, pet. You can come anytime you like in the next five minutes," he hissed between clenched teeth as he hauled her back to the center of his lap. Neither her hands nor feet touched the floor. One of his steely arms anchored her to him across the small of her back. Suddenly his hand landed on her ass. There was no reason for it to be the shock that it was. Except, he'd focused her attention on the dildos so completely that she'd forgotten this possibility. Hadn't prepared for it. Each firm smack delivered a deep sting and caused the large plug in her ass to rub against the massive dildo in her cunt through the thin membrane separating them. Black lightning exploded through her and fired her body into overload with each increasingly sharp smack. Her emotional response to the sensations and situation was complete. He'd mixed her need for humiliation with unbelievably intense sexual domination.

Prin began climaxing hard, really hard, screaming hysterically as the first shockwave of release took her on the third sharp slap. Her body thrashed wildly, totally out of control in a maelstrom of primitive pleasure and pain. The screaming orgasm demonstrated clearly how much she'd actually wanted this. His handling of her pleased the primitive woman inside her. That woman needed to know this man was strong enough to control her. The submissive little bitch within demanded this humiliating revelation of her sexual desperation.

The force of his spanking increased each time his hand met her bottom. Her ass glowed red, as he made sure to cover every inch of creamy, jiggling flesh with deliberate smacks. Each time his hand fell, it propelled her to a new level of intensity. Her orgasm surged higher and higher, not stopping, just going on and on. The boiling cauldron of sexual release ruthlessly thrashed her body and mind.

Finally, almost choking on her sobs, she felt the dildo in her gushing cunt fall to the floor. The spanking stopped and they both stilled, breathing hard as their spiraling emotions slid slowly back down.

She lay there across him in disbelief. Her tears dripped onto the carpet as she stared down with blank eyes. His heavy hand rested on her heated ass and she was forced to face the shameful fact that his command of her body and its reactions was total. He could bring her to unbelievable heights of pleasure as easily as that. Not that it'd been easy. Yet, he'd known exactly how she would react. He knew how high she would fly at his command. He'd just demonstrated the depth of his dominion over her. Even when punishing her, he was in complete control of her.

She felt naked right down to her soul. The urge to seek cover was elemental and instinctive. Her bones felt exposed. Gulping in air as she hung limply over his lap, Prin could barely comprehend what just happened. He could systematically strip away each layer of civilization between them. In an exceedingly short period of time he removed every delusion she held of being an independent, modern woman who enjoyed playing submissive. No, she was a submissive who lived for the pleasure of his every touch.

She'd all but demanded an orgasm. So, he'd delivered one with each slap of his hand on her ass. It couldn't be any clearer that he saw her attempt to assert control for what it was. He met her challenge even before she'd known she made it. The insertion of that nasty dildo in her cunt was to prove he owned every orifice. To show her he knew exactly what she wanted. Even the shameful, secret desires she could barely acknowledge to herself.

There was a knock at the door of the suite. He stood her up on shaky legs. Rising from the bed, he strode into the outer room throwing his directions back at her over his shoulder.

"Go wash your face and blow your nose."

She blindly turned toward the bathroom as the bedroom door clicked shut. In the marble hall he called a bathroom, she found herself clutching the vanity as she gazed at the disheveled woman in the mirror staring back at her. Who was she? No one Prin had ever met before.

Groping across the sink, she turned on the cold water, leaned down and weakly rested her elbows on the counter. Prin shut her eyes and repeatedly splashed the chilly water over her face. Wet, stringy hair dripped down, covering her face but she didn't care. Prin couldn't find the energy to pull it back. It just seemed like everything was too much effort.

Walking in the suite door this evening and looking into a face she'd only dreamed, was too much for Prin to absorb. His immediate and complete mastery of her could not be attributed to the original shock of seeing him. It was an unbelievable event unto itself. Moreover, it was complete. There could be no question what he was to her. He might as well have knocked her over the head with a dinosaur bone and dragged her by the hair into his cave.

His total mastery of her brought her to the realization that he'd not left her alone for a single second, until now. His walking out of the room without her was the scary thing. It felt worse than any punishment imaginable, almost unbearable. Where the hell had that come from? What was that? Oh, God in heaven, who was she?

He'd turned her ass into a red, burning pain center. This man humiliated her by forcing that shattering orgasm while he spanked her ass. He'd known she'd come so hard that the huge dildo would be pushed out of her cunt as he enjoyed the show. Nonetheless, his walking out that door into the other room made Prin feel sick. She knew he hadn't planned to be apart because he'd put the shirt on her. Prin was here alone because of her own actions.

This deep hatred of being alone frightened her. His demanding domination released her nasty whore. His tender care earlier in the bathroom, and just before she made that challenge, showed her how much he wanted the whore. He valued her. His every demand went straight to her craving to revel in that whore. He saw her secret desires and met each one with more than she'd ever dreamed. Gave her fantasies she'd never allowed herself to have.

She knew he wanted her with him every second of their time together. He truly wanted to share everything. The demanding, needy slut this mystifying stranger released in her could not face being without him. Yet, after that shattering spanking, he'd walked out the door without her. He let her feel this inexplicable sensation of abandonment. She realized this was the real punishment. This was the lesson. Don't make me leave you. It also demonstrated his complete understanding of the relationship he'd created between them. There was nothing independent, mature or even logical in the slut he'd released.

Leaning over the sink with her face shielded by dripping hair, her left hand reached out and groped for a towel. One plopped into her hand and she knew he was there. Relief overwhelmed her. Prin felt desperate and confused as she buried her face in the towel. These roller coaster emotions were ripping her apart, but jumping off the ride was too painful to contemplate. She stood there silently shaking. He allowed her to hide a little, to find her comfort zone in the unfamiliar situation they'd discovered.

The emotional turmoil she felt was incomprehensible. How could he affect her on this level? What was happening to her that she "needed" him? No, no, no, no. She couldn't afford to need. He could not be necessary to her soul. This was only one night of sex! That's all!

She stood there shuddering for a moment before she felt his arm lift under her knees. His other arm cuddled her close to his chest as he carried her out of the bathroom. She turned her towel-covered face into his chest and cried. His chin nuzzled the top of her head.

In the sitting room, he sank with her into a deep, leather sofa. He arranged her legs carefully along the cushions, as he turned her into himself with her hip across his lap. The position ensured her bottom never touched anything. Her arms crept around this devastating stranger's neck and she pressed herself into him tightly. His hands swept soothingly up and down her back, caressing her and pressing her into him gently with brief hugs.

His loving hold cherished her. He'd come back for her and simply picked her up. Used his body to assure her that she wasn't alone. The gentle cuddling said she'd never be lost in this new place. He'd taken her there, and would never be far away. Never leave her to fend for herself. The tears sliding down her face were the result of emotional overload. She wasn't sobbing or wailing. Just sitting in his secure embrace and letting go.

He dropped an occasional kiss on her bent neck. Gently he tugged the towel away from her to feel the tears against his skin. Those salty bits of her soul were precious to him. He could feel her groping emotionally in this new reality. He jealously hoarded each little piece of herself that she gave him. His big body shuddered while he held the one woman in the world who was meant for him.

He knew they were at a turning point. This whole night was the biggest gamble of his life. It wasn't like he'd planned what happened. He liked to have a plan. However, ten seconds after he came up with one, the little woman in his arms ripped it up and threw it out the window. She managed to do it every time. Then again, they'd gotten past all the garbage most people spent months uncovering. The relationship they created together was as raw and basic as you could get. He knew he still needed her more than she needed him, but it was a start.

When the tears subsided and she breathed easily again, he put a finger under her chin and turned her face up to his.

"Feeling better, pet?" he asked quietly.

She smiled weakly and nodded.

"How about we talk freely for a while? I need to know what's going on in that brain of yours." He carefully studied her face as he asked.

"All right." Her voice was a bit scratchy. She leaned back to look at him and winced when she rolled her hip to sit on her bottom.

A very masculine grin flashed across his face as his big hands whipped down to spread across both ass cheeks and gently adjust her back to her side. His hands remained there, petting her softly.

"Not yet, baby. Give it a few moments," he purred as he settled her against his chest. "I'll get you a drink in just a minute. First, I want to hold you. Now, tell me about those tears."

Her face buried in his throat again, she sighed deeply. "It's just so much. This isn't what I expected," she stated quietly.

"Are you disappointed?" he inquired.

"Overwhelmed…" There was a long pause. "Are you?" she asked. Prin felt him smile against her forehead.

"No. I'm a lot of things, but disappointed isn't one of them," he assured her. "This isn't what I expected either. I guess I don't know what I really expected. You're nothing like whatever that was."

They were quiet for a few minutes.

"I…I don't think I understand what's happening," Prin whispered into his neck.

"What don't you understand, Baby Girl?" The deep rumble of his voice was both soothing and wickedly sexy.

"You. Me. This thing we've become together. It's not right."

"Is it scaring you?" he asked.

"Oh, God, yes," Prin breathed. Her body shivered again as she acknowledged that.

"Then let me hold you through the scary parts. I promise, I won't let you go." His lips brushed her forehead again.

"You are the scary part. What you do to me is terrifying," she admitted.

"Come on," he murmured. "We need to get some food and liquid into you while we talk."

Standing up with her cradled high against his chest, he carried her to where a supper cart had been wheeled onto the balcony.

The spacious balcony seemed to be suspended over the river below. Tasteful shrubbery and careful architecture made it a private island sitting high in the starry sky. No other buildings were closer than across the wide expanse of water far below them. She supposed if you had a telescope, you could watch them out here. Other than that, they were alone in the balmy nighttime paradise. Discrete up-lights were dispersed in the private little jungle thriving out here. The diffused light was enough to see everything, but left them intimately immersed in the shadowy evening.

Chapter Four

ഇ

She noticed there was only one chair. Her dark warrior sat down with Prin across his lap once more. Holding an arm around her, he proceeded to uncover the light supper he'd ordered and pour them a glass of wine. There was only one glass, one plate and one fork. He brought the glass to her lips and held it while she drank.

It was still a bit uncomfortable to sit up like this and he smiled again when he noticed her shifting but made no comment.

"Do you like melon?" he asked while spearing a piece with the fork. Prin really had no opportunity to answer as he popped it into her mouth, so she nodded.

The rest of the meal went like that. He fed her, held her wine when she asked for it, then drank from the same spot her lips had touched. He ate a bit, but seemed more interested in tempting her to try just a bit of everything they had before them. The hand holding her to him never stopped caressing whatever he was touching. He often licked across her lips, lapping up whatever was left there, real or imagined, she suspected.

He told her about himself and his best friend who were always in trouble. The best friend sounded suspiciously like goddamn Dave to her. She didn't ask. After telling several stories, he asked her about her childhood. She told him some stories of her own and they laughed between the cuddling, petting and feeding.

When she was done eating, Prin leaned into him and rested her head on his shoulder. It settled into a spot that seemed to be made for it.

Their casual chatting brought the emotional intensity down to a manageable level. She knew he'd done it for her. He'd also kept her completely aware of him. The sting of her well-spanked bottom that rested on his thighs had kept her wet throughout the meal. He'd also told her personally embarrassing stories. Laughed at himself, and encouraged her to share more about herself without pressuring.

Now his clever fingers flicked open the buttons of her shirt and slid inside to rest on her hip, his thumb stroking the soft skin. With both arms wrapped around her, he sat there holding her in silence. The rightness of this moment melted into their bones.

Presently, he turned his face into her hair and asked quietly, "Who is the Dom in your dreams?"

Startled, Prin looked up at him. He met her gaze calmly and waited.

"What do you mean?" Prin nervously glanced away.

"Question thirty-two, you answered with the statement. 'I have a reoccurring dream that I must escape. He is a dark Dom whom I feel will not leave me until I have lived what he wants me to feel'," he quoted to her. "Who is he?"

Tension vibrated through her. He felt her tighten until she quivered like a strung bow under his hold. He soothed her with his hands, petting her hip and side. Earlier, she'd slipped one of her little hands inside his robe to absently stroke his chest. Now she withdrew it slowly. He considered that a bad sign. Still he waited patiently.

Looking down, she whispered, "I don't know."

"Tell me about the dreams, baby."

"I...I can't," she answered.

"Are they sexual?" he pressed. She nodded.

"Then you can tell me," he reasoned. "We agreed that you are mine to command sexually until six a.m., and I'm instructing you to tell me about them."

Prin hesitantly searched his eyes as she bit her lip. Slender hands started to twist on her lap. One of his large hands covered hers to stop them as he looked steadily into her eyes.

"I am waiting," he murmured.

She slid off his lap and he let her go. Pacing over to the balcony railing, she gripped it hard and started from the beginning.

"It started about two years ago. I began to have vivid dreams where a somehow ominous man dominated me. He was demanding, strong and relentless." She paused for a bit as he remained silent, willing her to continue.

"He came to me as soon as I fell asleep. Sometimes it seemed that I entered the scene after it already started. Like walking through a door and seeing yourself there, but knowing your consciousness just arrived. I can't turn around and leave again." She shivered and wrapped her arms around herself. He immediately went to her at the railing and folded her into his arms from behind. She leaned back on his broad chest and continued.

"He is like no one I've ever experienced, read about or thought of. The things he does with me are new. Things my husband never wanted or talked about. How can I dream something I've never heard of?" His arms tightened around her and his head bowed down to rest his cheek against the top of her head. He surrounded her and she continued.

"I started trying to avoid sleep, but no matter when I went to sleep, he was there. Then I tried sleeping pills, but I started to forget how many I'd taken. I'd wake up in middle of the night and take some more. They made me feel too groggy and hung-over. It seemed dangerous to continue that."

He breathed out a sigh of relief. "I'm glad to hear that, Baby Girl."

"He just kept coming for me," Prin continued. "Making love to me so deeply that I'd wake up crying, in need of a release that I never quite reached. Almost every night the experience repeated. I ached for him." She paused in obvious confusion. "He felt so intensely alone. There was so much pain and I couldn't understand what was wrong." Looking up at him with troubled eyes, she turned in his arms to slip her hands up his chest to link them behind his neck.

"When I stepped through the door tonight and saw you, it felt like you were him. Everything about the situation felt exactly like my dreams, but real. Like my one night of fun was something else entirely. As if you'd summoned me or something."

Holding her loosely, he studied her worried face. "Would it be so bad if I were that Dom, Baby Girl?"

She gave a self-depreciating chuckle. "How weird is that? I mean, how could that be? It doesn't make sense."

His severe features transformed as he smiled down at her. His silver-blue eyes twinkled and she caught her breath at the wickedly sexy bad boy he became.

"Just looking at me tells you I'm a Native American. Don't let the eyes fool you, sweetheart. They are the gift of a long-ago Scot who wouldn't be told not to wear his plaid after Culloden. He ended up in buckskins with his wife's people, but it was his choice. The blood in my veins runs thick with the, 'evil and heathenistic practice' that the 'good Christian Faithful' has tried to wipe out for almost a thousand years now. Those sacred stone circles can be found on this continent and in the highlands. Our ways include such things as 'Dreams'. Through them, we reach out in ways you might not expect. The Five Civilized Nations aren't as civilized as the general population likes to believe."

"But we've never met! I hadn't even heard of you before I told Marisa about my dreams. How could you, ah, what did you call it?" Her face crinkled in question.

"Reach for you," he supplied.

"Yeah. 'Reach for me', if you didn't know who I was?" Prin questioned, puzzled.

"I still don't know who you are, baby. But I've known what you are for the last two years. Mine." His arms tightened around her. "Why is it so hard to believe that some spirits are meant to be together? That already knowing the path, my soul would seek my mate as it wandered in the ancient ways."

Her eyes regarded him seriously, neither agreeing nor disagreeing. The generations of good Christian upbringing stood firmly between her and even the desire to accept what he was saying.

"Look, baby, it might be a strange concept for you," he said softly. "I understand that. Just open your mind to the possibility. That's all I ask. I know you're not stupid. You're aware that there are more things in this world than science can explain."

Prin nodded cautiously. He did make a good point, she mused. The compelling face and all that masculine confidence just oozing out of him made it hard to not automatically agree with him.

"What's happening between us is much more involved than just this one night. You know it is." His deep voice rolled down her bones, convincing and sincere. "We come together as male and female on an elemental level. One I've never experienced with another. I believe it's unique for you also. I also think you recognize it. Don't you?"

Prin hid her face in his chest again and nodded. One of his hands gently petted down her hair.

"Don't be afraid of it, Baby Girl," he whispered into her hair. "We're both in this together. What you do for me is scary as hell, you know. Just because I've got a clue why we are this way, doesn't mean I was prepared for it. It came as a surprise to me, too. It was one of the biggest shocks of my life when you walked through the door.

"So tell me why you told Marisa about the dreams? You obviously didn't believe the man in them might be a real person."

Her dark stranger smiled at her again and Prin shifted uneasily. Being the focus of so much attention was drugging. It wasn't casual or playful, it was concentrated domination in a way she'd never experienced before. Men had always been interested in her, but this dark warrior who looked at her with such intense eyes was more than that. She knew she'd answer almost any question he asked. Her complete inability to compartmentalize this night, this man scared her. Her desperate eagerness to please him overwhelmed her.

"Well, Marisa had noticed what condition I'd gotten myself into and insisted on knowing what was going on," Prin confessed.

"What condition was that?" Frowning down at her, his concerned expression appeared disapproving to Prin. What little resistance she had left sat up and took offense. She almost hated herself for it, but she couldn't stop. Answering his questions was as much a compulsion as breathing.

Huffing softly, Prin glanced away. "As I said, I tried to avoid him by not going to sleep. I was getting worn-out and tired-looking. My work was suffering. For a while there I didn't eat much and lost a lot of weight. Marisa is a bit of bulldog, you know. When she wants to know something, she usually finds a way to get it out of you. I was just so tired and strung-out that I couldn't fight her anymore. I told her everything one Sunday."

"Mmm, so she told Dave?" he questioned, trying to follow the train of events that brought her to him.

"Yeah, I really didn't expect him to...um..." She paused, and looked up into silver eyes as his lip quirked on one side. "Well, come up with a plan. He said that maybe one night of total submission would, um, oh...well, alter my subconscious brain enough to get rid of the dreams," she finished lamely.

That sinful smile widened as he bent down to rub his nose against hers playfully. "You came up with the plan, baby. I distinctly recall a long list of stipulations and conditions coming from somewhere."

Prin bit her lip and looked away again, blushing at his interpretation of her attempt to discourage him and her well-meaning friends.

He leaned back and looked at her seriously to continue. "Do you really think one night will take care of it? I don't think any Dom would release you so easily. Not even a dream Dom. I know I won't."

Her eyes rounded and shot back to his as his words sank in. She blinked and glanced away from him nervously again. "We have an agreement," Prin murmured quietly.

"Yes." The devil's own deep voice slithered across her flesh as his hands glided down to her sensitive bottom and squeezed gently. The dull fire of his hands on her recently spanked posterior, and the increased bulge beneath his robe narrowed Prin's focus effectively to her body and its needs. Her arousal spiked just that easily. His touch affected her wet core just as he meant it to.

"We have an agreement for this one night. But at six a.m. tomorrow, I am released from most of it. What happens then is up to us," he stated. His eyes took on a lazy slant as his hands massaged the globes of her bottom. He watched her grasp his intent. She didn't draw back, but studied him pensively.

"Free time is over, pet. The night won't last forever and I am afraid we have some ground to cover." He released her and stepped back.

"Take off the shirt." His voice dropped as his heavily muscled arms crossed over his chest.

She dropped the shirt to the floor. Prin adjusted her stance to the required position and glanced nervously at the panoramic view below them. He interpreted her apprehension immediately. His low chuckle drifted out into the night.

From somewhere behind the greenery, a low bench appeared and he placed it about a foot from the rail. His hand swept up indicating she should step up on it. Holding her hand to assist her up, he placed her facing the view.

"Spread your legs, pet. If anyone is watching, we want them to have a good view, don't we?" he teased knowingly. She widened her stance to the ends of the bench and felt her body blush with the rushing tingle of excitement. When did she become an exhibitionist? The possible humiliation was delicious. Who was this woman? she wondered.

"Now grab the railing." His deep voice seemed to resonate through her body as she obeyed.

Again, she was bent at the waist and fully displayed to him. The bench elevated her private flesh to just the right height. Light that poured out from the room behind them showed him everything that glistened and quivered.

"Damn, that is a picture," he mused.

His hand reached down and closed over a gently swaying breast. Blunt fingers pinched and twisted the engorged nipple absently as he contemplated her bent form. His slightly rough handling sent a decadent thrill through the submissive bitch he seemed able to summon up out of her at will. Her ass was still a bit pink from the spanking. Her plug and tail were lewdly prominent.

"Look at you, pet. Your pink little ass plugged and turned up for the world to see." His hand left her breast to slide around to the small of her back, pressing her down into a deeper arch. He used his foot on the bench to move it roughly closer to the railing, forcing her bottom to project over the back of the bench making her gasp. She desperately clutched the railing tighter for balance, while her breasts bounced. No other sound escaped her lips and he smiled. She was trying hard.

He grasped the nasty little tail and slowly squeezed, watching the enticing rosebud of her ass widen marginally. The dildo steadily enlarged as he worked the bladder while she panted through the sharp burn. The plug expanded more than it had ever done before. Prin squirmed as he stoked the fire in her ass. This decadent display fed every wicked appetite in the nasty whore who loved humiliation mixed with sexual demands.

A soft moan escaped her lips and her head dropped down between her arms. All thoughts of anyone possibly watching vanished. The monster in her ass grew to alarming proportions while her cunt clenched and wept in shameful excitement. All she could think about was her cunt and ass, and how he might use them. He'd never done one thing she expected. That knowledge left her suspended in anticipation, trepidation and uncontrollable excitement.

He dropped the little tail as the fingers of his other hand reached around in front of her. He spread the damp lips of her cunt from the front so his view of her exposed opening was unobstructed. As he held her open, the middle finger pressed firmly against her clit and started moving in small circles. Soon her hips began to rock in an enticing circular motion.

"That's it, pet. Move your little wet hole for me. Show it to me," he crooned as her hips moved faster on his fingers and she whimpered.

"Look at you drip for me, pet. Your slippery, naked hole is gaping open, begging to be admired. Look how swollen and flushed you are. I've never seen a cunt so needy."

He was driving her up again, but his fingers never dipped into her empty vagina. They circled then moved away, forcing her to follow those teasing movements. Compelling her to wiggle her cunt and ass up and down, swiveling and straining for his viewing pleasure. The tail hanging from her ass plug bounced drunkenly back and forth, slapping her inner thighs and reminding her rudely of his view. She knew it added to her pleasure with its dance between her legs. He was there, watching, seeing her jerk on his hand. Her body was willing to do anything, no matter how humiliating, to gain his attention.

"Do you want a fucking, pet?" he asked quietly, his laser eyes never leaving her squirming pink flesh.

She moaned and glanced back at him. He made no attempt to hide his enjoyment of her lewd little show.

"Yes, Sir," she gasped.

"Then beg for it. Your bad behavior hasn't been forgotten. Convince me you deserve my cock." His eyes sliced to hers as his fingers pinched her clit and milked it up and down like a little penis. Her hips bounced helplessly, her cunt gushing cream.

"Please, Sir. Please fuck my cunt, Sir. Please…" Her voice trailed off as his fingers stilled on her quivering flesh, then suddenly one thick digit from his other hand plunged into her.

"Is this what you want, pet?" he asked sternly as that one finger pushed in and out of the sopping cunt he held open. The frustrating movement separated her clenching, weeping channel with a slow, maddening motion. It was nice, but not the eleven inches of massive, pounding ecstasy she wanted.

"No…yes!! Please, Sir. More please!" She was panting heavily now, pumping back onto his finger frantically. Then a second finger sank into her.

"Bend your knees, bitch!" he hissed. "That's it. Fuck those fingers. Bounce on them, baby. Show me how much you want it." His voice was low and guttural as he watched his fingers disappear into her grasping flesh. Her moans escalated with each phrase and he knew she was as consumed with the images as he.

"Look at that greedy cunt slurp them up. You're so hot inside there. You burn me. Feel how hot you are?" He hooked his fingers slightly and dragged out of her, scraping gently.

Prin's head lashed back and she screamed. He plunged three fingers into her with a pounding force. Her body strained back at him for more as he pounded his fist back into her swollen, soft cunt.

Just as she was rising to the crest of release, he pulled his fingers out of her. She almost screamed in desperation as he left her gasping and trembling. It no longer mattered that her bottom pushed out and bounced in desperate hunger. Her head sank down between her outstretched arms again and she sobbed in gulps of air. Her body trembled uncontrollably as she froze in the obscene pose. Behind her, he vibrated with male domination.

"What do you want, pet?" he purred, each hand gripped a thigh, his thumbs stroked up and down her outer cunt lips, gently holding them open while teasing with the soft touch.

Her mind scrambled. He kept asking her that. Struggling up through the fog of intense sexual frustration she lifted her head and looked around at him. He watched her through narrow slits where his eyes should be.

Oh, God! Nothing she'd said up to this point had been right. Each time he asked her what she wanted she'd demanded satisfaction. He gave her something, but never what she wanted. Her brain struggled with the certainty that she must get it right this time. She would die if he didn't take her now.

Gazing back at his thick, pulsing erection it came to her. He wanted exactly what she wanted. But she was never going to get it without complete submission to him. Demanding her satisfaction denied him as her Dom. It made him as much of a toy as any dildo. He would not allow her to escape him that way. His ability to provide her satisfaction came out of his total control. It was an element they both needed.

He'd demonstrated over and over that he could give her what she needed. He would not let her lose the thrill his dominance gave her. He wouldn't allow her to waste one moment of this experience by taking responsibility for it.

Her head sank down between her arms again.

"Your pleasure, Sir." Her voice was muffled as she gazed down at the balcony floor below her. "Please, Sir, take your pleasure."

She heard the crinkle of a plastic wrapper as he quickly covered his cock with latex. His hands grabbed her hips firmly, and then red-hot steel plunged into her desperate cunt. The large bulb of his cock ripped into her narrow opening, its long, thick stock spread her mercilessly as he rammed in to the hilt with one powerful thrust. She screamed as the thick intruder slammed up into her.

He didn't stop. There was no time to adjust to his size. No chance to get used to the feel of that huge cock reaming into her narrow passage. His hips slapped her still sore bottom with each demanding thrust. His hands held her in place as he rode her hard. There was no room for her to move. No way to either meet his thrusts or get away from them. He was fucking her. She reveled in his domination as he forced her to take him as hard and deep as he wanted it, gorging her in the raw pleasure.

Leaning over her, never breaking the power or rhythm, he growled in her ear. "Take it, bitch. Take that thing between your legs, hard and deep. Don't you come until you're told to." His commentary continued as he panted between each word. "This is my cunt! My ass! My mouth! All my tight little fuck toys. You will never call them yours again. I will use them, fuck them and own them.

"Do you understand me?"

He suddenly stopped, pressed high and hard into her. Her head was thrashing back and forth, moaning with pleasure so long withheld that it was almost pain. She pressed back into him, shuddering in the fear that he meant to deny her again.

His hands on her hips, he shook her impaled body. "Do you understand me?" he demanded harshly.

Her head nodded.

"Say it!" he growled, giving her another little shake.

"Yours!" she cried out desperately. "Your fuck toy, your cunt, your ass, your mouth!" Prin knew she'd say anything right now, do anything and be anything he wanted. The knowledge burned down her belly to the fire pressed high and hard between her legs. Oh, God! It was so good! She needed this! That hot nightstick he wielded plowed into her deeper than anything she'd ever felt before. It stretched her over its hard width in such a way that her hipbones felt as if they were pushed wider.

He slammed into her with even greater force. Bending from his knees with each up-thrust, his whole body powered that monster cock into her. Her ass bobbed up in the air with each driving shove as he lifted her off the bench.

"Please, Sir. Please," Prin begged. "Please let me come, Sir."

He grunted and responded by increasing the power of his thrusts.

"No, my sweet bitch. Wait for it. Take it. Feel yourself stretched so tight around my cock. That's a good little girl." He continued pounding into her as he watched his dick disappear into her weeping hole.

"Beg for my cum! Now! Let me hear you say the words." His deep voice rumbled around in her dazed brain. Prin struggled to understand and do whatever it was he wanted. It was so hard to think.

The beast fucking his bitch lashed out at the need to wait for satisfaction. But that's what the man wanted from her. Not just her surrender, he needed her verbal acknowledgement of his mastery. She must admit to needing this, wanting this above all things. Saying those words would sear it into her consciousness. She had to accept that he owned her responses, her body. He didn't have the luxury of time to prove she was safe in his care. There was only tonight to show her, to somehow make her understand that her pleasure was the driving force behind every damn minute he spent with her.

Her cunt was so tight, dripping with that silky essence, it nearly drove him mad. He held onto his control by a thread, as he slammed into her and begged her in his mind to surrender. If she would just accept him, he could give her the most shattering orgasm of her life. His balls were burning, drawn up tight beneath his cock that couldn't stop jacking into her.

With the last two functioning brain cells she could muster, she gave him everything. "Please, Sir! Come in your cunt. I beg you, Sir!" Biting back a scream, she knew she was about to lose all ability to control the firestorm rapidly rushing up on her.

The relentless cock felt like it rammed up between her shoulder blades every time he entered. Her body shuddered convulsively with each pummeling thrust. Pleasure ripped her in white-hot flashes as he pulled out, and then slammed back up into her engorged flesh. He was driving her past all limits. Her unyielding warrior ruthlessly demanded her body's response twist tighter and tighter as he pounded into it.

"Good girl." His praise was a snarl. "Now come on my cock," he demanded in an almost unintelligible growl.

Her body clenched. She screamed into the orgasm exploding through every cell in her body. Interior muscles clamped down on him like a vise grip, squeezing and releasing so hard, he started swearing in a continual stream as he powered through her climax. The incessant fucking caused her release to roll into itself and rush right back up, overwhelming her.

Muscles she never knew could ignite flamed into life with the inferno shooting up from her crotch. Sensations so pure that pleasure and pain combined into something new, something that devoured reality and her with it. His seemingly effortless ability to focus every bit of her attention on those erogenous zones he manipulated magnified each sensation. It forced her to feel every reaction fully. He would allow no other input to distract her. Even the most obscure nuance of this brain-frying orgasm registered with her. Her mouth gaped open in a silent scream. Her body became a spinning, reeling receptacle of intense ecstasy. Her only reality was the flaming branding iron that would not let her stop climaxing. The orgasm flashed her entire form into such a high state of sensitivity that the night air seemed to caress her with a thousand fiery fingers. It was too much, and she went limp.

He felt her pass out as the head of his cock exploded. He held her clamped to him while the orgasm jerked his massive body in powerful thrusts. It felt like his cum shot up from his toes, burning straight up his dick in an endless stream of reality-altering pleasure. His head flew back and the beast roared his satisfaction. Every tendon and muscle clenched as he drained himself into his woman.

Her limp body still impaled on his cock, he dragged her off the bench. He staggered backwards to the chair, falling into it with her on his lap, sucking in great gulps of air while pulling her body upright in his arms. He held her head back against his chest. Large fingers checked the pulse on her neck and found its reassuringly fast but steady beat. He let himself slump back and turned his face up to the sky. Fucking her to unconsciousness probably wasn't a good idea. Sort of brought up the intensity issue that scared her so badly before.

Without even being aware of it, this woman broke him down to his most elemental nature. He was no more able to control their intense joining than he was able to stem his need for her. A small, delicate fist closed around his heart as he closed his eyes. He'd never imagined he'd find her. This woman who came to him in the dreaming, he'd hadn't believed she could live in his time. Everyone knew if you found your mate while walking with the spirits, you'd not know them in the waking times. That it would be at least another lifetime of waiting. He'd resigned himself to being alone except for the dreams. Accepted it. But here she was. Losing her now would be worse than dying — it would be a living death. Knowing she lived now and not being near her would be too much pain to live through.

She started to stir in his arms. He gently lifted her off his cock and disposed of the used condom. Swinging her up into his arms, he carried her to the bed. Her head lifted groggily as he lowered her to the pillows. Prin reached for him and he followed her down onto the mattress. His hands gently smoothed her hair away from her face and neck. He leaned over her, propped up on one elbow, as foggy brown eyes opened and focused slowly on him.

A little frown appeared on her brow. Dazed brown eyes searched his smiling silver-blue ones.

"What just happened?" Prin whispered.

"You passed out, pet." He grinned down at her. Male satisfaction oozed off him in near visible waves. If he'd had feathers, they'd have been fluffed, Prin surmised.

She struggled to move, but he pressed her back to the soft pillows and placed a finger over her mouth.

"Oh, no, you don't. Stay right there, baby. I'll be right back." He rolled off the bed, but turned back to her.

"Now, don't move," he purred again, and sauntered off to the bathroom.

She still gazed vacantly at the bathroom door when she heard the shower go on and he reappeared. Scooping her up off the bed, he carried her straight into the shower.

"Can you stand up?" he asked as he gingerly deposited her on her feet and held her carefully in case she fell.

She nodded. He set her under the warm spray and grabbed the shampoo. Putting a glob in his hands, he massaged her scalp. Prin's hands crept up to his slim hips to steady her swaying body. She relaxed into his care. After the shampoo was rinsed, he nudged her out of the spray. Soaping up his hands, he proceeded to clean every inch of her, tenderly smoothing his hands over the sensitive parts. He slid slippery fingers into every womanly fold and crack. After rinsing her thoroughly, he sat her down on a little bench along the wall and quickly washed himself. His eyes never left her. Prin gazed up at him dumbly.

Smiling tenderly, he picked her up again and stepped out of the shower, putting her down to brush a velvety-soft towel all over her body. He briskly rubbed her hair to a semi-dry state. Then quickly dried off himself.

"Do you need the toilet?" he asked quietly. She shook her head no.

"Okay, babe. Drink this and we'll take a little nap. You'll feel better after that." He held a bottle of water to her lips and tipped it up. She gulped several sips of the stuff and tried to shove it away. Insistently he brought it back to her mouth.

"You haven't had enough liquid, baby. Try and take some more," he commanded gently. She got about half of it down as the slight frown on his brow cleared. He finished the rest and lifted her easily into his arms, heading for the bedroom.

"I can walk, you know," she mumbled into his neck.

"I know." Sinful satisfaction was the only word to describe this man who carried her back into the bedroom. The fact that she hadn't gotten over that monumental fuck seemed to feed every male molecule in him. That was fine with her. He'd earned it.

He grinned down at her again as he slipped her into the bed and pulled the covers up, sliding in beside her. He gathered her into his side, arranging her head on his shoulder, grabbing her leg and hooking it over his hip, he turned her into him.

It was a surprisingly comfortable position. She draped an arm across his chest and let her eyes drift shut. Damn, was there nothing the man didn't know about her? It was too much of a struggle to figure that out and she sank into a deep sleep.

He resisted the urge to purr as she settled into him and dropped off to sleep. He grinned up at the ceiling, closed his eyes and savored the feel of her trusting little body in his arms. Baby Girl turned his heart over. Even her defiance made him smile. She handed him better scenarios than he could ever dream up on his own to show her what they were together. That damn contract had to go! This little nap gave him the time he needed to study the problem.

Chapter Five

෨

Groggily, she swam up through the thick fog of sleep. Damn it all! Was she dreaming again?

Her arms were stretched over her head and she felt her wrists secured with soft leather. Her legs were also immobile. Gazing down her body, she saw that each knee had been pulled up, and to the side. Wide, soft leather wrapped around her thighs just above the knee. The leather straps disappeared off the side of the bed toward the headboard. It was like being in stirrups, only more exposed. Both ass and cunt were tilted up and open.

Between her legs, a dark head bent as its avid mouth moved over her private flesh. He licked her like a big cat, and then sucked each fold in and out gently. His tongue bathed every morsel then moved to the next fascinating bit. She moaned and arched her cunt into him as best she could.

It wasn't a dream. Reality was so much better, she decided.

His deep chuckle rumbled into her womb as her head began to thrash on its pillow. He slurped contentedly, industriously sliding his tongue deeply into her. With each deep plunge he'd swirled it around as her inner muscles clenched, her cream sucked into his mouth. Lazily he dragged his flattened tongue up her slit to that throbbing bundle of nerves and circled around it. After tormenting her with those lazy circles, he sucked her clit hard into his mouth. She screamed. Releasing her, he turned his head and nipped her tender inner thigh to get her attention.

Gasping, she stared down at him. Her upper body was propped up with pillows so she had no trouble seeing his twinkling eyes gazing into hers.

"No coming without permission, pet," his deep voice warned her.

Immediately, his head dropped back down to lick, suck, nip and torment her. Her body broke out into a sweat as he ate her.

He just kept at her, seemingly unable to get enough of that cream. He demanded more and she gave it to him, over and over again. Soon she was desperately trying to stave off the orgasm rushing at her.

"Please, Sir. Your cunt needs to come!" she wailed, knowing there was next to nothing she could do to prevent it.

Suddenly his head pulled away and two fingers clamped down on her clit, hard. Intense pain shattered through her. It ceased as he immediately released. Sobbing with relief, she felt her clit gently sucked back into his mouth and his tongue lapping at it softly. The pain was almost instantly forgotten under his erotic attention, but her orgasm didn't come. He'd kept the intensity high, even driven it higher, but the orgasm was backed off. Her whole body writhed as he continued the torment. She began to panic. She couldn't take this. It was too much.

"Please, please, I'm begging you, Sir! Don't make me pass out again..." Gasping desperately as her body shuddered and shook.

Lifting his head slightly to gaze down at her cunt, he slowly slid two long fingers deep inside her. She was so sensitized that she shrieked at the invasion.

"Come on my fingers, pet. Now!" His arrogant demand released her. She did.

He watched her restrained body thrash wildly as he held those two fingers deep inside her. Hot and hard, she clamped down on him. Gushing her sweet cream until it flowed down into his palm. He leisurely lapped it up.

As her shuddering slowed down to deep breaths, he looked up from between her legs and slowly dragged the two digits out of her. Letting them slide down the slick flesh to her back entrance and circled the plug there.

"Was that good for you, Baby Girl?" he questioned softly.

She gulped and nodded—her big eyes watched him with apprehension. He smiled that bad-boy grin at her and grasped the wicked plug. Sticky fingers pulled it slowly from her body. The little hole gaped open as he removed the large implement.

His two wet fingers sank into her gaping ass. It felt good. He grabbed the lube from the bedside and coated his fingers as he pulled them out. Then shoved them back in and twisted to spread the jell around. Her body bucked into him.

"Oh, yes, baby. You like that now, don't you?" He looked into her eyes as he squeezed more lubricant directly into her ass. Three fingers easily slid into her as he spread the cool lube around her opening and deeply into her body. After careful inspection of the prepared area, he came up on his haunches and propped his latex-covered dick at her well-greased asshole. He reached down and slathered his cock with lubrication. Making sure she could see his every move as he stroked his huge, throbbing erection.

"Whose ass is this, pet?" he questioned as he pressed forward and the large head of his erection disappeared into her. His deep voice reached her through a sensual fog. Her body hummed in satisfaction and she realized how good that cock felt entering her. It stretched her as the thick stalk inched in, spreading her wider and wider. Adding to the pleasure was a minimal burn that created a new sensation she could not name. She pressed her head back into the pillow.

"Your ass, Sir. Oh, please, yes, Sir. More. Sir. Yes! Yessss…" Moaning and pleading deliriously, she felt him press in to the hilt. He stayed there a moment while her body tried desperately to buck back at him. She could feel the curly hairs of his groin pressed against her naked cunt. His balls nestled in the crack dividing her bottom. All the sensations rolled together on her. It was wicked! It was delicious! It was unbelievable! He was fully pressed into her ass and she wanted him to move!

Entering her ass after such an extended session with her cunt gave her no time to be afraid. Although his every action was deliberate and even methodical, she was still aroused from the orgasm he'd just given her. Being restrained removed any possibility of evading him, it never even occurred to her. Now here she was dying for him to fuck her ass. Willing to beg, plead whatever! But he *needed* to start fucking her ass!

His large hands gripped her thighs and he began to move. Slowly he pulled out, watching himself glide out of her virgin little hole. It was almost a spiritual moment for him. Her ass was his alone. No one else would ever see this sight. No one else would ever see his woman like this, period.

His possessive inner beast thrust back its head and howled in triumph. His woman was beneath him, willingly surrendering to this most intimate act. Her little body pressed eagerly back onto his cock as he shoved it into her. Her sweet voice begging him to fuck her ass harder, deeper. There could be no question later about what she wanted.

He gradually gave her what she wanted. Increasing the power and speed of his thrusts into that sinful, hot cavity of sensations. It was too good! As her rear squeezed down on him, he felt his control crumbling slowly. Each time she twisted beneath him, begging him to fuck her ass harder, a little more restraint vanished.

He drove three fingers up her cunt and she disintegrated into orgasm. He pounded away at her clenching ass through her first one, driving her ruthlessly into a second hard climax, and still he wanted more. She would be sore tomorrow, but he just couldn't stop. As she climaxed for a third time, his body arched into her and exploded.

He saw white lights behind his eyes as his seed ripped out the root of him buried deep in her sweet little ass. It felt like the release propelled his whole body into her shuddering flesh. He never wanted to leave this haven of extreme pleasure—she was so far outside all previous experience. He felt like he was barely hanging onto that rocket fireball, which swept through them every time they touched. There was no controlling it. He hung on and hoped to survive.

Tiredly he collapsed down onto her body. They were both panting gutturally as their sticky bodies vibrated with aftershocks.

Gingerly he pulled out of her. Quickly reaching to release her legs from the straps, he pulled each one down slowly. Her arms were released with gentle care taken as he pulled them down to her sides.

She lay there content to let him move her like a rag doll. Smoothing the hair off her brow he caressed down to her cheek. Her lashes drifted up to regard him. Staring down into her upturned face, he sank down and brushed her lips with his. She moaned softly and opened to him. Tilting his head for a better fit, his lips settled over hers and the kiss deepened. It was slow and lazy, a wordless communication that spoke of tender emotions. His lips worshipped her spirit, her heart—her very being was a miracle to him.

Sighing, he pulled away and slid off the bed to take care of business in the bathroom and dispose of the condom. He dumped salts into the tub while turning on the faucets. He left it running and returned to her. She hadn't moved an inch.

Scooping her up, he grinned as she curled into him naturally. Her arms wound around his neck and her head rested on his shoulder. In the bathroom, he stepped in the tub with her, sinking down into the steaming water. He sat with her in front of him and dragged her hair up over his shoulder and out of the water as she relaxed back on his chest. His cheek rested on the top of her head while long thick arms held her firmly. His legs stretched out beside her down the length of the tub. He surrounded her and Prin discovered she'd never felt more content. Presently he turned off the water with his toes.

Neither of them moved nor spoke for a long time.

The digital clock on the vanity glared at him, the red-lighted readout 4:45 a.m. He frowned at it. An hour and fifteen minutes left. His arms tightened around her and she murmured something unintelligible. Turning her head into his neck, she lapped her little tongue out to taste him. He guessed she was too tired to move and was trying to settle him down. Smiling tenderly over her, he began caressing her rib cage gently to wake her up.

"Hey, Baby Girl. Time to talk," he murmured, lifting his head from her hair. Her head bobbed once into a more comfortable spot on his collarbone and she mumbled.

"Sure, talk." Not bothering to open her eyes.

He dropped a kiss on the top of her head. "All right, I'll go first." His deep voice rumbled nicely under her cheek and she sighed drowsily as he started. "My name is, Gray Quinn Winston. My friends call me Gray."

Her head shot up off his chest to glare at him. All sleepiness vanished from her face as he continued.

"I own a security company that currently operates out of Miami."

She struggled to scoot away from him, but his hold on her would not allow it.

"Dave was a college roommate of mine before I went in the service. That's how we know each other."

"Wait a minute here," she interrupted, glaring up at him. "We agreed to no information! No names! What are you doing?"

"We agreed no information would be asked for or required," Gray told her patiently. "Nothing was ever said about volunteering it. I'm not asking you for anything. I'm not requiring anything from you. I'm just telling you about me." He smiled tenderly down at her and dropped a kiss on her scrunched up little nose.

"But, but…" Prin sputtered. "We have an agreement…" Her voice trailed off in confusion.

"And we still do. Right up until six a.m. this morning, baby," he assured her seriously. "That's why I need to get this in while you still have to listen to me. Remember the 'no talking until you're asked a direct question' part of that agreement?" His eyebrows rose as he regarded her.

Her mouth snapped shut in a mutinous line as she digested that bit of reasoning. Gray gathered her stiff little body back into him and continued. She didn't relax as he told her where he lived, how he handled the high-tech security as well as the corporate officers' physical safety measures for a national bank that had regional offices in town.

The water was beginning to cool so he lifted her out of the tub. Her sweet form remained rigid under his hands as he stood her beside the tub to dry her off.

It was a gamble. The only way he could figure to get around that damn agreement he'd personally made airtight. She couldn't "unknow" the information once she'd heard it. He wasn't breaking his word to her about anything they'd agreed to. Specifically, he'd agreed not to contact her after this night. If she made the contact, all bets were off.

Knowing the connection between them was lifetime-deep and getting her to accept it were two different things. Regardless of the damn contract, or if she contacted him, he would know where she was from this day on. She had no way of knowing that yet, but she had gained one of the most malevolent forces on the planet as her protector. He and the men he called friends would defend her with their lives, even if it were from a distance.

Standing there at the vanity as Gray brushed her hair out, he told her his cell phone number and made her repeat it back to him six times. Then his web address went through the same process. By this time, her hair was rippling down her back and her stormy eyes were snapping at him in the mirror.

They both used the toilet and he cleaned her as before. Back in the bedroom he slid one of his shirts on her, buttoning it up while he made her repeat his home address and number back to him with each button. He shrugged back into his robe.

A knock at the suite door announced the arrival of the coffee and croissants he had ordered for 5:15 a.m. delivery. Swinging her up into his arms, he carried her into the sitting room and deposited her on the couch. The bellman received his tip at the door and Gray wheeled the tray into the room himself. He parked it beside the arm of the couch where she sat. Scooping her up again, he settled into the seat under her and turned to the tray.

"How do you like your coffee, Baby Girl? Or do you prefer tea? I ordered both," he questioned.

"Coffee, black, one sweetener." Prin responded in clipped tones.

"Mmm, good. Me, too," he murmured. Ignoring her attitude he prepared one cup of coffee for them to share. Gray tested it against his lips and blew on it a few seconds before testing it again. Then held it to her mouth. Prin sipped gingerly at first then took a little more. Only then did he have some himself.

Gray's actions with the coffee demonstrated his care of her. Although he was a full Dom, not once had he taken a drink before he made sure she had one, he even monitored her intake to ensure she wasn't in danger of dehydration. That never occurred to her before. Not a morsel of food passed his lips before he made sure she had all she needed. He washed her and groomed her before seeing to his own needs at every turn. Prin felt his care on a cellular level. It bound her to him in ways she dare not accept. Her heart wept in desperate pain at each gentle touch. It wasn't supposed to be like this.

The need to protect him from the harsh reality of where her life was headed overwhelmed her. The strength to resist him built with each amazing moment in this man's care. Gray would not feel the pain she'd experienced with the death of her husband. Nothing on earth could now induce her to put him through that. She knew she loved him, loved him more than she'd ever loved before. Even the relationship with her husband paled in comparison, all the more reason to protect him.

Steely resolve crept up her spine. The coming pain would be hers alone. He'd eventually remember her fondly as one night of fun. There would be no lasting consequences, no lingering loneliness. She would miss him desperately until the day she died, but she refused to consign him to that fate. The day she died was likely to be many long years before he did.

When they were done with their second cup of coffee, he stood up and carried her into the bedroom with him. Setting her on the bed, he proceeded to dress. His office numbers were drilled into her until he was done.

Carrying her back into the living room, he gently sat her on the couch again. She figured that letting her walk had developed into a real problem for him. Grabbing her shoes, he slipped them on her and finally pulled her to her feet. Gray stepped behind her to help her into the coat she'd worn when she'd arrived, which seemed an eternity ago.

He again gave her that grin dipped in original sin as he buttoned it up and belted it tightly around her saying, "Keep the shirt. I don't want Dave getting a sneak peek on the way home."

Framing her face in his hands, Gray gazed seriously into her eyes. "You know my numbers, baby. You know how to get in touch with me, twenty-four/seven. I want to hear from you. I want to get together and talk about a relationship. I want you," he stated boldly. "You know I'm a Dom in the bedroom. What happens outside of it is up to us. I'll be whatever you need, honey. As little or as much as you want."

His eyes burned into hers with laser-like intensity and he didn't hide the emotion in them. It was tender and hot, even needy. He wanted her any way he could get her and he was letting her see it. This intensely dominant, arrogant male fearlessly handed her his vulnerability.

She gazed up into his serious eyes and started to tremble again. He'd asked for the very thing she must refuse to give him. Her future was no longer hers to hand out. An ugly turn of events last Thursday snatched that freedom from her. Dying inside, she stared up at him mutely. He gathered her into his arms and hugged her close for a long minute.

"I know this is scary for you, baby, even if I don't know why. I can't ask about that now, but I would like to as soon as you're ready." His quiet voice soothed her as it broke her heart.

Her arms were clutched around him tightly when he gently pulled them away and turned her toward the door. His hand at her back, he walked her out of the suite to the elevators. The lobby was empty as they strolled through it. Walking her out the front doors, Gray saw Dave's car pull up. He turned her to him and bent down to drink from her sweet mouth one more time.

The kiss was intense as he thrust his tongue deep into her addictive, coffee-flavored mouth. Steel-roped arms plastered her body to him and let her feel his immediate reaction to her. His kiss claimed her, cajoled her, and above all, loved her.

She was dizzy and blinked dazedly as he slowly drew back from her. Dave parked right beside them and leaned against the car as he watched with unabashed amusement.

Gray slashed him a scathing glance when he bent to open her door. Dropping another kiss on the top of her head, he bent across her to fasten the seat belt. Her door closed gently as Gray straightened and looked across the car roof at Dave.

Narrowing his eyes at the laughter he saw in his buddy's face, Gray growled, "Drive carefully. Anything happens to her and I'm coming for you."

Dave snickered and shook his head. "This from the 'Iron Man'. I take it you're gonna thank me later?" He chuckled as he slid into the car.

A deep rumble vibrated up Gray's chest at Dave. He didn't have time for the cocky attitude. Gray turned his attention back to the beautiful face gazing up at him while the car eased away from the curb. He stood there until it disappeared from view.

Six blocks later Prin still hadn't said a word. Dave reached over and squeezed one of Prin's limp hands. When he'd gently tried to ask her how it went, she'd mumbled something and turned toward the window. Now he was getting worried.

"Come on, honey. Do I need to go back there and beat him to a pulp?" Dave slid another worried glance at her.

She turned a wan smile on him. "No, no. I'm fine, really. Just tired."

"Do you want to come over to our house so you and Marisa can chat? I know I'm not the one you need right now. Would that help?" he asked. Her face seemed very pale to him and her hands were now trembling in her lap.

Dave's lips tightened as he started to have some serious doubts about his buddy Gray. Could this have gone terribly wrong? Dave was confident that he knew Gray, but after ten months in South America, the guy had changed. How much he'd changed wasn't something that had occurred to Dave before. Now doubts were creeping in.

She just shook her head no and gazed out the window.

"Did he hurt you, honey? Just tell me if he did and I'll go back there and take a piece out of his ass with pleasure," Dave asked, his grip on the wheel turned white-knuckle hard.

Prin glanced at him and recognized the grim look on his face for what it was. He was a Dom also. In a male-mind sort of way, he felt very responsible for her. He would never be anything but faithful to Mar, but the protective instincts of an Alpha male demanded he look after and defend his own. Dave was totally serious and intended to confront the big, dangerous man they'd left back at the hotel if she asked him to. Gray had four inches on him and around sixty pounds, as well as obvious experience in combat situations. But Dave was ready to take him on.

She laughed weakly, and gently squeezed his arm reassuringly as he drove. "No, Dave. He was great. He was wonderful, in fact. Stop worrying. It's not him. I just have some things to work out." *Territorial men!* Prin snorted to herself. God help her.

Dave grunted, but wasn't convinced. "How come it looks like you're about to pass out or cry then?" he demanded belligerently. Either prospect would be equally horrifying in Dave's mind. The responsibility for her pale visage weighed heavy on him. It'd been his idea, really. Damn. He couldn't live with himself if he'd exposed her to a dangerous situation.

"I'm not, believe me. Just get me home so I can sleep. I'm sure you understand when I say we didn't do much of that last night," Prin assured him softly.

Dave grinned cautiously and shot her a glance. "So it worked out then?"

Prin sighed, "Yeah."

Thankfully, they were pulling into her driveway. By the time he came around the car, she was out and walking up to the front door. He trailed along, still not happy about her pale face and shaky hands as she fit her key into the lock.

"All right, Prin," he said. "Please call Marisa. She'll be worried until she hears from you."

Prin smiled back at him as she stepped through the door. "Sure, but it will be late tomorrow. Don't worry. I'm fine." She felt a bit desperate to get rid of him as he stood there frowning at her. He nodded once and turned back to his car. Prin shut the door, leaned up against it and tiredly closed her eyes.

Shaking her head, she pushed away from the door and started to undo the coat. If she didn't get a move on, she'd sink to the floor right here and not get up. Carelessly shedding the coat, Prin let it drop while she toed off her heels and left them where they lay. Barely making it to her bed, she crawled in and pulled Gray's shirt tight around her. Sighing again deeply, she passed out.

* * * * *

Gray called Dave Monday morning to ask how his Sweet Baby Girl was doing. His legendary patience had run out by Sunday night. He'd been known to lie unmoving for up to forty-eight hours at a time to acquire his mark, then spend another three days stalking just to be sure no civilians were involved in the action. However, by Monday morning, he was ready to claw through concrete to see her.

Dave snarled at him. "How the hell should I know, man? I dropped her off and she hasn't been over since."

Gray sucked in his temper at Dave's inexplicable attitude and asked as calmly as possible, "Look, just go over there and check on her, okay? She looked pale when she left Saturday."

"I know she was fucking pale! I was afraid she might pass out in the car. If I ever find out you hurt her, I don't care what kind of Special Forces you were—I'm going to take a pound of flesh off your ass!" Dave's volume steadily rose with each word.

"Look," Gray's voice lowered warningly. "Just tell me where she is and I'll take care of it. If I did something to hurt her, I'll hand you the carving knife to work on me. But I need to know she's doing all right."

"Why are you yelling?" Marisa's faraway voice floated through the phone.

"It's Gray. He wants to know how Prin is." Dave made no effort to cover the phone as he answered his wife.

"Give me that," she demanded. Then a shuffle as the phone passed hands.

"Hi, Gray," Marisa's chipper voice sounded in his ear. "How are you doing?" she asked politely and waited for his response.

Gray gritted his teeth and stretched his back, arching his torso over the desk chair as he attempted to restrain his impatience and make polite conversation with her. He was willing to do anything for information at this point. He didn't really want to use all the tools at his disposal to hunt down Baby Girl, but he damn well would if this didn't yield the information he needed. What he was capable of was so far beyond stalking it was laughable. Not that she'd ever know it, but still, it might put a crimp in his trustworthiness if she ever happened to find out.

"I'm fine, Marisa. I'm just a bit worried about Prin." Gray slid in the name he'd heard Dave use and sure enough, Marisa didn't turn a hair.

"I talked to Prin yesterday, and she said she would be by next Sunday as usual. I think she's all right, though she sounded a bit tired. Of course, she's been that way a lot lately. Prin said she didn't want to talk about your evening, Gray. She wouldn't, you know."

Marisa prattled on as Gray listened quietly, gaining an astounding amount of information.

"She not that kind, Gray. She's a very private person." He made an agreeing noise, encouraging her to continue.

"In fact," Marisa plunged on. "She's been so tired lately that I insisted she get a checkup. Prin wouldn't even tell me what the doctor said."

Gray's head snapped up. Ninety percent of picking up information involved knowing what was important from what was garbage. That bit was not garbage. Silver eyes narrowed as the number of possibilities that statement opened washed over him.

"She just waved it off and changed the subject." Marisa blithely continued, "Said it wasn't importan—"

"When was she at the doctor again?" Gray interrupted with a gentle murmur designed to get information without disrupting her train of thought.

"I guess it was last Thursday. That appointment took her all day for some reason. We were going to go out shopping that evening, but she had to cancel on me. Said there had been a long wait. You know how doctors are," Marisa mused. "Anyway, you really don't need to worry about her. I'm sure she's fine. She would tell me if she weren't." Marisa paused and slyly inquired, "You guys got along, didn't you?"

Gray smiled into the phone. Dave obviously had left the room because he'd never let his sweet little wife chatter on like that. Marisa didn't have a clue how much information she gave away in her efforts to soften him up and get some details. Why not give her what she wanted? Getting her on his side could only help.

"Oh, we got along all right," Gray smoothly assured her. "Actually, I'm crazy about Prin and would really like to see her again. Just to talk. Work something out…" Gray trailed off knowing Marisa would jump right in.

"I'm so happy to hear that, Gray," Marisa enthused. "She hasn't seen anyone since Kurt died. It's been over four years, and I was getting worried about her. She lives alone and refuses to let anyone help her most of the time. She won't even let Dave take her car into the shop for service. I think that McFarley guy is ripping her off."

"She's been having car trouble?" Gray asked interestedly.

"I think so. She said she couldn't make it over here last Sunday, and I just assumed it was her car again. It's a lemon if you ask me. Of course, she had to go buy it herself. She wouldn't let Dave take a look at it first." Marisa snorted disgustedly. "Said she didn't want to be a bother. As if!"

Gray's grin widened and he settled back into the chair. He was already feeling better. Baby Girl was independent as hell. He liked that. Not having to beat off a flock of men who wanted to look after her saved him a lot of hassle, though this McFarley guy warranted some attention.

"I've known her since we were four and she has never been a bother to anyone in her life," Marisa stated in disgust over the very thought of that ridiculous notion.

Sinking further down in his chair and getting truly comfortable, Gray murmured another agreeing noise and let Marisa go.

"Why, at work, she's always the one who gets stuck there late. I think she lets them dump the hard projects on her because she doesn't want to go home to an empty house. That little cottage is not even the one she and Kurt had. Prin sold the old house three years ago. She said it was just too big to keep. But when she went back to work, I began to worry maybe there were some debts that no one else knew about. Still, she's a computer technician for gosh sakes, not an architect. Those high-falutin architects are just lazy, if you ask me. She spends fourteen hours a day at that office and brings home work on the weekends!"

Gray's eyebrows drew together as he digested the architects' office thing. Those places were filled with men. He scowled. Fourteen hours a day? That had to stop. Marisa paused for a breath and seemed to realize what she was doing.

"I guess all this isn't why you called. But I just wanted you to know that we see her every Sunday afternoon and I talk to her almost every day."

"I appreciate that Marisa. I really do. Do you think you could let her know I'd like to talk to her?" Gray's voice purred over the phone convincingly. "I'm really concerned about her and need to know everything is all right."

"Sure, Gray," Marisa agreed. "I'll see what I can do. It's been nice chatting with you. I hope this works out for you guys. It would be so good for her."

"Me too, Marisa, me too. Well, let me know when you talk to her." He waited for her agreement.

"All right, Gray," Marisa murmured.

They said goodbye and hung up.

Gaining access to her full name, home address and phone number, work address and number was no trick for a man in his business. A relatively short time later, he sat back from the computer. Now he could think of her by her real name. Princess Lilah Turner. He grinned at the name. Who would've believed her given name was Princess? He chuckled. No wonder she preferred Prin.

A bit more investigating and an hour later, her life was all but laid out before him. Possessing those facts directed him to an obvious plan of action. Get as close to this woman as possible. All he needed to do was find a way to seamlessly insert himself into her life.

Work involved extensive traveling. No problem moving his home base. Finding the right house here was the challenge. Where would she like to live? Gray was a master of assessing his options and coming up with tactical advantages. Position on a battlefield often decided the outcome. After Marisa's helpful chat, it took two seconds to figure out the "high ground" in this situation.

Two phone calls later and he'd nailed a prime location. Making an offer that couldn't be refused on the house he wanted didn't cause him one bit of pain. He could afford it. The business had taken off. His company was the best, and only the best could afford him. It wasn't that he didn't have a life to spend his money on, it was more that he seriously didn't need much to survive and never wasted his time acquiring more than he needed—until now. His needs changed completely the moment Prin walked through the door last Friday night.

By Thursday evening, Gray was pulling his Mercedes E Class into his new driveway. The quick flight to Miami to pack essentials and drive back was done in less than twenty-four hours after the house closing Wednesday. The amount of money required to have the place emptied and cleaned by the time he pulled up would have seemed excessive a week ago. Now, it was simply what it took to get the job done.

Glancing over into his neighbor's backyard where a man was standing in front of his sizzling grill, Gray grinned as he met Dave's eyes.

Dave's brows went up as he watched Gray heft the suitcase and bag out of his trunk and take them in the front door. Two seconds later Gray's cell phone rang.

"I just threw another steak on the grill. I take it you're the idiot who bought the judge's house?" Dave questioned into Gray's ear.

"Yeah. Thanks for the steak. I'll be right over." Twenty minutes later, Gray was slicing into a succulent, inch-thick steak at Dave and Marisa's patio table.

"So is this a new hobby for you, buddy? Tossing around stupid money on houses?" Dave asked casually. "I know you've always liked us. But hell, you could've rented the room over the garage if you needed our company that badly. The judge was nearly pissing his pants when he told me how much you paid. It's just cruel to get a guy that old so excited."

"Nice of you to offer the room. But I figure Prin will want her own house," Gray answered around a mouthful of steak.

"Ah. How are you thinking of getting her in there? She's already has a house, you know," Dave mused.

"Her place isn't really big enough for someone my size." Gray shifted in his chair. "This one seemed like it would suit us both."

Marisa laughed and put down her fork. "That place could house a small army, Gray. Is there anything in there? What are you planning to do with all that space?" Marisa asked in amazement then added the invitation of a bed as she realized the huge house had to be empty. "You're welcome to the guest room if you need it."

"Well, I thought we'd fill it." Gray smiled and raised his brows, the suggestive nature of how they'd fill it clear. "Thanks for the offer tonight. The bed and kitchen table are being delivered tomorrow," Gray added.

Both Dave and Marisa sat back and grinned.

"So how come she hasn't told me about the army you all are planning on?" Marisa asked around her smile. "I spoke to her just this morning and she didn't mention being pregnant."

"Haven't really run the plan by her yet," Gray murmured as he finished the last bite of meat. Purposely he concentrated on enjoying the taste, allowing his statement to drift off into the twilight.

"She hasn't called you?" Dave questioned with dawning concern.

"Not yet." Gray took time to enjoy the truly fine red wine Dave served with the meal.

The other two regarded him with a mixture of amusement and surprise.

"I looked over that contract before I handed it to her, Gray. It's a fine piece of ironclad writing there," Dave commented. "I've never known you to break your word."

"Isn't it though?" Gray leaned back and stretched his legs. "I outdid myself with that damn thing, I'll give you that, but if she contacts me, it's no longer binding."

Dave rubbed his chin and considered that. "Yeah. I guess you could read it that way."

"But she hasn't called you. How could you pay that much money for a house when she hasn't even called you yet?" Marisa wanted to know, her brow wrinkled in concern.

Gray gently smiled at her. "I need her to know I'm serious about us. I thought she'd like living next door to you, her oldest friend, so I bought it."

"It has nothing to do with the fact that she's here every weekend and will have to trip over you to get in the door?" Dave ribbed him.

"I wouldn't want to be un-neighborly." Gray shot back. "One has to work hard at being friendly when moving into a new neighborhood. I'm sure I read that in a magazine somewhere. I plan to make sure you guys are really secure in the fact that I want to fit in around here." Gray grinned as he leaned back and warmly regarded his friends.

Dave chuckled and Marisa shook her head. "So what? You're basically going to stalk her?" Marisa asked.

"If I have to," Gray conceded seriously.

"Careful with that, Gray," Dave cautioned. "She's not an idiot. Whatever her reasons are for not calling, they're not stupid or trivial. And she's not a pushover. Don't do something you will both regret."

"What happens between us is a private thing, Dave," Gray murmured softly. "You're not her father."

"No. But she doesn't have a father around anymore to look out for her." Dave's voice was no longer light or amused. Man-to-man talk was serious business. "We're pretty much it for her, if she's counting family members, Gray. Don't expect my loyalties to be with the big Special Forces guy if this doesn't go how you want it to. You can take care of yourself."

Gray grinned, and then chuckled. "Damn, I'm glad she's had the two of you around. I couldn't ask for a better set of friends for my wife. You stay in her corner, Dave. I wouldn't want it any other way."

"Wife?" Marisa squeaked. "You guys didn't fly to Vegas the other night, did you?"

"No, hon. When a guy like me makes up his mind, well, he's done. The ceremony makes absolutely no difference," Gray explained. "Men are sort of single-minded animals. Either a thing is on or off. No middle ground. I'm sure you've noticed that some time in the last eight years with this bas...uh, guy you decided to rehabilitate." Gray nodded toward Dave who was laughing and shaking his head.

"Ceremony might make no difference to you, buddy. But you're about to find out it's of pivotal importance to the sweet woman you think you're going to corral." Dave wrapped an arm around Marisa and nuzzled her ear. "I thought the whole ceremony thing would kill me before I managed to drag her down the aisle."

"Beast." Marisa laughed with Dave. "He was the worst. But seriously, Gray, just because it's a black and white world for you—do not think it is for her. We women don't just flip a switch like men seem to. It'll involve a lot more considerations for Prin."

"And I plan to be right there to help her with those considerations, Marisa," Gray smoothly confirmed.

"But buying a house and moving up here is pretty intimidating. You're used to being in command. Prin is not one of your little soldiers who's just going to fall in line as ordered." Marisa sat back and sadly shook her head at Gray.

"You looked at those guys lately, Marisa?" Gray smiled at her. "Not one of them could be called little, darlin'. But I understand what you're saying. I don't expect her to follow orders. I'm just removing obstacles. I don't want a long-distance relationship. I'm doing what it takes to move toward the objective, that's all. She doesn't have to do a thing except walk through that door over there. I don't expect her to uproot her life or leave the place she calls home. I'm willing to do all that. How is that bad?"

Dave was chuckling quietly. "Go ahead, Marisa. Explain it to him."

"Oh sure, leave me to do all the hard stuff. It's like talking to a brick wall," Marisa grumped to her husband. "Look, Gray. You've taken some really big steps here that involve both of you. Don't you see? Prin will feel like you're crowding her. Like you're sort of forcing her into accepting you."

"No. I haven't asked her to change a thing. I am simply willing to be present in her life," Gray defended himself. "I'd never force her into anything, Marisa. You know that."

"You just don't get it, do you?" Marisa sighed and shook her head. "Well, all I can say is good luck, 'cause you're gonna need it."

The early summer evening melted around them as they sat there on the patio. Gray and Dave chatted about sports and mutual acquaintances for a while. Marisa slid onto Dave's lap and soon drifted off to sleep as the low timbre of the male voices lulled her.

Gray looked at the contented couple and felt a burning ache in his chest. The relationship in front of him was the kind he wanted with Prin. Marisa was tired and not all that interested in the conversation. Instead of going in like most women would have, she would rather curl into the security of her husband's arms and drift off there. The complete commitment and loving trust between them was almost blinding. It burned into someone looking in from the outside. They didn't even know what they were showing him.

He missed Prin with every fiber of his being. Lonely and aching for the one soft body that belonged in his arms was a new and distinctly unpleasant feeling he seemed to be cultivating this week.

Chapter Six

ೕ

Friday morning came and Gray swore furiously as he paced back and forth across the den. He whipped around and paced back to the only bit of furniture in the room, his desk, and picked up the phone, only to slam it back down. A week, damn it! When he got his hands on her and finished taking her, she was going to find out just how bad an idea it was to make him wait.

He'd slipped into her dreams twice this week. Now that he knew what they did to her, he'd simply gone to her and held her. She'd been distressed and restless. He hoped it was the situation between them keeping her up. Holding Prin in his dreams was enough to tide him over, but he wanted her wide awake. He wanted her willing and trusting him. Dream Walking would no longer be enough.

He wanted her to acknowledge him as her man! He wanted to beat his chest and yell as loud as possible that she was his. Every male that crossed her path had to know she was his. The primitive necessity to mark her, to publicly declare his possession of her, was growing stronger every day.

For a week, his inner beast had been going nuts. That internal moron didn't give a damn about the acknowledgment issues. He just wanted her under him. The beast wanted his scent on her, in her. Every minute she wasn't in his sight he felt deprived, jealous and every obsessive emotion in the book. It was immature, intensely irritating and he hated it!

Gray stalked over to the bay window and scowled out at the wide expanse of manicured lawn. After watching Dave and Marisa last night, he felt his aloneness with a ferocity that twisted in his gut. She completed him in every way. Her sweet face soothed every past pain. She healed him in ways that he didn't even know he needed. Not having her was minute-by-minute survival. It wasn't living.

Gray's hand rested on the phone and he wrestled with simply calling her. Still, calling her would be breaking his word. She had to trust him for any kind of a relationship to work. She needed to know he would never, ever go back on a promise. He intended to make a lot of promises to her in the future, and he needed her to believe in them. His hands were tied by that fucking contract. Expletives hissed from between clenched teeth in a steady stream. He couldn't do it. Damn, he wanted to hit something.

His computer dinged the incoming instant message tone. He considered ignoring it. Hell, any distraction would be better than this! Gray slid into the desk chair and opened the message.

Prinlilah: Hello, Gray. I hope this isn't interrupting something important. I just wanted to let you know I'm fine. Mar said you were asking. Sorry for the inconvenience. Thanks

Gray sat there and gaped at the shy little statement on his computer. It was impersonal, to the point and intended to put a period on his concern. Not in this lifetime, Baby Girl. She'd opened this door of communication and by God it was his now. He almost grinned as his fingers flew across the keys in response.

Winstonsecur: Hello, Baby Girl. You are never an interruption. How are you feeling, hon? I've been worried about you. What's wrong? I can feel something bothering you.

He sat back and waited. Let her deal with that. She may not want to admit to Dream Walking, but she wasn't going to escape him and retreat back into some narrow Anglo-logic world. He could not allow her to dismiss him or what they had as simply an evening between strangers. God knew he could be patient, but apparently not about her acceptance of him. Baby Girl had no idea what she was in for if she thought he was going to let her curvy little self go!

Prinlilah: I am fine. REALLY. I just had a minute at work and wanted to let you know. Got to go. Bye

Oh no. Not so quickly, darling mine. This was not ending here. Gray slashed his response across the keys.

Winstonsecur: OK. When you get off work, we'll talk. What time will you be home? And, Baby Girl, I will go ahead and say what I have to say right here and now in front of whoever is leaning over your desk if that's what you want. Your choice.

Prinlilah: Fine. I'll contact you tonight when I get in.

His reply to her clipped little statement came back to show him Prin was off-line. A few seconds of hacking let him know she'd turned off the computer. He laughed and ran his fingers through his hair. Oh, yeah, Baby Girl was going to hear from him tonight!

Prin frowned darkly at her computer and flipped it off with a vengeance. Darrick was standing behind her reading her screen with interest. Turning jerkily to her boss she barely refrained from snapping at him just for being male. He chuckled as her stormy eyes rose to his.

"A new friend, Prin?" Darrick's voice rumbled in obvious amusement.

Darrick was a brilliant architect. His wiry frame and slightly balding head disguised a man in his prime. He looked unassuming and calmly allowed others to see him that way when it suited him, but it was a mistake to discount him in any area. He gave people all the room they needed to hang themselves, and quietly finished the job when they got to the hanging part. In business, it had made him obscenely rich at a very young age. Well, that coupled with a talent that hadn't yet reached its zenith. He was also a very good friend.

When Prin had first come to work here, she'd appreciated his gentle admiration. If she'd wanted it, they could have been an item immediately. He'd taken her tactful refusal in stride and they became friends. He never pressed her for reasons. For that, she was grateful. He never made her feel uncomfortable either. Right now, she was just happy he never pried as well.

"Mmm. Let me show you where I stored all the McDavish Building stuff." Prin ignored his question and got straight to business, hopping out of her chair to drag him off.

She'd just stopped in at work to tie up some loose ends. The events of the last two weeks required she take some time off. Upon hearing her news, Derrick assured her the job was secure and held her tightly in the warm embrace of a friend.

Comforting her didn't faze this man. Women were not the scary mystery to him that most men found them to be. He was that rare breed of man who understood women with sensitivity that never felt feminine itself. It wasn't just young women or pretty women. It was all women. Women knew it. It was scary actually. Prin didn't think he'd met a woman he couldn't charm. He didn't look like a lady-killer at first glance, but she was the only female that she knew of to turn him down. Even when his brief relationships were over, the friendship, or at the very least, gentle affection remained. Not once had she seen a pissed off, rejected female leave his presence.

His gentle empathy undid her there for a minute. When she got her emotions under control again, he sent her off to the bathroom to clean up her face. It was when she got back to her desk and saw that Darrick was tied up on the phone that she had screwed up her courage and sent the Instant Message to Gray.

Now, all too quickly, she and Derrick covered all the projects she was working on. By early afternoon, Derrick shipped her off home to take care of things there. He left her with a twinkle in his eye as he advised her not to keep her "barbarian" waiting.

It was nine p.m. Friday night. Her entire house was cleaned. The wash done and every possible detail attended to from lawn service to scheduling grocery delivery for the time she wouldn't be able to drive. Prin reluctantly sat down and stared at her computer. She still had no idea what to say to Gray. Prin suspected it would be a mistake to wait much longer. Flipping on the machine, she wasn't surprised when a message flashed across her screen as soon as she got on the 'net.

Winstonsecur: Hello, Baby Girl. It took you long enough to get home. Do I need to have a chat with someone at that office?? Just kidding. How are you?

Prinlilah: NO! You better be kidding. I take my job seriously, and I would take any interference there seriously. Am I making myself clear?

Winstonsecur: Calm down. I told you I was kidding. Now, what are you wearing?

Prin glanced down at her old sweats and raggedy football jersey. Why not? Computer land was just as make believe as the set-up in which they met. If he wanted to play, she could show him a thing or two. Letting her troubles lift for a moment, she giggled as her fingers glided across the keys.

Again, he had taken them in an unexpected direction. She'd worried all afternoon and evening about this conversation, dreading it, yet almost unable to stand the wait. But suddenly they were playing and she was laughing. How did he do that?

Prinlilah: Oh, a little of this and…well…none of that.

Winstonsecur: Ah…none of "that" you say? Good girl. No need for "that" between us. Now what's the little "this"?

Prinlilah: Oh, surely you know what "this" is. Every bad girl has one in her wardrobe, and you could make a bad girl out of an angel, Gray. You have seen "this" more often than I have, I bet.

Winstonsecur: Ah, a black lace French corset with thigh-high stockings and five-inch, shiny black heels. Yes, of course I know what "this" is. It looks lovely on you, darling, absolutely stunning.

Prin laughed. How she missed him. Missing him was the most dangerous thing she'd ever done in her life. She could not afford him right now. She couldn't resist him. This playful flirting was too fun, too tempting and too easy.

Prinlilah: I knew you could figure it out. You know it's cleaning day. Dusting wouldn't be the same without the correct outfit.

Winstonsecur: Baby Girl, the things I can do with a feather duster and you in that outfit are illegal in forty-six states. You're just being mean now. A visual like that could drive a man to his knees.

Prinlilah: Gray, the day I see you on your knees, is the day they spot pigs flying over the frozen gates of hell. And why only forty-six states? What's up with the other four?

Winstonsecur: If getting on my knees was all it took to get your attention, sweetheart, you would see me on my knees in the next ten minutes. About the states, I left out Alaska and Hawaii because I'm not sure about their Blue Laws. Nevada would want to sell you a license to do it, but California wouldn't give a damn. Why haven't you called?

Prin's hands trembled. *Here we go*, the serious stuff. Telling him what she faced in the near future was not an option. It's not like they really knew each other. There was no reason to drag him into her life. Even if she did tell him what was going on, what if he couldn't handle it? Oh, God, this hurt. Tears slipped down her face as she typed.

Prinlilah: It's not a good time in my life, Gray. You knew our deal was ONE night. A really great, naughty night. That's all we were supposed to have.

Winstonsecur: It wasn't one night—it's been two years' worth of nights. Is there someone else? Do you have a commitment you can't get out of? I need to know, Prin! Please be straight with me on this!

Prinlilah: No! It's nothing like that! Look, I don't want to talk about it. Please, Gray, there are some things going on in my life that I have no control over. I can't get involved! It's not like we even know each other that well. Can we please just let it go?

Winstonsecur: I don't think I can, Prin. We can't undo this thing. But we can go back to where we should have started. Baby, I want contact with you. I'll back off. We can spend some time getting to know each other. The one thing I can't do is go away. As long as I'm the only guy who gets to see you in that outfit, even if it's only in my mind, I can be a good boy and play nice.

Prinlilah: What does that mean—"play nice"?

Prin got up and started pacing. Could she do this? Could she have him in her life? Would he let her have just this little bit of him? The week had been hellish since she left the hotel last Saturday morning. Wanting him, needing the strength he carried so effortlessly, made her lonely right down to her bones. The loneliness coupled with the stress of her current situation was destroying her. Would he give her this?

No. She was grasping at an illusion because she wanted it so badly. He would want more soon. She knew it. Felt it with every feminine fiber of her being. Perhaps with him in Florida and her up here, it could work for a while, though. Was it worth a try on top of everything else? Perhaps by the time he wanted more she would know if she could give it to him. Maybe leaving this door open between them wasn't a bad thing. She knew she wanted this contact too desperately to deny him. It was better than nothing. He was backing off, letting her breathe a bit, and she wanted him too much not to let him seduce her with this ploy.

Winstonsecur: It means we talk. We play. We are friends, if that's what you want right now. It means I get to stay in your life, if only through this medium for a while if it makes you more comfortable.

Prinlilah: Will you do that, Gray? I would really like it if we could do that.

Winstonsecur: There is just one rule, no dating someone else in real time, Prin. I can't share you, not even a little bit. You have got to promise me that. Just that.

Prinlilah: That goes both ways? Right?

Winstonsecur: You bet!! However, you'd better be prepared to be naughty on this thing for me. If this is all I get, well, you know how I am! ☺ Just talking to you gets me hard, hell, thinking about you gets me hard. It's damn irritating too because you're on my mind 24/7.

Prinlilah: Poor baby, it's been a HARD week for you?? LOL

Winstonsecur: GRRRR… Yes, very hard. The little witch who got me in this condition should feel sorry for me, too. A man can only survive so long on the itty-bitty bit of blood that has been able to make it to my brain this week.

Prinlilah: Oh, so now you're holding me responsible for your troubles? Ha! A big bad boy like you brought low by a little thing like me? I don't think so!

Winstonsecur: Baby Girl, I am sitting here with my tongue hanging out and panting over the pleasure of being allowed to IM you. You, "little thing", can take me as low as you want! The outfit doesn't hurt either.

Prinlilah: So, back to the outfit are we? This corset is pinching a bit. Mind if I take it off?

Winstonsecur: Not at all, sweetheart. Here, let me help you. All those little hooks down the back are tough to reach. Besides, every inch of your back needs kissing. Right down to your naked little ass. You know how distracting I find those enticing globes. God, you have a beautiful ass, baby.

With a chuckle, Prin dashed the tears from her cheeks. He was infectious, distracting and the damn man was making her fall a little more in love with his big, possessive, sexy self. How was a woman supposed to resist a guy who was so macho he oozed testosterone, and yet so seemingly enthralled with her that he would back off when asked to? It was like having a big, unpredictable Bengal tiger agree to play with you.

Prinlilah: You are a silver-tongued devil! However, when that wicked tongue is busy on my body, how are we supposed to get to know each other?

Winstonsecur: Damn it, woman. How can I seduce you when you keep getting all logical on me?

Prinlilah: Poor Gray. It sucks to be you. LOL

Winstonsecur: Yeah, you're so much help with that. So, what's your favorite movie? Are you ever going to let me make love to you in the rain? Do you shop forever, or do you like to get in, get what you came for and get out? Do you insist on wearing panties every day? Do you like ice cream at one a.m.? Are you going to let me suck it out of you? How many pairs of shoes do you own? (The number of shoes is important info when reckoning a woman.) Do you like to eat out? Or is an evening in, by the fire more your style? Can I get you to have dinner naked on the floor by the fire?

Prinlilah: Yikes, Gray, slow down! LOL

Winstonsecur: Slow down? I thought that is what we are doing.

Prinlilah: There's a fireplace in Miami?

Winstonsecur: Well, this is getting to know you stuff. The fireplace could be anywhere. So, how about it? Naked, bearskin rug and Chinese? Sound interesting?

Prinlilah: LOL We have a lot of questions to get through before we get to that one.

Winstonsecur: Tease.

Prinlilah: Tyrant.

Winstonsecur: Yeah, yeah, start from the top. Just get to the naked part quick. I am a desperate man here. On the edge, as it were. Ready to explode with…um…curiosity?

Prinlilah: Oh, I believe you're ready to explode, Gray. Didn't know they were calling it "curiosity" these days. I'll just have to suck it up and start from the beginning, as it were. LOL

Winstonsecur: New rule. No mention of "suck" unless it's in connection to a body part and you're willing to continue until all the "sucking" is done! God, you make me crazy, woman!

Prinlilah: Stop it! I am gonna fall off my chair laughing. Damn, you're easy.

Winstonsecur: Oh Yeah! I am so willing to be easy! Thought you'd figured that out already. MEN ARE EASY for their women. We become a tower of Jell-O when you girls crook your little finger at us. Panting, begging, the works, we are there for you!

Prinlilah: Oh, RIGHT! Jell-O my ass!

Winstonsecur: Sure baby, I'd lick Jell-O off your ass if you like. Haven't tried that before, sounds interesting.

Prinlilah: All right, wise guy. What's your favorite color? Do you like anything besides action movies? Do you watch sports incessantly? Are you into politics? Do you golf? Is there a poker night with the boys? Do you like hanging out in bars? Do you believe in sending a woman flowers? Or is that a foreign concept for you? Do you cook? Do you do your own laundry? Do you expect a woman to pick up after you? Do you drink anything besides beer? Do you really think this long-distance relationship stuff is worth it?

Winstonsecur: YES! It's worth it! Don't ever doubt that. Damn, you ask the really hard questions. Before I answer that minefield of questions you must promise me that if you have a problem with any answer, you'll tell me and we will talk about it. We can compromise on anything, baby. Can you do that?

Prinlilah: Mmmm. We can compromise on anything? That goes both ways again. Compromise being the operative word here, Gray. Does the Dom/sub stuff stay in the bedroom for you? I really need to know.

Winstonsecur: Baby Girl, I am a protective, possessive, and since I met you, a jealous guy. I can't change that. I will do my damnedest to make you happy, though. I will never knowingly hurt you. That includes hurting you by not being able to bend. Yes, the sexual Dom/sub stuff stays private. I will always be an aggressive guy. I have a very high sex drive, and you know that. That's not all our relationship is or will be about, Prin. I want you all the time, in every way a man can want a woman. I don't need to Dom you to be with you, Prin.

Prinlilah: So you're telling me you're bossy, demanding and obsessed with sex.

Winstonsecur: Well, hell, woman. I am telling you that I want you any way I can get you. However, it's still *me* wanting you. Not some other guy you can make up in your head. It's always going to be *me*, Prin. Get used to it. I'll bend as much as I can on most things. But, baby, when it comes to your safety, or health or whatever is really important like that, I won't compromise. You're too important to be casual about, Prin. Do you get that?

Prinlilah: Gray, you don't play fair. How is a girl supposed to resist that?

Winstonsecur: It's working then. You're not supposed to resist, silly woman.

Prinlilah: Yeah, well, we are talking, aren't we? I don't appear to be resisting worth shit. I've got to tell you, Gray. I am an independent woman. I've gotten used to it and I like it. Don't expect a clinging vine because that is not who you're talking to. I'm afraid that my intense sexual needs might have given you the wrong impression. I'm still not clear you get that. Submission happens in the bedroom for me, that's it.

Winstonsecur: Oh, yeah. I get that from you, Prin. I know you have been alone a long time and are used to making your own decisions. So have I. But this relationship takes both of us being willing to bend, hon. We can do that. I know we can. I guess I don't want to imply that I am willing to be someone I'm not. I want you to know the real me, honey. I want you to want the real me. We can make this work, Baby Girl. We just have to keep talking. Keep being in each other's lives. That's all I'm asking for right now.

Prinlilah: You make it sound easy. This doesn't feel easy, Gray. Wanting you is hard. It's scary. You're scary. It feels like you are going take over my life until I just disappear into an obedient shadow. I can't do that, Gray. Yet, I can't stop wanting to feel your arms around me. I can't stop craving what you do to me. Oh, God, it hurts sometimes, Gray. How do we make it stop hurting without ripping each other up? Damn, it's late and I am getting all "girl gushy". Sorry.

Winstonsecur: Oh, my sweet Baby Girl. I want that "girl gushy" stuff more than I want to breathe right now. You feed my soul when you show me your heart. Please, don't ever be sorry for being honest with me. All I can promise is to be willing to move heaven and earth to make you happy, baby. I want to hold you 'til the end of time. I hurt with it, too. So, we are going to have to find a way to make this work.

Prinlilah: I hope we can, Gray. We are an intense combination. Even through this computer, you make me want. You make me need things I have never needed before. Will we burn each other up? I'm so tired, Gray. Yet, I burn. Would it turn to ashes if we burned like this on a daily basis?

Winstonsecur: I don't think so, baby. You just have to be there to find out. I can't stop wanting you. I don't think I ever will. We have to try.

Prinlilah: Okay. I have to get some sleep now. I need to think, too. You promised to back off a bit. Are you going to let us slow down?

Winstonsecur: Get some sleep, sweetheart. I will be here 24/7. The computer is always on. We'll talk some more tomorrow. You should know that my staff really hates you right now. I have been a bear this week. Don't make me tell them you are refusing to talk to me again. Things could get ugly.

Prinlilah: LOL As long as you don't know my address, I'm safe. I'll remember that.

Winstonsecur: Right. These people invade countries without anyone noticing. The things they don't know haven't been thought of yet. LOL Now go to bed!

Prin shut down her computer and sat back. What had she just done? That man was insidious—he snuck under each and every one of her defenses with effortless ease. Every one of her logical arguments drifted away into nothingness under his relentless attention. Resisting him was like trying to resist the wind. Hopeless. It was especially hopeless when she didn't want to resist him at all.

Dragging herself wearily to bed, she shucked the sweats and slid under the covers. But her mind wouldn't stop racing around in circles. Like a rat in a maze, she kept going over the same ground and coming to the same dead end. Nothing had changed. Well, none of the facts had changed. She'd just dug herself deeper into the Gray Winston black hole of emotional turmoil.

Falling in love with him had never been a question. That issue had been settled that night in his arms. She loved him. She loved his iron backbone, she loved his relentless sexual appetite, and she loved his tender possessiveness that could turn fierce and growly. She loved the way he was unafraid to show her he wanted her. She loved his humor, how he laughed at himself.

Curling into a fetal ball under the covers, she relaxed and sank into him. Pretending that he could really be all hers, just for a bit. Pretending nothing else mattered but them. What it would be like if they could be together? Together. It was a nice fantasy to fall asleep to.

Chapter Seven

🔊

Saturday morning dawned bright and clear. Gray didn't appreciate the fact that his view of it was uninterrupted by sleep. He was sprawled across his bed alone, watching the sun come up and thinking about the woman who should be tucked up beside him.

What the hell was it that she felt could keep her from him? He couldn't imagine a thing that would do it for him. He'd been real busy imagining since she signed off the computer last night. The shit he came up with only made him mad. It was useless. The logical side of his brain was disgusted with all this conjecture.

His inner beast had been making an awful racket. That idiot was beating against his cage and bellowing his displeasure at not having the woman here. Now! Regardless of whatever she thought she wanted. She belonged with him, damn it! His logical man agreed, but pointed out that they might need some sleep between now and that point in the future when she was here where she belonged. The beast screamed at the emptiness of sleep. He wanted to fuck. Fuck her until she couldn't move. Fuck her so hard and deep that she didn't remember the feel of life without his cock jammed up in her somewhere. Fuck her until she admitted she belonged to him. Fuck her until she agreed never to leave him.

Gray was afraid and he didn't like it. Not one damn bit. He'd never felt fear like this before. Ten months of torture hadn't produced fear like this. He'd never doubted there was an end to the torture. As long as he was alive, Rem would come for him. Anything could be endured if there was an end in sight. Even when he'd almost lost his life several times on missions, he hadn't been afraid like this. Damn it to hell and back! He needed that woman.

The sun was fully up now. Gray rolled off the bed and headed for the bathroom. He stood in the shower and looked down at himself. His erection stabbed up and demanded relief. His whole body hurt with wanting her. His head pounded, his chest ached, his eyes were scratchy and his legs felt wobbly. It felt like he'd spent the night in a bar fight instead of on the bed. Shit, damn and fuck!

Leaning a tired forearm against the cool tile wall, Gray rested his forehead on it and reached for his dick with the other hand. He suspected jerking off in the shower was about to become a habit. He took the job in hand and cursed in a steady stream, closing his eyes just long enough to picture her coming apart in his arms. His whole body convulsed as he spewed seed onto the shower wall in long, shuddering streams. It took a while for the trembling to subside and let him to get back to the business of actually having a shower. He shook his head in disgust. He was in deep, desperately deep.

Over breakfast, Gray contented himself with the thought that there was always Plan B. She'd damn well better work with him on Plan A, or at least Plan B. Gray knew Plan C would belong to the beast. She really wouldn't like Plan C. Nope, Plan C would piss her off big time and probably involve jail time for him. Neither of them would like Plan C.

Later that morning, he was again sitting at his desk staring at the phone. His hand actually rested on it while he listed in his head again all the reasons he couldn't just pick it up and hear her voice. The phone rang and he snatched it up.

"Winston," Gray barked into the phone.

"Get your ass over here, Winston!" Dave yelled. "Now I have both of them crying on my patio! Whatever the hell you did, you better fucking fix it!" The phone was already dead in Dave's ear.

Before Dave finished his sentence, Gray was out the door and sprinting across the lawn. Taking the four-foot stone wall dividing their properties was no problem. He vaulted it and landed in Dave's backyard. The patio deck was right in front of him where the two women sat beside each other, hugging and crying.

Dave burst out his back door just as Gray made it to the steps. His eyes only on Prin who was now gaping at him, her red eyes round and amazed.

Prin pulled away from Marisa just as Gray slid to his knees in front of her. His big hands rested lightly on her thighs. Afraid to gather her to him while she stared down at him in complete shock, he did the only thing a man could do in a situation like this. Promise to fix it.

"What is it, Baby Girl?" Gray pleaded. "Whatever it is, I'll fix it. Just tell me."

Her hand drifted across to his hair, as if to reassure her he was real. He grabbed that shaky little hand and pressed his lips to her palm, then held it to his thundering heart.

Big tears welled up in her eyes and slid down her face as she stared down at him. It was too much. He surged up, lifting her onto his lap as he slid into her chair. Bent over her, his entire body surrounded her protectively as he kissed the wet tracks down her cheeks.

Prin laughed shakily and turned her lips to his. Eagerly Gray molded his mouth to hers and plunged deeply into her. He drank in her sweet taste like the starving man he was. Sliding his tongue across silky flesh and swirling around her tongue, sucking avidly when she thrust her tongue into his mouth.

He needed to make her understand that he would do anything for her. Slay dragons, battle demons, follow her into hell if need be. Whatever it was. Someone would have to be stepping over his cold, dead body to make her cry again, ever! He didn't have the words. He'd never needed the words before, so he had no idea where to find them. He tried to show her with his kiss, his body.

Her shuddering little body melted into him like a liquid flame. His hands ran over every inch of her that he could reach, caressing, stroking. He was fevered in his need to touch her, feel her come alive in his arms, and she did. Somehow, her arms were locked around his neck and her breasts pressed pebble-hard nipples into his tensile-steel chest.

Her intense response left him with no doubt that she'd suffered as much as he had this last week. The reason she hadn't called him dropped to number two on his list of urgent questions.

He withdrew slowly from her mouth and felt her hands frame his face as she blinked up at him.

"What are you doing here, Gray?" Prin asked, still shocked at his appearance, vaulting over Marisa's wall. "Why were you at the judge's house?" She glanced at Marisa and Dave as if they could explain the mystery of his arrival from next door.

"It's not the judge's house anymore. It's mine," Gray growled. Breathing in deep to clear his head, he dropped a kiss on her forehead and repeated himself. "What is wrong, Baby Girl? Why were you two crying like that?"

Her big eyes gazed up at him blankly. "You bought the judge's house?" she squeaked. Her brow wrinkled as she tried to comprehend that.

Gray nodded, and waited for her answer to his question.

"Really?" Prin still couldn't comprehend it.

Smoothing a hand down her cheek, his thumb brushed away the remnants of her tears. "Yeah, really," Gray confirmed.

"Why?" was her next question.

He blew out a breath and realized that no further information would be forthcoming until she grasped his new home issue.

"Yes, Prin. I bought it last Wednesday. I needed to look at you at least once a week, even if it's only from a distance, just in case you decided to never see me again." He continued as fast as possible to get this part over with. "I thought buying the house next to yours might tick you off. Maybe make you get a court order or something. To avoid the appearance of stalking, I bought the judge's house. However, I'm willing to do the stalking thing if I have to. Dave just called me because you both were crying out here and he thinks I did something. I haven't done anything, yet. Could we get back to the question of why you were crying? Please," he ended earnestly. His eyes searched her face while his speech sank in.

Her brow furrowed and she leaned back from him. "You actually bought a gi-normous house so you could look at me?" she demanded loudly.

"Yes," he waited.

Prin hopped off his lap and darted across the patio to stand on tiptoes trying to look at his new house. Gray groaned.

Dave stifled a laugh as Marisa elbowed him in the stomach and it became a cough.

Gray turned to Marisa. Now here was a fountain of information if there ever was one. Surely, she could, as one of the criers, shed some light on the subject.

"Marisa, what's going on?" Gray asked as Dave turned to her also.

"I can't, Gray. It's Prin's news." Marisa shook her head and reached a shaky hand for Dave, who instantly wrapped his arms around her. They all looked at Prin again.

Prin plopped down on her heels and wrapped her arms around herself as she took a deep breath. Reluctantly she turned back to them and looked straight into Gray's eyes, she smiled shakily.

"I didn't call you because I didn't want to start something I couldn't finish, Gray." Prin answered his second question. For Gray, the answer was garbled female talk. It told him nothing.

He stood up, but didn't move any closer, afraid to spook her now that she seemed ready to talk.

"It's already started," Gray assured her. "How it ends will be up to both of us."

Prin shook her head and looked down. "No, not always."

Edging cautiously closer to her, he softly questioned, "Can't you tell me what the problem is?"

She shook her head and wiped some new tears off her cheeks. Her breathing got a little choppy for a second but she willed it back under control. Her battle for composure was ripping his heart out.

"You have to tell him, Prin," Marisa cajoled. "He's here now. Can you imagine the mess he'd make of my house if you don't? I'll never get rid of him."

They both laughed shakily. "I know, Mar. He's just so big."

Prin's eyes swung back to Gray and the weak humor faded from her face. Clasping her hands in front of her in an attempt to control the trembling, she gulped a few breaths and smiled at him sadly.

"Week before last they found a mass in my right breast," she stated quietly. "They don't know what it is. I've been having tests all week but both the surgeon and my doctor have never seen anything like it before."

Gray swallowed hard as the enormity of her statement rolled over him. He stepped closer to her but she held up a trembling hand to stop him.

"Don't, Gray. I'll never get through this if you touch me." He froze and waited for her to continue.

"They want to take it out as soon as possible, so I go in for surgery Monday morning. I came over to ask Marisa to drive me to the hospital that morning. I had to tell her about it and we both started crying."

Prin glanced at Marisa and smiled. "She's also pretty pissed at me because I didn't tell her until just now. I had to be sure before I said anything. You understand that don't you, Mar?"

"No, Prin. I should have been there for you during all those yucky tests. How could you not tell me? I'm really mad about that!" Marisa was at no loss for words and was about warmed up for a tirade when Dave dropped a kiss on her nose. "How about we let Prin finish before we take the rubber hoses to her?"

Gray slashed a grateful look at Dave and turned back to Prin. "Go on, sweetheart," he encouraged.

"I go in real early because—" she had to take a shaky breath, "—if what they take out is malignant, they will have to take out some lymph nodes to test also. If those test out fine, we're done. But if things don't go well they might have to do a lot more extensive surgery."

Gray felt every muscle in his body tighten. "May I hold you now, baby?" he asked quietly. She looked at him searchingly.

"Do you understand what I'm saying, Gray? After Monday I might not be a whole woman." Tears welled again in her eyes, her hands gestured wildly. "Or I might be a woman with a very short life expectancy. Even if, by some miracle, everything tests fine, they are still going to be cutting into my breast and taking a chunk out. I'll feel really shitty for around six weeks. Not much of a playmate for a while."

His gaze never wavered. His intent expression remained fixed and she tried again. "I can't ask you to deal with this, Gray. Death is hard. I know. There is no reason for you to go through this. We hardly know each other."

"Are you done?" he asked. She nodded jerkily.

Gray stepped forward and had her in his arms almost instantly, wrapping all of himself around her. She sank into him and giving up the fight to be strong. It felt like he'd been holding his breath until he could have her back in his arms again. Burying his face in her hair, he rocked her back and forth gently. Giving her the comfort of his body.

Dave and Marisa were holding each other tightly as they watched the other couple merge into what looked like one body. They turned quietly and stepped into the house, the door closed silently behind them.

After what seemed like a long while, Gray swung her up into his arms and started striding across the lawn.

"Where are we going?" Prin asked. Her voice muffled in his neck, her arms wrapped tightly around it.

"To my bedroom," Gray's low voice growled.

She smiled then giggled into his neck.

"What's so funny?" he demanded. The situation was a lot of things for him. Funny wasn't even close though. They'd reached the short wall and he sat on it to swing his long legs over it while holding her high in his arms. His pace quickened as he neared the back door.

Prin looked up at him and a smile hovered around her lips. "It's just such a male reaction." Her face got serious again. "Gray, sex isn't going to change anything. It's not going to make it go away, or fix it."

"Making love," he corrected.

"Huh?" Prin asked.

"Making love, Prin. Not sex." He glanced down at that sweet little face and quickly turned his attention back to the serious business of getting in the house. All he had to do was get through the kitchen and up the stairs.

"We are going to my bedroom so I can make love to you. Then it's going to be my turn to talk," he stated matter-of-factly.

"Gray! Have you even been listening to me at all?" she demanded exasperated.

At the open back door, Gray shouldered them in and kicked it shut. "I heard every word, Baby Girl. But it doesn't change a thing."

She smacked his shoulder. "We need to talk, Gray. For one thing I can't stay up all night."

"It's eleven a.m., I think we might be done by nine p.m. this evening if you have to go home and pack something. Then you have all day tomorrow to rest up and tell me how you want the house arranged." He was sprinting up the stairs.

"Gray!" Her voice rose as he shoved open the bedroom door. "This is crazy!"

He kicked the bedroom door shut and stopped. White-hot eyes looked down at her. "I'll tell you what's crazy. Thinking that I'm not interested enough to want you, regardless of what happens Monday. It's crazy to believe that what happened between us could stop, or fade or whatever it is your female brain has come up with."

He stood her in front of him and started undressing her. "I've waited patiently for a week, Prin. I'm done waiting." Her shirt dropped to the floor. "You're mine, I want you. I need you in my bed every night." Her jeans and shoes hit the floor.

Her mouth opened and he laid a finger over it. Gray reached behind her to unsnap the bra and flick it off her shoulders. "I know how monumental your diagnosis is. I get it that the future has a lot of questions in it. But there are several things that are certain." Her panties slid down her legs.

"I'm here. I'm the man who will to drive you to the hospital Monday morning." He started tearing off his own clothes, while she stood in front of him naked. "I'm the face you'll see when you wake up." His shirt lost all its buttons as he jerked it open and shrugged it off. "I'm the man who is going to take care of you afterwards." His belt whipped out of the pant loops so fast it swooshed. "I'm the one who will be there regardless of what comes next."

His pants thudded to the floor. "I'm the man who loves you." He stepped out of them and his shoes and socks at the same time. Gray picked her up and sort of tossed her on the bed, his massive body followed her, landing on top of her. Bulging forearms cushioned his weight from falling on her.

"I'm the man who is going to marry you." His mouth slammed down on her shocked lips, his tongue plunging deeply into her. He demanded her tongue in his mouth so he could suck on it. Her body arched up to reach him while his knees pressed down between hers, powerfully spreading them.

Rubbing his rock-hard erection up and down her slit, he coated it with the excess cream he found there. His hands grasped both her breasts and pressed them together. He tore his mouth away from hers and dived down to draw a taut nipple into his mouth. His tongue flattened against the hard nipple, he flicked back and forth sharply before nipping it gently.

Her neck arched back. Fire burned up from her clit as he mercilessly sawed his cock over her, deepening the pleasure shooting through her breast as he drew on her nipple harshly. He switched to the other breast swiftly, leaving her swollen flesh to be pinched and pulled by his fingers. He scraped a nail across the throbbing, abandoned nipple and she convulsed. He wasn't gentle. Manipulating those luscious globes of flesh consumed him. His fingers kneaded pliant flesh, milking it into his mouth insistently.

Her climax crashed over her hard. It ripped through her like an out of control freight train. He ignored it and kept tormenting her breasts, pounding at her mound without entering it. Prin writhed beneath him. Her fingers clawed down his back in a desperate attempt to press him into her, as he drove her back up to a peak of sensation that shattered her mind with the ferocious release it required. She came again. Her legs clamped high around his waist, her heels dug into him as she shuddered through it.

Gray grabbed her legs just above the backs of her knees and jerked them up. He pressed them into her chest and dropped his face to her drenched cunt. His mouth covered her entire mound and sucked in hard. Her body rose off the bed until only her shoulders remained on the pillows.

Her mouth gaped open in a soundless scream. She couldn't get enough air into her lungs. He narrowed his attention to her clit. His teeth gently clamped down on her swollen flesh and her bottom slammed back down on the bed. Her clit held in his teeth like that made her still beneath him in complete surrender. Her entire body focused on his next move. Gray's tongue snaked out, and slithered back and forth across it with mind-shattering speed.

Prin clutched the sheets and sobbed as her body jerked uncontrollably. "Gray, please. I beg you. Take your pleasure." His hands slid under her ass to lift her up to him, but other than that he ignored her again.

She gasped and pleaded. He switched his attention to her convulsing opening. His tongue sank into her deeply and licked out her cream. He rode her to such exquisite pleasure that she thought she would die. She begged him to fuck her.

Both man and beast were in agreement on this one. The woman he craved lay writhing beneath him and he wasn't letting her up. Getting his fill of her was an imperative he didn't even want to control. When he was done she'd fully understand where she belonged and to whom. Then they'd talk.

Both his thumbs were now gliding up and down the sensitive strip of flesh between cunt and back entrance. He drew her silky lubricant down to circle it around her tender ass and glided back for more.

Hot and insistent his mouth latched onto her clit painfully and she slammed into another climax, gushing her essence for him to press into her bottom. Hardly aware of his fingers there until two slipped inside her. He carefully stretched her. Sliding in and out of her then adding a third finger pressing into her little ass while his hot, devastating mouth sucked her through yet another hard orgasm.

Suddenly she found herself flipped over on her stomach. One of his arms slid under her, lifted her hips to make a space for the two pillows he pressed into the gap. She was dazed. He leaned over her and reached into the nightstand for some lubricant. Prin was gulping air desperately and had no time to pay attention to his actions.

He shoved her knees forward again so she was in a wide kneeling stance over the pillows that cushioned her. The lubricant tube pressed to her back entrance as he squeezed. The cold sensation of the cream shocked her into realizing what he was doing. Her eyes opened wide as the cool substance entered her. Yet resistance didn't occur to her. He was taking her, taking what belonged to him and not asking permission in any fashion. Exactly what she craved from him.

Gray leaned over so his face hovered above Prin and whispered in her ear. "Mine, Baby Girl. My cunt. My ass." The fat head of a plug slid past her opening. "My woman!" He pressed the plug in slowly. She squeezed her eyes shut as her tender opening strained to take the wickedly wide length of the dildo he pressed into her.

Her body was so strung out from the endless orgasms that he'd driven her to that the biting burn as he took her ass with the monstrous plug felt like a welcome relief. It felt so good as he inched it into her, so hard, and hot. Her flesh sizzled as it separated for the intruder. Prin strained to relax the tight ring of muscle and let the insidious invader take her ass, pressed back onto it with her last shred of energy as she accepted the final inch of it into her body.

"All of you. Every part of you is mine. I want it, Prin. I want the good stuff and the bad stuff. I want everything." He lowered his body onto her. His weight pressed down on her as she felt his now latex-covered cock slide into her weeping cunt at last. He was huge. She felt him slice into her like a burning branding iron. He relentlessly pressed up into her body to sear his mark on her womb.

"I know about death, baby. I know about pain. I would have welcomed that final answer two years ago if you hadn't held me in your arms and whispered in my ear that you needed me," he said. His body was fully draped over hers and he lay his cheek against hers to whisper, "Do you remember that night, Prin?" His eyes closed. "You Dream Walked me back to life and we have been together ever since. Don't ask me to leave you now over something that we can fight. I can't, baby. I won't leave you."

Prin's hands inched up the bed. Her fingers traveled around his elbows and slid over muscular forearms as she stretched up until her palms glided over the backs of his hands. Her fingers slipped down between his. Their hands clenched together.

"You owe me two years worth of sleep, Gray," she replied softly. "And then you owe me an explanation."

Gray lifted his head and peered down at her.

"You can start paying me back right after you finish fucking your woman." Her eyes were still closed but her lips tilted in a contented smile.

A grin crept across his face as his hips rocked into her slowly. "You know who I am?"

"Mmmm. As you said, I know what you are." She pushed back at him with every gentle thrust. Her body thrummed in an unbelievably desperate arousal, the blended pain and pleasure made her drunk, needy.

"When?" He lifted most of his weight off her and shifted back on his knees a bit for better leverage. Every inch of his cock was squeezed tightly as he drew out of her.

"When…?" Her breath hitched as his body pulled out and shoved back into her insistently. "What?" Tingling fire shot up her spine and her cunt convulsed as it bathed him in her silky fluid. Her tired body writhed weakly beneath him.

"When did you know who I am to you?" he asked again. He sat back on his knees behind her. He watched himself disappear into her as he looked down. So pretty. She stretched around him so tightly. His balls slapped her clit and splattered the evidence of her pleasure over both their thighs.

"When I woke… Oh, God, more, Sir… Saturday night… Please, Sir…and could think. Ah. I thought of… Oh, God. Yesss… Just like that… I thought maybe you…ah could be, um… Damn it, Sir, I ah… I can't talk and… Ohhhhh…"

Moaning loudly, she felt his fingers snake around her hip to trace every bare inch of her cunt. Gentle fingers tracked down the plump folds stretched so tightly around the root of him, and back up to her clit. His slow, sure strokes destroyed her ability to think a little bit more with every damp caress. She bucked back at him.

One hand clamped down on her hip while the other tormented her clit. He leaned over her again—powerful thighs steadily pounded his monster erection into her. "Who do you belong to, Baby Girl?"

Her hands now gripped the headboard to brace herself. Those insidious fingers never stopped pinching, plucking, and then gently soothing her swollen little clit. Pleasure tore though her and her body quivered on the edge of release.

Suddenly a harsh slap landed on her bottom.

"Come on, my sweet bitch," he panted, driving into her even harder. "Tell me who owns this greedy little body!" Another sharp blow accompanied his demand.

"You!" she screamed. "Only you!"

"Say my name, damn you!" The guttural growl was hardly intelligible. Steady spanks were raining down on her quivering ass, turning it a bright, glowing red as he rode brutally into her grasping cunt.

She thrust herself back at him. Lifting her pink ass for each smack and moaning deeply. The decadent pleasures became unbearable. The humiliation was in loving being spanked and fucked like a bitch in heat at the same time. It drove her over the edge of sanity. She screamed his name over and over again. Prin climaxed so hard her body bowed off the bed, supporting his entire weight on her toes and hands. He slammed her back down with a body-powered thrust.

The beast inside him roared his satisfaction. At last, he was dominating his mate through her climax, ramming into her convulsing cunt and forcing her to take more. The beast assured her submission by not allowing her to stop coming. He hammered her harder. Struggling to pull out and slam back in as her inner muscles gripped him so tightly. Finally, he exploded inside her. Clutching her, he jerked helplessly as endless streams of hot cum blew out the head of his cock. Incessant aftershocks racked his body. She responded with a shuddering tremble of her own each time he jerked in her. It took a long time for reality to creep back into the room.

Dazed, he pulled out and rolled off of her. Gray looked over at her limp, exhausted form and swore viciously. She was crying. Soft sobs shivered through her worn-out body as tears slipped down her cheeks. She lay there with her arms huddled under her, her legs spread wide in submission and wept.

Gray wanted to kick his own ass into next week. She obviously could hardly move. He knew all too well about intense pain. Pain too terrible to even let you scream. Had he caused her some internal damage? Being crazed with lust and banging the hell out of her was possibly the most stupid thing he could have done. Damn, like that was going to make the woman need his brainless ass. Scrambling frantically to sit up, he grabbed the pillows out from under her and searched the bedding for blood.

Chapter Eight

ॐ

"Where does it hurt, honey? I'll get a blanket around you and take you straight to the emergency room!" He rolled off the bed and searched for his pants as he flung the condom away carelessly.

"Get back here and hold me," the whispery little demand wobbled out softly.

Gray froze, and peered around at her. "You're not bleeding?" he inquired, still looking for any visible signs of injury.

She shook her head no and sniffled.

"Not in pain?" he continued, slowing his search as nothing seemed blood-spattered.

Rolling over slowly and holding up her arms, reaching for him, she shook her head no again.

He edged gingerly back up on the bed. Leaning over her but not touching, he worriedly searched her face. Her outstretched arms rested along his as he held himself up over her, a hand planted on either side of her rib cage.

He closed his eyes and grimaced. If it wasn't a physical pain, it was something worse. Steeling himself for what could only be a painful response to his question, he asked, "Tell me why you're crying, Baby Girl."

She laughed gently up at him. "Because I'm so happy. Because I'm scared."

He eased down onto her, his arms tunneling under her to fold the still quaking body into him. He frowned down at her in confusion. "What scared you, baby? Did I?"

She nodded yes.

A stricken look crossed his face. "Can we discuss it?"

Prin nestled into his shoulder and let him turn them over so she draped across his chest, his hands running gently up and down her back.

She shook her head again, sniffled softly and laughed at the same time. "I guess we'd better. I'm not getting over it."

Gray's body froze. He didn't even breathe. She wouldn't be sure his heart kept beating if her ear hadn't been pressed to his chest. Lifting her head to look at him, she frowned. "Gray, are you all right?" Her tear-bright eyes searched his pale face.

"Really? You're afraid of me?" Gray croaked. The realization that he'd damaged the only precious thing in his world shattered him. It had been a rough fuck, but he'd given her pleasure before, made sure she was ready. For a moment, when he'd seen she was crying, he'd been ready to do bodily harm to himself over it. But then she'd seemed to want him again. Now she was telling him that he scared her? That she couldn't handle what they were together?

"Of course, I'm afraid of you! I have no defenses where you're concerned. You touch me and I fly. It scares the stuffing out of me. You wander in and out of my dreams like you own them. That's spooky and not even fair. I can't say no to you. That's the scariest part of all." Her list of items didn't sound hysterical. It sounded—petulant.

Gray's body slowly relaxed as he digested her words and carefully analyzed the mood in which they were delivered. "You said you were happy, too. What are you happy about?"

"I'm happy about you. I need no defenses where you're concerned. You touch me and I fly. You wander in and out my dreams. I can't say no to you. You make me happy." Her voice purred this list. It was melodic and dreamy.

"The tears, baby, were they happy or afraid?" Gray pressed. He ruthlessly held the joy in check as he absorbed her second list. He had to be sure. There was no margin for error. A more truly life and death situation had never occurred for him before.

"Both," her tone turned tired.

"How am I supposed to know the difference? How can I fix it if I don't know the difference?" Frowning fiercely, Gray stared at her. The total concentration on her words manifested in his intense scrutiny.

"You just have to be there, Gray. You'll know the difference." Smiling into his chest her eyes closed again and tears dripped onto his skin. They lay there for a while. He kept thinking the tears would end, but a steady, quiet stream of them continued.

"Baby?" his tone still worried.

"Yes," she mumbled.

"We still with the happy tears?" he asked cautiously.

"Um-hmm," she assured him.

"I love you, Prin." His low voice reverberated into her bones, his tone and timbre a deep resonance as he held his heart out to her.

Prin propped her head up on his chest, watery warm chocolate eyes surveyed him. Smiling gently up at her dark, worried warrior, she reached out to smooth a hand down his tense cheek.

"I know you do, Gray. That's why I'm crying. I'll stop in a minute. I promise," she whispered in a reverent tone. His head turned enough to kiss her fingertips as they floated past his mouth, never breaking eye contact with her.

"Do you want to tell me anything?" he asked tightly.

Her smile widened and the silver tracks on her cheeks had a chance to dry as humor chased the storms from her eyes.

"Isn't this your bedroom, Gray?" she asked quietly.

"Yeah," he confirmed.

Prin just smiled up at him.

Gray frowned now as again he thought the worst was about to happen, he asked, "Is there a problem with it being my bedroom?"

Her eyes traveled around the bare room. Naked windows streamed early afternoon sunlight down on them. Bright white walls stretched around the unrelentingly empty, cavernous space. A shiny hardwood floor flowed from wall to wall, unbroken by carpet. In fact, the only thing in this room was the monster bed they were currently laying on and the nightstand beside it.

Eyebrows raised she met his gaze again. "Besides it being empty. No."

A mischievous grin played at her mouth as Prin prodded, "Thought you said when we got to your bedroom it would be your turn to talk. I don't want to get in trouble."

Warmth bloomed in his chest. Slow as sunrise on a winter morning, the soul-deep smile crept over him. Silver-blue eyes crinkled and glowed as his hands stroked purposefully down her back until they both cradled a plump butt cheek. Kneading them softly, his teeth flashed into a grin. With each squeeze of her delectable flesh, he made sure the plug in her ass was slowly pressed inward.

"Oh, Baby Girl, you are already neck deep in the stinky stuff," he purred happily.

Attempting a frown while her eyes sparkled produced a silly face that she couldn't hold onto, she collapsed laughing on his chest.

"Are you interested in the list, pet?" he chuckled.

"Good God! There's a list? I've only been here an hour or so." Lifting her head to try and glare at him. "How could I possibly have messed up that much?"

Gray rolled them over and propped his head up on one hand. His other hand started ticking off her sins.

"One, you didn't call."

"Two, you didn't call."

"Three, you didn't tell me about the doctor."

"Four, you didn't call."

"Five, you just had a gazillion orgasms without permission." Grinning triumphantly down at her, his hand dropped to her waist.

Prin lifted the back of her hand to her forehead in B-movie heroine drama, she clutched her chest with her other hand. Horror was written across her face and she gushed in response, "Oh, no! Gray, whatever is to become of me? Please, kind Sir, tell me what I must do?"

Gray scowled down at her when he noticed that the hand, which was supposed to be clutching her chest in remorse, was actually clutching her breast and running its thumb over a pouting nipple. His eyes remained glued to the enticing sight as he drawled in a rumbling B-movie villain voice, "For your first five crimes the price of moving in with me is required."

"No, no, not that!" she laughingly wailed.

He shushed her without taking his eyes off her breast and that fascinating little hand manipulating it. Gray continued, "There is nothing to be done about it, my dear. Your punishment has been decided!"

Her other hand slid under the neglected breast, lifting it. Slender fingers crept up to a distended nipple and squeezed, twisting slightly and releasing. Both hands worked her breasts as she watched his eyes glaze over.

"You said my 'first five' crimes. Are there more?" she whispered. Mischievous eyes danced over his enthralled face.

Gray nodded, swallowing tightly.

Her hands suddenly abandoned her breasts and smoothed down the slender rib cage to her abdomen. His gaze tracked them avidly. "What am I accused of, Sir?" she asked in the movie voice. "I lay before you an innocent, I tell you."

"Oh, *hell, no,* you aren't," he breathed as he watched her fingers glide down past her navel to trace circles on the sensitive mound of damp skin just above her slit. He could see her pink little clit swell and push out of its hood.

Snickering knowingly, she slowly spread her legs wide. She trailed a forefinger from each hand down the blushed outer lips of her vagina. A large paw snagged the leg next to him and hooked it over his own legs to open her wider still. Propped up higher on his now straightened arm, he sucked in a breath as her fingers hooked inside her swollen cunt lips and pulled them open.

She rimmed her inner folds, sliding up and down the slick surface of that first deep groove sensuously. *Mmm, that was good.* Teasing like this lost her the advantage. Prin found herself adrift in the decadent thrill of being watched as she fingered herself. It was a new, wicked pleasure. Only nasty girls did this. She'd never done it in front of anyone! The exhibitionist inhabiting her body was delightfully disturbing. She seemed willing to come out for him on a regular basis. Prin drowned in the seductive power this new play fed her.

Her back arched slowly as heat burned its way up from her core. Gasping softly, her fingers met again over her clit. It pulsed in excitement as she held the concealing lips open while one finger gently circled the throbbing bundle of nerves. The other spread her inner folds and glided down to her dripping opening. Eyes drifted closed as hips lifted up to press her desperate little pussy up into her own hands. Prin rocked her steaming cunt slowly into her own deliciously twisting fingers. Delicate heels dug deeply into the mattress while her body vibrated above it.

Breath shuddered out of Gray as he watched two creamy fingers sink deeply into her pink flesh. His face was flushed, nostrils flared, his body actually trembled when those fingers slowly drew out. The slippery action was accompanied by slurping sounds as if her body were trying to suck them back in. Prin sank them back in to the hilt, as she rose off the bed to meet them again.

"Ooooh…" Prin breathed. "Ohhh, yesss…" Moaning quietly to herself, her hips rotated in a circular motion on her deeply embedded digits. The fingers over her clit squeezed and rubbed, sending the breath out of her in shuddering groans. Each gust of air caused her magnificent breasts to jiggle sweetly. His eyes darted back and forth, overwhelmed with the abundance of sensually undulating woman.

Gray thought his head might explode and he wasn't sure which one would go first. He'd never seen anything as beautiful as Princess Lilah pleasuring herself. She flowed like a fine wine. That taut, willowy body danced slowly to an erotic beat only she could hear. Her creamy skin flushed from head to toe as her pulse pounded through her veins. She gave herself up fully to the hedonistic pleasure, willingly exposing this most private moment for his viewing pleasure.

His mouth dropped open as he watched her. He'd seen beautiful women do sexy things before. This was off the scale. The moaning porn queen in his bed blew him away. Damn, she was fine!

Suddenly, he was very clear on why wars were fought over a woman. How whole nations could be plunged into turmoil to recover one man's obsession. If someone, anyone at all, tried to take her from him the struggle would be to the death. No doubt about it. No holds barred, no quarter given, no prisoners. Moreover, he damn sure wouldn't be the one dying!

Fingers glided in and out of that snug little opening as the glossy inner folds clung to them. Her body curved up in a liquid ripple to meet each thrust, then sinking away as she pulled out again. Her slender neck arched up as her head rolled back and forth across the pillow. She was a living flame, burning him to the bone with her slow climb to climax. The need to grab her was only overpowered by his astonishing inability to move due to extreme fantasy fulfillment.

Prin no longer cared if the whole town watched. The fire in her cunt started at a slow burn, but now it licked up every sensitive nerve in her body. Each languid touch drew it to new heights. This wasn't the mind-numbing inferno Gray gave her. It was gentler, but still insidiously hot.

"Mmmmm, ohhh." She couldn't help the breathy gasps of pleasure and didn't try to. She needed to drag air in deeply as she pressed harder into her drenched cunt. Her mouth felt dry, her throat parched as the heat consumed her. Prin's fingers slowly tormented widely displayed flesh, each moment of smoldering indulgence drawn out leisurely.

She milked her pleasure center shamelessly as she slid her fingers up and down and pinched her clit firmly. All the while fingers thrust rhythmically into her. She ground her hips into them. Her lower body swiveled and rocked in slow motion. She was close, so close. The rush tingled up her legs. Her body trembled as she dug her fingers deeply into a visibly constricting cunt. Fingers pinched her clit sharply as she pulled it up into full view and flung herself over.

Her pale body arched off the bed. Hips thrust upward as her mouth gaped open in a long, soundless wail. She crashed onto the shores of bliss with unexpected violence. Wave after wave of molten heat folded her into velvet pleasure while her fingers stroked her swollen cunt through it. Clit and cunt lips swelled impossibly fuller as her intimate tissues flushed deeply in wanton feminine satisfaction.

Slowly she sank back to the bed. Her fingers gently pulled out of her cunt. She dragged the liquid clinging to them up her body to trail it over pebbled nipples. Sticky fingers squeezed pouting nipples firmly. The distended points were puffy, swollen and achy, needing the attention to calm down. She massaged them tenderly as her breathing returned to normal. Her legs remained wide open and her hips rocked soothingly as if rubbing against a phantom lover while she petted herself into calmness.

Her lashes drifted open and she looked up at Gray. He stared down at her with a shell-shocked expression on his face and he seemed pale. She frowned, puzzled.

"Are you okay?" her voice was still breathless and soft.

He snapped his mouth shut and gazed down at her mutely for a moment, then sank to the bed beside her. His big body was shaking.

"No, I don't think I am," he mumbled.

Prin rolled to her side to prop her head on a hand and looked at him. His eyes were closed. His arresting face was somehow drawn and tight, both hands fisted at his sides, biceps bulging with some suppressed emotion with which he seemed to be wrestling. A sickening suspicion began to sneak up on her.

"Did I shock you, Gray?" she asked, worried now. "I'm sorry if that upset you," she hurried on. "I thought you would enjoy it. It never occurred to me that you would hate it…" Prin trailed off as a bark of derisive laughter erupted from him.

He dragged a big, shaky hand down his face. "Hate it? Baby, I barely survived it." He turned his head. Those pale eyes burned into her through a sheen of unshed tears.

Gasping, her hand shot out to cradle his clenching jaw. He seized that hand and brought it to his open mouth. His face pressed into her palm as he squeezed his eyes shut and inhaled deeply. Her body's perfume already drifted lightly around the room. But here on her hand he could drink in her unique scent deeply.

"You are so beautiful, Princess," he groaned. "What makes me think I deserve someone as fine as you?"

She sank into him, scattering kisses as soft as the brush of butterfly wings across his chest and neck. Steel-banded arms wrapped around her and hugged her to him in a rib-crunching hold. "But I can't let you go, Baby Girl." The ragged desperate words were whispered into her hair.

"Who asked you to?" she replied. Her smile hidden in his chest was beatific. *So, that's how you wrecked a warrior? Who knew it could be so easy?* Sliding her hands up and down his sides, head pressed to his chest, she heard each one of his shuddering breaths. He was barely in control. She'd done that to him. Deep within her, a whole new kind of satisfaction bloomed. There was nothing like having one or two weapons stashed away. Time to let the big guy off the hook, she supposed.

"Umm…Gray?" She gently nudged him.

"Yeah, baby," he rumbled.

"I need to breathe soon." Humor edged her comment.

"Oh. Sorry." His hold loosened marginally, but his face remained buried in her neck. He still breathed in a choppy gasp. His body felt so tightly clenched that the skin was a thin layer of leather stretched across a steel statue.

"Gray?" she tried again.

"Yeah?" his mumble remained muffled.

"Do you think you could let me get up soon?" Prin felt a bit more serious about this request.

"No." Still a murmur into her skin. His rejection of that idea managed to convey a spoiled little boy who wasn't even going to think about giving up his possession. His hands smoothed up and down her body. He just couldn't touch enough of her. The curvy miracle that was Prin overwhelmed every one of his senses. He wanted to tie her to himself in every possible way. She hadn't told him she loved him. Nor had she responded to the moving in thing, much less the marriage statement. Momentarily, he considered asking her again. Romantically, like he should have done the first time. Oh, hell, no! Asking was out. A desperate man did not ask for what he needed. Too risky.

The only option left was simply taking. Yep. No choice here. Baby Girl had just written her future out in stone and his dick was hard enough to do the chiseling for her. His beast enthusiastically agreed with the "just taking" plan.

"Mmmm, got a bed pan?" she inquired.

Soft laughter rumbled in his chest. "Perhaps we can make a deal."

"It'd better be a quick deal," her response warned.

"You say yes, we head to the bathroom." His arms tightened again, holding her to him and preventing any escape.

"Yes! Now, Gray!" Prin's urgency grew with each word.

Grinning like a fool, he scooped her up and sprinted to the bathroom.

Ten minutes later, Prin was once again clothed in one of Gray's shirts and had just been deposited on a kitchen chair. His care of her in the bathroom was a repeat experience from the hotel. She calmly let him clean her. It was cute actually. He was so intense with his attention to detail. So serious in his duties that pampered her in every respect. The only furnishings she'd seen in the house besides the bed were the kitchen table and chairs. Gray grabbed things out of the fridge to make them sandwiches. It probably shouldn't be amusing that he did it without allowing her to help. He hadn't let her do a thing yet. It was also amusing that while her feet had touched the floor several times, she had yet to walk a step in his house. However, she had a pressing question, which pushed all else aside.

"Gray, what did I agree to upstairs?" she cautiously asked.

He glanced at her as he transferred the sandwich materials to the table, and then sat down beside her to make them. "Everything," he responded seriously.

Her eyebrows climbed her forehead. "What 'everything' are we talking about?"

Shrugging, he stated, "Everything I want. You said yes. I figure it applies to everything."

Laughing, she turned more fully toward him. He handed her the first sandwich. "That 'yes' was given under severe physical duress. No court in the land would uphold it."

"Don't much care what the courts think," he responded taking a big bite out of his sandwich.

She frowned at him. He looked at her again and frowned, too. "Eat, baby. Tomorrow you can't have much before surgery." She took a big bite, mulling over what just occurred. He seemed entirely serious about his "everything" theory.

Chewing thoughtfully, she went over what she knew of him. He was a Dom. He waited on her hand and foot. He was an incredibly loving man who could barely bring himself to put her down. He was decisive and ruthless in his demand that she know all the pleasure he could give her. He'd apparently moved into this house to be near her, uprooting his entire life instead of asking her to uproot hers.

He anticipated her needs consistently. He displayed a possessive tendency that might be a problem. Now, though, it was sort of cute. He was a bit of a control freak, she suspected. He might be disturbingly cute now, but required caution in the future. He was painfully honest in his intentions. He exposed his weaknesses to her fearlessly. He gave his entire being into the effort, whatever it was. He'd apparently honored his word about no contact after their night with great difficulty, but he had done it.

She slipped out of her chair. His entire body tensed as pale eyes narrowed. She padded over to the refrigerator and grabbed the gallon of milk. Prin rooted around in the cupboards until she found some glasses and came back to the table. Pouring them each a glass, she sat back down. He relaxed and continued chewing.

She almost giggled, but struggled to school her features and remain composed. Sipping her drink to hide the smile, she then finished the sandwich. Barefoot, only dressed in one of his shirts, and the man stiffened when she got up to walk around. Yep, logical thought was not driving her big warrior at the moment. That she had put him in this place amazed her. She knew exactly what he was feeling because she felt it, too. She needed him in ways that were primitive, elemental and scary. However, Prin was done being scared. Every moment was precious now. He knew the truth and still wanted her, so be it. She'd take everything he gave her and return it back to him. But the big idiot needed to understand that.

"Do you want more?" Gray asked.

"No, I've had enough. Thanks," Prin assured him.

"Mm," he grunted and turned back to eat his second sandwich.

She watched him speculatively. Obviously, he was willing to do whatever it took to keep her. His body tensed as she moved around the kitchen, never relaxed until she again sat back down. Those eyes tracked her without blinking. Big boy was making sure she didn't head for the door. Obviously, he'd made a decision and was going to paste her "yes" on it.

Well, damn! Looked like he'd just signed on for the full ride. Time to rescue him from the emotional ledge the big lug had worked himself out onto. He needed to trust her, too. To know he was safe with her. Watching her like a hawk every time she got near a door would get old quick. The temptation to tease him with her knowledge died a quick death as she looked at the powerful man beside her. He'd already reached into her body and captured her soul. His gentle grip cradled it in his heart and she couldn't breathe when she thought about what might have happened if he didn't want her.

When he finished eating, she quietly said, "Ask me again, Gray."

Instantly alert, Gray studied her. She sat beside him placid as a pond on a windless day. Pale eyes searched her face but found nothing to give away her feelings. She simply regarded him and waited. His stomach twisted as he realized what she was doing. It was a test. Would he give her the freedom of choice?

He knew if he didn't give her that choice, he could never be sure of her. Never know for sure where her heart was. If she didn't choose him, could he live with it? *Hell, NO!* Beast roared. *Mine! She's mine and we are not giving her up!* Squeezing his eyes shut, he did not attempt to hide the struggle that was raging in his mind as his face grimaced. She'd obviously figured it out already anyway.

The dainty little woman just marched herself right into the lion's den fearlessly with that request. She didn't know what he was capable of. She couldn't realize how dangerous the man sitting beside her could be. However, he knew that she did. The power had never been in his hands and they both knew it. In her submission to him, she'd enslaved him to her. Now it was time to cowboy up, to take it like a man. Time to put the money on the table and pick up the cards. He couldn't think of any more corny sayings. Getting down to business was the only thing left to do.

He took a deep breath and left his chair to sink down on his knees in front of her. Once again, his hands rested lightly on her thighs as he looked up at her.

"Marry me, Prin." It still wasn't a question, but it was the best he could do.

She smiled down at him. Her hands rested over his, holding them to her thighs.

"I love you, Gray," she said, her hands stopping him from surging up to her.

He sank down. Perhaps it was a good news, bad news thing. If that was the good news, the bad news was going to suck. The dark warrior kneeling at her feet tensed as he waited. Whatever she said next sentenced him to a half-life of pain, or the gift of everything.

"I need you to really think about this, though," her quiet voice continued. "Monday night there is a good chance that I will no longer be the same woman I am now. I don't even know how I'll handle it if there is only one breast on my body by the end of the day. On the other hand, if the worst happens and we're talking months instead of years for a future, then what happens? I don't know what happens next." Prin squeezed his hands as he started to interrupt her. He subsided.

"I know for me, since the moment we met, it's been a really strange time. I'm not saying my feelings aren't real, it's just everything is more intense. I know you read me somehow. Perhaps you're picking that up. I don't know. Perhaps both of us should just slow down until we know what's going to happen. Let our emotions settle."

"What exactly do you mean, 'settle'?" Gray questioned cautiously.

Prin sighed. "I don't know. Not do the wedding thing. Just get through this before we try to plan a future."

"I can do that." Gray gazed at her seriously, not moving.

"You're waiting again, Gray. I don't know what you're waiting for." Prin frowned at his still form. He was kneeling at her feet and he should have looked at least a little humble, instead he looked like a panther ready to pounce. He was holding himself so still the leashed power rolled off him in waves. The unwavering, unblinking regard of those pale eyes as his whole attention focused on her was disconcerting.

"I want to make sure you know I hear you, Baby Girl. That I am listening with my whole being to everything you have to say. Everything that scares you or makes you uncomfortable needs to get out in the open now, so we can handle it," he explained.

"I guess that's what I have to say. I don't really know what I expect you to do about it. I just needed to say it." Prin released his hands on her thighs.

Gray didn't pounce. He slid his arms around her waist and nestled his cheek into her tummy. Closing his eyes, he thought about what she was saying, as Prin ran her fingers through his hair. She'd said she loved him. That mattered more than anything else. If he had that one, he could deal with whatever she needed. Marisa was right, she felt crowded by the house, his moving, all of it. On top of what she was already dealing with, it was too much. How could he become an asset instead of a burden?

The last thing he wanted to be was another worry. He needed to find a way to do this in the next two minutes, before she got around to the female notion that they needed time apart. Or, came up with some other idea designed to shove a man away. Tightening his arms around her, he started talking. Unconsciously slipping into a different speech pattern as he related the secrets of his heritage.

"When a man releases his soul to the universe in Dream Walking, he has no control of its destination. The universe ebbs and flows at will. Those things that draw his soul to them in the great expanse do it because they recognize one of their own. That's how we know our spirit guides. They draw our souls and speak to them.

"I have heard in legends of a soul finding its mate in the Dreams. This is only spoken of reverently and with great fear. If you find your heart in the Dreams, you will never find it in the Waking Times. Only the past or the future inhabits the Dreams. Never have I heard of one soul drawn to another when both live in the present. Never have I heard of one soul traveling unerringly to that other soul, over and over again.

"I asked my Grandfather about this. He also has never known it to happen. He seemed very troubled about it. He said if two are drawn so strongly that the Dreams are not a path to the universe, but only a path to each other, they are a pair who has been searching for each other a very long time. He advised me not to look back for the reason we search for each other so desperately. Whatever pain separated those two souls in the past must be so great, it would be best to leave it in its own time.

"I know the Dreams are not part of your culture. The concept of Dream Walking and all it represents is strange to you. Prin, you know it exists. You know I have held you in my arms for around two years now.

"Honey, even if I didn't find your spirit brave and your thoughts fascinating, I would still love you. There is no event or circumstance that will stop me from loving you. You will always be the most beautiful creature in the universe. My soul will fly to yours every time it is set free. For it is not free at all. It is yours.

"I will do whatever it takes to make you comfortable through this difficult time. Except leave you. I will not do that. I will back off if you want. I will go as slowly as you want. However, I will not go away. I cannot go away. It is not possible for me to rip my soul away from yours. Do you understand what I'm saying? I am powerless in the face of what you are to me. You are my mate. The only woman in this life, or any life after who can complete me. My love, I tell you this to explain. Not to trap you or burden you.

"The house, my moving, all these things mean nothing compared to you. Nothing will drive me from you. Nothing that occurs Monday has any hope of altering my feelings for you. My only wish is to ease this for you. Tell me how to make this easier for you."

Gray remained bent over her lap, his massive arms wrapped around her sweet body and waited for her to respond. He'd laid his being at her feet. All that he was or would ever be was contained in this one little woman. He couldn't think of another way to explain it to her. That would have to do.

Her hands continued sifting through his hair during his entire speech and didn't pause now. The silence between them wasn't strained or uncomfortable, rather peaceful and gentle. Finally, she took a breath to speak.

"You don't give a girl much wiggle room, Gray," Prin commented quietly.

He turned his face and pressed an openmouthed kiss into her abdomen. "I give all that I am, Prin," his voice rumbled over her pelvic bone.

"I guess we have a lot of work to do," Prin answered.

"Work?" he questioned.

"Yeah," she sighed. "The house is empty. It looks damn big, too. I absolutely refuse to have the wedding anywhere else but the backyar—" She couldn't finish the sentence because he shot off his knees and his mouth was clamped onto hers.

Laughing into his mouth, she felt him scoop her up again and set her in his lap. When their lips eventually separated, she looked up at him through her lashes and continued. "I also insist on the right to walk around at will. You will wreck your back by carrying me everywhere. I need that back in full working order. It's attached to those lovely hips that come in very useful regularly."

He laughed into her neck as he nibbled on it. "I'll work on it. No promises."

"I also need you to take this thing out of my butt. I have to take a Fleet tomorrow, you know," she insisted.

"I know, Baby Girl," he mumbled into her hair. "That's why I used it. Makes it easier for you."

She leaned back from him until she could see his eyes and raised her eyebrows.

An entirely masculine grin spread across his face at her look of disbelief.

"That, and the fact that I really like doing it for you," he purred.

Epilogue

හ

The mass in her breast turned out to be just that, a "mass", not malignant, not even a cyst, just a "mass".

The doctors were relieved to be able to bring good news to the dark giant pacing in the waiting room. His laser eyes had speared them going in to surgery. "Take care of my lady." His rumbling command held a faint threat. It was an involuntary primal reaction to back away from him and the look on his face.

The folks with him all sat back and let him prowl, only safe thing to do actually. After they wheeled her away, he'd gone nuts. No one could get close to him. He just snarled and paced back and forth. His face strained and set in a fierce scowl.

The others with him all looked normal enough, except for one, the silent one sitting with his back to the wall. He was too big and fierce. It made a person nervous just to look at the blond sentinel sprawled in deceptive casualness across two little hospital chairs.

That morning Gray expected Dave and Marisa to show up at the hospital. However, it was a surprise when Remington Morgan glided into the room. He supposed it shouldn't have been. Rem was the quintessential intelligence-gathering machine. The big Florida native always showed up when you least expected him. Uncanny in his knowledge about when you needed him as well.

Gray didn't know whether to be insulted or amused as he saw his long-time friend and sometimes partner enter. Obviously, Rem was keeping tabs on him and Gray hadn't been aware of it. Rem was unbelievable at uncovering information. The only one better was Gray himself. Rem knowing about Prin's surgery, his knowledge of the time and location even though Gray hadn't known about it until Saturday, begged the question of how long Rem had been keeping tabs on him.

"Rem," Gray greeted him as the two men shook hands. "Been watching my back long, buddy?"

"Only since you got lost in the glades, my man," Rem answered back with a smile. That incident happened when they were eight, and it was the only thing they disagreed on. Gray insisted he hadn't been lost, Rem just grinned and shook his head when it came up.

Now Rem sat there on guard duty. The large golden man with his startling black eyes caused an instinctive shiver regardless who it was looking at him. The nurses could hardly take their eyes off the almost feline features of his face—the men instinctively knew a predator when they saw one. Though he sat quietly in contrast to Gray's pacing, a field of nearly visible energy sparked around him.

Gray wouldn't have admitted it, but Rem calmed him on several levels. Rem was a familiar security measure. He'd been at Gray's back almost all their lives. Not following him, but moving in tandem. From their wild childhood in the Florida Everglades to combat on the Special Forces Team, Rem was a constant. They'd been two halves of a powerful whole that barely needed to speak to function as one. Moving like the avenging hand of God with a three hundred and sixty degree field of vision.

Rem was the one who never believed the State Department statements about Gray's "death" two years ago. It was Gray's final mission and he was sent in solo. The political landscape changed overnight, as it often does, and Gray was "lost" in enemy-controlled territory.

Rem and the boys never stopped searching for him. When Rem uncovered a hint, a mere wisp of intelligence on Gray's possible location, he gathered their disbanded team and went in. There was no backup, no support personnel. In fact, they made sure no one in any official capacity had any idea what Rem and the boys were up to.

The boys, all civilians now, had gotten together and taken a "vacation" to South America. Returning with a breathing Gray caused a stir in official circles, however. The government hurriedly backed off its demands for an official investigation of the "vacation" into restricted territory when five sets of hard eyes turned on them.

The government was informed that an investigation would be welcome. It would bring to light how a highly trained government specialist was abandoned in the field, even declared dead without a body being found, among other things. The "among other things" part was delivered while all five men grinned in an identical menacing fashion.

This conversation took place in the hall outside Gray's hospital room shortly after his return. The government decided to leave well enough alone. The boys were a bit more difficult to convince to do the same. At the time, fresh off a recovery mission that was personal, they'd been hungry for blood. The realization that the government itself had trained them with the very skills they needed to find the administrative malfunction and eliminate it, did not exactly escape the government's representative. His recommendation had been for someone to take an early retirement. Preferably in Nepal.

Amazingly, the doctor's good news turned Gray's face a ghastly shade of white, he sat down hard in a chair. His head sank into his big hands and he shuddered.

"Do you need something, sir? A glass of water?" the doctor asked worriedly.

"Ah, no." Gray straightened then stood up again as the doctor continued.

"The surgery went well. All the tests were good. She will be in recovery for about an hour and then they will take her back to her room. You can see her then. We want to keep her overnight for observation and we'll probably release her tomorrow morning. As far as her recovery, she needs rest for about ten days, another two weeks after that and she'll be able to go back to work. There will be some pain and soreness for about six weeks. She'll have a pain prescription to deal with that. So, she looks great. We couldn't be happier with the outcome of this procedure." The large Mr. Winston shook their hands and the two doctors left with some relief.

Both doctors had a chuckle back in the scrub room. When this guy came in for a baby delivery with that little woman, he was going to be a mess. There was no question that it would happen either. Virility rolled off him in waves. Every nurse in the place found a reason to peek in the waiting room just for a glimpse of all that masculinity in motion.

Gray's face was the first thing Prin saw when she opened her eyes back in her hospital room. Confused from the sedatives, she frowned. This was an unfamiliar face to her. He was smiling over her, tears slipping silently down his cheeks.

Gray laughed at her confusion. "These are happy tears, Baby Girl," he assured her. "Everything is going to be fine."

Her hand tightened on his. "How am I supposed to know the difference?" she whispered.

"You just have to be there, Princess. You'll know the difference," he assured her.

Prin surrendered back into sleep. If Gray said it was fine, that was good enough for her. Worrying was a waste of time, he did enough of that for both of them. This time there was a slight smile on her lips as she surrendered into dreamless slumber.

Two weeks later, Prin laughed to herself as Gray brought breakfast to her in bed again. At this rate, even she would believe they'd amputated a leg instead of taken a mass out of her breast. Her recovery time in his house had been spent being carried around wherever she wanted to go. He'd never left her side. Not even the night she'd spent in the hospital. He'd spent it staring at her from the chair. Every time she opened her eyes, he'd been looking at her.

The only time he'd been away from her was the hour he spent going to her place to pack some of her clothes and personal items. He hadn't even wanted to do that, insisting she looked great in his shirts, right up until Rem agreed with him while admiring her legs as she sat on the couch. Gray had gotten up, directed Marisa and Dave to take care of her, grabbed Rem and driven straight over to her place.

Taking Rem had been a security measure and made her laugh even more. The man was obviously making fun of Gray with his comment. Rem had been nothing but sweet and brotherly since she'd met him. In fact, she knew she owed him a debt as he quietly found himself a bedroom and camped in the house with them. He'd been there to do whatever needed doing while Gray hovered over her.

Rem was the guy who found a decorator that magically understood her taste from a remarkably short conversation. Gray had insisted they didn't tire her. Rem had grinned and taken the man from the room.

The next day, after a morning of trucks coming and going, the den and kitchen were fully furnished, as was the patio and several guest rooms. The decorator's ideas for the formal dining room and parlor were so lovely she'd simply nodded. Rem and his monied background seemed to know exactly how to make things happen with the least amount of fuss.

Prin smiled at her soon-to-be husband and kissed his cheek as he settled the tray across her lap. "Thank you, darling," she murmured having learned days ago it was useless to argue with him that she was perfectly fine to get up.

"So how long do you think Rem will be staying with us?" she asked as she sipped her fresh-squeezed orange juice.

"Right up until he decides I won't lose my mind if you cough." Gray grinned down at her as he admitted that. "We are part of a unit, honey. Get used to the boys dropping by. Especially if they think something might be wrong. Rem might be the only one here, but believe me, the rest are getting daily reports." Gray shook his head. "You'll meet them all at the wedding. Until then you're not allowed to look at them."

Prin laughed. "What, you don't trust me looking at handsome men?"

Grays eyes twinkled. "It's not you, Baby Girl. Believe me, it's not you."

SLIP KNOT

ଉ

Dedication

❧

Allen for his patience, Char for her insight and Patti for her expertise. Also to Ida for her sharp eye.

Trademarks Acknowledgement

The author acknowledges the trademarked status and trademark owners of the following wordmarks mentioned in this work of fiction:

Porsche 911 GT2: Dr. Ing. h.c. F. Porsche AG Corporation

Boy Scout: Boy Scouts of America Corporation

Spandex: Monsanto Chemical Company Corporation

Jacuzzi: Jacuzzi Inc.

Glock: Glock, Inc.

Jeep: DaimlerChrysler Corporation

Kit Kat Klub: Kit Kat Klub, LLC

Kevlar: E. I. du Pont de Nemours and Company Corporation

Prologue

‰

At four in the morning the night was deep velvet shadows in moonlight relief. The balmy Florida breeze whispered around that wicked hour when it's both much too late and way too early. A black Porsche 911 GT2 prowled the upscale condo community and backed into a driveway. The driver jumped out and stepped around the car to hand out a willowy blonde. Sweeping her into his arms, the two figures merged.

They kissed deeply while his hands roamed down her figure. Her eager body responded against him as the kiss heated. Her date undid the single bow of her halter-top and peeled the two sides down slowly. That protracted descent offered her the option to object before being bared to the waist. The loose top fell to the ground as his deep kiss never faltered, male hands glided up and over naked breasts. The man's fingers toyed with her nipples, driving her to lean back and boldly offer up the perfection of her breasts for his pleasure.

Her pale body glowed in the soft moonlight. Long, smooth legs strained up on tiptoes. Her delicate rib cage was clearly visible below trembling breasts. Head tipped back, she arched her neck as her date nibbled his way down. Silky blonde hair became a shimmering waterfall of spun gold behind her. It cascaded down to skim the butt barely concealed under a spandex skirt. Her ass flexed as her lover's hands roughly and thoroughly caressed those firm curves.

Enthralled, the two lovers never heard a sound from the dark vehicle parked in the shadows of the neighbor's garage across the street. He'd even left the window down for the handheld digital video camera and the small audio amplifier sitting on his dash and they still had no idea. He could everything. She stood right there in public and let the man slide his hand up under her skirt. The instant her panties were pushed aside for the young man's fingers to shove into her was unmistakable. The Observer gaped at them as the couple indulged in public lust. Disbelieving shock racked him as the scene became increasingly bawdy.

Her date sucked her breast in steady pulls that obscenely lifted and stretched delicate flesh to disappear into his mouth. His left arm pumped upward between her legs, the silhouette view clearly outlined the repeated thrusts of a forceful invasion.

The Observer's lip curled in disgust when the man stopped. He could hear the blonde moaning and begging the bastard to fuck her. Her lover's response was a chuckle.

"Oh, no, baby. You don't get an orgasm that easy," the date responded.

"Brad!" she wailed, "Damn you! I'm so close. Do it now! I need it now!"

"Then lose the panties," her date demanded.

The blonde reached under her skirt and yanked down flimsy panties. They slid the length of her legs to the driveway.

"Come on," the young man whispered, leading her to the front of the car. "I'll give you what you need."

The young man positioned her with her back to the street — he placed a firm hand between her shoulder blades and pressed her down. Her hands automatically came down to support herself as the luscious body bent over the darkly gleaming hood of the low sports car.

"Now spread those pretty legs for me, baby," her date ordered.

Looking back over her shoulder at him, she sputtered. "Here? Someone might see us!"

"No one's up!" he hissed. "Besides, you didn't have a problem when you thought you'd get a nice little finger-fuck all by yourself. Now spread those legs. I've wanted to see this for a long time." Her date never raised his voice above a hushed whisper. Nevertheless, the Observer easily overheard the entire conversation. Stunned disbelief had given way to disgusted outrage as the show across the street became increasingly explicit. Anger stabbed its steely dagger into his brain as he watched.

The blonde spread her legs while her date rolled the spandex skirt up to her waist.

"Oh, God in heaven, that's beautiful!" Brad reverently breathed as he stepped back to look at the living art he'd created. A Porsche GT2, six-cylinder, turbo-charged *Beast*, with *Beauty* draped all over it.

Bent over the hood of the black phallic symbol, her pale flesh all but sparkled in the moonlight. Standing at an angle, Brad could see her perfect, champagne breasts swaying gently. The skirt made a bandanna around her waist, cinching it in tightly. Her ass arched up, pale globes of succulent temptation. Widespread legs showcased the slick folds of her bare cunt. Her head turned to the side and flung white-gold hair across the glossy black hood.

The Observer sucked a breath in silent gasp at the sight she made. He was glad the digital video was set on auto, because he could barely hold it. She created a fantasy of cream and silk, sleek femininity in all its youthful perfection. He couldn't turn his eyes away from the vision. At the same time, he couldn't stand watching it. Bile rose in his throat as his dick hardened in his pants.

Seeing her date's reaction, the blonde smiled that mysterious, languorous invitation women have issued since Adam and Eve. Her hands slid wider to lower her upper torso until puffy nipples barely kissed the hood. Tammy's graceful back stretched and arched dramatically. Ass and cunt presented in blinding, carnal glory.

"Is this what you want, big boy?" she taunted the young man softly. Her hips undulated slowly with her words, causing both men to groan. Tammy and Brad were so completely involved with their own lust—they didn't register the Observer's reaction to her nasty invitation.

"Oh, yeah," Brad breathed. "That's it, you evil little witch. Show me what you've got. Show me what you want." His tone turned ragged, almost strangled in his need as he encouraged her.

"Come over here and finish what you started," she whispered. "Shove that cock of yours in me and prove this car is really a fuck machine."

Her date smiled wickedly. His left hand snaked out to finger her pussy again. His devilish manipulation stroked and plucked private flesh. The burning desperation for release quickly rekindled within her. Rudely he spread her cunt lips and stared down at the exposed flesh. He held her open while he sank three fingers from the other hand slowly into her eager opening. Her body shuddered and thrust back onto the thick invasion.

"That's right," Brad said softly. "Come on. Work for it! You want a finger-fuck? I get to watch! And if your neighbors are up, so do they. Imagine that old man across the street, peeking out his window watching you fuck yourself like the nasty little bitch you are." Her head thrashed as her body convulsively quivered in response to the exhibitionist fantasy he created for her.

"Earn this cock," he continued. Her hips surged back on his fingers while he taunted her with the possibility of being seen. "Put on a show, Tammy. Oh, yeah. Look at that pussy in heat. Come on. Do it harder! You know you want it harder."

He didn't help her. He just held her open and watched her greedy cunt push onto his fingers. The Observer gritted his teeth to keep from screaming at her as he watched the delicate body writhe and thrust itself on that horrible hand. She moaned and panted—shameless in the public fuck she gave herself. She behaved like a street whore. The Observer's zoom lens provided him a close-up view of her show. Probably better than the monster she did it for. He hadn't been prepared for this at all. The Observer felt pinned to the truck seat by the force of chaotic emotions watching the nasty scene unleashed.

Her date let her come on his filthy fingers, not removing them until her convulsions ceased. His eyes remained trained on her like a fucking vulture. The Observer hated him for debasing her like this. Bitter contempt swept through him as he watched them perform their shameless peepshow. Anger and disgust were familiar companions that gave him the power to remain hidden and let the trash before him condemn themselves.

When she finished, her delicate little cunt dripped with juices while the young man stepped back and to the side again. The blonde remained spread and bent over the hood. Unrestrained, she chose to stay there. *Good God, was she going to continue this vile display?* The Observer watched the bastard rip open his pants and shove them down just far enough to release a respectable cock. He stood directly in her line of vision to smooth a condom down his hard tool.

"All right, my sweet little bitch—let's see what you really want." Brad stepped behind her and paused to stroke her ass. He rubbed the thick head of his cock up and down her wet slit. She thrust back at him but he moved so she couldn't impale herself.

His hands curled around her hips to hold her still. Rubbing against her again, yet never quite entering, he bent over her back and growled, "Tell me what you want, Tammy. Say the words for me. Show me what a dirty mouth you have."

"Enjoying your little fantasy fuck are you, Brad?" she hissed in frustration. "You'd better earn it with the best bang of your life, bad boy! Now spank me. Then I want you to fuck me hard and deep."

Her voice carried clearly across the early morning mist. The Observer spat out his window as he heard her sweet voice wrapped around those revolting words. He trembled with rage. It thundered through his skull and down his body. He hadn't expected this. Not in his wildest imagining had he dreamed this could happen to his Angel—Tammy.

Brad straightened up and kept the bulb of his dick pressed to her opening, but not penetrating. His hand rose and fell on her lily-white ass rapidly. It wasn't a hard spanking. However, the smack of his hand on her flesh sounded as loud as a rifle report to the Observer. Just when her head jerked up in intense pleasure, Brad thrust his hips brutally and sliced into her.

The Observer fumbled with his own fly. Grabbing his dick, he began jerking off roughly while still holding the camera. Little slut wanted a fuck, did she? He'd show her hard and deep! His cock was twice the size of that pansy-assed bastard's who pounded into her. Little boy out there was already about to come. In a frenzy of wild hatred and lust, the Observer pumped his cock in time to the show before him.

He could see that thrusting ass quiver as the prick tried to hold back an orgasm. The slut beneath him moaned and gasped like a gangbang junkie. Right there! Out in public like a fucking bitch in heat. She displayed herself and took it from behind. A white-hot rage burned over the Observer.

He saw her body stiffen as she plunged into orgasmic bliss. The bastard in her cunt joined her, jerking like a monkey on a string as the orgasm controlled his body. There was nothing smooth or elegant about the raw fuck these two shared on top of the car.

The Observer let go of his erection in disgust. He was rock-hard, but couldn't come.

The young man flipped Tammy over and laid her out across the hood of his car again. After smoothing on a new condom, Brad grabbed her knees and shoved them high and wide. Plunging back into her, he began pumping hard and fast. She cried out in a thin, feathery wail, coming on his cock again. The prick kept fucking her.

The memory disk had long since filled, and the Observer put the camera on the seat beside him. A dark shadow, he sat there watching them fuck like minks in her driveway. Tammy writhed in release once more before the prick noticed a blush of dawn creep over the horizon. With a last powerful thrust, he emptied his seed in her once again.

Tammy's legs slid down his sides as Brad lowered his body onto her. Both of them were sweating profusely and gasping for air. Turning his head to press a soft kiss to her lips, Brad pulled out. They lay there wheezing like racehorses.

"Stay right there," Brad commanded as he finally straightened up off her. He drank in the sight of her spread pussy as he stood above her. It glistened, all swollen and puffy from the abusive pounding. She lay for his viewing pleasure as he tucked himself back in his pants. Her lewd display in contrast to her date being fully clothed burned the Observer to a new level of rage.

This was the fault of that stripper bitch. Tammy would never behave like this if it wasn't for the influence of that whore she lived with. That goddamn roommate was the one who'd created this ugly slut out of the ethereal beauty that had been Tammy. The Observer cursed under his breath as he realized the huge mistake he'd made. He'd actually been fond of the whore roommate. At one point he'd thought he could save her. Under the influence of the damn pills, he'd let the filthy bitch infect his perfect Angel with her diseased self.

That disgusting stripper could cover her obscene body with all the dowdy clothes she wanted. She was still a stripper, a whore who took off her clothes for money. An abomination who contaminated the very air Tammy breathed. Where else would Tammy have learned to act like this?

Being exposed too long to that rotten gutter trash Kathryn Melinda Saunders had soiled perfection. He should have rescued Tammy long ago. It was really his fault after all. Just like last time. It was his fault Tammy was forced to endure these ugly creatures. They took advantage of her sweetness. His fault that she no longer knew how to behave like the Angel she was. This would never do. He'd have to fix it. Now that he knew not to take the pills, he could fix it.

He watched as the prick peeled her off the hood of his car. Her legs were shaky. Brad smoothed her skirt back down for her. Reaching to the ground, he retrieved her halter-top and secured it on her body. The Observer could clearly hear the low tones of their conversation via his audio amplifier.

"So," Tammy murmured, "have you decided to come down to the ranch with us?"

"Come on, baby, that's two weeks away. Besides, I'm not really a 'meet the folks' type of guy," Brad hedged.

Tammy laughed softly. "Get over it, bad boy. I'm not about to drag you down the aisle. It's a huge party and I thought you'd enjoy it. Forget it, I'll find someone else to entertain me."

Chuckling, he swatted her ass. "Oh, really? Well, we'll see."

The Observer watched as Brad finished dressing her and walked her to the door. Her hands were shaky as she inserted the key and let herself in. The prick pressed a brief kiss to her lips and then turned back to his goddamn car as soon as the door clicked shut.

Again, the Observer's face was twisted in disgust. He watched Brad slide into his expensive sports car and cruise away. It was a forgone conclusion that the bastard must die. As the Observer's vehicle followed the flashy black sports car, a malevolent smile crept across his face. A plan formed slowly in his mind, as he knew it would.

The Observer parked down the street and watched the prick slither into his apartment. He carefully made note of the address, as well as the license number of the disgusting car. This was almost too easy. The prick didn't even look around when he got out of his car.

First, he needed to get rid of these two grotesque influences on Tammy's life. It would be easy to manipulate the Kathryn whore. She had the brains of a fruit fly. Her stupid Pollyanna attitude made her a revolting but easy target. She'd do as she was told, just like she always had. The boy was an unknown, but not for long. Once they were gone, he would save his Angel. Sure, she'd be punished for her shameless behavior. It might take a while to cleanse her after what she'd just done, but he could heal her. Transform her back into the delicate flower she was meant to be.

When Tammy realized how wrong she'd been, then training could start. He would help her. Just like he had for Mother. She looked so much like Mother. That's what caught his eye all those late nights ago in Atlanta. Tammy had the very same delicate beauty Mother had, along with a shining splendor that opened her to the attention of *all those men*. Yeah, men who wanted nothing more than what he'd just witnessed between Tammy and Brad. At first Mother just wouldn't listen to reason either. Not until the end.

He knew it was a curse to be surrounded by vulgar whores all his life. He'd tried to help them, but it was too late by the time they stepped up on stage. At that point, they'd already given their souls up to the demon. He'd tried to cleanse some of them in the beginning, but it never worked. Tammy was so like Mother. It would work for her.

Tammy would worship him when she understood what he did for her. How he'd saved her from these filthy bastards. When she thanked him, that angelic face would glow as gentle tears slipped down her blushed cheeks. Then he would set her free. Free to fly with the angels where she belonged.

He would fix this. Lovely Tammy would be clean once more.

The Observer's dark vehicle glided off, heading for his place to work out details of the plan. He loved making the plan. It brought much-needed amusement into his daily struggle with the voices. The only relief he could find lately was watching cops flounder about like idiots after he brought another soul back to her destiny.

It wasn't fair that he was so much smarter than they were. But then, life wasn't fair, he supposed. Look at the mission he'd been given. That wasn't fair. Not fair at all to expect one man to make such a big difference in a rotten world.

The Observer calmed himself by thinking again how she would thank him when this was all over. Reaching down for his still exposed dick, he finally found release while picturing her angelic face glowing up at him in gratitude.

Chapter One
Two weeks later
The Rolling R Ranch, Central Florida

෨

Remington R. Morgan turned his face up to the ice-cold shower and closed his eyes. Damn it to hell! Kathryn was burned onto his eyelids. Frigid water sluiced down over Rem's body as he ran a weary hand through his hair. Still his cock ached and his body clenched in a demented hunger for her.

It'd been this way since the first time he'd seen Kathryn three and a half years ago. A long-ago Saturday night when he'd been home on leave after a difficult mission. They'd classified that mission as a success, but Rem would never feel that way about it. The civilian death toll was unacceptable to him. Even one, much less the number that'd gotten in the middle of a senseless struggle like this one had been.

Early that evening Rem received a call from Cappy at the rickety excuse for a bar about five miles down the road. His sister Tammy and her friend were about to cause a ruckus. Whatever that meant.

The bar was little more than a large shack that had once boasted a cabana theme. It had existed in this spot since before the super highways. In its heyday, it sat on a main road down to the Gold Coast playgrounds. Now all its twenties' luster was long gone. The tattered remains of tropical tourist charm were now just sad and silly.

Pissed as only an older brother could be, he stormed down to the bar. Slamming doors and squealing tires the whole way. Tammy and her friend had no business being in there! He'd told Tammy to stay away from the place! Little sister always thought she could handle herself. Not in this place. It catered to rough types, dangerous or just plain bad-asses.

He damn well had better things to do than bailout Tammy and one of her silly little princess friends. He hadn't actually seen Tam's buddy, but shit, they all looked alike. Every one of them was an anorexic idiot, flighty as hell and brick-stupid. Whatever the trouble was, they'd probably brought it on themselves. Some damn day he'd leave Tammy to straighten out her own shit!

Rem strode into the bar, filling the doorway with six-foot, two-inches of heavily muscled hard body. As he paused, his posture warned of predatory power constrained under military discipline. All bulging biceps and flexing thighs, masculine aggression rolled off him like the ominous vapors of a receding fog.

A high and tight haircut emphasized sleek, almost savagely feline features. Black eyes, under deceptively lowered lids, could not disguise the menace he embodied as he scanned the smoky room. Strong cheekbones and straight nose, with nostrils flared in irritation, above an expressive mouth now drawn in a grim, tense line, signaled the limited patience he was willing to expend. Grooves down his cheeks jerked while his rock-hard jaw clenched. His chiseled features were intensely focused on finding truant babies as he looked through a thick fringe of masculine lashes.

It wasn't hard to spot them. Four biker types were hanging all over Tammy and her little friend. Sweeping the bar door open with a bang, he'd turned every eye in the room on him. The four men straightened instinctively, predators who recognized a new beast challenging for the room. As he stalked across the filthy floor, Rem's eyes flicked down to the girls at the table once. Flashing black eyes blazed briefly over an elfin face with luscious lips. Those pillowy lips were currently hanging open in a tempting little "O". Something about the woman zipped right down to his dick and yanked hard. Instant and intense, the animal within demanded sexual ownership of the female staring up at him. Shit! Now he really needed a good brawl to work off the startling sexual response to seeing her pouty, pillowy lips.

Rem didn't hesitate a step as he sneered at the four fools lined up between him and the girls. He came straight at them, his intent clear as people scrambled out of his path. No talking, no taunting. This jungle's inhabitants could already smell blood in the air and were scuttling out

162

of the way. All four bikers tensed and crouched in ready position with fists clenched. Two of them held knives at their sides in warning. Rem smiled darkly. They were threatening him with weapons. Good.

One moment he was walking, the next he became pure energy exploding in blindingly graceful fury, striking multiple targets in staggering combinations of martial arts kicks and hits. Still, the power felt leashed. The effect was chilling as bystanders witnessed strength so tightly restrained that it roiled just below the surface in deadly quiet. That lethal control never lost its grip on the inner beast straining at its bindings. Piercing black eyes held death in the face of his opponents, offering them that option with emotionless intent. In near silence it happened so fast, four men were lying on the floor groaning, Rem had both girls by the upper arms marching them out.

His firm grip on the green-eyed witch's trembling skin shot a different kind of lightning down his adrenaline-drugged body. Rem gritted his teeth. This creature was not the usual type his sister hung with. Lush, round curves bounced as he dragged them out. Her willing acceptance of his touch felt like submission as compared the screaming banshee Tammy made. His face twisted into a grimace as he contained the insane urges his steely erection roared at him. The victorious beast within demanded he take the woman of his choice, bend her over a table and fuck the fight out of his system. Since when had he become a Neanderthal? Unable to deal with this grinding lust and the dominant fuck it demanded, he dismissed it as his intense sexual appetite rearing its head. Anger was the only socially acceptable avenue to channel surging aggression.

He dragged both girls out of the bar with little regard for grace or dignity. In a voice harsh with controlled violence, he turned on them. "Go home, little girls! I catch your asses here again, I'll tan them both!"

Rem immediately jerked away from a dismayed nymph's face as Tammy's friend gaped at him. Desperate to escape her, he turned back to the bar. He couldn't deal with this pulsating hunger over a curvy body barely visible under remarkably loose clothing. Rem ignored Tammy's hysterical screams at his back and stalked up to the brassy blonde who'd followed them out.

This woman he understood. She barely wore a tank top and one could almost say she had shorts on. Her face was heavily plastered with makeup and her hair needed the roots done. The invitation in overdone eyes was explicit and direct. Rem didn't bother answering, just backed her up with his body. When they hit the building, he proceeded to burn off some energy, grinding his hips into her willing body as he slammed his lips down on hers. Base gratification of the screaming urges still pounding through him was his only thought as he took what was offered. Denying himself this outlet didn't even enter his head as the warrior took his due.

Tammy hauled a still gaping Kathryn across the dirt parking lot into her car and squealed off, spewing gravel and dust in her fury.

The young woman who watched out the back of the fishtailing car had a great view of his jeans-clad ass thrusting hard. His rough hands wrenching up the tank top to prowl over bare breasts. Thick fingers pinched and twisted nipples rudely while the trashy blonde wrapped a leg around his waist. He'd glanced over his shoulder to see Kathryn's face disappearing down the road while he crudely attempted to remove her from his mind.

Now there was nothing Rem regretted more than the way he introduced himself to Kathryn. That was a little over three years ago. She had still been in college and way off-limits as a "kid" to the hardened Special Forces officer. His encounters with her after that showed him a glowing, gentle spirit who crept into his mind with uncanny ease. Her appeal was both intensely sexual and pure feminine perfection.

A year later she'd come down to the ranch with Tammy again. He'd only been home one night and Tammy had shown up with her friend. Kathryn had smiled shyly at him and become busy helping Maria in the kitchen. After supper he'd cornered her on the short walk between dining room and kitchen to apologize for the last time he'd seen her. She'd simply looked down and shook her head.

"No, no. You were right, Rem," she'd insisted softly, glancing up at him with those huge green eyes and blushing furiously. "We shouldn't have been in there. Thank you so much for, ah, for what you did. It was really nice of you to get us out of there."

Rem had been stunned. She'd thanked him for something Tammy had yet to forgive him for.

"Ah, well, it's okay," he'd mumbled, totally forgetting the reason he'd started the conversation as his eyes focused on the lush bottom lip she was biting. "It's what big brothers do," he'd finished lamely.

"Well, thanks again. I'd better get these into the dishwasher." Kathryn had then inched around him with the stack of supper dishes she'd been holding to rush into the kitchen.

Essentially stunned, Rem had stared after her a moment and frowned. He should have offered to help her carry the dishes. He should have finished apologizing. He should have done a lot of things, but once again instant lust had swamped him as soon as he inhaled her delicate honeysuckle scent. He'd stood there and floundered through a half-assed statement and she'd completely stumped him with her gentle "thank you". As she disappeared into the kitchen he had felt like a fool. Rem had not liked the feeling, nor had he liked the driving need to grab her. It confused the hell out of him.

Again, he'd tried to fuck her out of his mind when he returned to base. He had looked down at the moaning woman under him the next night and suddenly she'd looked too harsh, too tough, not Kathryn. He'd fucked her with a renewed purpose, squeezed his eyes shut and tried to ignore the fact he knew he couldn't come. That night he'd gotten stupid drunk after the woman left.

He'd seen Kathryn again at her college graduation. She and Tammy were in the same class. After graduation he and two of his unit buddies Charlie and Miguel had helped the girls move from Atlanta to Orlando. During the two-day trip, he'd tried to stay away from her. It had been impossible to ignore her gentle personality. She was kind and thoughtful in a way that was totally captivating. Tammy actually mirrored some of Kathryn's qualities when they were together. Rem had been amazed. He'd never seen his spoiled little sister exhibit kindness and thoughtfulness.

Each time he'd seen her since only deepened the attraction. For a part of him it had grown into that burning full-bodied emotion, which makes a man think about coming home to her every night, babies and anniversaries. Another level centered much lower on his body—he craved the lush, curvy body she inhabited. The animal need to cover her shuddered through him at his first sight of her every time. Controlling those dark desires became a battle he was tired of winning.

He'd done his bit for country. The need to protect and serve that drove his personality was now narrowed down to one sweet woman. He was ready to settle down. Perhaps it was retiring from the Special Forces—perhaps it was just his age. Could be he'd finally found a woman who turned his body to rod-iron and his brain to boot-leather.

Resisting the attraction was no longer an option. At first he'd done it because she was so dang young. Still on active duty he'd known she was out of his reach. When he'd retired from the service, it had become clear there would be no other woman for him. Her close relationship with his sister as best friend, business partner and roommate meant his family had included her in their circle. His parents seeing her as a daughter was exactly the relationship he wanted, but he wanted it with her as his wife. The frustration of what he wanted being so close, yet so seemingly unattainable ate at him.

He'd just gotten a close-up view of what finding your heart beating in the breast of your mate looked like. His best friend Gray was the luckiest bastard alive as far as Rem was concerned. Gray had found his Princess and claimed her with what appeared staggering ease to Rem. While he was damned to years of looking, wanting, needing and not touching.

Even now, Kathryn barely spoke to him. Whenever he came near, she managed to quickly move away, keeping a nervous distance from him at all times. It didn't matter how he bent himself into being gently attentive and polite. He'd become a fucking non-threatening Boy Scout for that woman. Even though the sound of her voice could light a fire in his soul, he'd tamed it for her. He showed her only the gentleman, never again the warrior. He'd done every damn thing he could think of to remove the memory of that night in the bar. Through it all, the fierce need to possess her built with each failure to reach her. Now, simply knowing she was on the property was enough to drive him to the cold shower.

One of his specialties was seeing past a disguise. Kathryn had a spectacular body she did her best to disguise. She seemed shy and intimidated by her own sexual appeal. She was only twenty-three—she needed time to get comfortable with herself. It didn't take Special Forces Intelligence and Espionage training to figure that one out. Any idiot could see her self-depreciating personality was a sign of self-esteem issues. That very fact pointed to the possibility she was a virgin.

All this psychology babble got him exactly nowhere in relation to the steel pipe he was sporting. Reasoning with an Elite Forces-trained, A-1 National Security-rated brain meant zip to the cock and balls. They were blue, hard and wanted Kathryn. Not an hour ago, they'd seen her emerge from her sensible little car, in her sensible clothes. No amount of brilliant analysis could convince them that the woman they wanted wasn't about to come within their reach. Even an ice-cold shower could not drive the point home to them.

Sweet, young, naïve, she was all of that and precisely the things that normally sent him in the opposite direction. Yet, now, his mind was consumed with sensual thoughts of her soft pussy as it yielded to accept his hard invasion. How he'd spread her legs, hold her puffy little cunt lips open and jam his face into her. Keeping her there until he ate his fill of her. Until her cream coated his mouth, his lips, his face and dripped off his chin.

It was unexpected—this incessant need to taste her, know her private scent and slather his body in it. In the past it had always been nice to fuck-face. He'd returned the favor when the situation called for it, but he'd never needed it, fantasized about it. Damn. Last time the girls came to the ranch, he'd almost slipped into her room and stolen a pair of her panties. Just so he could hold them to his face and inhale her essence. Pathetic bastard that he was, he'd probably do it this time.

Rem knew she wasn't ready for his sexual appetite. She certainly wasn't ready for the possessive, slobbering beast who wanted to lick her in every nasty way he could think of. The fact was he didn't deserve her after the way he'd spent the first half of his life. His needs were dark and danced right on the edge of totally reprehensible. He'd indulged every one of them through the years. First it was the freedom of too much money. Then being part of a combat unit whose missions took him deep into the underbelly of the world community had expanded those urges with endless opportunity. Being part of a unit of crazy daredevils didn't help either. It wasn't a vocal challenge, but the boys did compete on every level. Sexual prowess was certainly not left out.

He'd never wanted anyone or anything as much as he wanted this woman. He refused to doubt his ability to gain what really mattered to him. So, he valiantly struggled to ease them into some sort of casual friendship. If he could get her to loosen up and let him near her, things would develop until she became confident enough to play on the intense level he instinctively knew she was capable of.

He normally liked women who were tall, busty and brash. If the woman could just barely squeeze it into spandex or paint it *Do-Me* red, that's how he liked those parts. But this woman, with her lemon-fresh face and barely glazed lips, mystified him. She represented almost a polar opposite to his normal choice. Yet for over three years now, her face and form haunted him. He couldn't stop looking at her face.

That Kathryn was a natural redhead showed in every feature. His experienced eye saw it in bright green eyes that tilted up, giving her an elfin look. A pert little nose with faded freckles sprinkled across it. He knew she was trying to hide them, but he loved those freckles. And her mouth! Her redhead's complexion was pale, except for her lips. There, she was berry pink. They were lush and full in the fashion most women required injections to achieve. She never wore lipstick. If she ever did work up the nerve to put on the shiny red stuff, her mouth alone would stop traffic.

He wasn't playing when it came to this elusive spirit. No, this woman already lived in a much deeper, intimate place in his soul. Her essence seemed to invade him in ways that at first disturbed him then humbled him. She'd shown him what an arrogant, selfish prick he'd turned into without even saying a word to him. The very fact that his struggle for self-control was an effort where she was concerned highlighted his usual attitudes in a harsh light. He'd not thought of himself as a self-empowered user until he'd realized there was nothing he had or was that would get him Kathryn.

Wanting her had become a constant in his everyday life that spiked to painful need unexpectedly when he'd see something and want to show her or get it for her. Then the reality of her not being his would slam into him again. He'd actually resisted the impulse on countless occasions to get whatever it was for her anyway, cursing his inner man's inability to get the picture. She wasn't his to provide for. Her smiles were not his to earn. Thinking about it made him crazy sometimes because she was so far away. However, she would not get away when he finally tempted her into his life.

His teeth gritted through the brain-freezing water and he mentally yelled at his enflamed genitals. *Listen up, boys! This is the last time we do this. One more cold shower and you guys will behave like the goddamn adults we are. She leaves tomorrow. 'Til then, STAY DOWN!*

Rem resigned himself to the torture of another futile day attempting to talk to her, be near her, just to stand next to her without Kathryn melting away like a shy doe. He dressed in his usual jeans and western shirt. His only concession to the party was that the shirt was not really old. With a grimace he headed out to face the annual party already happening on his lawn. A few paces down the hall loud voices from behind his sister Tammy's door stopped him.

"No! Absolutely, fucking—NOT! There is no way in hell! I will not wear this shit, Tammy!" Kathryn yelled.

"Kathryn, you look great! I mean, really GREAT! You have to wear it!" Tammy insisted.

"Great? This is not great. I look like Jessica Rabbit!" Kathryn sneered. "This thing stamps 'TRAMP' on my chest and 'FUCK ME' on my ass. I am not going out there in these minuscule excuses for clothes!"

Rem had come to an abrupt halt as the voices smacked him in the face. Had that language come out of shy little Kathryn's mouth? Well, damn! Rem frowned darkly and crossed bulging arms over his broad chest. Narrowed black eyes glared at the door. Unrepentantly he commenced to eavesdropping on the unbelievable girl talk. Obviously, Tammy and her partner Kathryn were entirely different women behind closed doors.

"Kathryn, you haven't had a date in a year and a half, much less sex," Tammy continued. "Every guy in the place is going to sit up and pant when they see you walk in tonight. You'll have your pick."

"You've got that right!" Kathryn snapped at Tammy. "They're gonna think they took a wrong turn and ended up at the Kit Kat Klub!"

"It's not that bad, really. It just shows off your assets," Tammy insisted.

"My assets? More like it shows off rack and ass," Kathryn said. "I need a bra, I need hose and I need more clothes!"

"Awe, come on, Kat. A little jiggle in your wiggle turns men on," Tammy cajoled.

"I know exactly what it does to men, Tammy. Have you forgotten college?" Kathryn demanded. "This is a new place, a chance to be more than just a 'rack and ass' chick. No jiggling, no wiggling, no begging a guy to tie me up and fuck me. That dance is done! I'm not doing it again!"

Rem's mouth dropped open. *Tie me up and fuck me??? Begging??? Rack and Ass???* His stunned brain started to agree with his cock. Little honey wasn't some innocent flower.

"Besides," Kathryn continued. "I've been perfectly fine, thank you. I've got two BOBs and extra batteries in the fridge."

"Right, Kat. Like a battery-operated boyfriend is gonna do ya. This is me you're talking to," Tammy scoffed. "You're cranky all the time. If someone doesn't spank your ass soon, I'll have to send you to Marco for more than a weekend fuckfest. Now, wouldn't it be so much cheaper on the business to find a local bad boy? I'm sure we have someone here who knows how to tune up a woman's ass for a good long ride."

Marco! Who the fuck was Marco? Rem silently sucked in wind through his teeth and stepped closer to the door. If Kathryn needed a spanking and a "long" ride, her delicious ass was right where it needed to be in his house. Five steps down the hall, through one closed door and she could saddle up for the goddamned duration. She could make this trip real cheap! No need to walk, he'd carry her.

Rem was fiercely certain this woman belonged to him. He'd gone slowly for her. Now he discovered she hid a bad girl under all that clothing. That pissed him off a bit. Nevertheless, he sure as hell wasn't about to let her waltz off to some Marco creep! As his hand reached for the doorknob the girls' voices stopped him.

"Cut it out, Tam," Kathryn huffed. "You know there's only one guy who flips my switch. Just because I can't have him, doesn't mean I'm willing to bag up the *trash* and take it to the curb."

"Yeah, I know," Tammy answered. "I was hoping you'd gotten over that already. Besides, you do *'trashy'* better than anyone I've ever seen. And I mean that in a good way. You can't wrap yourself up in boring clothes and call it a life."

"Yes, I can, Tam. I know I don't look it, but I'm too old to screw around." They both laughed softly. Rem leaned his forehead against the door in an effort to hear every word as Kathryn continued in a sad voice.

"I've seen what I want, Tam. Even if he's out of my reach, I can't settle for less. My heart is his in ways I didn't know it could be. Guys see me dressed like this and they'd never see anything else. It's not enough. If he saw this woman and came on to me, I'd die. I want more. I want him to want all of me, not just my 'assets'. I want a home. You understand that, don't you?"

"Oh, Kat. I'm so sorry, sweetie. He's a blind, stupid idiot. Haven't I always told you that? He won't ever give you what you're looking for," Tammy said quietly.

"Yeah, well, unfortunately he's the only idiot who wets my panties," Kathryn confessed. "Until he stands in front of the preacher and says 'I do' for someone else, I'm stuck with BOB and Marco. Now, hand me back my clothes. We're already late."

"Come on, Kat. How about we compromise? Wear the sweater at least. And try to be nice to men. That's all I ask. Just look," Tammy wheedled.

"The sweater *with* a bra. And I get to wear my own skirt," Kathryn clarified the deal.

"Don't forget the 'be nice' part!" Tammy insisted.

"Yeah, yeah. 'Be nice.' I got it. Okay. Time to shop around for cock and balls," Kathryn agreed.

Rem pushed away from the door and quietly glided down the stairs. The girls' mind-boggling conversation ran through his head in a continuous loop. Moving away from the party, he stepped into the garage. He needed time to make sense of this. He was used to picking up information at a fast clip, but this changed his world on several levels.

Rem allowed his brain to shift into analyze mode so the new facts could rapidly arranged themselves. Threaded through their conversation was one theme that bothered him the most.

She was in love with someone. Someone she would see here tonight, someone who didn't love her.

After a deep breath, Rem went down the list of fucking bastards—guys also known as his friends—presently here or coming this evening. No one jumped at him. No, this wasn't working. Start at the beginning, he had to be missing something.

Kathryn was actually a nymphomaniac—remember to investigate that.

She had a spanking/fuck-buddy named Marco—killing him would be at the top of the next list.

She had two—a tool and a spare—battery-operated boyfriends with backup batteries on hand—oh, God, he wanted to help her use those, both at the same time with his dick in her mouth.

She liked rough sex as indicated by spanking reference— nirvana! A woman who wanted her ass tuned up for a "long ride".

She knew she was hiding a killer body under all those clothes. She kept it that way for some reason to do with the bastard she loved.

The bastard wasn't married yet, but she thought he would be at some time in the future.

Tammy thought she'd wasted her time waiting on this guy. Kathryn agreed.

The "in love with" bastard would be here tonight. He'd never seen her looking "trashy"—fucking blind bastard. How could he not know she had something spectacular under there? She didn't want him to just want the "*rack and ass*" shit still didn't add up. He was missing something.

With his back against the wall, he slid down until he was in the cowboy-sit position, ass resting on heels, powerful forearms on knees. His golden head sank down to stare at the concrete floor. He needed to loosen up his spine and get some blood back to his brain.

Perhaps if he stood on his head some blood would make the return trip from cock to brain. Running a distracted hand through his hair as his brain took in the new reality of Kathryn he couldn't resist the fantasy.

He could see her in his room bent over the metal railing at the end of the bed. If she was as naughty as he suspected, her cunt would be shaved and dripping with her excitement as his hand fell repeatedly on her ass. The sharp little spanking would turn her creamy globes a bright red. Just to warm her up, the last spank would be a gentle upswing, directly on her swollen pussy. That smack would make her scream as his cock plowed into her dripping little hole. He'd shove it in all the way in and ride her hard. Making sure each thrust fucked her as deeply as possible.

Well, shit, he felt his balls tighten. Blowing out a hard breath, Rem straightened and adjusted the painful erection.

Time to get serious about this. No distraction with her body. Treat it like an op.

One. Kathryn hadn't had sex in over a year and a half.

Two. Kathryn liked an edge to her pleasure, possibly domination.

Three. Kathryn did trashy well.

Four. Kathryn was in love with some bastard who didn't know she was alive.

Five. Tammy thought Kathryn should move on and ditch the disguise. Kathryn refused to move on or ditch the disguise.

Six. Kathryn was thinking of visiting her spanking/fuck-buddy.

Seven. Love Bastard was someone she knew around here. Love Bastard didn't know Kathryn any better than he did.

Eight. Time to relieve Kathryn of her clothes and her old fuck-buddy. Time to become her new fuck-buddy.

Okay, come up with a plan. If he couldn't have her heart immediately, he'd damn well be her fuck-buddy. This plan involved about sixty years of convincing Kathryn he was the only man for the job. Abruptly Rem felt a savage urgency to stake his claim on her enticing little self, certain that once he got her, he'd find a way to keep her.

This past year had proven him a hopeless failure at polite and thoughtful. Time for what he was good at. Let her know he liked it raw. Apparently she got off that way, so they should be doing it by midnight.

Rem straightened away from the wall and strolled back into the house. He snagged a beer in the kitchen and stepped out onto the patio to survey the assembled crowd. His family's Central Florida ranch was a large, sprawling spread. Even though it was an operating ranch, it made up barely a fraction of the family's actual assets. Something most people didn't realize, which was fine by the Morgans. They didn't live like they were in the top one percent income level and none of them ever would. Well, except Tammy, she did princess damn well, he acknowledged. Over by the pool, a bunch of his buddies from the Special Ops unit were joking and talking under the pavilion.

Through narrowed eyes Rem sized up each man. Which one of them could be the blind idiot she loved? Deep inside the question gnawed at him with jagged teeth.

This annual gathering started by his father over forty years ago had grown into a massive community event. Back in the day of peace marches and race riots, it had begun as a personal effort to integrate the community with all the divergent cultures present in Central Florida. It was Robert Morgan's answer to making a difference where he lived. Giving people a place that was basically neutral to meet and get to know each other. Christmas was simply a handy reason for those who needed it.

It was a warm afternoon even for Florida in December. Winter sunlight glinted across the massive lawn with its deceptively casual landscaping. Decorated pine boughs fastened to every possible structure added the aroma of Christmas to the air, right up until the gentle breeze changed and brought the sizzling scents of an open bar-be-que pit to invaded the senses. No one, and pretty much nothing, was refused admission to the Rolling R Ranch on the first weekend in December. Everywhere one looked there were kids and families. Some even brought their pets.

Years ago his unit members were naturally included. Rem, the Unit Exc. Officer and his best friend Gray, the Unit Commander, were both local boys. Now, they were all civilians. Gray was the last man "in", but he was back and safe. Gray had married recently and was happy as hell. Thank God, he couldn't be "the bastard". Being married already took him out of the scenario.

In another time, Gray would have been royalty. Pounding through his veins was the blood of a thousand generations of Seminole warriors. He would have effortlessly moved to the front of any war party. Each of his ancestors had gained the position of leadership through blood, sweat and pure animal cunning. They had remained there by surrounding themselves with men who didn't need to be led. As commander of the unit, Gray picked men he knew were his equal or better. Gray led them with the respect they deserved, creating a fighting force that never saw defeat. A unit that presented an interesting mirror of Gray's heritage played out in modern times.

The relationship between Rem and Gray was closer than brothers. They'd spent their childhood in the Florida everglades, two wild ruffians. No one but the two of them understood their unique connection. As soon as they'd met, at that long-ago December party, they had become inseparable. Joining up in the military together seemed natural. Being assigned to the same unit was a testament to their superior officers who saw a pair, when put together, became a single fighting entity of awesome power.

The other men in the unit melded into that unique relationship through training and battle. Coming together under severe circumstances built ties forged in blood. As civilians, they were still a unit. There was no doubt they'd come together to oppose any threat aimed at any one of them.

These men who were more to him than his own flesh and blood seemed the very men most likely to stand between Rem and his woman. Rem scowled. Was this the thing that could separate the unit?

Rem spotted Kathryn and Tammy out by the Jacuzzi talking to Miguel and nearly swallowed his tongue. The sweater Kathryn wore at Tammy's insistence was a clingy, fuzzy, pink confection. The thing just barely wrapped itself around her awesome chest. Its wide neckline displayed her neck and shoulders then draped in loose folds over impressive cleavage. Those soft folds, resting on the slopes of her creamy breasts, were the only place the sweater was loose. Down over the swell of her breasts it pulled tight to hug her in mind-numbing faithfulness to her waist. It ended just above the waistband of the skirt. The tight flesh it revealed tempted a man to touch.

Just looking at her made him dizzy as blood rushed south. Dragging his attention to Miguel, Rem noticed the bastard's eyes kept dropping. Suddenly, he remembered Kathryn promised Tammy to be "nice" to the men. As she laughed at whatever Miguel said, Rem felt fierce jealously claw up his spine. He normally liked having a woman other men looked at, as long as she was securely attached to his arm. He'd no problem with other guys drooling and lusting. In the past, he'd even arrogantly encouraged it. But this was different. Very damn different!

Problem number one, she wasn't attached to his arm in any way, shape or form. Problem number two, she was shopping for "cock and balls". Tammy was right. Every man in the place was sitting up and panting over her luscious body.

Could Miguel be the bastard she loved? The sniper of their unit, he was a cool customer. The fabled Latin temper all dialed down into intense concentration and an eerie calm that only cracked in quiet humor occasionally. Now he smiled and said something to the girls, flashing those dents in his face he called dimples and acting all casual.

Like hell. Rem set out across the yard only to be frustrated as he was soon hip-deep in acquaintances he couldn't actually ignore. As the "Son of the Ranch" and managing owner, this party was now his shindig. In that position, he was forced to acknowledge folks when they spoke to him.

His mother and father were present, but off with their cronies. Perfectly happy to let the "young people" be in charge. In fact, they were cutting out early this afternoon, catching a cruise to the Caribbean for three weeks and not coming back until just before Christmas.

When Rem finally looked up again and located her, Kathryn was talking to Charlie. Shit! Another member of the unit, he was a monster of a man. Charlie had muscles on top of muscles, black as sin and twice as mean except when pursuing a woman. Then the big commando became smooth as thick cream. Not this time, Charming Charlie. Dodging a football, Rem tried to make his way over to them. Again, it didn't work out.

In the center of the backyard an ornate Victorian gazebo served as the bandstand. In front of it, a large wooden platform was laid out every year to serve as a dance floor. At the four corners tall posts rose to support the strings of Christmas lights strung around the floor. To one side a huge party tent was set up so even if it rained, people could sit around and eat or visit. By dusk, when the band started warming up, it seemed to Rem he'd seen Kathryn talking to every man present, except him. Something or someone came up every time he'd get close to her. Before he knew it, she was way across the endless expanse of people again.

The band had started their first set around eight p.m., right after everyone was finished eating. Since then, she'd stayed away from the dance floor. That was a relief.

The frustration simmering through him snapped and snarled at the constraints of civil behavior. Each time he saw her talking to a different man, a little more patience faded away. At least it didn't appear she'd made a choice with the "shopping" crap yet. She damn well was about to!

An hour later, Rem gritted his teeth and powered through the crowd. He finally made it behind Kathryn just as the band struck up its first slow dance of the evening. He slipped an arm around her waist and growled, "Dance with me," in Kathryn's ear as he propelled her onto the dance floor.

Chapter Two

ॐ

Kathryn turned a startled face to Rem and gasped in surprise. He felt her brace as he pulled her against his body. Not about to give her a chance to refuse, he moved effortlessly around the floor.

At last! Her soft body pressed up against him from knees to chest. The light honeysuckle perfume of her surrounded him in mind-numbing delight. It had to be a powder she used, he decided as he dragged a deep breath. He looked down into her stunned face and smiled a slow, satisfied grin. That tempting little mouth was rounded in an "O" of surprise.

"Put your arms around my neck," his low voice instructed her.

Kathryn's mouth snapped shut and she frowned at him. "Loosen up, Rem. There is no need to flatten me. I don't feel like dancing. Take me over to the edge and let me go!" Her voice became firmer as she listed her demands.

"No. Now put your arms around my neck and enjoy the dance." The satisfied grin on his face wouldn't fade as he looked down into her snapping eyes.

"What?" Kathryn sputtered. "Did you just refuse to let go of me?"

"Yes. Here, let me help you." Rem reached up and arranged her arms around his neck. Now every possible inch of her pressed against the front of him. Perfect.

Kathryn's bountiful breasts rubbed into his chest. Her soft abdomen, which he suspected was flat as a pancake under that heavily gathered skirt, cradled his mounting erection. One of his steely thighs worked its way between her legs so she practically rode it. He felt firm muscles flex as her legs moved. No way those were chubby.

Kathryn battled a wave of flaming heat as the object of her fantasies wrapped his bulging, flexing and rippling self around her. This was the magnificent man whose intense regard turned her panties into a drenched mess, pressed flush against every part of her and moving to the music with a smooth catlike grace that was uniquely his. His golden hair ruffled in the evening breeze and his dark eyes dropped lazily as he looked at her through wicked lashes. His entire body seduced her with its hard planes and fluid movement.

She'd been lost from the first moment she'd set eyes on his painfully beautiful body, those sharp features and sinful, sooty eyes. He'd overwhelmed her in cunt-clenching, nipple-knotting, gasping lust. The physical display of power on that long-ago evening wasn't even the main reason she'd fallen like a brick. All that intensity and beauty had been bent on rescuing the damsel in distress. So, he'd been there for his sister, it didn't matter, he'd rescued her, too. Regardless of how many times she forcibly made her brain grasp the fact he hadn't been there for her, the end result was the same. Shamefully obsessed with a man far out of her reach both socially, and well, economically — he came from the "disgustingly rich" bracket — she might as well be another species. Still he was her Knight in Shining Armor. The silly fairy tale would not let her go.

He'd never danced with her before. Although she was now a business partner with his sister in their small web design company, Kathryn had always made sure she didn't hang around and lust after him like a starstruck teenager. Her response to Remington Morgan was too uncomfortable for her to dare spend any time around him. So this demand for a dance came as a shock.

"Remington Morgan! What are you doing? Let go of me this instant!" Panic shrilled through her voice. Her body vibrated with the need to escape. Self-preservation was an instinct she'd learned before she could walk. When every receptor screamed danger, Kathryn got the hell outta Dodge. Right now danger was dancing her around the floor. She felt her inner idiot rising fast. Even allowing herself to enjoy his hold for one dance was likely to lead to stunningly stupid behavior.

Rem couldn't resist ducking down to suck her plump bottom lip into his mouth for a fraction of a second. One of his hands drifted low on her back to keep her in place riding his thigh. Not quite copping an ass cuddle—but close. Anyone who cared to look at them knew he held this woman intimately. Exactly the impression he aimed to convey.

"What I'm doing, Miss Kathryn," he rumbled softly as he released her lip, "is stating to every male present that you are no longer free. I'm also enjoying the hell out of feeling your luscious little self pressed up against me at last."

"What? Why would they care? You're not making a bit of sense and you're creating a spectacle. Everyone is looking at us. I don't appreciate being made the laughingstock of this party! Now, Let! Me! GO!" Kathryn battled the panic twisting up her gut. Did he know her telltale body gushed its pleasure at all those hard muscles pressed against it?

If she'd heard him correctly, he'd just told her he wanted to warn other guys *off* her. Why would he do that? And why was this imposing man who'd always been frustratingly polite, looking at her like a condemned man regards his last meal?

This uncharacteristic behavior pointed directly to her deepest fear. She'd seen how he behaved with a whore. It was burned into her memory. She'd even been jealous of the woman at the time, wishing she hadn't put on the frumpy disguise to visit Tammy's folks. Later, she'd been incredibly relived when she realized he reserved that behavior for "throwaway" women.

"Why do you think anyone is laughing?" Rem glanced around. Sure, a lot of people were checking them out. Naturally, they would when he was nearly molesting her in middle of the dance floor. But no one seemed to be laughing. Looking down at her again he noticed her face was turning a bright, blotchy red.

Interesting. It was hard to concentrate on the puzzling parts of her questions as her body moved against his.

"Remington! What has come over you?" Kathryn hissed as her eyes darted around at their audience. "Why are you behaving like this? Or is it just my turn? Have you worked your way through all the acceptable women present? Are you humiliating me because I'm all that's left?"

"Humiliating you? Why would you think that? Hon, if I step away from you, everyone present will know just how much I enjoy being this close to you." He pressed his erection into her with a shallow thrust. "Do you think that should humiliate me? It won't. This is the first time all year, much less today that I've managed to get close to you. I don't know what you mean about all the available women present, but I've been trying to talk with you all day. I did intend to talk to you first. But, well, the music started and I needed my hands on you already. So we're talking now." Confident he'd explained it, Rem smiled down at her.

"Talking? You call this talking? This is a full-body tackle in front of everyone. This is not talking!" she spat at him through clenched teeth. Kathryn didn't know what this was, but it had almost nothing to do with dancing either. It was more a public statement of some sort. Her heart sank as she absorbed what type of public statement he was making. Arrogant and crude.

This dance made her feel dirty even though she'd spent the last three years using Rem as the hero in every single one of her fantasies. But not like this. This felt like a man who assumed he could handle her any way he wanted, public or private. This was about her value as a person being less than every other woman here. Perhaps she could slip out and salvage some dignity.

"Would you rather go some place private to chat?" Rem asked calmly in the face of her hissing little cat fit.

"Yes! That way, when they find your body parts strewn across the lawn tomorrow, no one will know for sure who did it!" Kathryn was trembling now. She hoped he thought it was rage. Better that than the real reason. She could feel herself melting from the inside out. His effect on her nervous system seemed to be catastrophic failure.

"Snappy little thing, aren't you? Come on. Let's show everyone how much I like you then sneak off. I'm sure they won't get the wrong impression." Rem grinned and moved to release her. Her arms suddenly clamped around his neck like a vise.

"Don't you dare, Remington Morgan! Dance us over to the side of the platform and step down into a dark corner." Splotchy red marks were spreading across her face—he could see them down her throat.

Rem obediently danced them to the edge of the platform. He couldn't stop grinning into her scrunched-up, splotchy face. A step down and he had them back on the lawn as gracefully as possible. Kathryn grabbed one of his wrists and started dragging him away. Chuckling, he noticed she headed for the lawn shed.

"Shut up, Rem!" Kathryn directed over her shoulder.

Stomping across the lawn created an interesting "jiggle in her wiggle", Rem decided. Not minding at all, he trailed behind her.

People seemed inclined to let them pass. Rem figured her fierce face as she marched him away had something to do with it. Could be they thought he was about to receive the sharp side of her tongue. He was going to get that tongue all right and it was only eleven p.m., ahead of schedule.

Off on the far side of the lawn they came up to the shed, Kathryn yanked on the side door and found it locked.

"Let me get that for you," Rem murmured. He moved around her to unlock it. Rem pulled out the master key set and grinned back at her. "We didn't want the kids getting in here," he explained to the smoldering object of his obsession.

She stepped back and folded her arms under magnificent breasts. Her foot tapped in irritation beneath the long yards of skirt. She looked like a pissed-off pink kitten. Rem swung the door open and gestured her in with a polite half-bow. Marching through the door, Kathryn whirled on him as soon as it clicked shut. When the faint lights from the party were closed out, darkness descended on them. There were two windows, one on either side of the shed, but the dim light allowed by those only outlined the large riding mower and various rows and stacks of equipment, chemicals and sundries required to keep the lawn in shape. If everything had not been meticulously ordered in neat rows, stacks or hung on pegboards, there would have been no room to move around at all.

"Doesn't this thing have a light?" Kathryn's cantankerous voice demanded. The enormity of her mistake coming in here dawned on her as she glanced around. While the shed appeared large on the outside, it was so crammed with lawn equipment on the inside there was nowhere to move away from him. The trembling effort to control her surging lust and turn it into the cool detachment required to get through this little chat was going to be monumental.

"Yeah, but then everyone would know where we are," Rem reasoned. "I thought you wanted some privacy?" The close quarters were perfectly all right with Rem. She could hardly take two steps away from him in any direction. The murky darkness was a familiar place, it held no secrets his eyes could not see.

"Right. This'll do," she snapped. "What in the wor—Oufff..." Her tirade came to an abrupt halt as big hands pulled her curvy body against his hard one and firm masculine lips locked onto hers.

One steel-banded arm snaked up her spine to hold the back of her head in his palm. It allowed him to control her upper body and press it against him. The other went right for the tempting ass. Wrapping around her and sliding his hand down the plump curve that'd been making him crazy for so long, Rem curled his fingers to palm it and squeezed roughly.

He groaned as her mouth dropped open and he tilted his head for a better fit. Rem drove his tongue deeply into the sweet, punch-flavored depths of her. He insistently inserted a rigid thigh between her legs. His bent leg propped against the door behind them and lifted her to her toes on his thigh.

He'd only meant to warm her up. Kiss the resistance out of her and show her a taste of what they were together. But his damn control was whittled down to nothing. He'd spent way too many hours watching her float around the property flirting with every man present. Sometime during the frustrating afternoon, he'd lost the ability to stop.

Of course, it could be the three-plus long years of needing to taste this forbidden mouth. Every time he touched a woman these last years, he'd pretended it had been Kathryn. He could pound into a woman until his body trembled with exhaustion, his dick ached with reaped releases and still he hungered for Kathryn. Having her suddenly in his arms in a private space blew the last of his control. His body took over. It claimed her on an animalistic level.

Kathryn gave up rational thought as he forcefully pressed his rock-hard body against all the right places. Her hands clutched bulging biceps while he held her immobile. Her breasts ached and nipples puckered painfully. That wicked tongue plunging into her mimicked his lower body with each thrust. The hard bulge under his fly made her graphically aware of how much he had to work with.

A carnal combination of lust and longing exploded across her body like a wild brushfire. It didn't go in one direction, just blew out to every extremity with a white-hot intensity that burned away time and place. It left her spineless in his arms as pleasure incinerated the last remnants of resistance. Every inch of her needed his touch and she pressed herself desperately into him. The heat of his body drugged her with his unique taste, feel, barely there soap and man smell.

A deep growl reverberated up Rem's chest when he felt her melt against him. Unable to taste enough of her, he dragged his tongue down the side of her face. He licked his way to the tendon between neck and shoulder. His teeth clamped down on it gently and he sucked hard. Her head fell back and her body surged up at him. God! She was sensitive.

The hand on her ass slid up to investigate the waistband of her skirt. He needed that thing off her. Determined fingers found the button and flicked it open. The thing didn't even have a zipper—it just fell open in a pocket arrangement.

His mouth moved across her collarbone, sucking, nipping and soothing the stings with long licks. He no longer had to hold her in place so both hands reached down to shove the ugly skirt off. As his hips pulled back for a particularly fierce thrust, the skirt fell to drape over his thigh. Rem's hands immediately clamped onto her delectable ass. His mouth shot up to hers again, swallowing the shocked moan as she felt his fingers curl around her bare flesh and discover the g-string she wore as they investigated the cleft of her bottom.

Her eyes flew open and she stared up into his ferocious gaze. Still working her mouth in the deep kiss, he very deliberately drew his hands up her sides pulling the sweater up. His eyes narrowed and hers widened as he drew it over her breasts to her armpits. Her arms were already around his neck so the quick move to pull back and whip it off was simple. Kathryn was now perched on his leg in g-string and bra.

The feeble amount of light filtering in the two small windows was enough for him to see exactly what he'd uncovered. She stared up at him with a dazed expression like she couldn't quite figure out what was going on. Good. Just a few more seconds and he would explain it to her in detail.

The contraption she called a bra looked more like a flack jacket. Hell, it was coming off.

In a fluid motion, he reached behind her and flicked the row of six hooks open to drag it off her shoulders. Her hands immediately shot to her chest as she attempted to cover the heavy globes that fell out of the pseudo-flack jacket. Rem leaned back a bit and looked down at her futile attempt to cover the mounds that spilled out above and below her little hands.

"Let me help you with that," he rasped. At the same time, his hands skimmed up the undersides of her breasts and determinedly tunneled under her hands. As rough fingers roved over plump nipples, he clamped the stiff berries between thumb and forefingers with a sharp pinch and twist. Sure enough, her hands reattached themselves to his biceps as she almost fell off his leg sucking in a moan at his actions. He released immediately, his palms rotated until his fingers cupped each heavy breast and held them up for his inspection.

"Remington," she gasped. "What are you doing?"

His eyes were glued to her incredible rack. Her breasts had to be way past DD. He'd never held such large, incredible breasts. Thank God, for good night vision! The view was spectacular.

Spilling out of his palms were two world-class tits. Pale flesh quivered in his hold. The areolas surrounding her fat nipples where puffed up and crinkly with excitement. They rose from the smooth flesh around them in swollen invitation. Her nipples themselves were perfect strawberries of succulent temptation. Below the unbelievable breasts, her rib cage was slender and her waist tiny. He could span it with his hands as he'd discovered while removing the skirt. Her hips curved roundly out while her thighs hanging over his leg were firm. Oh, yeah, Jessica Rabbit in living flesh! And he hadn't even seen her ass yet. Have mercy!

The sight of her, even in the dim light, snapped the last available expanse for mental traffic in his brain. His cock and balls were fine with that. They knew what to do and now they had the right body to do it with.

"Rem, uh, what?" Kathryn breathed. "What are you doing? We can't, we can't do this." Kathryn desperately clutched at a shred of awareness. Her body gushing in screaming overdrive, she gulped in air and tried to remember why this was wrong. Why this huge, savagely sexy man who inhabited her dreams should not be claming her body.

One thought snuck past the blockage her body created in Rem's brain. He hadn't heard a "no" or a "stop" in whatever it was she said.

Tenderly Rem lifted a breast to his mouth and sucked it in. His ravenous mouth opened wide to take the whole areola in. His actions gently bent her back to offer up both breasts to his mouth like the juicy treats they were. Sucking in hard, he twirled his tongue around the plump nipple, investigating that bit of stiff temptation greedily. His other hand fastened around the neglected breast as thumb and forefinger clamped on her nipple. They stroked from root to tip in insistent demand that it stand up in swollen splendor. He could feel her silky excitement seeping through to his jeans.

Her head fell back and her body writhed on his leg. Her hips jerked with each pull on her breast and she moaned so softly he could hardly hear it. Her fingers dug into his arms as her body shuddered under his mouth. His suckling mouth and tormenting fingers moved over bits of flesh so sensitive, so needy for his touch that she felt as though he reached into her body and stroked her from the inside out. He propelled her right past turned-on into foaming-at-the-mouth insanity.

Abruptly, she slammed into an unexpected orgasm. He felt her legs clamp around him while her body pumped on his thigh as the fierce climax jerked her uncontrollably. His greedy mouth switched to her other breast. He turned his head sideways and bit down on her engorged flesh with dull molars. The sharp pressure forced the areola to puff up further. He drew on the sensitive tip incessantly, slurping loudly and growled in satisfaction.

He couldn't get enough of her taste, her scent and her squirming, flexing, tantalizing body. His hands caressed her with almost bruising force as he tried to fill them with all of her. They pressed into her with ferocious need, while the reality of her flooded his system. Hard palms skidded over silky ass and thighs, occasionally his fingers clenched uncontrollably. Immediately he forced himself to release, terrified he'd bruise her, unable to stop touching. They swept over every available inch of skin, save one. He couldn't reach down between her legs. If he did that, they'd be fucking on the shed floor before he had a chance to taste her. He needed to taste her. Then, when she was creamy and dripping wet, then he'd show her a "long, hard ride".

He switched to the other nipple again. She started begging.

"Please, no, Rem! Not again. Please… Aaarrgg…" Kathryn gasped deeply, as he bit down gently on the overly sensitized nipple and released her. She slumped slowly onto his chest.

Both panted harshly while he cuddled her limp body, she from the excess of release, he from the lack of it. He felt like a bull in heat. His breath bellowed hard in the fight for control. She'd said it! "Please, *no*, Rem." A soft, breathy request, but it constrained him like a straight jacket.

He fully identified with the male animals' need to paw the ground, stomp, toss his head around and roar his displeasure. He'd like to make a big production of convincing her that *No* was not a good idea. But as the soft woman in his arms slowly regained her senses, he simply held her tightly.

The sensual fog began to lift from Kathryn's mind. She realized she was mostly naked, cuddled against a fully clothed Rem. *Yeah right. She was all naked.* The damp, twisted g-string couldn't be considered clothing anymore. It was barely dental floss at this point. She buried her face in his hard chest and groaned. This could not be happening! Her body still trembled with orgasmic aftershocks. The trembling morphed magically right into shaking from extreme humiliation.

Kathryn's mind whirled into action, had he somehow seen her obsession with him in her actions at the party tonight? Did he know what an idiot she made of herself over him? Had he finally done a background check on her and discovered what she'd done to get through college? *Well, sure he had, stupid! Why else would a normally reserved guy grab you and strip you in a shed?*

His rough hands glided up and down her back while he pressed little kisses into her hairline. His big body was shaking, too. Kathryn was pretty damn sure it wasn't the same thing she suffered from. The length of pipe poked in her abdomen told what was ailing him. His own damn fault! She wasn't the one who ripped innocent people's clothes off them.

Her life experience welled up to warn her this would only go downhill. No good alternatives presented themselves in her mind. Growing up, some of her earliest memories were of what happened to her mother when her stepfather was pissed. It didn't matter what he was pissed about, a beating occurred. She'd learned the value of making oneself invisible and her mother had taught her the skill. Life as a stripper from the age of barely eighteen had only reinforced those early lessons.

Unable to handle the ugly situation that bore down on them relentlessly, she figured the most reasonable thing to do was leave. She didn't want to talk about this! She didn't want to continue to the only available conclusion she could imagine, the one that included an angry, horny man and what he did when a woman said "no" to him. In her experience, there were only two options. One was bad and the other worse. Both were events she'd like to avoid. Clothes were required to leave.

Kathryn glanced around frantically—she found her skirt was still draped under her across Rem's leg. Leaning down to retrieve it, too late she realized the motion dragged her breasts down Rem's chest. He groaned deeply.

"What are you doing, honey?" His deep voice rumbled quietly as she straightened and buttoned the ugly skirt.

"Dressing." Her reply dripped ice chips. Showing any emotion at all only made the situation worse. Survival, as far as she was concerned, depended on her ability get away. Angry men could smell fear, panic, desperation.

"I see that. Why?" Rem asked carefully.

Sliding back off his leg, she searched for her sweater in the near dark. Kathryn assumed the darkness that kept her from seeing him clearly would also protect her as she groped around the shed. Bumping into yard tools added a pointy hazard to this exercise. She ignored him and kept looking. Silence was a refuge, she knew there were no correct answers in this situation. Better to be beat for silence than give the man something to use as an excuse for the beating.

Actually, he'd no trouble seeing her and her breasts bounce around the shed. Night vision was not a problem. Watching her hurt herself on sharp lawn tools was. He blew out a breath and tried again.

"Kathryn, I've got your sweater right here. Now, calm down and come back over here so we can talk," Rem directed quietly.

"Talk? Last time you said we would 'talk' my clothes came off. I'm not getting anywhere near you. Toss it to me." She held out a hand for the sweater and backed up as she said that, only stopping when the mower blocked her path.

"Yes, you are," Rem countered arrogantly. "But this time, we really will talk first. What's happened between us isn't over yet. We need to hammer out a few things, honey. I'd like to hold you while we do it." He was a long way from finished touching all that velvety skin. This little taste of her was like giving a starving man one small pea to eat. He needed more!

He pushed away from the door and moved toward her.

She scrambled backwards and he frowned. Her jerky body movements indicated fear. Her increased breathing and defensive stance didn't require his highly trained observation skills to figure out they pointed to one thing. Kathryn felt physically threatened and she was ready to run, the only reason she hadn't left yet was because he was still holding her sweater. Deeply puzzled by what he saw, Rem knew his eyes were not deceiving him. He quickly reached over and swiped up her bra as well. Better have all the clothes he could if he wanted to keep her here.

"Look, sweetheart," he tried to soothe her gently. "You've got to admit this was good for you, too. An orgasm and a sweet wet spot on my jeans tell me you were with me all the way." In his struggle to lighten the mood, Rem stumbled on the line of reasoning that hit like a knife slicing into her heart.

Kathryn gasped and her body jerked as if she'd taken a blow to the breastbone. Her brain registered the direct hit on sensitive "dreamland" territory. Apparently, this could get worse. It hadn't seemed possible a minute ago when she found herself draped naked over a fully clothed man. But listening to the object of your Happy Home Fantasies list the reasons that made you an easy slut-fuck was worse. She actually heard her Mayberry house explode. Shrapnel from its destruction ripped into her and left a wretched, blood-soaked mess. So this was how to kill a fantasy? It had to go down bloody. Even in her fear she'd apparently held onto that silly, little girl dream. Now it, too, was gone.

"I know what happened, Rem. Now give me my clothes!" Kathryn demanded softly. Her whole body trembled with the effort of not doubling over in pain. She had to get out of here!

"No. Not until we talk about this." Rem knew her tone had gone from cold to arctic ice. Somehow, she put a type of distance between them that could not be mapped and moved through. Why? How had they gone from tropic heat to this cold place? He frowned, unaware the scowl made him appear like a man ready to simply take what he wanted. She'd seen that face on a man before in the worst possible circumstance.

"All right, asshole," Kathryn responded. "You want your pound of flesh? Here it is. Yes. I came. Yes, all you had to do was touch me and I acted like a cheap whore. I am apparently shamefully easy where you're concerned." Her voice cracked. "How much more humiliating does this have to be for you to give me my clothes?"

Rem was stunned.

"No, baby! That's not how this was!" He stepped toward her again, confused in his agitation over her perception of shame and humiliation. She jerked back as far as the riding mower would allow and he froze. No! No! No! She wasn't supposed to be afraid of him. Why did she feel physically threatened? He had to find a way to reach her. He needed some way to reverse her ugly perception of the most beautiful event of his life.

"There's nothing to be ashamed of! We're both adults. This was fantastic, mind-altering foreplay. The type of thing a guy dreams of. I had the most incredibly gorgeous woman in my arms who responded fully to my every touch. It was beautiful. Please don't hate this. We didn't do anything wrong! How can I make you understand?" He pleaded now, desperate to get them back to the touching part, impatient to hold her enticing little body in his arms again.

"Perhaps refusing me the dignity of dressing gave me the impression I'm only the entertainment. I'm not your entertainer, Rem," Kathryn's voice chilled even further.

He knew it could only be considered low to deny her the right to dress. It was a control tactic on the lowest levels of the man/woman relationship scales. He didn't get the entertainment thing. But hell, he didn't seem to be getting about seventy percent of what she said. Why was communication such a struggle? Why did so much of what she said make no sense?

He thrust her clothes at her and she snatched them from him. She jerked the sweater over her head and wadded up her bra to stuff it in her skirt pocket.

"I'm sorry, Kathryn. I wanted you to stay and talk to me. I'd no intention of demeaning you." He talked to her back now. He supposed it could be construed as another control tactic to stand in front of the door. How did this get worse and worse? Somehow, he couldn't reach her. It felt like the harder he tried, the further away she moved.

She nodded. "Fine. Can I go now?" The acid tone of humiliation and rigid line of her shoulders told him she expected him to deny her that also.

He didn't want her to leave. Oh, God! If she left now, she would leave him. He knew it. Things between them were screwed up beyond all comprehension. Her mind twisted this into some sort of nasty little game on his part. Yeah, grabbing her on the dance floor was a bit caveman-like. However, losing his mind over her body should have been a compliment. Why did she feel insulted, humiliated? What had gone wrong?

"Kathryn, please listen to me. I lost my mind in here. I know that. It was me who lost all control. I've wanted your sweet body for way too long to be able to turn it off after what I overheard today. Touching you blew me away."

Kathryn only heard one thing out of all that. Discounting all his self-depreciating confessions was easy when she heard that one phrase.

"What you heard today?" She turned slowly to face him and squinted into the darkness.

Her low, deadly tone silenced every other thought in his brain. Oh, God in heaven! Why was everything that fell out of his mouth exactly the wrong thing? Her demeanor left him with no doubt it was about to get a shitload worse.

"What did you hear, Rem? What did you hear that gave you the right to treat me like the crap you walk through in the barn?" Her flat voice was almost a whisper in a scary sort of emotionless way. It chilled him to the bone.

"Kathryn! It was nothing like that. Didn't you hear a thing I just said? Were you even in the same shed with me?" He ran a distracted hand through his hair and tried to think. This didn't make sense! How was everything he said twisted around to push her farther away?

Kathryn stared at him with dead eyes. It really didn't matter anymore. She had nothing left to lose it seemed. Inside she'd accepted that there would be no escaping this now. He stood in front of the door, she couldn't get out the front of the shed because that was locked. Besides, she'd never make it over all the equipment fast enough to evade him even if it was open. The only option was retreat to the one place no one could reach her. Her mother had shown her how to do that, too. Deep within there was a place to hide. A place the abuser couldn't touch no matter what he did.

"Oh, yes, Rem. I've been in the front row all evening. I was there on the dance floor when you decided to display your control over me to your buddies by handling my body as rudely as possible. I was right there when you figured no asking was required and jerked my clothes off. I sure didn't miss the part where you proceeded to amuse yourself with my sexual responses. And let's not forget being present for the special humiliation of you telling me that I liked it because I came for you, and you have the wet spot on your jeans to prove it."

Tears gathered in her eyes but she gritted through them. Emotional displays were deadly, she almost panicked when she realized she wasn't as detached as she needed to be. Damned if she'd let him see her cry! "Last but not least, the absolute treat of having to beg for my clothes! I am right here living it. Now, we've moved on to the new and exciting game of 'What humiliating thing does Kathryn have to do to be allowed to leave'. I am once again, live and in person."

Rem's mouth dropped open. Her account of events stunned him. Shit, it absolutely floored him. What in the hell happened here? He was used to being in fast and fluid situations. Deep into a firefight, bullets whizzing by, he could still analyze and focus on the most relevant information to improve the unit's position and act on it without breaking a sweat.

The words out of her mouth bore no resemblance to the events as he knew them. Except the events occurred in exactly that order. They both had the same facts, but the interpretations were poles apart. So that made perception the key here.

"All you have to do is listen to me a minute," Rem responded softly. "What I overheard was you and Tammy talking in her room this afternoon. From that conversation, I discovered that you *know* you're hiding a spectacular body under the starchy clothes and do it purposely. I also heard about your fuck-buddy Marco. I've been trying to get next to you for over a year, Kathryn. Then this thing about Marco, well, it sort of twisted my brain a bit."

Nervously Rem ran a hand through his hair again. She just stood there looking at him. Her arms were crossed as she leaned away from him on the mower. All indications were cold, very cold.

"So, yeah," he continued. "I was a bit direct on the dance floor. I want you, Kathryn. I've been trying to talk to you all afternoon and couldn't manage to reach you. One damn thing after another kept getting in my way. I was frustrated. I guess when we came in here I wanted to prove to you how good we could be together. I've spent over a year treating you like *spun glass*! That never made an impression. I can't even get you to have a conversation with me. So it seemed like a good idea to just show you. You don't need that damn Marco bastard. I'm sorry if I offended you. I never meant to hurt you." Rem looked away, unable to meet her intense gaze.

Kathryn sat down hard on the mower seat. Actually, she was sitting sideways with her legs dangling over the big wheel. It was sit down or fall down. *Trying to get her attention for a year!* That couldn't be right! When he smiled at her, she'd been nearly catatonic in sexual hysteria. AND WHAT THE FUCK HAD SHE SAID TO TAMMY???!!!!

Damn. Damn. Damn. If he heard about Marco and her refusing to give up the conservative clothes, he must have heard about the toys and the take the trash to the curb comment. Oh, God! He heard what they said about her being in love. Had she or Tammy mentioned anyone but Marco's name? Had she said who it was that flipped her switch?

Okay, rules to the Ultimate Humiliation Game. Admit nothing! Kathryn was beginning to feel like a pro at it.

"So what were you trying to accomplish, Rem? You showed me how good we could be. What did you think would happen next?" Kathryn asked, regaining the cold emotional control required to live through this.

"What I thought—" he stalked over to her and rested a hand on the steering wheel of the mower, the other hand on the back of her seat and leaned down into her. She'd finally asked a question that made sense to him and he didn't want there to be any mistake about this next part, "—was that you and I could come to a mutually gratifying agreement on me being your new 'fuck-buddy'. I'm local. I am willing as hell and I usually know how to behave in public. I like all the stuff you girls were talking about. That's what I wanted to happen next."

Kathryn stared up at him, her mouth dropped open and she appeared to have trouble with the new information again. Good. While she wasn't talking she couldn't twist this into something it wasn't.

"I'm willing to audition for the part properly tonight," Rem continued. "I know exactly how to 'tune a woman's ass up for a good, long ride' as you girls so appropriately put it. Afterward, you can draw up a contract for all I care. But the position will be mine. No Marco! No one else! The toys will be allowed but only when I use them on you. Sometimes I might want you in a costume. It'll just be for me, so don't go getting bent out of shape over it. That's what I want."

Kathryn gulped. Her mind did the TV-on-the-fritz thing. It'd flash scenes from the scenarios he listed then go completely blank. Serious overload. He wanted to be her "fuck-buddy"? He wanted to *audition* for the part? Costumes, tune up her ass, the works? He thought he could regulate her use of the BOBs!

"You want to, ah, to audition?" Kathryn questioned in amazement. That specific terminology left her in no doubt that he knew about her former profession. All this shit could be narrowed down to one thing. Insert "whore" for "fuck-buddy". His own personal whore is what he thought he could demand. Everyone knew strippers were whores, right? He assumed she'd fall down on her knees in gratitude that the prince of the Rolling R wanted her for his private entertainment.

"Oh. Yeah. All night long, Kathryn," his voice dropped an octave. "I am gonna do you until you can't remember your name." He straightened up slowly. Crossing his arms over that massive chest, he regarded her seriously. "I'm in charge in bed,

Kathryn. What we do out of bed is negotiable. You've got to know that going in. Now, say yes."

Chapter Three

ഇ

The pause between them was long and fractured with an emotional tension that jumped and sparked as they stared at each other.

"No." Kathryn's reply froze the air between them.

Rem frowned darkly. "What?"

"I said, 'no'. I don't want to be your whore." Winter's cold, blue hand gripped her heart and squeezed as she looked at him and continued. "I know it might come as a shock to you, considering the trash I come from and what I've had to do for a living. Regardless, being a rich man's whore is something I'll never be able to stomach. Now that I can make a living doing something I love, well, it's even less appealing. So, no."

Her ugly summation of his offer hung between them for a moment.

"A rich man's whore?" Shocked, his volume increased with each word he repeated. "What the hell are you talking about?" She flinched and shrank back for a second as he yelled those questions.

"Either let me out of here or get on with the beating, Rem. Yelling at me isn't going to change anything." Bleak and emotionless, her quiet tone flayed him. Her face was now a clear pond of nothingness. Those lovely green eyes were fixed and empty. The woman who sat before him was a shell. Nothing remained of the vibrant personality and dry humor he'd known before.

Her assumption that he could become violent with her sliced into his soul in a way he never saw coming. Her razor-sharp words struck so hard, he staggered backwards as they ripped coldly through his core. The action effectively cleared her path to the door. Like a shot, Kathryn was up and out before he could gather his thoughts to respond, leaving with the speed of someone who knew better than to waste any opportunity to escape.

He lurched back against the shed wall and stared after her fleeing form. Blinking blankly, he debated his immediate impulse to follow her. No. The minefield that was her prickly female brain would perceive that all wrong. If he'd learned anything in the last half-hour, it was that Kathryn didn't trust him. She certainly didn't trust him as a man. She didn't trust him as a friend. Now she was physically afraid of him in every way.

The fact she was afraid of him seemed inconceivable to Rem. The rock-solid foundation of his personality was protection. Protect the weaker ones. That included every woman and child on the planet. His need to protect got him in trouble sometimes. Women were seriously independent these days.

Pain radiated through Rem. Heaven had been in his arms and somehow he'd managed to hurt her so badly, she ran from him in fear. He knew it wasn't all him. But he'd been the one to poke at some deep wound she carried, clumsily scaring her in his ignorance of its existence. He was responsible for her pain and fear right now. He'd somehow made himself the new boogeyman in her life. Damn it to hell!

Gathering up the remains of his trampled ego, he tried to amble casually back to the party. With each step the weight of the world settled heavily onto his shoulders. No question, his ignorant ass had fucked up with Kathryn. How they ended up with such different perceptions of the heat between them was a real mystery. One he needed to get solved.

The enormity of this fuck-up could only be called world-class. Right up with not noticing the iceberg in front of the ship. He didn't even need two hours to sink his boat. Forty-five minutes tops, that's all it took for him to send it to the bottom. That's all it took to hurt the most important woman in his life so badly she ran from him.

Rem found himself standing beside Gray a few minutes later. Gray was joking with Miguel as he watched his pretty wife dance with Charlie. Gray raised his brows and glanced around behind Rem. The question conveyed was, *I saw you latch onto then hustle off that little lady. Where is she and what happened*?

Rem frowned looking out onto the dance floor and lifted his chin slightly. Gray clearly got the reply. *Hadn't you better be watching your own woman? Charlie can't be trusted.* Gray turned back to the dance floor with a grin. Rem wasn't going to discuss whatever had happened.

Miguel chuckled softly beside Gray. The sniper caught the whole conversation clearly. No problem with his eyes. He'd been hanging out with these guys way too long. It was spooky at first to watch these two communicate without speech. Yet after learning their unique form of signing, it made perfect sense. Rem scowled at both of them.

Rem and Gray knew each other so well that over time they'd developed a nonverbal form of communication. It involved Seminole sign language, some obvious Anglo gestures, quite a bit of American Standard Sign Language and a lot of military signals. But when it was just the two of them talking, it dwindled down to a few obvious gestures and the complete understanding of each other. Combat-honed, their unique communication turned into a very distinctive tool that the entire unit could read and use.

The three of them stood beside the raised dance platform, two large men grinning, and one scowling darkly. The music ended and a laughing Charlie handed Prin, Gray's wife, back to him.

"You are one lucky bastard, Gray," Charlie teased. "If this woman ever gets tired of your sorry ass, she can come see how a real man treats a woman."

"I'll be the last man standing, Charlie, my man," Gray casually responded as he gathered his wife to his side.

The party noise subsided in one of those odd lulls for a second. Into that silence a bright flash appeared through the trees down toward the road. A muffled boom immediately followed it as a fireball shot up into the sky. Scattered around the party the members of the unit immediately shifted into alert mode. Hyper-awareness of unit members' positions and the snap of danger zipped between them. Suddenly every person at the party became theirs to protect. They went from guests to grim warriors in the flash of that explosion. Across the crowd, two more heads swiveled toward Gray and Rem. Rem met Gray's eyes briefly and then jogged across the dance floor to step up onto the bandstand.

Gray squeezed Prin's hand. "Call 911. Find Tammy. The two of you make sure everyone follows instructions," Gray murmured, already turning away with Miguel and Charlie.

Rem moved in front of the microphone. "Everyone, please stay here. The boys and I will investigate and let you know what happened. Just to be on the safe side, please make sure all your family members are accounted for. Above all, it's important you stay here. We don't want to trample whatever's out there."

By the time Rem loped to the front of the main house, two SUVs waited there. Five sets of eyes regarded him calmly while handguns were efficiently checked. Rem raised a brow at the amount of firepower present and grinned at them.

"Well, gentlemen. We all recognized that flash-boom," Gray stated the obvious as he handed Rem a Glock nine millimeter semiautomatic pistol. The group of big men slipped into unit mentality as easily as pulling on a comfortable old sweatshirt. Rem checked the gun out of habit as Gray continued speaking, assuming command as they all expected him to. It was how they functioned, not what they needed. "It's probably not what we think, so try not to shoot any civilians. Remember, the cops will consider it their scene. Don't touch if you don't have to."

Silently the guys loaded into the vehicles. They weren't exactly somber, but what could you say? The situation was serious for someone.

Three quarters of a mile down the main drive, they found the wreckage burning beside the road. Silently filing onto the asphalt, six men stood there a moment surveying the scope of the site. It was obvious no one survived the crash, no need to rush in. The burning remains provided enough light to see a black Porsche 911 GT2 had slammed into a large pine tree. The car blew up, somehow, as well. As he looked at the fire, Rem cocked his head to the side slightly and frowned. Gray grunted a low, menacing sound.

"Yeah," Miguel agreed with them. "It's burning too bright. Shouldn't have combusted in the first place. They build safety features into this thing out the ying-yang."

One of the men stepped forward to the edge of the asphalt nearest the crash and inhaled deeply.

"You got something, Blaster?" Gray questioned sharply.

"Nah. Just a whiff when we stepped out here. It's gone now. Probably won't show up at the lab. A bit more C-4 than I would have used though." The slow-talking Southerner shook his head. "Not an amateur, not a pro. Interesting."

"Anyone see him leave?" Rem asked the group. Everyone knew whose car it was. The jerk was trolling the party for clients—something heavily frowned on at this event. Rem knew Tammy hadn't been with him. She and the jerk just finished a big blowout over his behavior, besides he'd seen her across the dance floor back at the house.

"Yeah," Jackson spoke up. "I was out front with, well, with someone and saw him leave. He had a girl. Not someone I've seen here before. No idea who she was."

"Well, shit!" Gray spat. "If it was just him I wouldn't mind so much. But if he took one of ours with him, I'm gonna be pissed."

Sirens could be heard in the distance.

"Guess I'd better get back and let folks know what happened," Rem said as he stepped back into his SUV. "Time to see who's is missing. Anyone want a ride back?"

Charlie and Miguel piled back in with him. He carefully turned the SUV around without leaving the asphalt and headed back to the house. He already knew Gray, with his highly honed tracking skills, and Blaster, the munitions expert, would deal with the cops. Subtly making sure they didn't miss anything. Jackson was just nosy enough to stay and watch everything. He had a strange talent for seeing the big picture on things, sort of like a natural bent for the overview.

Rem sighed heavily—he did not need this shit right now. Finding a way to make things right with Kathryn should be at the top of his To-Do list. Now he was stuck making sure he had everyone's name and number for the cops before he could let them go. There was still the matter of discovering who'd been in the car with Brad. Not to mention telling Tammy that her boyfriend just blew up. Although they'd fought like cats and dogs twenty minutes ago, it would still be a shock. Kathryn would have to wait. At least this kept her at the ranch a bit longer.

Already at the house, Rem had to smile as he saw Tammy, Prin and Kathryn actually blocking the drive to keep people from leaving. Two of the three women seemed relieved to see him drive up and take over. Rem pulled the SUV sideways across the exit before he and the boys stepped out. People gathered around them immediately, asking questions and generally making a racket.

Talking loud enough for his voice to carry, Rem told them most of what they knew. "There was an accident up near the highway. The car spun out, hit a tree and caught fire. The gentleman driving didn't survive. The cops were arriving as we left. I'm sure they'll be down here shortly, folks. That's all I can tell you for right now.

"Please make use of the house if you have kids who need a place to sleep. We'll all be here a while." Rem looked over at

Kathryn and asked quietly, "Would you please help folks into the house? I need to talk to Tammy."

The quiet tone and look on his face as he asked her that also asked her to put their differences to the side. He was requesting her help for Tammy, not himself. Kathryn read exactly what he wasn't saying and nodded. The exchange wasn't lost on Tammy, she gasped, realizing who the driver had to be.

Prin immediately joined Kathryn in heading for the house. Soon they both had tired toddlers on their hips as they assisted frazzled mothers herding little ones in. Tammy stood there and stared up at Rem. He didn't have to tell her who was in that car.

Rem opened his arms to his baby sister and she sank into him. She might be a tiny bit spoiled, but he'd been one of the people who'd spoiled his parents' surprise child. She was the beautiful cherub who ran over them all with sweet, angel feet and he hated to see her hurt. He was relieved to realize there were no tears. Perhaps this wouldn't be as bad as it could have been. He walked her into the garage for privacy before he asked the next question.

"Do you know the woman he left with, sweetheart?" Rem questioned gently.

"Someone was with him?" Tammy gasped again. "Oh, no, Rem! How awful. Is there no chance they survived?"

"Sorry, darlin'. None. Do you know who it was?" Rem pressed.

"No, no idea," she breathed. "Rem! Someone here just lost a daughter, sister or, God forbid, a mother. How do we find out who it was?"

"We'll know shortly. The family missing a member will come to us." He sighed heavily. That was going to be ugly. No easy way to ask a family if the woman was one who might go off with a stranger. As soon as he asked that question, they'd know.

* * * * *

Far to the north, the Observer chuckled arrogantly. The plan worked beautifully. He knew it would. It really would have been nice to have more than two weeks to implement, but the prick and his self-gratifying habits constrained him. Good to be rid of that irritating prick bastard and the slut witch. Regardless of how difficult the task had been.

As the dark vehicle glided into Orlando, the Observer lamented the fact he couldn't share the brilliance of this plan with someone. Despite the rush, he'd come up with a truly exceptional plan to get both the evil bitch and bastard prick into that cursed car and at his mercy. Poetic justice is what it was, sending both of them to hell at the same time. Absolute poetic justice.

He pulled into the garage and wearily got out of the vehicle. Absently he clicked on the perimeter security system and deactivated the interior security to enter the house. He glanced around at the mess and sighed deeply. This had to be cleaned up before he brought Tammy home. She wouldn't like a messy environment anymore than he did.

The kitchen table was strewn with electronics and tools. It spilled over into the dinning room where the huge computer, essential to complete the plan successfully, was located. A superior smile spread across the Observer's face as he surveyed all the tools necessary to dispose of those two in the proper fashion. It wouldn't have been right to just kill them. No, his mission mandated that those who could not be saved must understand the punishment they faced was for their sins. A tall order in this case. Finding a way to destroy the car with them, while making sure they were clear on the reason, was complicated. Happily, he'd found a way to make the car both his voice of judgment and executioner. It was most satisfying now that the deed was done.

Altering the computer controls in the Porsche to accept a few remote control instructions had been difficult. It actually required he learn the specs of the obscene machine. Getting access to the GPS screen and sound system in the car proved to be challenging. He wished there had been time to put a camera in the rearview mirror so he could have watched their faces when he flipped on the video.

The video was a work of art in its clear portrayal of both their sins. It cut back and forth between her sleazy dancing in the club and the prick's disgusting attack on Tammy. That's how he thought of it now. It had to be an attack. The video was short but very effective, he thought. He needed to be sure they understood, so he'd taken a chance and used audio to list their sins for them and let them know judgment was at hand.

Mother would be proud of her smart little man. She was always proud when he took care of things. It was so much better now that he could hear her again. Those damn pills took Mother away from him. They made him see things differently. They were the things that made him stupid, not the other way around.

Wearily he took himself off to bed. All in all it had been a very long day, at almost four a.m. It was defiantly time to sleep. Cleaning it up later would be all right. Tammy wouldn't be here for a few days. And he wanted to be up in time to watch the evening news. It would be on by then. He so enjoyed the news when they showed one of his accomplishments. They never knew what they were talking about, but the visuals were gratifying.

* * * * *

It was six a.m. by the time Rem walked into the den at the ranch. He stood in the doorway and scowled at the room full of sleeping people. His displeasure directed mostly at Miguel.

The huge sectional was strewn with bodies. On one long arm of it Gray and Prin slept. Gray had someone's chubby toddler draped across his chest and Prin tucked into the sofa against the back. Both of them wrapped an arm around the baby. On the next section Miguel stretched out with Tammy sandwiched in between him and the sofa back. Miguel also had a little one sprawled in baby bliss across his chest and abdomen. He held Tammy's hand across the child's back to corral it.

Kathryn curled up on the third arm of the couch. Someone's preschooler clutched her as they both slept peacefully. Charlie in one easy chair, Blaster in the other and Jackson made himself at home on the floor.

Rem envied all of them the few minutes of sleep as he rubbed a hand down his face. Well, except Miguel. That man was far too comfortable cuddled up with his little sister.

Just moments ago he'd almost gotten to the place where he could find a sofa to stretch out on, too. Then the call from an old friend at the crime lab came in. That disturbing call fired him right back to red alert. Now he needed Gray's equipment to untangle this.

Rem glided soundlessly over to Gray and crouched down on his haunches a few inches from Gray's face. Immediately, Gray's eyes flicked open, brows went up and his head lifted off the pillow. Rem nodded and jerked his chin toward the door. Around the room male eyes opened as soon as Gray's did. Rem's body vibrated danger on such a high level that the others felt it immediately.

Swiftly, the guys who needed to extracted themselves from babies and women and ghosted out the door. Rem indicated the coffee machine as they entered the huge country kitchen. Everyone retrieved a cup and sank into a chair at the long ranch-style table. Rem remained pacing until everyone had a seat. No one spoke. They waited.

"I just got a call from Pat Case over at the county crime lab," Rem informed them. "Since we're back door to the Rocket Ranch aka NASA they watch things carefully in these parts now. He thought I should listen to something he pulled off a piece of the car. After nine-eleven, anything unusual makes those boys jumpy. They retrieved a transmission. It's less than thirty seconds, but he recognized a name on it. The name he recognized was Tammy's. He didn't know who Brad and Kathryn were. It mentions all three of them in some sort of narrative that ends with the statement 'Judgment has come'. Case is sending it to your website, Gray, so it stays secure. He's notified the detective already. We'll probably have him all over us soon," Rem concluded.

Charlie whistled low, expressing the group's feelings of foreboding.

"Where's your laptop, Gray?" Miguel demanded with uncharacteristic urgency. Miguel was the loner of this group. As the sniper he was often stationed high above the action to act as an extreme backup and lookout. He was the one who assessed an unknown threat moving in on whatever the operation was. It was often solely his decision to eliminate the threat or allow it to show friendly or unfriendly status. His personality was normally an almost spooky calm.

"Up in the room we were using," Gray replied as he got up to retrieve it. Slipping in and out of a room without disturbing the sleeping occupants was a simple task for anyone in this group.

Jackson, Blaster and Charlie stood also. "We'll do a perimeter check," Jackson murmured as the three of them left the room. Everyone clearly understood the crash was a hit. They'd suspected it before now, but assumed it only involved the jerk's life. He was unscrupulous—no surprise if he'd stepped beyond boundaries in the financial world. Brad had tried hard to play with boys bigger than himself.

The mention of Tammy and Kathryn changed everything. One or both of them was assumed to be in that car. So the killer wasn't finished. The killer was trained enough to rig the car to blow without leaving obvious tags, bright enough to alter the internal workings of the machine and demented enough to actually do it. "Scary bastard" came to mind.

Gray returned shortly with the laptop. He flipped it open and plugged it in swiftly, booted it up and logged onto the secure site. The download was fast. Rem and Miguel leaned over his shoulder as he played it.

"Look at you two grotesque pieces of refuse. Writhing there in the depths of your debasement. See your sins! Your kind does not deserve to know my angel Tammy Morgan. She must be cleansed of your filth. Kathryn Saunders, Brad Schwartz, your crimes are known, Judgment has come." The voice was digitized. A lab could probably strip it down, but the chances of the real voice being in the system was low. Voice IDs had been passed up for DNA identification some time ago.

The three men sat back and stared at the screen.

"Fuck!" Rem exploded. "The bastard is coming for Kathryn! Oh, hell, Tammy, too!"

"Not damn likely," Miguel growled fiercely.

"Calm down!" Gray barked.

"Calm down for what?" Prin wanted to know from the doorway. Kathryn and Tammy were right behind her. All three of them had sleepy children on their hips who were fussing.

Gray snapped the laptop lid shut and got up to take the toddler away from Prin so she could get the drink the baby was asking for. The other two men did the same for Kathryn and Tammy. After the kids each had a drink and were settled in someone's lap at the table with fresh fruit to munch on, Prin looked back up at Gray.

"Calm down?" Her voice made it a question.

Gray frowned. "Not in front of the kids."

Kathryn and Tammy both glared at Rem and Miguel. The two big lugs hung over them like great dark shadows. They did some complicated dance around the women that involved inserting their bodies between the women and the windows at all times. It made the toddlers nervous. The tension could be felt rippling from male to male like radio waves.

"What is going on?" Tammy demanded as she glanced from one chiseled male face to the other.

"We received some news about the crash," Rem answered. "We need to get the remaining families out of here as quickly as possible."

"What are you going to do?" Kathryn asked. "Wake them up and kick them out?"

"Pretty much," Gray answered for Rem.

Chapter Four

ഇ

As the last family disappeared down the drive, Blaster sauntered into the kitchen and grabbed a soda out of the refrigerator. "What level we at, boss?" he asked Gray.

"Red," Rem shot back at him.

Blaster whistled. "Last time you said red, our position was overrun. What do we need to know?"

"Is everyone in a position?" Gray asked.

"Yep," Blaster assured him. "Y'all couldn't sneak a fruit fly into this house. What're we looking for?"

The three women listened quietly. All realized this was the information they hadn't gotten earlier.

Rem sighed and glanced over at the women. His already rock-hard jaw clenched further.

Gray shrugged and made a quick motion with his left hand. Two fingers hit his chest and flashed in a wavy pattern behind him. Blaster's brows shot up and he stepped back in surprise.

"What are they doing?" Kathryn asked the other two women as she frowned at this strange behavior.

"Talking!" Prin and Tammy answered in identical disgusted tones.

"No way!" Blaster sputtered. "Some stupid bas...um, idiot wants the women?"

"Just Kathryn and Tammy," Gray answered.

"What?" Tammy and Kathryn both exclaimed.

"Start talking English now!" Kathryn demanded. Fear floated around the room like a ghastly aroma.

Rem turned to her. "Were you supposed to catch a ride back home with Brad last night?"

"Uh, yes I was," Kathryn stammered in surprise, both at the unexpected question and the situation as a whole. "We...we were both supposed to meet, ah, a client early this morning. That reminds me, I forgot to call him." Kathryn rose to reach for the phone.

"Don't!" Rem snapped.

"How did you know that anyway?" Tammy questioned suspiciously.

"It's involved," Rem answered quietly. "But basically the killer transmitted a message into the car through a GPS system. We just listened to it. All three of you were mentioned. I mean, Brad, Kathryn and you, Tammy. He seemed to think Brad would have Kathryn with him in the car."

Turning to look directly at Kathryn, Rem continued. "So our problem is, he missed his mark. Half a kill is never good enough for a mind like this. He'll try again. If we can keep him from discovering your location for a bit, we have a chance to get him before he gets you.

"He'll know he didn't get you as soon as the evening news comes on," Rem stated calmly. "The story about the kid's date getting killed in the crash will be all over it. Especially since she was a tourist. So we only have a few hours before he starts looking for you."

Kathryn's mouth dropped open in an "O". Rem needed to steel himself from looking at those succulent lips, so he turned to Tammy. "He seems to think you need to be what he called 'cleansed'. Guys who talk like that are usually sick bas...idiots. They often kidnap the person they want to 'cleanse', and do it forcibly. You understand what that means don't you, Tammy?"

Tammy's mouth also gapped open and she shook her head no. Traces of fear etched into her pretty face.

"It means that he probably wants you more than he wants Kathryn." Rem sighed deeply. "Just killing her is good enough.

You, he has plans for. It means he knew *your* boyfriend would be driving Kathryn back instead of you. He knew it long enough in advance to rig a pretty sophisticated bomb on the car and make it all look innocent for the cops."

Turning to Kathryn, he asked, "When did you know you were driving back with Brad, Kathryn?"

"Just two hours before we left to come here," Kathryn whispered.

Gray nodded and picked up the explanation. "Well, then that was part of his plan. Your appointment was a setup. We need the name of the client you were supposed to meet. That guy has to be involved."

Kathryn paled. Her gaze jerked to Rem and skittered away. "He…he can't be involved," she stammered out as her hands twisted nervously.

Gray noted her reaction and slid into his smooth, cajoling voice. "Just give us the name, Kathryn. We'll take care of it. If he was manipulated by the, uh, idiot, everything will be okay. We just question him a bit and move on." Gray knew the appointment guy was involved, but she seemed so reluctant that he added the possibility her client might have been manipulated to calm her.

"No, no. You don't understand. He couldn't have anything to do with this. I just know it!" Kathryn insisted.

"It's all right, honey," Gray assured her. "We need to start somewhere. Just before you came down here, both you and Brad were maneuvered into the drive back together. You've got to admit it looks suspicious that the killer knew this. We only need to talk to your client for a minute."

Kathryn shook her head and stared at the floor. She stared biting her lower lip viciously.

Inexplicably, Rem stiffened and turned to Kathryn. His whole body seemed to expand. Rem sucked in a breath and stalked over to stand in front of Kathryn. Cold black eyes glared down at her. She shuddered a tiny bit at his frontal intimidation tactic, but glared right back up at him.

"It was him, wasn't it, Kat?" Rem questioned. "You were meeting your buddy," he drew out the last word like a curse word. "Weren't you?"

"His name is Marco Muslovski," her voice was quiet and cool. "He is a personal friend of mine as I told you. I can't imagine he could be involved in this. He was to deliver a package and needed to get back out of town in a hurry because of business commitments. That's why I agreed to meet him so early on Sunday. Brad was meeting with him about something else entirely. I've no idea. I would presume it involved Brad being a stockbroker."

Remington gritted his teeth. His hands fisted at his sides while his body radiated heat. Every muscle tightened as he struggled to contain the anger. It was all twisted up with frustration, possessiveness and just plain, dirt-ugly jealousy. He could feel the blood pound through his skull.

"Well, start imagining it, sweetheart!" Rem spit out between clenched teeth. "Because I'd bet anything we'll find your Marco never showed up in Kissimmee either. Why would he when he expects you to be dead this morning?"

"Oh, my!" Tammy gasped, her eyes bounced back and forth between her big brother and her best friend. "My, my, my…" she breathed out and grinned.

"Absolutely not!" Kathryn snapped. You could almost see her back arch as she hissed at him. "I don't believe that for one minute!"

"Why don't you give us his address and phone number so we can settle this right now," Rem growled.

"No," she responded calmly. The flash of power refusing him gave her was gratifying right down to her toes.

"NO?" Remington bellowed. "This bastard wants you dead, and you say NO! Let's get one thing clear, *little girl*—" Gray flashed out of his chair and grabbed Rem by the back of the neck, jerking him backwards and spinning him around. He only managed the move because Rem was so focused on Kathryn and literally trembled with rage. As it was, the two of them froze in a hold that involved a large hand around Gray's neck. Rem pulled back when he realized who'd grabbed him. Gray had two inches on Rem and a handful of pounds. However, at this moment, a lot less desire to beat the shit out of something. Rem's killing rage could have taken Gray to the mat and they both knew it.

"How about you let me handle this, buddy?" Gray suggested smoothly, as if it was a casual conversation. "Before you say something to your lady you'll regret," Gray's silver-blue eyes flashed into the molten black fire burning in Rem's. Rem stared at him a hard moment, took a deep breath and stepped back. He backed up silently until he leaned his butt against the kitchen counter and crossed his arms over his chest.

Gray turned to Kathryn and smiled. Just as he opened his mouth to continue, she cut him off.

"I am not his woman!" She enunciated each word clearly. Her lips thinned and red splotches were creeping up her neck. "Don't refer to me as such again."

"Yeah, I see that," Gray agreed smoothly as he sat back down at the table. "But that's not really important right now, is it?"

Kathryn jerked her head no.

"What is important is for us to discover the extent of this threat. That involves ruling people out as suspects." Gray's maneuver ensured Kathryn couldn't see Remington.

To Prin, he murmured, "Would you mind getting Kathryn a cold drink, Baby Girl? This has been a shock to all of us."

Having Kathryn with her back to Remington was a necessity. Gray almost snorted in disgust as he glanced at his friend. The poor bastard had no idea how deep the pit of snakes and worms he'd dug with that one little phrase could be. Rem really needed a refresher course on women. Calling the woman you wanted to sleep with *"little girl"* in that tone got your balls removed. If the woman in question was one you'd fallen in love with—well, shit—Hell hath no fury, etc., etc.

This entertaining turn of events had Blaster lounging against the opposite kitchen counter from Rem, grinning like a loon. A sharp glance from Rem whipped the smile off his face as he dipped his head down to examine the soda in his hand. His big body shuddered a couple times as he coughed back his amusement. Miguel sat quietly next to Tammy. His habitual calm replaced by intensity that rivaled Rem's. He wasn't exactly hovering over her, but his body could easily be mistaken for a coiled spring.

Prin handed Kathryn a tall glass of ice tea and sat herself down on Gray's thighs facing Kathryn. Tammy moved over to slip into the chair beside Kathryn and wrapped an arm around her. The women were closing ranks around the injured party. Rem restrained himself from snorting and settled for a loud sigh.

Prin patted Kathryn's arm and gently explained, "Gray can call this man's number from his computer. He'll make it sound like a sales call from a carpet cleaning company or something. If the man doesn't answer, the guys will search a bit further to see where he is. But right now, he's all they have to go on. They need this information, Kathryn. I know you understand that."

"Of course I do," Kathryn snapped. All the petting and support was nice, but Rem's attitude still pushed *all* the wrong buttons. She could feel him smolder behind her. Her refusal to answer him and his ugly manner was a knee-jerk reaction.

Gray's fingers flew across his computer as he programmed Prin's suggestion. Gulping the cool drink, Kathryn relaxed back into her chair. She looked over at Tammy's pale face and smiled weakly. They were in this together it seemed. Being "cleansed" didn't sound much better than being killed. Probably worse.

"Are you ready for the number, Gray?" Kathryn inquired politely.

"Any time you are, hon. Need someone to get your purse?" Gray offered helpfully.

"No, I know it." At that, there was another huff from behind them. Gray's jaw clenched once, but he smiled at Kathryn.

"It's 555-121-0055." Gray typed it in and the computer dialed as they all listened. On the fifth ring, a gruff voice answered. "Yeah?"

Kathryn's hand shot over her mouth as she gasped. Marco's gravelly voice was instantly recognizable to her. The computer started its spiel and the phone slammed down.

Huge tears spilled down her cheeks. Kathryn buried her face in her hands as she gasped through the shock. Tammy hugged her tightly and Prin leaned over to cradle her head. Rem pushed away from the counter, drawn to her distress because he couldn't stand to see her cry. He completely forgot the reason had he stood so far away in the first place.

Neither Gray nor Blaster had forgotten, though. Both men straightened to shoot him dark looks. Kathryn obviously knew the guy who'd set her up. The information in her head took them a long way down the road to unraveling this thing. They could probably get there without it, but why do it the hard way? Whatever festered between Rem and Kathryn messed with the flow of information in a big way.

Gray would have sent Rem outside if he could. But this involved Rem's sister and woman. No one could move the man if he didn't want to go. It was also his damn ranch.

"He was supposed to drop off a package for his boss," Kathryn finally managed to say. "He could have canceled the appointment. They couldn't get a hold of me last night." Now, that she'd thought of a plausible reason Marco was still at home, her head lifted and she glanced around the group hopefully.

"Yeah," Gray agreed gently. "That area code is Atlanta. Why don't you—" he was cut off again.

"Oh, right!" Rem exploded. "Defend the sick, fucking bastard who set you up to die, Kathryn. How much evidence do you need to—"

"Shut up, Rem!" Gray bellowed. "If you can't be helpful, go outside and do something useful. Like beat your head against a rusty nail! For God's sake! Quit antagonizing the woman!"

"Antagonizing her? Damn it to hell, Gray," Rem hissed. "She refuses to see that bastard for the scum he is!" Rem's big body literally pulsed with rage as he moved toward the table again.

"Look, you dense Cracker!" Gray almost shouted. "We need more information from her. You keep riding her this hard, she won't tell us anything. God knows I wouldn't talk to you! What the hell is your problem? Did she take a bat to your head in that shed?"

"Stop!" Kathryn yelled at them. "You want to know all about my life in Atlanta? Just ask him." She pointed at Rem. "He investigated the hell out of it and has the attitude to prove it."

"What?" Both Rem and Gray looked at her blankly.

Her lip trembled as she stood up and gazed at Rem. "Go ahead. Tell them how I earned my way through college. Tell them all about what I did just to afford food. It doesn't matter anyway."

Kathryn turned and ran from the room. Tammy shot her brother a killing look and followed. The four other people in the room looked at each other blankly.

"What the hell is she talking about, Rem?" Gray asked exasperated.

"Not a clue. I never investigated her life. She was Tammy's roommate for two years before going into business together. I never questioned it beyond that," Rem shook his head in wonder. "She thinks I know something and it's upsetting her. What the hell?" He headed after the girls.

Gray snagged his arm. "Hold up, hotshot. Don't you think you've cut off enough of your nose to spite your face yet?"

"You know, buddy," Rem's tone turned into a soft threat as he looked down at Gray's hand on his arm. "I've had about enough of you handling me this morning." That said, Rem did change direction and headed out the back door.

Gray shook his head.

"Is he all right?" Prin asked quietly.

"No," Gray sighed. "His woman and his baby sister are threatened. He hasn't slept since Friday night and he can't seem to stop inserting his foot in his mouth."

Gray chuckled and cuddled his wife on his lap. "I, however, am in fine form, Baby Girl. Two hours sleep and I'm raring to go." Nuzzling her neck as he delivered that line had her laughing softly and turning into his body eagerly to kiss him. The two of them sank into openmouthed mating.

Blaster cleared his throat and shuffled his feet. Realizing the kissing couple hadn't even heard that noise, he grinned and ambled outside to find Rem. Miguel pushed away from the table, cast a dark glance in the direction Tammy and Kathryn disappeared in and then left through the door to the other side of the house.

Rem stood on the patio frowning out toward the pool.

"Perhaps a little sleep before the detective gets here wouldn't hurt you, man," Blaster commented as he came to a stop beside Rem. "We've got the perimeter locked down, Miguel and I are patrolling the house," Blaster pointed out, "and Gray is gonna do some of his slick investigation shit on the computer. He has the guy's name and number. We know he's in Atlanta. Shouldn't be too hard for him to dig up who this Marco's contact is and connection to the girls. You're the only one who didn't get any sleep last night. Take a load off, buddy." His soft, Southern drawl cajoled Rem. Blaster's influence on the group was always an easy calm. His features just naturally smiled at the world as he moved through it in lighthearted unconcern. It was a mistake to believe the air of slow-moving, simple guy he projected. Folks usually figured that out right after it was too late.

"Could you sleep if it was you?" Rem asked quietly as his temper dissipated into tired worry.

"Well," Blaster hesitated and scratched his ear. "You ain't gonna do any good if you've fallen down from exhaustion. They need you up and sharp when the time comes. Think on that." Confident he'd imparted all the wisdom required on that subject, Blaster moved off.

Remington sighed deeply and agreed with Blaster in his head. It was only nine-thirty a.m. He should grab some downtime. Just an hour or so, he assured himself as he trudged in and dragged himself up to his bed.

* * * * *

The detective arrived just after five. Once again, Rem, Gray, Miguel, Prin, Kathryn and Tammy were gathered around the kitchen table. The other three men were out on patrol. Gray had pulled together information during the afternoon, which he hadn't shared with Rem yet. He'd also been in contact with the sheriff's office several times, sharing information, going over details so everyone was on the same page.

The surveillance outside was now arranged into a schedule so everyone could eat, sleep and shower. But the arrangement couldn't go on forever. Three of the unit worked for Gray, but the rest had regular lives to get back to.

The buttoned-down Detective Glisic with his average haircut, his mid-range suit, scuffed shoes and standard government-issue car, flipped open his laptop and cleared his throat.

"Okay, folks. I'm here to nail down some facts on this situation. We have the audio transmission only. It was a narrative to a visual of some sort. But the visual transmission, if there was one, was short-range site to site. We know the car had a GPS screen in it, which could have been used. No way to pull that from the wreckage."

"The men—" Detective Glisic glanced at Gray "—found impressions by the main road that indicate there might have been a vehicle parked there. Casts have been taken of the tire marks. We're waiting for a tread match and possible vehicle types list."

Detective Glisic consulted his computer and continued. "The guy in the wrecked car was your boyfriend, correct, Miss Morgan?"

"Yes. Well, ex-boyfriend actually. We broke up about ten minutes before the crash," Tammy clarified.

"Mmm." Detective Glisic smiled at Tammy. The tall, slender blonde made an impression he couldn't resist. "Obviously, you didn't have time to rig this in ten minutes."

Turning to the redhead, he continued. "I understand you were supposed to be in the car, right?" She nodded. "Why weren't you?" he pressed.

"Ah, I, well, we weren't supposed to leave until one a.m. Brad wanted to stay at the party as long as possible." Kathryn stumbled over her explanation and the detective frowned.

"I didn't even know he'd gone until I heard about the crash." Her voice strengthened as Kathryn looked directly into the detective's eyes and explained. "He apparently decided to leave early with someone else. He hadn't bothered to tell me. We didn't get along all that well, so it doesn't surprise me. The only reason we were civil to each other was our connection to Tammy. If that was over, he would certainly take off without a worry about me."

"Interesting," Glisic continued. "So you both were scheduled to meet Marco Muslovski around six a.m. You stated to Mr. Winston here that the arrangements to ride back up to Kissimmee together were only finalized two hours before you drove down here. Right?"

"Yes," Kathryn confirmed.

"You also stated to Mr. Winston that the only people who knew about this arrangement were you, Tammy, Mr. Schwartz, Mr. Muslovski and his boss, Mr. Deesly."

"Yes," she agreed.

"The same Mr. Deesly who was your boss for four years when you worked in his club Daryl's Doll House?" Glisic smoothly questioned.

"Yes." Kathryn's answers remained clipped and cold as he outlined her life.

"Would these two men have reason to kill you, Miss Saunders?" Glisic wanted to know.

"No," Kathryn answered firmly.

"Are you sure? You were a headliner. Losing you had to affect the business?" Glisic pressed, his tone implied more than the actual words.

"One stripper, more or less, isn't all that important. I'm sure you're aware of that, Detective Glisic." Kathryn's voice remained frosty in the face of the implications.

"Well, perhaps you're more than a stripper, Miss Saunders?" he mused softly. "Perhaps they were pissed when you took their 'Money Maker' out of town? Perhaps there is a whole different business at the Doll House, a *side* business that you're unwilling to admit to, Miss Saunders?"

Kathryn gasped and shrank back in her chair. Rem's body lunged flat out across the table as he grabbed the detective by the neck. Both men crashed to the floor in a swift, fluid motion the eye could hardly follow.

Rem crouched over the strangled detective as he held him up by the throat to bring them nose to nose. "Perhaps you want to reconsider how you talk to the lady?" Rem growled. His hand opened swiftly to allow the man's head to slam down on the tile floor. Rem rolled smoothly back up to stand over him.

"What the fuck is your problem?" Glisic screamed at him between gasps for air while he scrambled up off the floor awkwardly. Turning to Gray, he demanded, "Get that man out of here if you want to avoid a shitload of trouble!"

The detective dusted himself off and glared at Rem who stood with arms crossed and regarded him silently. His unmoving body radiated a deadly threat no one doubted he could back up. At the table, no one else moved. The women all wore slightly shocked expressions. The men watched the action with carefully bland faces.

"I mean it, Winston! Get rid of him or I'm gonna call down a shitload of whoop-ass on your little party here!" the red-faced detective bellowed, in an attempt to reassert his authority.

"It's his house, Glisic," Gray spoke slowly, as if instructing a not-so-bright five-year-old. "It's his woman and sister who are threatened and his property where the crash occurred. He doesn't go anywhere unless he wants to."

"I will not be assaulted by a raving maniac while doing my job!" The detective straightened his tie, gave his neck a twist and rubbed the back of his head. "You come at me again, you lose a body part. Am I clear, Morgan?" he demanded antagonistically as he glared at Remington.

"Are you clear on the requirements for this interview, Officer Glisic?" Rem shot back at him in a low, lethal tone.

Both men bristled with hostility as they regarded each other. Finally, the official shrugged.

"I'll do my best. But the material is ugly. If you're too squeamish to listen, perhaps you should leave, Morgan." Picking up his chair, Glisic sat down at the table.

Kathryn turned to the detective. "I believe your question was if Mr. Deesly and Marco were my pimps? Let me explain it so you'll understand."

Kathryn straightened her shoulders and laid both hands on the table in front of her in an odd sort of schoolgirl way. Her eyes drifted to the wall across from her and went blank. Her voice was firm yet flat. All expression or inflection removed from it.

"I went to work for Mr. Deesly five and a half years ago. I'd just turned eighteen and was in a new town with nowhere to live. How I got there is irrelevant. Mr. Deesly hired me off the street. I didn't know how to dance. Yet he gave me a three hundred-dollar advance. He told me to go get something to eat and about a place I could stay for thirty dollars a week until I could afford something better.

"I was the youngest girl at the Atlanta club. Mr. Deesly told Marco to walk me out to my car every night. One night it was very busy and I didn't want to bother Marco. I went out alone and a customer grabbed me. He managed to shove me into his car and raped me. Marco found me before the guy was done and beat him severely. Mr. Deesly took me to the emergency room. He had to make them run a rape kit," Kathryn's voice never faltered. In a quiet, detached monotone she outlined the hideous events as if she listed the ingredients to a recipe.

"The detective who came to the hospital told me that even though the rape kit proved I'd been a virgin before the rape, no one would believe a stripper in court. The man used a condom so there was no semen. No real evidence. And besides, the medical transcript was the only thing we had to keep the man who raped me from pressing assault charges on all of us.

"I didn't recover well. Marco taught me how to defend myself. Marco also taught me not to be afraid anymore. When I graduated from college, Mr. Deesly gave me a thousand dollars and told me never to darken his stage door again. Then he kissed me goodbye. Those are the two men everyone seems to think want to kill me. They are the only men who have ever treated me like more than a piece of meat. I will not believe they are doing this."

Everyone in the room sat still and silent as she told her tale. Now people shifted uncomfortably. Her intense story, related in such a flat, strong voice was moving in its bareness. The emotional impact she tried to avoid intensified.

A stark, hungry, homeless and desperate eighteen-year-old had entered the room with them and glared around defiantly, daring anyone to feel sorry for her. The expressionless recounting of her rape and subsequent betrayal by the justice system haunted the room with its barren despondency. Rising eerily from the ruins of her young life was the struggle for self-respect and recovery. A ghostly cloak of wishes, dreams and a heart that would not be defeated, settled around her shoulders.

Rem stared at her and felt her tale burn into his chest. Every word and action in the last eighteen hours clicked into perspective. The enormity of what she assumed he wanted from her. Why she reacted the way she did. It all crashed down on him, gutting him with her pain and his own contribution to it. Was it possible to fuck up more monumentally than he'd done with this woman? The only guy lower than he was the asshole trying to kill her.

Blinking rapidly, Rem pushed away from the table and paced over to the kitchen window. Powerful forearms, knotted with tension, gripped the countertop. He leaned over the sink with his back to them. Rem struggled to absorb each painful event as her deep wounds ripped opened new and fresh in his mind. He'd no defense against the repeated blows as each devastating event occurred for him as she told it. She'd had years to deal with them, yet still the covering was so thin and fragile she dared not disturb it with anyone's compassion.

That she didn't want anyone's pity couldn't be more obvious. He'd none to give her. Her rise from the mangled wreckage life handed her made him so proud, he could taste it. His part in making her feel shame over it cut him off at the knees.

He couldn't even flinch from the blows. She would see it. He knew for a fact she'd think he was repulsed by her life. Her entire mindset suddenly became crystal-clear. The more he understood her thought processes, the colder he got. He saw his very words play into her deepest fears. His actions in the shed mirrored the most gruesome event of her life. Oh, God, he prayed the rape was the only truly dreadful event of her young life. He didn't know if he could take any more. Yet that sketchy outline of her life left several black holes of missing information.

Rem squeezed his eyes shut and fought through the intense need to sweep her up in his arms and hold her closely until all the pain went away. Her brave soul would never have allowed it, even if he hadn't just spent the weekend alienating her in the worst possible way. Swallowing tightly, he ruthlessly beat down the urge to throw up. The need to shred the bastard who'd hurt her closely followed. Yeah, eventually he'd have the name and pay someone a little visit in Atlanta. There were records, he consoled himself. There would be a name. Grimly, he let that promise of retribution be enough for now.

Kathryn glanced at Rem's back and turned to the detective. "Do you have any more questions?" she asked calmly.

Tammy reached over and took Kathryn's hand. Knotted in support their hands rested on the tabletop.

Detective Glisic cleared his throat and squinted at his computer. "Ah, yes, Miss Saunders. Please tell me how your appointment with Mr. Muslovski was arranged? That seems to be the key. It gets both you and Mr. Schwartz in the vehicle together at the time of the crash."

"Last Friday, I received a call from Mr. Deesly. He sounded as though he had a really bad head cold. He wanted me to do a website design for him and I agreed. Since he was feeling so poorly, he said he would send Marco down with the specs and outline that I would need to get started," Kathryn explained.

"He also told me about his problems with his stockbroker. We were just chatting as friends and I recommended Brad. Even if I didn't like him much, the man knew how to make money. So, I guess that's how Brad got involved. Mr. Deesly often used Marco to check someone out."

"I see," Glisic mused. "So the voice on the phone was distorted, wasn't it?"

"Yeah, I guess it was," Kathryn frowned.

"Was it Mr. Schwartz who came to you with the plan to drive back with him?" the detective questioned.

"Uh, yes, it was," Kathryn concurred.

"Please, consider carefully. Is there anyone else who knew of your connection to Deesly and who might want to hurt you?" Glisic pressed on in the effort to drag the information out of her.

Kathryn bit her lip as she thought back and sifted through the people in her old life. Rem had since turned around to listen intently. His face was as bland as the rest of the men in the room. They all waited for her reply.

Tammy suddenly spoke up. "That cousin of Deesly's didn't like you much, Kat." Both she and Kathryn chuckled at the mention of him.

"Tell us about him," Gray encouraged softly.

"Well, he thought he was some sort of preacher," Tammy supplied. "I talked to him quite a bit actually. He was always outside the back door of the club at closing time. Anytime I went to pick Kat up, he would come over to the car and try to convince me not to associate with 'that kind of people'." All four men stiffened as Tammy recounted her memory of the man.

"Tell us exactly what he said to you, honey," Miguel bit out. His eyes were fierce in a way that made Tammy frown at him in puzzlement.

"Well, I don't really remember it word for word! Last time I saw him was over a year and a half ago," Tammy shot back bristling defensively at him.

"Tammy," Gray prompted. "Can you remember exactly how he referred to the people he didn't want you being with?" His deep voice inserted calm encouragement into the situation and soothed her enough to get her back to remembering.

Gray sliced a glance over at Miguel as Tammy thought. His frown conveyed the "It's not the time to push yet!" message.

Glisic typed away at his computer as he created an accurate record of the interview. He was content to let the others ask questions since they were the same he'd have asked anyway. In spite of his own outburst earlier, he agreed with the frown Gray shot at the volatile hotheads around the table. The women held the key to this and information flowed much easier when they were calm.

"Yes, actually. He always referred to them as 'That Kind'. As if they were a different species or something. It was strange. But he never did anything. He always carried a bible and seemed really harmless," Tammy mused.

"Tell us everything you know about him," Gray pressed gently and included Kathryn in the request.

"As Tammy said. He is Mr. Deesly's cousin," Kathryn answered. "Jonathan named the club Daryl's Doll House just to piss him off I think."

"Jonathan?" Rem asked sharply.

"Deesly," Glisic supplied. "Jonathan Deesly."

"Yeah, well—" Kathryn pointedly ignored Rem, "—Daryl is the cousin's first name. Jonathan said he'd been a pain in the ass since they were kids and laughed about him. One time, Jonathan mentioned that he'd felt sorry for him, too. I took it to mean that when they were kids Jonathan felt sorry for Daryl over something. He only talked about him the one time when he explained why he didn't have Marco remove Daryl from the back door. As long as he was harmless, Jonathan wanted us to ignore him."

"Anything else you can tell us?" Glisic tried again. "Description maybe?"

The two girls looked at each other and laughed. Tension was strung across the room entangling them all. Their nerves needed an outlet and laughter at the remembered visual gave it to them briefly.

"He's really odd," Kathryn mused.

"Yeah, a real fashion disaster," Tammy supplied with a grin.

"We're looking for something a little more concrete here, sweetheart." Miguel growled. "Like height, weight, hair and eye color?"

Fire flashed in Tammy's eyes at Miguel's tone. "You can quit calling me your silly pet names, jerk. I am not your anything! Got it?"

Gray sat back in mild surprise at Miguel's continued intense attitude. The normally cool sniper actually did have a Latin temperament hidden under all those steely nerves. Apparently, Tammy supplied the spark required to ignite it. Rem caught the possessive undercurrents also. He glowered darkly at Miguel.

"Ah, right," Glisic injected into the tense atmosphere. "So, how about that description, ladies? Anything you can give us will help."

"He was so strange-looking. He had a military haircut, wore a long, black parson's coat with a white collar under it. But his pants were fatigues, tucked into military boots. The boots were really shiny, too," Tammy clarified her position.

"He's about six feet tall," Kathryn finally supplied his physical description. "Brown hair, brown eyes, maybe a hundred and ninety pounds, around forty, appeared in okay shape. You'll have to talk with Jonathan if you want more information on Daryl."

"Okay," Rem blew out a breath and summarized the situation. "We have three suspects, ah, avenues to investigate," he amended quickly at Kathryn's dark frown. "It's after six-thirty, so the local news is over and our boy knows he missed on Kat. Time to get the girls out of here—we can't keep the team here indefinitely anyway. No reason to give him a static target with both marks present."

"Yeah," Gray agreed. "We've got three light planes out there. I suggest they all take off and go in different directions. We can load the women in boxes so if he's watching, he has no idea which woman is in which plane. That ought to buy us enough confusion to run this information down."

The men around the table all nodded in agreement.

Prin frowned. "We all have to get in boxes?"

Gray grinned at her. "That's right, Baby Girl. This could be fun." Prin slapped him on the shoulder as his eyebrows wagged at her suggestively.

"Sounds like a good plan to me," Glisic agreed. "Now, just tell me where the other two ladies will be and I can let you get to it."

"NO!" Rem and Miguel barked in unison.

"Excuse me?" The detective glared at both of them.

Gray chuckled and turned to the detective. "They'll check in with me, Glisic. I'll contact you as we need to. The less information out there, the safer these women are."

"That's acceptable." The official frowned and clicked his computer shut. No need to use the department's expenses if they were willing to do the work themselves. Looked better on his budget.

"Just make sure you contact me if you learn anything, gentlemen. Our department will pursue this vigorously." Glisic glanced around the table one more time as he gathered his things up efficiently. "I expect cooperation if we need more information from the ladies. I'll be in contact." With that, he stood and found his own way out to his car.

"So, what now?" Kathryn asked into the silence after he left.

"You and Tammy pack your bags," Rem answered her. "We'll go tell the rest of the team our plan and bring in boxes."

* * * * *

In the suburbs of Orlando, the silent and still Observer sat in front of his TV after the first edition of the early news. The volume was turned down and his eyes unfocused as he let the

232

color blur and jump on the screen. He knew if he didn't hold on very tightly, he'd explode. Mother hated it when he lost his temper and wrecked the house. So, he sat real still. It helped to count his breaths. It took his mind off the storm of random violence that raged through him.

He almost thought he might need one of those pills. No, no. No need to do that. They infected his brain. When he was a bad boy, Mother always made him take a pill. He hated them. It wasn't his fault. He hadn't been a bad boy.

Follow directions was all those idiots needed to do, such a simple thing. But no! They couldn't even do that right. It messed things up so distressfully when people didn't follow directions. Yes, it was the best plan. No, no, nothing wrong with the beautiful plan. It was the trash he had to work with who messed things up so abominably. You truly had to do everything yourself to get it done right.

That grotesque stripper just lost the privilege of a quick death. Nope, now she'd earned herself more of his attention. Wasting his time came at a cost. Hadn't he taught her that lesson once already? No, no. Someone else had taught her. But still, she should know. How many times did he have to tell her to do something? Did she think she was too good to do as she was told? Oh, she'd know who was the boss again shortly. Yes, yes, she would know who was the boss again.

He'd been kind to her, fatherly even, and look how she repaid him. Wasn't he the one who'd ordered the most expensive gigolo in Atlanta to make her his special project? He'd known she was a moneymaker the first moment he saw her. The filthy kid had a sensuality that glowed about her. He'd known she'd make a first-class whore after her usefulness on stage wore thin. But no, even back then the bitch had defied him. After he invested all that time and effort into educating her to be an elite whore, she'd fucking finished school and left him.

His lips curled back in a snarl. There were would be no more opportunities for her to defy him. No, no, the fucking whore was about to learn who the boss was again. This time the bitch would do what she was told.

Where was she, still at the ranch? Still with Tammy?

Would she know she was meant to be in the wreck? Probably not, but someone else might. The audio-visual had been a risk. It fulfilled his needs so beautifully that he hadn't been able to resist using it. But now it left him open if anyone retrieved the message. He needed to move. His fingers started to tap out a jerky rhythm on the arms of the chair.

Clean the house and move! Must get things in order. There was no way the transmission could be traced. Must move. It was done off a stolen laptop, which he'd already destroyed. He still felt the gnawing need to cover his tracks. Wouldn't do to ignore that. Got to move. His fingers tapped faster. Mother always said to go with your heart. Dear, sweet Mother. Yes. Need to move.

He had just one thing to do before he moved. Kill the stripper.

It took two hours to make it back down to that fucking ranch. Half a mile away he parked near some brush and got out. Better to come in the back. Damn, stinking bitch. Look at all the trouble she'd made him go through. He should have known she'd be trouble. All that compliance before had been an act. Lying whore. It was wrong to disobey him, he was the boss of everything. Yes, yes, the boss.

Just as he entered the tree line of scrub pine, the distinct sound of a light plane's engines taking off roared overhead. He watched the private plane gain altitude as it headed north. A second plane immediately followed, it made a wide turn and headed west. Then a third did a complete turn and headed south.

The Observer watched them wearily. So they thought they could outsmart him, did they? Well, whoever they were, they would find out differently. This just meant he had more time to form the plan. His Angel would contact him—he had no doubt of that. She needed him. Yes, yes, needed him. He knew he'd be able to hear her, too, in a few days. Mother would be so pleased. Mother would be proud of her smart little man.

Chapter Five

🆂

Kathryn crawled out of her box as soon as she felt the plane level off. She slid into the copilot's seat and took the headset Rem handed her. *Why bother*, she thought as it settled over her ears. They had nothing to say to each other. Rem only spoke to her in spare, clipped tones since the detective had left.

The plan for her to go with Rem and Tammy with Miguel seemed to spring fully formed into the collective male minds. No amount of logic about the need to get projects, which had deadlines from their apartment made a dent. Three tough faces just stared at them blankly, like they were idiots or something.

Gray finally responded to them. "If you want to live to finish those projects you'll go now."

The only thing further anyone said about it was when Rem stopped Miguel just after they loaded Tammy onto his plane. Rem gave Miguel a dark look and reminded the man that it was HIS sister in there. Like there was any doubt, Kat snorted to herself.

"Where are we going?" she asked, breaking into the desert-dry silence between them.

Surprisingly, he grinned over at her. "Down to an island off the coast of Belize. You're gonna love it. Sun, surf and me to cook for you."

"You cook?" Ah, here was a safe subject. Kathryn hoped they could have a civil conversation.

"Yeah," he confirmed sheepishly. "It's kind of an obsession. When I figured we'd go there, I called ahead on the secure line and had the kitchen stocked with everything I haven't had time to try."

"No shit." She laughed. "Who would have guessed it?"

In that little statement, Rem heard her relaxed use of a curse word with him for the first time. Maybe she'd dropped the good-girl disguise. Maybe she finally felt relaxed and able to be herself with him. Lord only knew, they'd both been acting up a storm this last year. If he accomplished nothing else, he wanted to make her comfortable with him. Get her to trust him. A little dependence from her and he figured he'd be in seventh heaven. It should have been a shock that he wanted her to depend on him.

In his past, a long list of women tried that one. As soon as he felt that slipknot slide around his neck, he was out. Gone so fast, the dust in his wake was settled and had a family by the time the women looked up.

"Why don't you take a nap?" Rem suggested. "The flight will be a few hours and you didn't get much sleep last night. There's a pillow and blanket just behind you."

"What about you?" Kathryn asked suspiciously. "You get any sleep at all? Or am I flying with a dead pilot?"

"Relax. I got four hours this afternoon," Rem grinned at her. "Good for another seventy-two, honey, ah, I mean, Kat. Sorry if the pet names offend."

"Another seventy-two? Right!" she scoffed. "Maybe back in the day, old man, but you're a geezer now. Sure you can make it?"

"Geezer? I'll have you know I'm only thirty-six, you disrespectful infant," Rem shot back at her. He could hardly believe they were joking. She'd never ribbed him. What did it mean? Was it a good thing? Or did she see him as a comfortable old sock now? Shit. When had he become this Nervous Nelly?

"Yeah, as I said, geezer. And I know the pet names are a habit you old guys can't break. No sweat. Go ahead, put on the elevator muzak you like so much. I am gonna unplug a bit." Kathryn leaned around looking for the bedding.

"Unplug?" Rem's brows went up as he repeated the slang.

"Uh-huh, known as nap by the terminally decrepit." Chuckling, she snuggled down in her seat and closed her eyes. Next time he looked at her, she was out.

Rem marveled at the new personality she showed him and smiled to himself. This was the woman who faced life and survived it. Damn, he liked it.

Kathryn's eyes were closed and she was doing her "sleep" impression for him, but something about this moment wouldn't let her relax. Abruptly it dawned on her. He was rescuing her again. The fizzing pop in her blood was the resurrection of the damsel in distress fantasy. Disgusted with herself and the childish dreams she couldn't seem to kill, Kathryn tried to reinforce the logic of this situation. The only reason she was with Rem instead of Miguel was because it was obvious for Rem to protect his sister. The switch was simple strategy, nothing personal about it. Not that it would be hard to figure out, but any little bit of confusion the guys could throw at this bastard was not to be overlooked. Sometimes it was the simple things that a brilliant strategist missed.

This change in the way they were responding to each other was startling and disturbing. The careful distance she liked to maintain had been shattered in the shed. Each unbelievable event following it simply shoved the unfinished business aside. It was still there lurking like a winter-starved wolf ready to lunge into the room.

Exhausted both physically and emotionally Kathryn decided it was time to employ survival tactics. Concentrate on the one thing she could control, herself. That basic fact had been a constant in her life. It was her ability to disconnect from a situation in which she was a victim and focus on how to change it that had gotten her out of the small Georgia town she'd been born in. Away from the horror of degrading abuse at her stepfather's hands while her mother watched in codependent dismay. It had allowed her to see there was no point in staying. No one could save a woman who didn't want to be saved. Not even her own daughter.

She chose to remember her mother as the strong, beautiful woman who'd taught a first-grader how to hide when the man coming up the porch steps was stomping and stumbling. The woman she'd looked at that last day in the shack on the bad side of town was not the mother who'd saved her as a child. She wasn't the loving creature who'd read *Cinderella* over and over again by candlelight because it made Kathryn feel better. They weren't allowed to use too much electricity. Her stepfather declared it was a waste to burn it to read fairy tales to a stupid kid. The mother she remembered snuck in with a candle and Kathryn's favorite book while the TV blared in the other room.

That flickering, treasured memory soothed Kathryn now. It allowed her to drift into the hazy place between sleep and waking where one rested without losing area awareness. Not that she was on guard—Rem was busy flying and didn't seem a threat at present. It was simply part of the survival formula that could not be disconnected from the rest of it.

They touched down just after midnight. The little island boasted a lighted, paved runway. Amazing to Kathryn's mind, but she supposed it was the way people in Remington's income bracket lived. Not like she would know.

Rem helped her out of the plane and grabbed the bags. A Jeep was parked there to take them to the house. It was empty with the keys resting on the seat. Kathryn made no comment. Rich people seemed to know how to make the "convenience" elves appear. Those mysterious creatures who arranged things in the perfect place and then magically disappeared. She'd commented on it once to Tammy who'd shrugged and laughed while she admitted Rem was the best at it. "If you really needed a plan to work, put Rem in charge of it," she'd advised.

The place they arrived at couldn't really be called a house. More like Dream Greek Villa on the Beach! Kathryn's mouth dropped open as they drew near.

Everywhere lights flickered as if illuminated with a thousand candles. Not one harsh electric light in sight. White columned porches surrounded it. The beach side porch stepped down directly onto pink sand. The other three sides enclosed a fantasy garden, full of mysterious shadows, half-hidden sculptures, fountains and winding paths. The mingled tang of crisp ocean breezes and tropical night-blooming flowers added an unreal perfume to the warm night air that drenched the senses in the lush unreality of the place.

Rem pulled up in front of it and reached over to gently place two fingers under her chin. A light push upward closed her mouth. Kathryn gulped and stared around her. "You like it?" he questioned not moving, just watching her take in the view.

"Um, aren't they gonna miss this place on Mt. Olympus? Seems like they would notice a whole villa disappearing," she breathed.

That smart mouth again, she made him smile. Rem slid out of the Jeep and grabbed the bags.

"Ready?" he questioned.

"Yeah, huh," Kathryn mumbled.

Her head swiveled from side to side on her neck as they entered the house. If she could have twisted it around entirely, she would have. Kat had heard about places like this. They usually came with Robin somebody giving a tour and talking way too loud in his bad English accent. Trying hard to keep her mouth clamped shut, she followed him until he opened a set of double doors into the goddess Aphrodite's bedroom.

Kathryn hesitated to enter although he'd dropped her bag at the foot of the cloud bed, which seemed to float in a huge seashell. Holy shit. The room had more flowing, gauzy curtains and draperies than she'd ever seen.

The furniture was light and feminine. White with pale pink accents and gilded gold framed everything. An entire wall opened out to the ocean view. The phosphorescent, moonlight-crowned waves seemed to roll right through the room in pagan splendor. The muted pounding of the surf provided a deliciously erotic, throbbing heartbeat to the whimsy the room embodied.

The villa wasn't really lit with a thousand candles. Gaslights created the unearthly glow. Since they had to generate their own electricity, Rem explained, only a few appliances used it. Kathryn nodded dumbly. He showed her the bathroom attached to the dream bedroom. It was bigger than the whole town she came from. Kat decided not to mention that.

He'd said to make herself at home. If she needed anything, she could probably find it in the drawers and various cabinets. This was Tammy's room, after all. Tammy never packed to come down here. Said it was easier to just leave what she needed. Kathryn nodded mutely, again. If she really couldn't find something she had to have before tomorrow morning, he would be down the hall, just the next set of double doors.

Rem received more silent nodding from Kathryn.

"Are you okay, Kat?" Rem questioned worriedly.

"Oh, yeah. Sure. Fine," she assured him distractedly.

"Okay then, good night." Rem smiled gently at her and left the room.

"Yeah, um, night, Rem," she mumbled, still staring around the room.

Rem shook his head as he closed the double door silently on her stunned figure. Maybe he'd gone too far having the whole place lit up for their arrival. The juvenile urge to impress her out of her mind wasn't a new one. He'd lied when he said that was Tammy's room. It was her room. Tammy had never set foot in the place.

He'd bought the villa as a broken-down wreck of a twenties relic. Restoring it took on an interesting turn when he had met Kathryn. He hadn't even realized he'd been doing it with the one aim of impressing her. Not until the construction reached that room. That's when he'd recognized he'd planned to make this the place he took her. Only her.

The whole thing was a nod to his hedonistic, sensual appetites. But her room was everything lovely and enticing, soft and alluring. Her room was a homage to the goddess she represented to him. At the time, he'd no idea just how limited her background actually was. But damn, her face when she saw it made every penny spent worthwhile.

It's not like he owned the island, but he wouldn't mind if she thought he did. How stupid was that? Yet here he was, strutting around his room like a fucking gorilla, ready to beat his chest and bellow like an idiot just because she'd been impressed. Pausing to gaze out at the ocean, he had to laugh at himself.

* * * * *

Kathryn managed to move around the room after a few minutes of gawking. Damn, she felt afraid to touch anything. How was she supposed to relax in here? It kept feeling like the real owner would glide in and order her banished to Hades or some such place. The bed did look inviting. She hadn't really slept on the way down. Just closed her eyes and pretended so she wouldn't have to talk to Rem.

The banter thing that happened between them confused her. She didn't know where to go with it, how to act now that he knew everything about her. She felt stripped bare—or set free. She couldn't decide which. His gentle playfulness soothed her and worried her. It was like they were two new people. But in the background all their baggage hung over them ominously. She'd reinvented herself before, it had been necessary to move on with her life. She'd done it when she arrived in Atlanta, again after the attack, then again when she'd graduated and put her stripper's life behind her. Every time she'd carefully gathered all the information she could on the personality she wanted to display and then acted on it until it was real. Now maybe it was time to see who the real Kathryn was.

At last, time to let all the jagged pieces of her life meld together and simply be the person they made her. There was nothing to hide anymore, nothing to defend. This time she could simply be herself. She knew in her soul that the real Kathryn was a combination of the gentle child, brash stripper and conservative computer geek.

She took a quick shower in the hedonistic bathroom. It could only be called hedonistic—just looking around at the yards of gleaming white tile, the glowing brass hardware and decadently huge clawfoot tub made one feel wicked. She hurried out of there.

Back in the bedroom, Kathryn finally gave up. Why fight it? The place was appallingly sinful. It seduced her with plush textures, inviting vanilla-scented silk sheets and feather pillows. Naughty fantasies danced around that shell bed like forbidden temptations. It reigned queen-like over the entire room, requiring a two-step bench just to get into it.

Kathryn dropped her towel and introduced the bed to the real goddess in the room. Laughing to herself in sensual freedom as the room emboldened her. She tipped her head back and slid the towel off her hair. Running her fingers through the masses of red-gold curls, she let them tumble down her back in abandon for the first time in years. Not even on stage had she let her hair free. Now it flowed past her butt to frame her hips in flaming wantonness. Standing with her head tipped back and her arms raised to sweep the hair off her face, her body glowed in the flicker of the gaslights like molten gold.

Rem who'd told himself he was simply doing a quick check of the property stood in the shadows of the veranda, watching her. The sight of her exploded through him with such force he sank to his knees. Seeing this goddess in all her glory for the first time beat him down. It sucked the air out of his lungs and turned his bones to water. The voluptuous figure stretching in innocent abandon left him floundering in a maelstrom of sexual desperation. He remained unable to move long after she turned out the gaslights and slid under the silk sheets. Naked. Gloriously, fabulously naked. He wasn't sure if he'd be able to crawl back to his room anytime soon.

This was not good. He didn't think she'd be too interested in a relationship if he turned into a catatonic, slobbering idiot every time her clothes came off—they'd never get beyond the emergency room. Because that's the only place she would be taking him if she saw him like this.

Finally, he managed to drag himself into his room and collapse on the bed. Not that he could sleep much in this condition. His balls were so blue he couldn't even feel them anymore. He lay there and prayed for the strength to cherish this woman as she deserved to be cherished. Having her in his life, his bed—just his, period, went way beyond a need. Perhaps this was what deranged obsession felt like. Rem closed his eyes and tried to rest as the sun crept over the horizon. Sleep deprivation couldn't make this situation better, he supposed.

The next morning, after she'd pampered herself to within an inch of her life in the sumptuous bathroom, Kathryn couldn't bear to face those dull clothes in her suitcase. Those clothes weren't her anymore. Her determination to simply be the real Kathryn demanded something else to wear. Turning to the closet, she decided to investigate. It contained an explosion of jewel tones. The contents were silky sarongs, floaty sundresses and flirty little shifts. It didn't seem like Tammy's taste. Maybe she felt different down here, too. Kathryn knew she was a different woman this morning. So, what the hell?

Rem knew the type of woman she was now. If something was going to happen between them, she might as well enjoy it. This Kathryn could certainly handle a man who saw her as simply a sex object, when it was on her terms. She'd been doing that her whole life. Now she'd just do it with style.

Kathryn slipped into a silky sarong that draped across one shoulder and hugged her unrestrained breasts lovingly. The naughty little number pulled tight across her ass and made her feel like the sexual queen of the universe. The slit up her thigh almost came to the top of her hipbone. Slit like that, the short skirt was almost inconsequential. Her g-string, masquerading as panties, didn't have anywhere to hide so she got rid of it. Kathryn smiled in satisfaction as she looked at the woman in the mirror. This woman could handle any man, dressing like this was simply flexing the female power of being who and what she truly was. Not bothering with shoes, Kathryn padded out of the room to investigate the palace.

Damn, maybe she'd been wrong. Who knew you could walk into the kitchen and find Adonis, clad only in brief shorts and an apron? She'd never seen him without a shirt before. There he stood over the stove. His massive back rippled with fascinating muscles every time he moved. His tight ass, clearly outlined under those shorts, did things to her that involved changing her panties on a regular basis. Standing there, sans panties, could be trouble. Towel anyone? And his legs! Two long examples of muscled male perfection carried his body around the room. Oh, yes, perfection that required much more study.

Whistling softly to himself and moving about the kitchen in a loose-limbed symphony of all things right in the world that came with muscles, he didn't know she was there. And what a phenomenal aroma coming from the pan he was tending!

"Morning," Kathryn ventured from the door.

Rem whipped around at her voice, his grin faltered as he spotted her framed in the doorway. He swallowed roughly as his eyes traveled down her and up again. He closed them tightly and sucked in wind, not bothering to hide his reaction. The aroma changed from the pan on the stove and he whirled back to tend to it.

"Morning, Kathryn," he managed in a horse voice.

"Got something interesting over there?" she inquired with a smile. Oh, yeah, big boy liked the view. That gave her the confidence to move into the kitchen and perch on the stool beside him. Kathryn crossed her legs just to get even after that peek at his bare chest. His eyes watched every move peripherally. He swallowed hard again and became very busy at the stove. The growing bulge under his apron told its own story.

"Nah, just a little thing I call, 'Blow Your Socks Off Breakfast by Rem'." He coughed and cleared his throat.

"Smells yummy and sounds a bit dangerous with all that blowing going on." Kathryn purred deliberately.

"Mmm, I guess you went for dressing on the safe side this morning, then. Not much to blow off. You look great." Rem glanced at her again and smiled.

"You like?" Kathryn smoothed material that wasn't wrinkled down her rib cage.

His head turned to her slowly and his eyes traveled at a leisurely pace over her. A warm flush crawled down and back up her flesh with the movement of his gaze. Little shivers vibrated down her spine then gathered to do a two-step on her pelvic bone. All she had to do was remember that she didn't love every golden hair on his head. She could do this. He's just another man.

Clearing his throat again, Rem turned back to the stove and served up two plates of food. Grabbed one in each hand and smiled at her.

"I thought we'd have breakfast on the patio. Could you bring the coffee, please?" He indicated the pot with his chin, turned and headed out to the table. It'd been set with fresh fruit, coffee cups, water and pretty little glasses of orange juice.

A frown crossed Kathryn's brow as she followed him. All the signs were there, but he wasn't acting on them. The man was looking but not touching. How was that any fun?

Seated across from him after they both finished the truly excellent breakfast, which had to have about gazillion calories, Kat sighed. There had been a delightful white cream sauce full of mysterious ingredients over fluffy biscuits, eggs that had been altered in ways that defied her taste buds to identify, perfectly browned sausage or bacon to choose from. Next to each plate sat a small pie-like confection. She had no idea what it was besides cheese-covered and abdominally delicious. She hadn't meant to finish any of it, just taste. But now her plate was clean.

"What's wrong?" he asked in concern. The entire meal had passed in pleasant conversation. It was like both of them circled the elephant in the room, afraid to confront it. The elephant in this case was sex. No way she'd mention it after the shed incident. But she was pretty sure he wouldn't either for much the same reasons.

"I was thinking about what I have to do to use up all those calories you just fed me." She shifted in her chair and leaned back.

"Take a swim, hon. Problem solved. All I ask is that you don't go in the ocean alone. I don't know of any rip currents here but it is still the ocean, you know." His smile was worried, as if he thought she would argue with him.

"Of course," Kathryn agreed. "It would be foolish to take a risk like that. Do we need to clean this up? I haven't seen any help around here, is there?"

"Do you mind? I asked them to come only twice a week. I thought we could look after ourselves most of the time." Rem's eyes searched hers for reaction to that bit of news. If he expected a spoiled Tammy-like reaction, the man was about to be disappointed. She had no problem looking after herself.

"Perfect," Kathryn murmured. "No one to bother us. That means I don't have to worry since I can't find a bathing suit that fits. Let's get this cleaned up. I can hardly wait to swim!"

Kathryn bounded out of her chair and gathered up plates. She hauled them into the cavernous kitchen. A few minutes later Rem followed her in. She already had the dishwasher loaded. Thank goodness, they used the electricity for that appliance.

"Kathryn?" Rem asked.

"Yes?" she murmured taking one last swipe at the countertop with the dishrag.

"Did you just tell me you don't have a bathing suit and you want to go for a swim now?" he questioned quietly.

"Yes, you coming?" She turned a smile on him.

"Can we talk about something first?" Rem leaned against the counter across the room from her.

Kathryn stopped and turned to him, raising a brow. The long, muscled man across from her seemed strangely hesitant as he jammed his hands into his pockets.

"Look, I know I made a monumental ass of myself. I wanted to apologize for it." His voice had gone low and cautious. "I've never run a background check on you, Kathryn. All I know about you is what you told all of us yesterday. If I'd known, well, ah, I wouldn't have been such a bastard in the shed. I know how I acted. How I sounded. I didn't mean it like you thought," he trailed off.

"Apology accepted." She smiled brightly at him.

His eyes narrowed. Unless he was mistaken, that was a stage smile. One meant to dazzle but reveal nothing of the person behind it.

"I believe I also need to apologize in advance for the effect your body has on mine. I'm really sorry if it bothers you that I'm pretty much turned on the moment you walk in a room. I'll never lose my mind again and grab you. I'll try to deal with things, well, you know, better. But you, swimming naked in the ocean, well, I'll look."

"Of course, you will. You're a man, aren't you? I'd be insulted if you didn't." Her breezy tone bothered the hell out of him.

"Yeah, I'm a man. One who wants you so much he's been known to turn into a monosyllabic imbecile. But that doesn't mean I'll take what isn't offered. You have to come to me if anything is to happen between us. I just wanted to clear that up before we went outside," Rem stated decisively.

Her eyebrows climbed up her forehead. "So you're saying, unless I specifically ask for it, you won't touch me?" Kathryn questioned.

"Yes," he confirmed.

"Okay?" Her answer was slow and cautious. She drew out the response to a question.

"That okay doesn't sound okay to me." His eyes were serious and his tone sincere. "You do understand I want you. That hasn't changed."

"Um, well, no, I don't understand, Rem. A little over a day ago, you stripped me in a shed. Now that I'll do all the work for you, you want me to beg for it as well?" Kathryn frowned and crossed her arms under those impressive breasts.

"Oh, Kat, please! Let's not start this kind of misunderstanding again. I am willing to beg you, baby. I will happily fall down on my knees and follow you around the property if that's what you want. What I refuse to do, is take anything from you that you don't want to give!" His big body shuddered as he finished that statement. "I will do anything you want, Kat. Anything you need, even if it's not touching you. I'll find a way to do it." Rem stepped away from the counter toward her, his hands outstretched, palms up, his whole body was involved in trying to make her understand.

Her eyes looked at him with every year of her hard life in them. They were skeptical as she regarded him. "Really, Rem. No need to make such a production over absolving yourself from any blame in what happens here. I understand we are both adults. We're basically alone on an island and will often be unclothed or close to it. These things happen. You don't need to worry that I'll cry rape later or go for child support," she stated, exasperated.

"You brought me here for my protection. You're doing me a huge favor. I'm living in the lap of luxury and you've every right to expect something for all this. You already know I don't have the cash to hire you. I'm not going to quibble over a little poke and tickle. Shit, I might even teach you a thing or two." Her tone was neither cold nor warm. These were the facts as she saw them.

Rem paled and backed up. She'd already counted the cost of his "protection". Her reasoning was sound in the world she came from. One paid for everything. She'd been paying for a very long time. He sat down hard on a kitchen chair.

"Kathryn—" he had to clear his throat again, "—the protection is free, the stay at the island is free and the food is free. The plane ride was free. Don't you understand? I want to do this for you because I care about you! I can afford it and am good at it. You don't owe me anything. I am not buying you. I am trying to give you the respect and protection you deserve as a woman." By the end of his statement, his voice was raised and firm. Once again, she wasn't listening to him.

"No, Rem. Nothing's free. I will owe you. It's a debt I can't pay. Even if you never ask for a cent, never touch me, we will not be equals. We will never be on the same playing field if that's what you're going for," she answered quietly.

"Yes, we can," he insisted. "Why can't you accept this? Let it go. Let us get to know each other. Explore each other as much as we want? Why does it have to be about owing? That has nothing to do with the relationship I want with you." Rem searched her face looking for a way to reach her.

"I don't know. I just can't," Kathryn sighed. "Perhaps I've never learned how to accept a gift. It's usually a trick. I don't mean you want to trick me. But, how do I explain this to the prince of the Rolling R Ranch? I've learned the hard way, the only thing worth having is something I've earned myself. Otherwise, someone else has all the power. They can take it away from me."

Pacing away from him, she looked out the windows at the sea longingly. "I understand if you don't want me because you think I'm cheap. If it matters at all, you should know that I've only been with two men. The, ah, rapist and Marco."

"Damn it to hell, woman!" Rem exploded. "What matters is that you are trying to sell me your body to salvage your pride. I won't have it! You'd hate me if I took you up on that offer. Besides, I don't just want your body, spectacular though it is. I want you, Kathryn. As I heard you tell Tammy about the mystery bastard you are in love with, 'I've seen what I want, and

I can't settle for less', I agree with you entirely!" Standing up abruptly, he stripped off his shorts. Naked, his thick erection swung out heavily as he turned to the door.

"I need a swim. If you don't want to swim, fine. But we agreed no swimming alone. So please sit on the veranda or something so I won't be breaking my word on that." Rem strode off swiftly toward the water. He never saw her dress hit the floor.

She'd seen a lot of cocks in her day. Customers were always flashing strippers. As if looking at that was gonna turn a girl on. Well, it would have if they all looked like Remington Morgan. Holy Moly! That man was hung. Staying on the veranda while that collection of body parts was bare and, well, visible—just wasn't an option.

Kathryn ambled to the water at a leisurely pace. She intended to enjoy every second of watching his long legs flexing as he strode across the sand. But above all, she watched those delicious dents in the sides of his ass expand and compress with each stride. Oh, God, the flexing power of that ass had her thankful she was about to sit down in the surf. At least she wouldn't be the only thing surging and foaming.

Chapter Six

ɞ

As she sat at the edge of the surf, Kathryn watched him slice through the water like a sleek dolphin. He swam out beyond the break line. She watched intently until she saw him turn around and start back.

Kathryn sat far enough up the beach that only gentle fingers of spent waves flowed up her legs to her naked waist, then receded like a shy lover returning again and again to caress her. Leaning back on her arms, she closed her eyes and let the sensuous, petting foam wash over her. Presently he splashed out of the water beside her.

"What are you doing?" Rem growled at her.

"Sitting here in the lap of luxury, basking." She cracked her eyes open enough to see him standing over her.

"Well, damn it woman! I had this all taken care of." He waved a hand at his erection. "Now look what you've done to me."

"I see," she murmured. "Want me to take care of that for you? Offer's still open, big boy."

"No!" Rem plopped down on the sand beside her. "Touch me and I'll scream rape."

Kat smiled and turned back to the ocean. She slowly spread her legs wide and arched her knees. As the next wave rushed up her it broke right on her now sensitive, swollen cunt. She gasped and lifted her hips up off the sand in reaction. The receding water left tiny bubbles of sea foam on her that popped with featherlight explosions of sensation. Another wave hit her with even greater force and she felt a little of the warm ocean push up into her vagina. It pulled out quickly as her reluctant tormentor rushed back down the beach.

Kathryn no longer paid any attention to Rem. These wicked new pleasures consumed her. She dropped back on her elbows and let her head sink into her shoulders in surrender. Eager to welcome whatever caresses this relentless but shy aqua lover would give her. Kathryn spread her legs wider. The ocean rushed up her body again and this time its foaming fingers reached her swollen nipples as it also pushed into her gaping cunt. It swooshed back down her to leave its bubbly symphony of explosions behind.

Normally her body wouldn't be this responsive to every stroke of sand and surf. However, at this point she'd been so primed and needy by the exposure to, and denial of, Rem's magnificent person that she reveled in this wet embrace.

All her naughty parts were swollen and flushed, begging for contact. The gentle but insistent invasions of the throbbing surf and repeated explosions of the popping foam drove her slowly up the path to bliss. She gave herself to it. Breathless as each wave investigated her. She thrust back as it pressed gently into her, shivered while it slid over her stiff nipples persistently, and flowed down her abdomen and legs in ever-changing patterns of advance and retreat.

Rem sat beside her, dazzled. She'd become a water nymph writhing in the surf. An erotic vision who moaned urgently as she spread her legs wider still in surrender to the sea god Triton's pleasure.

Flowing and undulating in the perpetual motion of the waves, she became one with the surf, sensuously oblivious to the world around her. He trembled at the absolute splendor laid out before him.

Her large breasts shuddered as each wave washed over them. The fat berries on top of them were stiff and straining up toward the sun. Her slender rib cage and flat abdomen undulated with her harsh breathing as the pink, swollen pussy between her legs pushed back at the surf with each swell.

He could see her clit distend out of its hood as she arched her hips up into another gush of water. Son of a bitch, that plump bit of secret flesh nearly undid him as he watched it eagerly presenting itself to the foaming surf. Each receding wave left an offering of froth enveloping it. The bubbles burst and tremors shot up her body. He realized even those minuscule caresses stroked her to pleasure. The smoldering eroticism of the moment engulfed him. She convulsed into orgasm as the surf rushed up her again and he'd no choice but to join her.

His ejaculation shot across his chest and abdomen in fiery ropes of frustration. The surf cleaned it immediately from his body and he sank down on his back beside her.

"Oh, damn. I had no idea," Kathryn whispered as the surf now petted and soothed her.

"About what?" Rem croaked.

"The ocean! I've never been to the beach before." Her confession stunned him again.

"You live in Florida! How can you not have been to the beach?" he demanded in consternation.

"I work. The beach is for play. I haven't gotten around to it." Kathryn hadn't opened her eyes yet after that little trip into oblivion.

Forgetting for a moment her obviously restricted childhood, Rem demanded, "Hasn't anyone ever taken you to the beach to play?"

Turning her still flushed face to him, she smiled gently. "Sure they have. You just did."

That sweet smile shot deep into his heart. The child in her peeked up at him and he couldn't resist her. He needed to cuddle her, play with her. Most of all he needed to show her all the fun the world had to offer. All the things she'd missed.

"Come on, my little sea nymph. Let's build a sandcastle." Rem grabbed her hand and hauled her up to move out of the surf.

"Oh, Rem, I'd love to!" The naked little girl glowed and skipped beside him as they found a spot and he showed her how to dig out a moat.

Then construction of the sandcastle took on serious importance. Cups, spoons, mixing bowls and several spatulas from the kitchen were required. No utensil could be spared in their quest for the ultimate creation. The two of them frolicked all morning in childlike hedonism, naked and utterly carefree.

Later, as the sun climbed high in the sky, Rem sat back on his haunches and grinned at her. "Better cover some of that pink skin of yours, sweetie. The sun can bite your ass in a big way."

Kathryn glanced down at herself and made a silly face. "Yeah, you're right. I haven't developed leather for skin yet like you. Do you ever wear clothes on the beach? There isn't one tan line on you."

Grinning at her innocent, yet naughty conversation, he stood up with her and surveyed their half-finished creation. "We can finish this later," Rem pronounced, mildly anxious to get her in now that he'd noticed her reddened skin. Holding out a hand to help her up was natural and they strolled up to the outdoor shower.

Watching her under the cascade of water chased away the little boy. The man stood there and appreciated a beautiful woman performing a simple task. As she finished the shower and turned toward him, a smile crept across her face. Grabbing a fluffy towel, she dried off gingerly as he rinsed. His washing process consisted of turning without taking those hungry eyes off her. Stepping out just as she finished drying, he snagged her towel and used it, too.

"There's some aloe vera bath oil in your bathroom. Maybe a cool soak in the tub might help you out," Rem suggested as they stepped into the den. "I'll whip us up an ice-cream sundae lunch and bring it in to you."

"Ice cream!" Kathryn gasped. "Oh, no, you don't. I can't eat ice cream after that breakfast. You want me to be big as a house by the end of the week?"

He frowned. "There's not an extra inch on you that isn't put to good use. You don't have to worry about that. Besides, you can go for a run with me this evening if you're so concerned about it."

"Run? No way!" Kathryn scoffed. "If I tried running, these things—" she held up her luscious breasts, "—would knock me out!"

He couldn't help it, he burst out laughing at the visual she painted. Dragging in a breath Rem just had to ask, "So what do you do?"

"I dance." Kathryn stated huffily.

"Ah? Dance?" Rem questioned.

"Yeah. The first time I quit dancing, I gained twenty pounds in two months! It was awful." Her face scrunched up in disgust.

"The first time?" Rem's grin turned into a scowl.

"Not for anyone, silly. For myself. You've got to admit my body is uniquely fitted to that form of exercise. It's aerobic and a great way to work off all my little oral sins." The last sentence ended in a purr and a wicked little smile.

They were standing in front of each other totally naked, engaged in the type of everyday conversation men and women always have. Teasing and flirting with each other, entirely relaxed. Rem almost shook his head in wonder. The many facets of this woman stunned him, her childlike enjoyment of the sandcastle, her wicked pleasure in the surf, her petulant insistence she needed to watch her diet. She'd wrapped her curvy little self around his heart without even trying.

"Okay, brat, fresh fruit and veggies for lunch. Now, get in that bath before you turn crimson."

"Eeek," she squealed and looked down at her rapidly reddening body. Turning on her heel, Kathryn rushed off toward her room. He leaned sideways and cocked his head in that very male way of watching a woman bounce out of a room. Whistling low under his breath, Rem did shake his head this time as he tried to remember what he was supposed to be doing next. Ah ha, lunch. That's it.

Twenty minutes later, he sauntered into her bathroom with a tray of fruit and vegetables as promised. He set the tray down on the shelf that curved around the back of the tub and stepped his naked self into her bath. Easing himself down at the other end, his long legs slid up the outside of hers.

"I didn't realize I was sharing," Kathryn commented mildly.

"Well, if I'm going to feed you woman, I insist on being comfortable at least." He picked up a strawberry and held it to her lips, "Now stop complaining and eat."

Laughing around the fruit she protested, "Not complaining, doofus."

"Could've fooled me," Rem groused and dipped down to sluice the water over his head.

They munched in silence for a while. Eventually Rem leaned his head back and closed his eyes. Kathryn watched his body slowly relax. The big lug was naked and in a huge Victorian tub with her. A tub which happened to be in the dreamiest, most romantic Victorian gone crazy on Greek revival bathroom and he was falling asleep.

Nudging him with her foot, she huffed, "You tired of looking at me already?"

A slow grin crept across Rem's wickedly handsome face but his eyes didn't open. "Not likely, Kat," he murmured. "But someone got me all hot and bothered last night. Dropped her towel and stretched like a cat on a scratching post. Then took herself to bed leaving me high and dry. I didn't get much sleep."

"You were watching me?" Kathryn gasped.

"Oh, yeah." Rem's voice was a totally satisfied growl.

"Well, it serves you right! It's not nice to watch people when they don't know it," Kathryn huffed.

"But it's rewarding as hell." He opened his eyes slightly and they sparkled at her under heavy lids. "Now I need a nap though, Miss Kit Kat."

The obvious pet name brought an immediate frown to Kathryn's face. "Call me that again and I'll remove whatever body part comes to hand, bad boy!" she threatened.

"Ah. There is a story there." Rem grinned. "Care to share it?"

"No. Forget it." Kathryn turned her head and looked away.

Rising slowly, Rem stood at the end of the tub and stretched. They'd been naked more than dressed today. Still her petulant gaze was drawn to him. Reluctant but powerless to resist, her eyes ate up every flexing muscle on the taunt body before her. Magnificent! The man defined the term.

"Come on, brat. Get your lovely butt out of the tub and let me get some rest." He stepped out, grabbed a towel and tossed it to her then snagged one for himself.

He headed back into her room when they'd dried off. Rem whipped off the bedcover and held up the silk sheet. "In, woman."

"Uh? We're going to bed?" Kathryn crawled in as she asked the question. First, he wouldn't touch her, now he ushered her into bed?

"Nope. We are taking a nap," he grumbled.

Sliding in beside her, he immediately turned on his side into her. His head snuggled into that sensitive spot between her neck and shoulder after he'd arranged her arm to wrap around his neck. Eyes already closed, Rem sighed contentedly. She lay there looking down at him in surprise. He'd managed to cuddle his big self around her without actually stroking anything erogenous. Then he was sleeping. Just like that. Out.

Smiling softly, Kathryn contemplated the amazing man in her arms. She'd never been in bed with a sleeping man. Not without having sex first. It was a nice feeling. Not exactly relaxing right now because she wanted to fuck him so badly, but the implied trust and comfort level was nice. *Okay, it feels fucking fabulous*, she conceded to herself. Being the one holding

Remington Morgan while he slept fulfilled dreams she hadn't even known she had.

Kathryn gently rested her cheek on the top of his golden head and inhaled the scent of him deeply, quietly taking him into herself. She closed her eyes almost reverently. This moment, this perfect moment in this perfect place would shine in her heart forever. When she was alone on cold, dark nights, she'd remember this. Just close her eyes, and pull this crystal-bright moment out and let it warm her. He had no idea what he'd given her. She was going to hoard the treasure of it. The secret fact was, this was the first time ever, in her entire life, she could remember feeling the way she felt right now.

This unbelievable combination of happiness, physical safety and emotional security enveloped her in warmth that melted every cold and empty spot in her soul. It wasn't just the complete absence of fear. He'd filled the void fear left with joy. Playing with her, teasing her, pampering her like a princess and yet, not. Kathryn sighed deeply and decided analyzing this might wreck it. Sleep was probably a good idea, though she hated to miss a single second of this. Without even realizing it, a tiny crack was opening in her heart. Trust peeked out shyly.

He woke her with gentle kisses on her neck and shoulder. The late afternoon shadows stealthily crept across the room. His lips explored her shoulder and his hand at her waist lightly caressed, but never strayed up or down. Playing possum, Kathryn wandered what he'd do next if this didn't rouse her. The possibilities were too tempting to pass up.

She felt him grin against her shoulder. "I know you're awake," he whispered. He reached up and nipped her earlobe. "Time to get up and get dressed."

"Owww!" Kat squealed and scooted away from him as he chuckled and rolled off the bed.

"Dressed? What for?" She lay watching him arch his back and scratch his chest.

"We're going for a run. I've got some energy to work off. A run is the only way to do it." Rem grinned down at her, his heavy erection showed just how much he liked looking down at her sprawled across a bed. And where most of that energy was centered.

"Run? You know how I feel about running. I'll just wait here, thank you," Kathryn responded absently.

"Nope. Part of the service, sweetheart, I never let you out of my sight. Besides, you'll be driving the golf cart. So get up and get dressed." Rem grinned at her.

Pouting, she sat up and stretched her back also. Just to be mean, she rolled out the other side of the bed and with her back to him reached down to grab her ankles. Stretching, of course. Her legs spread just wide enough to display her wet, pink cunt clearly.

Rem groaned and pivoted to the door. "Ten minutes. I'll meet you in the kitchen. Remember your clothes!"

"Why?" she yelled after him. "It's not like you haven't seen everything."

"Yeah, I have," he called back. "But the folks on the other side of the island haven't. I'd like to keep it that way."

"Other side of the island?" Kathryn mumbled to herself as she headed for the closet. The man planned to burn off a hell of a lot of energy. Damn she was good. Laughing softly, Kat chose a silk sundress. The short little number whispered around her like a naughty promise. Perfect. Let him try to work off this much energy.

He ran along the beach as the sun slid down the horizon in spectacular fashion. The extravagant splashes of pink, orange, red and purple that painted the sky turned their surroundings into a dreamscape. As Kathryn watched his bronze form move effortlessly in a ground-eating jog, she willingly surrendered all pretense of restraint. He was perfection on the hoof as it were. No big surprise there, but the visceral pleasure of watching him glistening with sweat as every edible inch of him moved in animalistic grace was something she didn't even attempt to disguise. The cards were already on the table. He knew she wanted him.

They rounded the point and went about halfway down the other side before he turned around and headed back. Off in the distance she could see what appeared to be a village of some sort. As they returned to the house, the sun was just sizzling into the sea.

His indulgent smile as he helped her out of the golf cart beside the house said he'd been fully aware of the ogling he'd gotten and loved it. The sneaky exhibitionist had fun torturing her. Kathryn grinned up at him.

"I need another shower, hon, then I'll grill us some steaks. You can make a salad to appease your rabbit-food addiction. Come on, I'm hungry." Rem retained his hold on her hand as they entered the house and started down the hall.

"Uh, Rem? Where are we going?" Kathryn asked, mildly interested since the kitchen was the other way.

"Just through here," he directed.

They entered his room. It was as large as hers, but masculine in a lord-of-the-manor sort of way. The bed was huge. It was dark wood with tall columns at the four corners that held up a canopy. The canopy gathered in the center top like a crown. His hold on her hand didn't loosen as they reached the connected bathroom. He lifted her up and sat her down on the black tile vanity as soon as they entered.

"I'll just be a minute, honey. I hope you don't mind waiting here for me. It's important for me to be able to see you at all times." He kissed her forehead and started stripping off socks and shoes. "Do you mind?" he asked again when she didn't answer.

"Oh, no, no. I don't mind at all. Sorry. I got involved watching you strip. Forgot how to talk." Kathryn laughed into his eyes.

"Vixen! Comments like that will get you kissed by a sticky, sweaty man." Shoving off his shorts, he stepped over to her and pressed a gentle kiss to her lips. No pressure, just sweet, grazing lips.

"Hey, that wasn't a kiss!" Kathryn complained to his back as he stepped into the shower. It was a glass enclosure so his eyes truly never left her as he rinsed off in the cool water.

"Not a kiss? I see. Your one of those high-maintenance women, aren't you? Rating a man on every little thing?" Rem shook his head in mock disappointment.

Perched on the vanity, Kathryn suddenly realized she was giggling. Amazing. Had she ever giggled when there was a naked man in the room? Had she ever felt so utterly secure? He never let her forget she was a sexy, enticing woman. At the same time, the "real" Rem never let her feel pressure or obligation. Whatever their relationship was evolving into, it wasn't about what she owed him or what he expected from her. He played with her, teased her and talked to her.

Her head tilted as these new thoughts blossomed. His quick shower over, Rem stepped out to dry off.

"What?" he asked softly.

"Humph?" Kathryn snapped back to the present and frowned as he took his naked self to the sink and grabbed his razor and shaving cream.

"What were you thinking so hard about?" he asked as he lathered his face beside her.

"Ah. I'm happy. I was thinking about it. Someone is trying to kill me. We're on the run—in the lap of luxury, but still on the run—and I am happy. It made me wonder why?" Kathryn answered honestly.

"Mmm. Come up with a reason?" he questioned, not looking at her as he carefully stretched his neck for the razor.

"Yes," Kathryn responded.

Rinsing his razor, Rem glanced at her with twinkling eyes. "Not gonna tell me?"

"No. You've already got one big head. Why encourage the other?" Kathryn leaned back and smiled as he kept shaving.

Finishing up, he rinsed and put the toiletries away. Rem stepped over to her, gently moved her legs so he could stand between them and rested his hands on the vanity beside her hips. With her leaning back already, they were nose to nose. His eyes positively sparkled as he looked at her and then turned his cheek and rubbed it against hers.

"How's that?" he asked softly, his lips just brushing her earlobe.

"How's what?" Kathryn breathed. All that shockingly in-shape man leaning over her and gently rubbing his cheek against hers short-circuited mental functions. What was he asking? And what made him think she could talk when he did that anyway?

"How's the shave?" Gliding his face lightly across hers, he turned his head the other way to give her the opportunity to test that cheek also. Oh, yeah, soft and smooth. Her eyes closed to better enjoy his warm breath caressing her neck. His face slowly, gently stroked her face.

"Ah, nice. Very... Hey, come back here! I'm not done testing!" Kat protested as he straightened away from her.

Laughing softly, Rem plucked her off the vanity and again moved them into his room. At the massive bureau, he grabbed some shorts and pulled them on. Stepping back over in front of her, he fitted his hands carefully under her arms and lifted her up.

"Wrap your legs around my waist," he instructed.

Her legs encircled his slim waist and her arms naturally looped around his neck. One of his hands slid under her—under the little skirt—to span her bottom. Casual as you please, Rem sauntered out the door.

"Where are we going now?" Riding him wasn't a problem for her. But this new arrangement got all her naughty parts hot again.

"I'm so hungry I could eat leather. Lettuce for lunch isn't gonna cut it, darlin'. So we are going to the kitchen. You weren't done testing." Glancing at her, he grinned slyly. "I just wanted to fulfill all your needs. This way you can test anything you want and I can still cook."

They were in the kitchen. He held her anchored to him with one arm. With the other, he gathered his ingredients. Rem moved around the kitchen easily. Glancing over her shoulder, Kathryn saw he was lining things up to facilitate the one-handed cooking procedure.

Eyes questioning, she looked back up at his face. He winked at her and continued preparing the meal. His body flexed and shifted between her legs as he moved. The hand supporting her ass wasn't squeezing or in any way encouraging. He just held her flesh to flesh. Puzzled, Kathryn glanced back at the counter.

"Relax, sweetheart," Rem purred. "It'd help if you leaned up against me. That way I wouldn't be afraid you might fall over backwards." His calm tone soothed something inside her. Suddenly she realized how much she needed to be held. The sensation unfolded slowly across her body. So this was how it felt to be close to someone for no other reason than it felt good.

Relaxing her upper body into his chest, Kathryn tightened her arms securely around his neck. He shifted her weight so she sat on his forearm and hip. His approval of her movement was conveyed by a kiss to the top of her bent head. Rem casually tossed the steaks on the gas grill and turned slightly so the spatter would hit him, not her.

A comfortable quiet enclosed them as she watched him make supper one-handed out of the corner of her eye. He never grunted or shifted her weight. He simply held her firmly to him and continued with the job at hand. She waited for a suggestive comment or provocative touch. When he asked if she'd like some wine, she thought it was coming. He poured her a glass and held it up to her lips as she sipped it.

"Let me know when you want more," Rem murmured as he set down the glass to turn the steaks. Her arms and legs tightened around him slightly, just to see what he would do with the reminder. He kissed the top of her head again, as if to reassure her he wouldn't drop her and continued grilling.

Turning her face fully into his neck, she felt something deep inside her start to break apart. No one had ever just held her. As far back as she could remember there'd never been one time when someone offered her this kind of holding. This feeling of touching, safety, being close to someone else because they want you near them. Not because of what they wanted you to be for them, to them, with them. This felt like...like her existence was good enough. He wanted to hold her essence to him in some elemental way. This felt so good it hurt.

Suddenly there was pain and pleasure so severe she sucked in air sharply. The breath whooshed out of her again in a sob. Kathryn began shaking as crumbling barriers shredded her from the inside out. Long-ago pain shattered into sharp pieces of her past. The emotional whirlwind stabbed them into protective walls in her soul.

Immediately, both his arms wrapped around her and his head dipped down to her ear.

"What is it, baby? What's wrong? Am I hurting you?" Worriedly, he attempted to pry her arms from around his neck so he could look at her face. She locked them firmly and shook her head no.

"Please, Kat! Tell me what's wrong. What did I do?" His tone edged toward panic as her body shuddered in what felt like nearly silent agony. That one sob as it began was all the sound she made besides breathing heavily.

"Keep holding me. Please," her broken whisper barely reached his ears even though his cheek was pressed against her temple.

"Honey, tell me one thing. Is this a seizure? Is there some medication you need?" It suddenly occurred to him he knew almost nothing of her medical history.

Her head shook no.

Frowning darkly, Rem shut off the stove and carried her to the den. Sinking slowly onto the sofa, he carefully unwrapped her legs from his back so she wouldn't hurt herself and leaned back, taking her full weight onto his chest. She stretched her legs down the front of his legs and silently shivered in his arms. It felt like her bones rattled together as he wound himself around her tightly and held on.

The trembling subsided slowly, but she was still dragging in great gulps of air as if she couldn't get enough.

"Slow down, baby," he whispered in her ear. "Easy now, just breathe, honey. I've got you. It'll be okay. Whatever it is, we can handle it. Just breathe. That's it, slow and easy." He never stopped crooning to her softly until she could finally lie there taking deep, gentle breaths. As she relaxed, his hold loosened until he was stroking his hands lightly up and down her back. Little tremors rippled through her irregularly so he didn't move.

"Tell me what just happened, honey. Please trust me enough for that. I need to know." His earnest request drew a long sigh from her and he tensed. Afraid he'd said the wrong thing again. When would he learn to read her?

"You held me," her soft voice confessed.

"Yes. Did I hurt you?" Rem prompted gently, still worried that this might be another incomprehensible misunderstanding. Something he'd done in ignorance again.

"No. Yes. Some." Her face was still buried in his neck so he didn't even have her facial expressions to help him.

"I'm really good at figuring things out, baby, but you've got me on this one. Which is it?" Rem persisted.

Kathryn laughed weakly and pushed herself away from his chest. He didn't let her go, just glided his hands down her arms until he was holding her hands. If she was trying to put distance between them, he would have a problem with that.

"I'm sorry, Rem. I made you ruin dinner. Come on, let's finish it. You were starving before my meltdown." She pulled on him as if to get up.

"Kat, honey, I will wither up and die of starvation on this couch if that's what it takes to get you to tell me what's going on inside you. What happened?" Rem insisted as he refused to budge.

She stared down at him a minute and exhaled noisily again. "You sure you want this?"

"More than I want to breathe. I need to know. It wasn't just you, baby. It had something to do with me and I know it. Now help a poor, ignorant man out. Help me understand why holding you hurt so much?" His eyes searched her face as he asked.

"I've, well, no one's ever… Ah, it's just…" Kat stammered and looked down at his chest so she wouldn't have to see the pity in his eyes when she finally spit this out. "I guess it's that no one's ever held me before. I mean, not like that. I didn't know, um, I didn't know about holding like that. It sort of snuck up on me and I flew apart. I'm sorry." The last part was a whisper as she studied his breastbone.

Rem frowned hard as what she was trying *not* to say sank in. "Don't, Kat! Don't say you're sorry to me one more time!" His hands raced up her arms and wrapped around her again, pulling her down onto his chest. His face turned into her hair and he clenched his teeth. Taking deep breaths through his nose, Rem tried to stem the jolt he felt deep in his bones.

No one had ever held this beautiful woman! How could that be? That little fragment of information blossomed in his chest like a slowly expanding cloud of dark awareness. The utter bareness of her life impaled him on its jagged edges. She actually apologized for delaying his supper! His arms tightened around her.

He'd been loved unconditionally all his life by so many, his parents, his sister — in her own bratty way, Gray, the guys in the unit. Not that the guys said it, but they gave it to him time and again. She'd had nothing, no one. It was becoming disturbingly clear how void of love her life had been. If a simple thing like holding did this, what kind of grim life had she been forced to live? And now she thought she needed to apologize over such an insignificant thing as food? That destroyed him in six different ways.

Her slender arms locked around him. Firm legs slid to the sides of his and squeezed tight. She returned his hold fully as he tried to grasp the emptiness in her confession. It racked him. Sweetly she returned the comfort he'd given her by holding him tightly. He realized he was the one trembling now as she unselfishly tried to comfort him. It tore him up. But he needed it, needed to hold this woman.

Almost panting for air, he raised his head enough to ask quietly, "Why did it hurt you, Kat? Tell me how not to hurt you. Tell me how to protect you."

"Some pains make you stronger, Rem," she whispered back. "You know that."

Softly she explained it to him. "It hurt because, well, because it was discovering a pain I never knew was there. Suddenly I recognized all the times I'd missed this. I'd seen people hold their children, their lovers, their family, but it was like watching a movie. Not real, you know. Suddenly it's real. You gave that to me like it was nothing — I don't mean that bad!" He'd sucked in a breath at her statement. "It was something unbearably precious. Then I knew. I knew all the times when it wasn't there. That's what hurt me. I'm sorry if it disturbs you."

"Oh, dear, sweet God in heaven! Don't you dare apologize to me again or I'm gonna tan your hide, woman!" His voice trembled with emotion so the threat didn't quite have the punch it might have.

Kathryn laughed softly. He was still holding her so tightly it was a struggle to breathe. No way she was complaining. He could clutch her until her ribs broke. A cracked rib would be nothing new. Being held was.

"How about we get that supper, honey?" Rem whispered desperately. He needed something to do! There was no one to beat down. No enemy to seek out and destroy. No target, no tangos, nothing he could do to fix this. It was agony for the action-orientated warrior inside him. He'd built his life around the unit and what they did. They fixed what needed fixing and did it better than anyone else. They rescued. They liberated, overthrew dictators. They got supplies into places no one else could. His job as one of the strategists meant he knew everyone's secrets and could call in favors from here to Moscow.

Yet, all he could do for this woman was hold her. He understood living through pain. He didn't know what to do about living within emptiness. Here she was smiling at him as he stood up and carried her back into the kitchen. He could barely breathe with the glimpse of deep emptiness she'd shown him. How could she be this sensitive, caring, gentle woman? The tender heart that thought of others before herself was a miracle.

At this point, the possibility of putting her down didn't exist. Unsure if it was for her or for him, he just knew they needed to hold, touch, feel, to be as close as possible a little while longer.

When supper was complete, they both picked up plates and he carried her out to the patio. The velvet, tropical night seemed like the right place to be.

Sitting with her on his lap, he fed her bites of his steak and held her wine. It was necessary. She let him surround her with his desire to right all the wrongs in her life. She understood that he needed to do something with his response to her stupid weaknesses. So she rested her head on his shoulder while he finished. She snuggled into him, twisted her luscious body to face him from the waist up.

"You okay?" she asked after they'd sat there in silence awhile.

"Mmm," he confirmed.

"I need you, Rem." The statement was made in a voice soft and serious.

He lifted her off his chest and looked into that sweet face. Whatever she said next, he wanted to understand it completely. No misunderstanding, no screw-ups.

"No, not for anything. Not because of anything. Well, because I've been lusting after you for as long as I've known you." Grinning at him mischievously, she continued. "And because you've been holding me for hours, Rem. You know how you said you'd like to do costumes sometimes? Does that include fantasies?"

"Well, yeah," he answered cautiously.

"I want my first kiss. I want you to kiss me like you mean it. Like it's something you've wanted to do forever. Could you give me that?" Her eyes searched his worriedly now that she'd made her request. "If you don't want to, I understand," she hurried into the pause. "I just thought you'd be really good at it," Kathryn trailed off lamely.

Rem studied her face and felt his heart contract in pain. He had a dark suspicion that whatever happened at her real first kiss had not been a good experience. The mission to erase every one of her bad memories was a job he intended to do right.

"Yes, Kathryn. A thousand times, yes," he breathed as a smile broke across his face. "Come on." He stood her up carefully as he rose from the chair. "Time to get dressed!" He grabbed her hand and dragged her into the house.

"Dressed?" she squealed and glanced down at her already clothed form as she hurried to keep up with him. He hustled them to her bedroom door. "I asked for a kiss!"

"First date dressed. I'll knock at the front door in about half an hour. Let me be your first date, Kat. Let's do this right, baby, please," Rem cajoled.

His intentions delighted her. This wonderful man had somehow seen way past her request to the heart of her need. She refused to let that bother her right now. His plan was too much fun to pass up because it embarrassed her that he saw her so clearly. It obviously didn't drive him away, so why worry about it? Laughing at him, she stood on tiptoes and kissed his chin. "Get lost, Rem. I need to change." The door shut behind her.

Damn, half an hour to arrange this. Time to be the magic man. Well, with a bit of help.

Chapter Seven

ဆာ

Thirty-one minutes later, the doorbell chimed. Kathryn glided to the door dressed in an emerald sundress that hugged her chest and waist. Wishes and tiny little straps held it up. Around her waist, a knotted sapphire scarf floated down the full skirt. The scarf and skirt frothed around bare thighs and a lethal length of leg. Strappy sandals presented her slender ankles and narrow feet. A matching sapphire scarf cascaded down below her waist with her rippling mane as it held her hair back.

Whistling low as she opened the door to him, Rem grinned at her. "Hello, Kathryn. You look great. Ready to go?"

"Yes. Do I need my purse?" she asked.

"I've got it covered." Her hand slid under his arm and he led her down the steps to the Jeep.

"Where are we going?" Kathryn asked.

"Sightseeing," was his vague response.

"Mmm." She glanced at him suspiciously.

"It's something I think you'll enjoy." That bad-boy grin gave her a jolt as he handed her into the Jeep. Laughing irrepressibly, she let him buckle her in.

"You don't look so bad yourself," Kathryn commented. He was dressed in charcoal slacks that hugged his ass and draped down his legs to Italian leather shoes. A black, silk shirt completed the look and set off his fair-haired warrior good looks. He was a tall, golden god wrapped in night shadows. His eyes, black as the night sky, shone down on her warmly.

They wound across the island on a dirt road that took them up for about twenty minutes. They came to a flat spot and Rem pulled over to park. Kathryn didn't see anything around but trees and brush.

"I don't want you to ruin your shoes, so let me carry you." He slid an arm under her legs and scooped her up. He took an almost invisible path and strode further up the hillside. Rounding a curve, they burst into a magical clearing at the hilltop. Around the perimeter flickering hurricane lamps cast dancing shadows on Mayan ruins, lighting them but not chasing away the night.

Kathryn gasped at the beauty of the place. A pagan place, a mystical place where past and present converge under the weight of ages. Rem set her down gently and let her take it all in.

The clearing floor was strewn with huge, toppled stone masks and fallen columns covered in glyphic writing. At the center of the clearing, on the apex of the island's central hilltop, there remained the bottom of what must have been a step-pyramid. Only the monster base lingered in this age. The top was now a flat expanse of grass.

"Can we look around?" she asked reverently.

"Sure," his low voice confirmed.

Holding his hand tightly, she approached the nearest mask. It was lovely and fierce. Depicting some long-dead ruler or perhaps a god—it appeared to rise out of the hillside at the call of night birds and ancient rituals. The flickering lamplight added the illusion of dancing forms swirling around these sacred wonders of the past. The two of them moved slowly through the megalithic monuments of the past until they came to the pyramid base.

Skimming the back of her hand with his lips, Rem smiled down at Kat. "Do you trust me?" he asked quietly.

"Of course." Her big eyes were serious in agreement.

"Then let me turn back time," Rem murmured. Bending slightly, he again lifted her high in his arms and climbed the pyramid. Atop it, the panoramic view of the island and surrounding sea was unearthly in the dazzling moonlight. In the center of the grassy pyramid top, a large, black silk cloth with gold embroidery had been laid out. It, too, was covered with Mayan symbols and glyphic writing. Rem took her to it and gently laid her down at its center.

He stretched out beside her and leaned on one elbow to look down into her eyes. His hands brushed away the scarf holding her hair and spread it out across the black and gold silk. He stared at her in wonder and reverently smoothed his knuckles down her neck to feather them across her collarbone. Reclining there like a primeval sacrifice, Kathryn absolutely glowed in the moonlight.

"The first kiss," Rem whispered.

Leaning down slowly he brought his lips to hers. He brushed back and forth to feel her softness as he pressed gently to savor their pliable fullness. His tongue tasted them in featherlight strokes. Her lips parted on a sigh and he gently slipped inside, a shallow invasion that worshipped her and pulled back. He kissed her chin, her cheeks, glided his lips up to feel her eyelashes flutter across them.

"Ah, Kathryn," Rem breathed into her forehead. "You are beauty even the stars must bow to."

Returning to her lips, he sank into them. Kathryn's mouth opened beneath his and he drank from her. Sweeping his tongue deep into her silky depths, Rem explored as if every surface he stroked tasted of ambrosia. Licking her, consuming her essence insistently, his free hand drifted from cheek to neck and back up again, caressing baby-soft skin with tender fingers that glided over bone and flesh in gentle adoration.

Her hands slipped smoothly up his straining biceps, cataloging each bulge and hollow, up to his wide shoulders and neck. One hand sank into his hair, caressing his scalp while the other explored his muscle-roped back. Her body arched into him endeavoring to press her ample breasts into his rock-hard chest, needing to rub those throbbing mounds against him, but he was so far away. Suspended over her, only his mouth and fingertips touched her.

Kathryn clutched him and moaned a plea. Instinctively her nails raked his back lightly to bring him closer. He resisted, still attached to her in a deep kiss.

Tearing her mouth from his, she gasped, "More, Rem! I need more!"

"Yes," he agreed as his lips dragged down her arching neck.

"Now! Please. Touch me now!" Her body rippled on the black and gold background. Shifting and straining to reach him with a dancer's grace. Every muscle worked in concert to make her body undulate in naturally staggering sensuality.

Rem looked down at her. Her face glowed softly with passionate heat. Her body shifted restlessly in the grip of her need. Her hands traveled over his body gently, asking, needing. She wanted and she asked. Not demanded, no shrill insistence, just a sweet, soft request.

As far as he was concerned, she had a right to demand the world worship her fearless spirit. If he could lay the moon and stars at her feet, he would do so. If there was a way to soothe every hurt, he would find it.

Rem glanced up to make sure his helpers really had left the premises. His eyes searched the shadows that surrounded the clearing. He would kill the man who looked upon her with anything but reverence. Convinced they were truly alone, he sank back into her. He allowed the passion to rise between them as he kissed her deeply. His hands tunneled under her to find the zipper holding sundress bodice together.

The zipper eased down slowly and his hands slipped inside to caress the velvet skin of her back. He explored every undulating inch before he peeled it off her shoulders and pushed it to her waist. Deftly plucking the scarf from around her waist, he dragged the dress down her legs to toss it aside.

Propped up on his elbows over her, his hips still pressed into the ground beside her, he slid his hands up under her incredible breasts to cradle them gently. Inquisitive fingers stroked over the smooth expanse of flesh until he reached her distended nipples. He pulled away from her mouth to look down at what he'd uncovered.

Her breasts spilled out of his hands, trembling with each breath. Her areolas puckered around plump nipples as he tormented them with a light touch that made her moan and beg for more. Kathryn arched her back up into his hands and offered herself to him, a living vision.

In this place, she became all that was feminine. The earth goddess whose lush body held life and death for her worshipers. Her large breasts drew the air from his lungs. Her slender, undulating waist and flat belly ensnared him and drew his gaze to her generous hips and glistening, naked cunt.

This was the temple he intended to worship at until the end of time. If in his devotion, she received the impression he thought she was the embodiment of a sexual deity, so be it. At least he would have done something right. Time to start explaining what worshipping her meant.

His soft caresses flowed over Kathryn with sensual insistence. Every delicate touch ignited wicked sparks of sexual need. He strummed her body with a masterful touch she'd never felt before. It wasn't lazy, yet it wasn't rushed with male impatience. The slow climb as he investigated her, built a fire of white-hot embers. The heat outdid any quick inferno she'd ever felt.

Rem sat up and tore off his shirt. All the impatience he'd lacked in his touch, now focused on the task of shucking off his clothes and shoes quickly. Kathryn watched the magnificent male body emerge and spread her legs wide. She expected him to fall on her and have at it.

Rem smiled at her actions. He could read her expectations now that he knew a bit of her past. The wide part was very nice, but he planned to show her how a man paid homage to his goddess.

He stretched out beside her and taking her arms, placed them over her head. He applied a gentle pressure to indicate he wanted them kept there. His lips glided down the inside of her arm, licking, nibbling and tasting down over sensitive tendons just to the inside of her armpit, wending a leisurely, wet path to her breasts. His hands trailed lightly over her fascinating nipples again, wringing a frustrated moan from her as they passed down to explore her ribs and waist. His mouth climbed the slope of her breast just as his fingers inched across the silky skin of her pubic mound. His inquisitive hands and mouth fondled every inch of her lovingly.

He sucked her plump nipple into his mouth just as his fingers curled down and pressed insistently into damp folds. He slowly spread those fingers wide, holding open the gate to paradise for the universe to admire. She convulsed under him and arched her hips up into his hand. Her slender back bowed to press inflamed breast into his mouth. Little gasps escaped her as his fingers spread her and explored her creamy cunt.

Kathryn drifted in a hazy, sensual mist. Rem's hands guided her higher and higher. His gentle but insistent touches immersed her in an insidious delight. Drawing each touch out, stretching it into the next torturous caress, his mouth glazed her body with decadent explosions of pleasure. His tender, masterful, patient lovemaking unfolded a whole new universe to explore. Perfect trust melded with pulsing desire. He drowned her in waves of indulgent emotions she dare not examine.

The soft, black night dripped with diamond stars and highlighted in moon silver engulfed her. It folded her into ancient reality where there was no past, no future, only now, only this man.

Between her legs, Rem gently drew her moisture up over each plump lip. Explicitly focused on the need to paint every millimeter of her flushed cunt lips with fingertip and cream, sliding between the plump lips, reaching to her opening for more and drawing it up sensitive flesh. He circled her swollen clitoris slowly then drifted a light touch across it quickly. He could feel her swell beneath his fingertips. Her cunt became engorged and puffy as her shy little bundle of intense need pushed up to reach his elusive fingers.

Working breast and cunt with slow intent, he stroked her carefully, determined to guide her slowly over wave after wave of dripping pleasure. Rem remained fully in control, but not as she'd ever experienced before. His entire being with all its awesome strength commanded to focus solely on her journey into rapture.

Her gentle moans and whispered mewls melted into the night around them. Those barely discernable sounds joined the timeless voices that writhed here in ages past. Rem realized, in her most intense moments, she became quieter and quieter. This incredible woman was so accustomed to hiding emotion at an elemental level that now it was natural for her to suppress her desire. Just as her intense pain had been almost silent, so was her intense pleasure.

That sad window into her psyche drove him hard. This woman would scream for him! She would let herself go. Her trust became a precious prize he was determined to claim as his own. Someday she would trust him enough to let go. His soul bled each time her joyless life manifested itself physically in her. The fact she was capable of humor commanded all his respect. Whenever her mischievous child peeked out shyly, the little imp entranced him. Yet every time he saw that elfin face, he wept for her. The shinning gift of her trust wouldn't be given tonight. He knew that was asking too much. A lifetime of being alone — alone right down to her soul — required a bit more time to undo.

Rem switched to her other breast and suckled her gently. Licking the nipple tenderly, catching it between his teeth to bite down on it while he flicked it hard with his tongue. She clamped her mouth shut and offered up both cunt and breasts. She was ready, almost there, her silence screamed at him.

Suddenly, he shoved two fingers up into her tight opening as he opened his mouth wide and dragged her hypersensitive nipple in hard. Two heavy thrusts into her convulsing body and she flew apart in his arms. His fingers, buried deep inside that steaming, wet cunt felt her inner muscles clamp down. Her body milked those digits desperately as her head arched back and she exhaled fierce and quiet. Rem opened his mouth wider and sucked fiercely as he pumped those two fingers into her firmly through her climax. He stretched her tight opening by twisting as he thrust into her yielding flesh. He drew out her response as long as possible with knowing use of fingers and mouth.

Rem withdrew his fingers slowly as he felt her gradual spiral back to earth. Easing his big body between her legs, he let her breast fall out of his mouth with a little pop. He dragged his face down her body with openmouthed licks and kisses. He whispered praise to her fervently between each touch.

"That's it, honey, look how beautiful you are," he crooned. "My sweet goddess of the night. So perfect. So lovely."

He covered her breathless rib cage with homage of his lips then suckled gently around her trembling belly. Inched down slowly, until his face rose above the apex of her widespread legs. Breathing in a lungful of her scent, he gazed down at her, watching the moonlight bathe her damp folds in silver shadows. Such a mysterious collection of hills and valleys made up a woman. More specifically, this woman who'd become the air he breathed, this spectacular, stunning woman who grabbed his heart and ripped it from his body.

His hands splayed her inner thighs while his thumbs hooked around her sensitive outer lips and opened them for his mouth. Closing his eyes and extending his tongue, he sank into her. Rem flattened his tongue against her and licked a long slow swipe from ass to clit. Then slurped back down in a zigzag pattern, dipping firmly into her swollen flesh. Rem was pressing his face into that heavenly cunt at last. He felt drunk with need. He wanted to rub her scent over his face, his hair, his body. She might object to his bestial obsession with the thick cream he wanted to bathe in. He contented himself with lapping it up and demanding more.

Kathryn felt the hilltop spinning around her. New sensations pierced her body like arrows cutting through flesh and bone. His busy tongue delved deep within her, compelling her back up into the glittering sky. She felt his feral growls deep in her womb as he literally worshiped her with hot, damp devotion.

Rem lost himself in carnal oblivion. He sucked her clitoris into his mouth and sent her flying again. Kathryn moaned softly and let go. Rem remained between her legs through her climax, avid in his need to suck up her cream as fast as she could give it to him. He ravaged the pink swollen bits of her with teeth and tongue. Between licks, he'd nip her as if he couldn't help himself. Soothing every little hurt with long bouts of suckling each fold carefully into his mouth and adoring it. He reveled tirelessly in his need to consume her taste, her scent, her very being. Kathryn came for him again before she started begging.

"Please, Rem, I need you in me… Oh, yes," she sighed, as he immediately moved up her body, kissing it lingeringly as he worked his way up. Reaching her face, he smiled gently down at her. In a quick move, he flipped them over to sit her on his clenched belly.

"Oh. Oh, my!" Kathryn gasped and adjusted to the new position.

"There you go, honey. Take whatever you want." Rem's hands caressed her thighs.

"Take?" Kathryn's upper body sank down onto his chest. "Whatever I want?" She stared into his eyes, puzzled.

"Yes, sweetheart, whatever you want, however you want it, anytime. What's mine is yours, baby. You'll get that someday." Liquid black eyes drank her in as he lay there beneath her.

Biting her bottom lip, Kathryn studied him and let his gentle petting soothe her doubts.

Her body shifted back so the broad head of his cock caressed her sopping wet opening. She rubbed herself on it as the red-hot shaft slid through her folds and up to press her clit.

Her hips swiveled and stroked as he arched up into her torment, Rem's hands descended off her legs to fist in the cloth below them.

Kat smiled at the moaning man beneath her. This was nice. The cat in her demanded she rake her nails down his chest. She scraped his nipples and he sighed his approval. Oh, yes, this was very nice.

Kat sat back on his thighs and gazed down at the thick erection standing straight up between her swollen cunt lips. The massive thing reached up to her belly button. Its broad stalk pulsed with his heartbeats and the wide, plum head glowed in the moonlight as a steady stream flowed from the little hole.

A curious finger reached down to explore the tip and rub the silky moisture down his cock. They both watched her learn him. Enthralled, she ran fingers through his thick patch of blond curls to discover the heavy balls under his cock. She fondled them gently, examined them with a single-minded fascination that amazed and tortured him. His cock twitched on her belly as if to knock on her womb and remind her he was still outside, instead of inside where he belonged.

Glancing up, she looked into his eyes. "Condom?"

"Pants, left pocket," Rem rasped.

She stretched across his body to retrieve his pants, unknowingly tormenting him with breasts, belly and cunt. He closed his eyes and gritted his teeth. *Oh, please, let her find the damn thing fast*, he begged the gods of desperate men. Her sweet explorations drove him up faster and higher than the practiced manipulations of the most depraved women in the world. His whole body demanded he thrust up hard, screamed at him to take her fast and deep.

Delicate fingers trembled as she ripped open the condom. With agonizing care she smoothed it down him, using two hands to span his engorged width. Kathryn came up on her knees to position him at her entrance. A gentle hand fit the fat head of his cock between wet folds. Then the little witch paused.

She arched back and reached up to lift the hair off her neck. Rem closed his eyes again. It was too much. The sight of her magnificent body perched atop his dick nearly ended it all right then. His cock stood at the entrance to heaven while her body above him seemed to float in the stars. She became a promise of perfection in that shuddering moment before fulfillment. This woman took his soul for all time.

"The first time, Rem," her whisper floated softly into eternity as she pressed down. Her small opening took him in slowly. With brazen deliberation, she stretched around him one millimeter at a time. Her tight little cunt admitted his thick intrusion grudgingly. Wet and swollen, she squeezed him to the point of pain. Such a delicious, deliriously decadent pain, it forced him to give up all pretense of holding some part of himself back.

"Oh, please, Kat!" he begged shamelessly. "Please, baby, more. I need more! Please, please! Oh, God, yesss. Yes, baby, just like that!" Groaning raggedly, he slid all the way into her, tunneling through velvet tissue, which clasped him in its silken fist, pressing up to her womb. His cock throbbed, expanded, lengthened even as she took him.

She sat him like a queen atop her kingdom. And she was. This woman could rule him with her whims if it meant he could be here. Deep inside the hot, tight, paradise-inducing place that was Kat. She loomed over him very straight, as if his cock reached all the way up her spine.

Her face flushed with passion as she watched him beneath hooded eyes, a waiting look, one that made him nervous. The meager amount of blood making it to his brain started to panic. Then he got it. Right here was where most men would take over and seek their own pleasure. Rem lay perfectly still.

Pain coursed through him as his body clawed its demands into his gut. The need to thrust, plunge, drive himself in and out of her flayed him. This animal instinct driven by a lust almost three years denied ripped through his tortured body. Sweat coated him as deadly discipline held him still. The fierce restraint loved her with all his power, all his control and all his heart. He waited.

Cautiously Kathryn began to move. She slowly realized he wasn't going to do anything she didn't want him to. A smile crept across her face and her hips picked up the pace. Rem had to grit his teeth to hold back his release. Yet as he fought for control, he watched her relax. Felt her cream drip down on him like hot wax as she came to believe in his control. The thick root of him stretched her tight. That wondrous small opening didn't accept him easily. Even though she dripped with her excitement, she had to force him in with her weight every time she shuddered down his cock.

Kathryn took his hands and placed them on her breasts. At the edge of desperation, he obeyed her and kneaded the full globes as she bounced with more enthusiasm. He soon discovered the harder he plucked her nipples the faster she moved on him. Oh, yeah, heaven.

His body couldn't help itself—he pushed up into her thrusts. His head arched back in the battle for control that was slowly escaping him.

"Yes," she breathed, releasing him to thrust. "Yes, that's it. Want me."

Rem went nuts. His hips thrust up hard as they slammed together over and over again. His big dick sliced into her soft interior mercilessly to demand her release. The red-hot invader commanded her surrender as she conquered his core.

Heat washed over them while ancient voices wailed in the wind. Timeless whispers whirled in a vortex of unintelligible refrains as the sexual melody echoed once more between past and present. A wickedly licentious storm of passion erupted over them. His shout of completion pushed her over the edge of the universe. Pumping furiously, Rem fucked them both through his climax in a pagan dance of fertility. The ages approved. Once more, life was reaffirmed on the altar to forgotten gods.

Sinking down onto him, Kathryn surrendered her limp body into his arms. They lay joined for quite a while. Groaning softly, she lifted off and rolled over onto her back.

"Damn, Rem. All I asked for was a kiss. What happens if I ask for a fuck?" Her shivery whisper was almost fearful as the mood of the place settled around them.

"I show you the Pirate Caves," Rem's deep voice rumbled. A little humor seemed appropriate at the moment. The weight of the powerful joining they'd just shared pressed down on both of them. Rem actually wondered if he should have looked into the history of this place a bit more. Something felt different. Almost as if coming together in this particular place might have sealed them together in ways neither of them was ready to understand. It bore looking into.

"You get to be the governor's daughter. I, as the pirate, have rescued you from the evil governor. Or perhaps kidnapped you. Depends on your mood, darling," he teased softly. "In any case. You get fucked by the pirate."

"I see you haven't put much thought into it," Kathryn mused shakily, not yet over the bout of reality-challenged sex.

Rem disposed of the condom and sat up slowly to search around for their clothes. Dressing her carefully before sliding into his own clothes, they were both silent as he picked her up and climbed down the pyramid.

All the lamps around the perimeter had flickered out. A consummate planner, Rem made sure only enough fuel was in them to last about two hours. He didn't want the helpers showing up too early to clean up. Unable to put her down just yet, he carried her back down the path to the Jeep.

"Can I come back in the daylight sometime?" she shyly asked.

"Sure. Any time we're not in the Pirate Caves." His bad-boy grin flashed down at her.

"Ah, I sense you're eager to get there," Kathryn teased.

"Okay, you got me. A little pillaging is right up my alley," Rem confirmed on a chuckle.

"Do you think we could manage some sleep first?" Kathryn yawned tiredly as he deposited her into the passenger side of the Jeep. Carefully he buckled her seat belt and dropped a kiss on her lips before heading to his side of the vehicle.

At soon as he slid behind the wheel, Rem reached over and grabbed her hand. Holding it, he used their combined hands to shift so he didn't have to let her go then rested it on his thigh under his hand.

"Sure," he murmured. They were quiet for the rest of the ride down, both a bit awed. As they pulled up to the villa Rem turned to Kathryn. "Could we sleep in my bed tonight?"

Laughing up at him as they got out and walked in, Kathryn responded. "Anything you like. Are we taking turns?" she teased.

"If you want we could. It is your room, you know, built for you with your things in it. I expect you'll want to spend some time in it before we move you into my room." Rem's voice was neither teasing nor laughing.

Kathryn stopped, effectively stopping him and turning him to face her. "You said it was Tammy's room."

"I lied." Serious male eyes regarded Kathryn cautiously.

"What? Why?" Kat demanded.

"I'm an idiot?" Rem supplied as honestly as possible.

"It's not Tammy's room?" Kathryn had to clarify again.

"No," his deep rumble confirmed.

"Well, whose things am I wearing? Because if some girlfriend of yours comes slamming through that door demanding her clothes, I'm going to be pissed, Rem!" Her hands now gripped her own hips and the storm in her eyes was flashing lightning.

"It's all yours, Kat." Rem insisted.

"I think I'd remember that shopping spree, Rem. These clothes are not mine," Kathryn stated.

Rem felt her anger clearly. But it was different this time. Different from the shed incident in some way he couldn't put his finger on. Not being able to read her was a dangerous thing. It would be wise to proceed with utmost caution. Fuck, if he was wise, he'd have kept his damn mouth shut.

"I bought it all for you. That's what I'm trying to tell you. It's your room, your clothes, your everything. Tammy has never been on the island before. She knows about it, but she's never been here. Nor has any other woman. I mean, any woman I brought here." Rem stopped when he realized he was starting to babble. He never babbled!

Kathryn cocked her head to the side and narrowed her eyes at him. Rem felt the bottom fall out of his gut. This part felt suspiciously familiar. They usually ended up in the mother of all misunderstandings after this part. Perhaps tomorrow would have been a better time to bring this up. Yet he wanted to tell her everything. Show her everything. Give her everything. It'd just fallen out of his mouth.

"Take me to bed, Rem? I'm too tired to deal with this tonight," Kathryn finally asked wearily.

"No problem, honey." He scooped her up and strode down the hall to his room, relieved to the very bottom of his tired bones.

Laying her down on his big bed, Rem efficiently stripped off her dress and shoes. Kathryn groaned and snuggled under the covers expecting Rem to join her. Too tired to keep her eyes open long enough to notice him head for the bathroom.

After a quick shower, Rem returned with two wet washcloths. Gently he pulled back the cover and rolled her sleeping body onto her back. Carefully he ran the damp cloth down her neck and around her breasts, down her torso. Nudging her legs apart, he wiped up both of them from knees to crotch. Tenderly he spread the pink folds of her cunt and cleaned her carefully.

"What are you doing?" Kat mumbled.

Leaning down as he held her open to drop a soft kiss on her exposed clitoris, he glanced up into her barely open eyes and smiled. "I didn't want you to wake up sticky and uncomfortable, baby. Now turn over so I can get your back." Obediently she rolled over.

"You don't have to do this," she protested weakly as she enjoyed the fresh, cool cloth sluicing down her back and butt. Firm fingers spread her ass cheeks and he gently pressed the cloth up the crease.

"I take care of my own," his deep voice growled as he eased off the bed to return the washcloths to the bathroom. A second later he slid in behind her and wrapped a firm arm around her. They slept.

Chapter Eight

ဢ

The door to Rem's room burst open. Rem leapt out of bed with a Glock nine millimeter pointed squarely at his sister's chest.

"Damn it to hell, Tammy!" he bellowed. "What the fuck are you doing here?"

"Stop yelling at me and put that gun down!" Tammy yelled back.

"I almost shot you!" Rem lowered the gun but didn't release it. "Where is Miguel? What happened?" he demanded as possibilities exploded in his head. The only way Tammy could be here was if Miguel sent her because he was too wounded to accompany her.

"I don't give a flying fuck where that bastard Miguel is!" Tammy screeched.

Her entire attention to this point had been taken up with her brother. She suddenly noticed Kathryn regarding her serenely from the bed.

Kathryn had seen Tammy in this mood many times. She felt relatively certain Miguel was okay. Well, in the physical sense at least. This was Tammy in high hysteria.

"Oh. Hello, Kathryn," Tammy sputtered in surprise.

"Hey, Tam. Ditched him, did you?" Kathryn asked calmly.

"You're damn right I did!" Tammy shot back having found a familiar, sympathetic listener. The fact that Kathryn was in Rem's bed seemed self-explanatory to her. So Tammy moved on to her own pressing problems.

"That bastard wanted to tell me what to do every minute of the day. And I mean every minute! He actually insisted I leave the bathroom door open when I need to go. Can you imagine?" Tammy marched around to Kathryn's side of the bed and plopped down. Kathryn tucked the sheet under her armpits and adjusted the pillows so she also sat up.

Rem felt his mouth drop open as the two women settled in for what looked like a familiar routine. There he was naked, standing by the bed holding a gun and no one was paying attention to him. Running a hand through his hair in amazement, Rem headed for the dresser in the closet. At least shorts were required, he supposed. A glance out the window at the sun just over the horizon told him it was only around six a.m. Already the day was fucked up beyond repair.

"Oh, I can *not* tell you how mad I am at that barbarian!" Tammy continued. "He threatened to spank me because I wouldn't listen. Can you imagine? Now, you know I don't mind it in play, but nobody pulls that shit on me for real!"

"They do now!" A deep voice spoke through clenched teeth from the bedroom door. "And it would seem it's long overdue."

Rem strolled out of the closet resignedly. He'd known Miguel would show up on her heels as soon as Tam admitted ditching him. Now his bedroom was bristling with barely restrained violence and way too many people.

Tammy whirled around to face Miguel. "What are you doing here? I told you, your services are not required anymore. That means you're fired, you thick-headed Neanderthal!"

"And I told you, you need to learn some manners, little girl!" Miguel's tone dropped even lower as a vein in his temple pulsed.

Rem shook his head, walked over to a barely visible door in his wall and swung it open. Kathryn's brows climbed her forehead as she watched him step into her room through a sneaky little secret door. A minute later, he reappeared with shorts, a tank top, panties and a bra for her.

Scowling around at the arguing couple, Rem raised his voice over the screeching. "Out! Everyone out! Kathryn needs a shower and I go with her wherever she goes. Even the bathroom." That last part was directed at his frowning sister.

"Well, it's different for you," Tammy huffed. "She's in love with you."

"Oh, yeah?" Rem's head swiveled around to Kathryn and a grin spread across his face.

"Tam!" Kathryn did some squealing herself. "Will you shut up?"

"All right," Miguel growled. "Time to leave the adults alone, angel face." He reached over and hauled Tammy off the bed by her arm.

"Get your hands off me, you disgusting little man!" Tammy pretty much screamed up into his face. The need to look up at him sort of negated the "little man" comment. Yet it made the comment even nastier with its implication of what precisely she considered little.

Miguel simply hefted her up over his shoulder. His large hand landed with a resounding smack on Tammy's bottom.

"AAARRGGG!! Put me down! See how he treats me, Rem! I'm going to be black and blue from head to toe!" Miguel walked out the door, apparently ignoring her kicking and screaming. As the door closed behind them, another loud smack could be heard. Miguel's deep voice corrected her while she upped the volume of her tirade. "No, just your ass will be black and blue."

"Oh, my God, Rem. Do you think Tammy is all right?" Kathryn asked worriedly while he pulled back the sheet and scooped her out of bed to carry her into the bathroom.

"No, she's not. But I suspect she will be eventually." Rem grinned as he deposited Kathryn by the toilet and turned to the shower.

Kathryn glanced at the toilet, then at his back as he adjusted the shower temperature. So that's how it was? She shrugged and took care of business then joined him in the shower.

Rem washed her carefully while she laughed at him and protested she was perfectly capable of taking care of that herself this time.

"Mmm, mine," he responded briefly. "I take care of what's mine."

Kathryn gave up and left him to it. His slow, meticulous hands investigated every fold and crease until she moaned and begged him to fuck her. Happy to comply, Rem grabbed a condom from the shelf in the shower. Massive shoulders barely strained as he hefted her legs over his forearms and her back against the tile wall. With his mouth molded over hers, Rem lowered her until her slippery cunt rubbed the fat head of his dick. He shifted his weight to lean heavily into her upper body and thrust up hard. A flaming spike spread her tender cunt swift and deep. The thick pole pounded right up to the hilt. Her arms tightened and she bit his lip. He took that as a request for more.

Rem dragged his mouth down her throat as his lower body rammed into her fierce and fast. Oh, sweet heaven, she drove him crazy! He got his dick jammed in her for two seconds and he wanted to come. His goddess was spread wide against a wall as he pounded into her. She clawed his back! Rem tipped his head and howled. It felt so good he didn't even try to hold in that base, male response to fucking his woman.

Kathryn retaliated with a sharp nip to his neck as her body jerked into orgasm. Rem slammed into her clenched cunt. He fought desperately to hold off, but her cunt clamped down on him and milked him with fierce contractions. He had no resources left to resist her and exploded hot and deep. It felt like his spine liquefied and poured out his cock and into her.

Panting harshly as he held himself within her quivering body, Rem shut his eyes and tried to calm down. This was not the time to just keep nailing her. There were people out there and things to do. Besides, it was a tight fit. She could hardly hold him even as he relaxed slowly like this. She had to be sore. That's what it took to convince him to pull out—in a minute.

"You okay, honey?" he asked concerned. The silence worried him. How was he supposed to know if she was in pain or pleasure?

"Oh, yessss, I'm fine," Kathryn breathed. "As soon as I figure out how to walk again, I'll be fine."

"Not a problem. You just sit right there on that handy seat I've provided, and I'll carry you anywhere you want to go." Rem grinned into her hair, still pressed tight up against her.

They discovered laughing could be felt deep in a woman's cunt. That led to kissing, and his hips just started moving all on their own. Shallow, gentle thrusts.

"Rem?" Kathryn said softly.

"Yeah?" he answered.

"Are we doing this again?" She wanted to know.

"I think we are. I'll be gentle, baby. Just slow and easy," he promised.

"I want to taste you," Kathryn whispered shyly.

Rem stopped moving. It wasn't necessary. Her hesitant little request nearly sent him to his knees again. Fire licked up the back of his legs and centered in his balls as he processed what exactly she meant by that.

"Now?" his voice was strained.

"Well, whenever you'd like. I just thought you might like it now," Kat hedged.

Working swiftly, Rem pulled out of her and removed the condom, tossing it in the toilet. He rinsed by twisting his lower body slightly. Kissing her deeply he reached between them and parted her roughly, driving his cock into her hard. He needed to feel her, be in her, just this once. Her little request took him over the edge of sanity. It stripped him of reason. Oh, God, how was a man supposed to resist this?

Rem shut off the shower. Still holding her perched on his cock, he walked into the bedroom ignoring the fact they were dripping wet. He crawled up on the bed carefully and lay down with her still deeply impaled. Her body once again balanced on him as he lay beneath her.

"Anything you want, baby." His hands dropped to his sides and he watched her.

Looking down at him, she frowned briefly. This dominant, alpha male was once again laying beneath her in surrender. Once was nice, but that wasn't the man she fell for three years ago. He lay still and patient, waiting for her to decide her pleasure.

Sliding off him, Kat smiled sweetly as her mouth leaned down to flick his hard nipple. A pink tongue did a naughty dance around the copper disk and stiff male flesh. Suddenly, her mouth opened and she sucked in hard. Rem's back came off the bed and he shouted as sensations burned from nipple to cock in an entirely new experience for him. She nipped her little teeth down to capture his sensitized nipple and grinned around it as he froze. They both knew he was completely at her mercy. Kathryn's hands slid down the clenched abdomen to wrap around his thick cock.

She held him there, gripped tightly in both hands and teeth. The display of female power shook him with new, unfamiliar sensations. This woman knew what she was doing. She knew how he felt—both excited and afraid. Pain or pleasure, both were hers to dispense. Her choice and she was taking a damn long time to decide.

She released his swollen nipple, but her hands tightened around his erection. Rem groaned and closed his eyes. Surrendering in shuddering gasps as her hands stroked up and down his thick shaft. Kat's body moved down his slowly. Her mouth explored rigid muscles lazily. Sometimes she licked and kissed, sometimes she stopped to suck him in hard again and nip pinched flesh. She left a trail of stinging red marks down his body.

Every time she marked him, his hips jerked up into her hands and a little more pre-cum spilled out of him. Finally, her face was directly over the large, purple head of his cock. She blew on him gently as her hands stroked him, studying him, mapping each vein and ridge, but not touching him with her mouth.

"Do you want my mouth?" Kathryn questioned softly.

"Yes, oh, damn yes," Rem moaned.

"Is this my cock?" her wicked whisper continued.

"Yours, honey, all yours!" Rem wasn't above putting some beg in his voice.

"Are these my balls?" One of her hands slithered down to lift his testicles. She weighed and rubbed them roughly. Rem gasped in air hard as her hands moved over him.

"Yes! Your balls," he wheezed as her hand closed around them and gave them a firm squeeze.

"They're full for me, aren't they?" Quiet and wicked, her voice snaked up his body. The dangerous game she played astonished him. He was not a submissive. He'd never had a submissive bone in his body. Yet for her, he lay there trembling under her hands, his entire being on fire as she teased and wielded her power fearlessly.

"Yes," he breathed.

Suddenly he was free. His eyes shot open to find her standing beside the bed.

"Then come fuck your woman, Rem. Don't be gentle or careful. I won't break. I want your strength. I need your dominance. Don't think it takes something away from me. I know I can dominate you. Now, you do, too. But it's not what does it for us, is it?" Her strong voice was calm.

Growling fiercely, Rem didn't bother answering her. He jackknifed up off the bed and was behind her in an instant. Forcing her upper body down over the bed, he shoved her feet apart so she was bent over and spread wide for him. Only then did he stop.

"A nasty little game you played, Kat. A man gets his dick that close to your mouth, he wants it sucked." Rem stepped back to regard her body.

"I think you're going to have to clean up after yourself when this is over," he growled. "But for right now that white bottom is just too tempting. Stuck up in the air and spread open like that. What do you think I should do with it, my wicked little goddess?"

"Oh," Kat moaned.

His hand landed on it heavy and sharp. "That's for being a tease."

Another biting spank landed on the other cheek. "That's for pretending with me."

The third slap shocked her. His hand swung up and landed flat and firm on her cunt, lifting her to her toes as fire exploded through her sensitized body. "That was because I wanted to."

Then he was behind her, shoving his enormous cock into her burning cunt. Driving it home and ripping it out again in near frantic need. He held her hips in a ruthless grip and fucked her hard. He watched his cock slice into her red, swollen pussy. His balls slapped her sensitive lips every time he rammed in. He used his whole body weight to shove himself up her. His body wrenched up on his toes with each hard thrust.

Searing shocks burst through Kathryn. Her entire being became focused on her engorged cunt with that third, harsh little spank. That particular sensation quickly followed by his monstrous cock shoved into her inflamed flesh, flashed every pleasure receptor to frenzied action. Rem gasped and grunted gutturally with each deep invasion. The merciless sexual demands sent sharp, spinning stars of flaming heat whipping through her. His brutal pummeling drove her into agonized ecstasy. She crashed into orgasm, convulsing hard on his plunging shaft.

He fucked her fiercely through her climax and then increased the power of his thrusts. He snarled with each penetrating plunge. Letting her have everything he'd been holding back. Fucking her like an animal. Just as she screamed into another intense orgasm, he let his release take him with her.

Boiling hot semen jetted deep into her womb. He propelled it in with feral grunts and growls. Jerking his hips against her to jam as much of himself deeply inside her as he could. Holding himself there, high and hard, until the wrenching bursts ceased.

When it was over, he slumped down on the bed beside her bent form. Flat on his back with his legs hung over the side of the bed. It felt like the marrow from his teeth had been sucked down and shot out his dick with that reality-altering orgasm. Rem's large body panted harshly as he tried to regain some shred of composure. He needed to reclaim his body from the base beast who couldn't stop fucking this woman.

Resting there panting, several things burst on his numb brain at once. She'd screamed for him. He hadn't worn a condom. She'd seen his fear of hurting her and found a way to free him from it. She wouldn't accept anything less than the man he was, even if he was doing it for her again. She could take him to a place he didn't even know existed. Have mercy! She could be pregnant!

Kat recovered first. She slid off the bed and knelt between his legs. Soft lips sucked his balls into her mouth. She cleaned them gently with each lick and stroke of her tongue. Kat dragged her open mouth up his cock to swirl her tongue around it. Happily she licked up every drop of their combined juices. As her lips reached the fat head of his cock, she sucked his semi-hard penis into her mouth. Busily she worked her head from side to side. Tongue slurping up and down, seeking his essence industriously. At last, satisfied he was clean, she sat back on her heels.

Rem sat up slowly and leaned down to rest his forearms on his knees. Both hands ran through his hair as he looked into her eyes. "I didn't wear a condom," he told her quietly.

"I know. I've never… Even the first time there always was a… I'm clean," she whispered back at him.

He grinned a sheepish look into her worried face. "Me, too. Not once. Ever."

"You don't have to worry about, ah, well, I wouldn't make you... I'll take care of... It'll be mine, you don't have to..." Kathryn trailed off as Rem frowned fiercely.

"Oh, no, you don't! It's ours! Yours and mine! Together, Kat. I take care of what's mine! I keep what's mine! And most of all, I keep the mother of my children with me! Don't even start with that evil little brain of yours. MINE! You. It. MINE!" His voice rose steadily as he tried to hammer his point home. There could be no mistake about this. Nothing on earth would induce him to let go of this woman now. He was damn glad he hadn't worn a condom at this point. No need to confess that. It's not like he planned it. Perhaps he should have. It was a damn good plan.

She grinned at him then laughed. "You're not going to start treating me all gentle again, are you?"

Grabbing her hands, he hauled them both up and headed back to the bathroom. "Well, not always," he conceded out loud to her in slightly mollified tones. At least she wasn't arguing. In his head, he wondered if she knew how precious she was to him? Perhaps in bed they might play a little rough, but even the slobbering, possessive beast in him wanted to pamper her, protect her, wrap her up in every wish or dream she'd ever had.

A short time later, they both stepped out of the shower again. Rem handed her a towel and never took his eyes off her as he dried. Laughing she chided him, "Cut it out, Rem. I'm not the runaway here. Can I use your toothbrush? Mine is far away, you might slip and fall chasing me into my room." Her twinkling eyes as she teased him calmed the possessive idiot who seemed to jump up like the bogeyman whenever she scared him.

His bathroom came equipped with double sinks and a vanity, just like hers. Only his tile was black against white walls, where hers was white. He handed her his toothbrush as he retrieved his razor.

"So it's me?" he mused.

"What are you?" she mumbled around toothpaste.

"The guy who wets your panties?" He almost cut himself just saying it.

"Ah, that famous conversation. I told you so yesterday, anyway." She shook her head.

"No, you said you'd been lusting after me. Not the same thing." He had to grin into the mirror at that one.

"Sure it is!" she insisted in disgust.

Sharp black eyes sliced into her green ones. "I'm glad, honey." That statement seemed to be way too serious for this conversation, Kathryn thought.

"Well, it's settled anyway. Was beginning to worry me some," he continued.

"Why?" Kat demanded. She'd finished with the toothbrush and was now leaning against the sink watching him shave.

"Didn't want to kill one of my friends over you. It looked like the only answer last night," he calmly replied as he finished up.

Kathryn cocked her head to the side and studied him pensively. This was not a casual conversation, and he seemed to be telling her something that wasn't exactly clear. "Rem, do you have something to tell me? Is there another surprise?" she asked suspiciously.

Black eyes turned on her after he stashed the shaving kit. "I guess I do. Shouldn't be a surprise though, sweetheart. You are mine. I don't care how we go about this as long as you're with me from here on out. I've wanted you a long time, Kat. You've spent a couple years avoiding me. That's over. We can deal with all that after this thing is settled. I will not go back to some distant relationship with you, honey. Am I being clear enough?"

Kat smiled and walked into the bedroom for her clothes. He followed, leaning against the bathroom doorjamb brushing his teeth as she dressed.

"Think I'm kidding?" he asked after rinsing and coming back to pull on shorts and a shirt.

Kathryn looked at him and shook her head. "No, Rem. I think you're very serious. I also think there is a lot of garbage to work out between us. I agree that the present situation is way too intense to make any long-term decisions. We'll talk about it when this is over."

"Nope," Rem corrected softly. "I said you're mine. Not that we'd discuss it when this is over."

Kathryn finished pulling on the tank top and shorts. She looked at him contemplatively a moment then smiled. "We'd better get out there before they kill each other."

"Mmm," was his comment as he grabbed her hand and opened the door. Tammy's strident voice carried across the house from the kitchen. Thankfully, the smell of coffee accompanied it.

Entering the kitchen hand in hand with Rem who refused to let hers go, the scene was much as Kathryn expected. Tammy was clutching her cup of coffee while telling Miguel exactly how to impregnate himself. Miguel stood by the window scanning the surrounding grounds, ignoring Tammy.

Tammy paused as they entered and beamed at them. "So, that was an interesting shower."

"Couldn't hear a thing over the screeching in here," Miguel's deep voice mused.

"You call it screeching? You imbecilic, single-cell organism. Could you just shut up and let the humans chat?" Tammy turned back to Kat.

Rem handed Kat into a chair at the kitchen table and headed for the coffeepot. Getting two cups down, he made them both and came back. He handed one to Kathryn then pulled his chair next to hers and sat down. One arm rested around her back and his fingers caressed her shoulder idly.

"I see your internment hasn't turned out so bad." Tammy smiled at Kathryn.

Kathryn grinned guiltily but couldn't think of a single thing to say.

"Have you talked to Gray?" Rem asked Miguel.

"Yeah," Miguel answered, never taking his eyes off the outside landscape.

"He knows?" Rem pressed.

"Yeah," Miguel answered shortly again.

"Think it's out?" Rem wanted to know.

"Knows it." Miguel used two words in a row. Improvement, Kat thought.

"Reinforcements?" Rem asked.

"Yeah." Back to one word from Miguel.

"ETA?" Rem questioned.

"Nineteen hundred," Miguel supplied.

"Tango ID?" Rem's hand continued gently caressing Kathryn as he asked.

"Yeah, only one UL. It's him." Miguel moved to another window.

"Movement?" Rem shot his questions between sips of coffee.

"Stealth. Gray hasn't got him yet," Miguel murmured.

"Damn," Rem breathed. "Who's incoming?"

"C1 and C4." Miguel grinned as he confirmed that.

"Toys?" Rem wanted to know.

"Full load," Miguel responded.

"Will you two cut it out and talk like human beings!" Tammy exploded. "The only thing worse than this is when you let your fingers do the talking. I swear, I am sick to death of all this testosterone buildup."

"She really related to you?" Miguel questioned Rem.

Everyone laughed except Tammy who scowled in a good imitation of Rem's scowl.

"It's perfectly clear," a smiling Kat interpreted for Tammy. "Gray knows you left Miguel. Gray thinks the bad guy knows. Charlie and Blaster are coming down and will be here around seven p.m. tonight. Gray has narrowed the suspects down to one that he can't locate and he thinks the suspect is on the move. Charlie and Blaster are coming armed."

All three occupants of the room looked at Kathryn in surprise.

"Damn." Miguel grinned at Rem. "Do you realize how short your leash just got, Rem? I bet she can read the sign, too." Miguel chuckled and turned back to his study of the surrounding grounds.

"How'd you follow all that, baby? And how did you know who C1 and C4 are?" Rem asked as his laughing eyes sparkled at her.

"I'm not an idiot!" Kathryn huffed, offended. "C1 has to be Charlie. He's the only man whose name that starts with C in the unit. C4 is just obvious for Blaster. I've heard you guys talk before, it's not like it's a secret code or something."

"Yeah," Rem agreed still amused. "But there is a secret code. Can you read that, too?"

"No. The only sign language I know is American Standard Sign Language," she sniffed.

"No shit. Well, then you do know about half the secret code." Rem nuzzled her ear and whispered, "I'll teach it all to you for a price."

Tammy snorted. "She just needs to see you using it and two hours later she'll be teaching it to you. She picks up on these things. How do you think she learned sign language?"

"Really?" Rem mused. "How did she learn sign?"

"A neighbor kid is deaf. She watched him talk to his mother for two days. On the third day she went over there and joined in the conversation. Now we have lots of deaf clients thanks to her. They use the Internet a great deal, you know." Tammy smiled, looking as proud as a mother hen over Kathryn's talent.

"Oh, it wasn't that easy. I really sucked at first. But they were so glad someone wanted to learn that they taught me. That's all." Kathryn glanced down, flustered with all the attention centered on her.

"So how does Gray know I ditched Miguel anyway?" Tammy questioned.

"You didn't ditch me, brat. You just got a bit ahead of me," Miguel corrected her testily.

"I ditched you! Would we be on this lovely island if it was up to you?" Tammy insisted.

"No. You ran away like the spoiled little girl you are, Tammy. You've endangered everyone who is trying to help you, but mostly you've put yourself and Kathryn in danger. That's what you've done," Miguel finished quietly.

"Oh, get over yourself, Miguel!" Tammy blew up. "Look around, you melodramatic, old women. Everyone is fine! There is no bad guy following our every move. Sure, there might be a sick, obsessed person out there, but there always are!"

Rem spoke up. "Stop it, Tammy. Miguel is right. Do you think the six of us spent the last fifteen years of our lives *knitting*? When we say there's a problem, we don't say it casually. I know you've never experienced anything like this before. That just means we've done it right so far. But this time you're in it. It's coming for you. Stop being an ass and let us do our job."

Tammy stared at her brother and frowned. Kat suspected she hadn't been taking this seriously at all. Hearing it from both Miguel and now Rem was shaking her faith in her invincibility. Before whatever "it" is happens, one always believes that "it" only happens to other people. Especially for the beautiful, privileged young woman Tammy had always been. It's not that she was deliberately arrogant—she just had no idea what being helpless and overpowered meant. There was no time in her life when she couldn't have exactly what she wanted or who she wanted. Even when she went too far, there was always someone to bail her out. Kathryn could fully understand her inability to accept that the world was a radically different place than she'd thought.

"How Gray knows is that—" Rem continued, "—however you got here without Miguel triggered his 'watch' command on the computer. If he knows you're moving and where to, it's only reasonable to assume the Bad Guy who's as smart as this one, was triggered, too. That means trouble is coming here or already is here, depending on where the Bad Guy is based."

"Oh," Tammy mumbled.

"So, what do we do now?" Kathryn asked. She wasn't really concerned, but Tammy needed a break from all the male disapproval focused on her.

"Well," Miguel took up the conversation. "That depends. We hope Gray can locate the tango in transit. We're using this to get him moving. As long as there's a hot lead out there for him might as well use it as bait."

Rem leaned down and dropped an openmouthed kiss on Kat's shoulder, lapping indecently with his tongue before pushing away from the table. "I'm hungry. Anyone else want breakfast?"

"Oh, gosh, it's been forever since he fed me!" Tammy perked up. "I don't suppose you're gonna make that delicious French toast thing you do, Rem?"

Kathryn realized both men avoided using a name for the Bad Guy. So it had to be bad news. They were trying to protect her. That was just peachy by her. Reality was overrated most of the time. She'd hang on to this dream world where Rem treated her like a goddess for as long as possible.

* * * * *

By noon, the Observer lounged atop the pyramid in the Mayan ruins with a pair of high-powered binoculars trained on the villa below. Everything was ready. Now all he had to do was wait.

Tammy had called him. Her actions begged him to rescue her. He could do no other but comply. She'd brought him right to the bitch and he would reward her sweetly for that. Perhaps her cleansing wouldn't take as long as he'd thought. It warmed him to be so close to his Angel.

When he got her "message" last night and un-coded where she was leading him, a lovely plan laid itself out in his mind. The location couldn't be more convenient. The added audience only enhanced the experience for all of them. The plan was perfect for punishing a wide range of individuals. He marveled that he hadn't thought of this before. How amusing to know they could flail around all they wanted and still he would best them. There was no doubt he could run mental circles around all those big, nasty-looking men who kept buzzing around her. But they were as ignorant as the rest. He would best them and have the satisfaction of seeing them suffer. So much better this way.

His check-in to the fishing camp on the other side of the island had been simple. Securing a room for the equipment, quick and easy after he hacked into the reservations they already had listed. He would be long gone by the time the real client showed up.

His walking off on a hike appeared the most natural thing in the world for a tourist to do. Now he'd found this perfect place for the transmitter. It offered him a direct line-of-sight to the villa and the fishing camp. His plan was falling together better than he'd dreamed. Perfection was so simple when one did things right.

He still depended on another to get the ritual site prepared. But that one had never failed him in the past. It should be fine. He'd left detailed instructions for the other to follow. This time, everything would go right. After all, he was the boss. Yes, yes, the boss. He'd correct his mistake with the bitch. How he ever could have imagined her to be a good person he didn't know. It was the pills, they confused him. The bitch would not escape again. She'd escaped him in Atlanta. Yes, yes, escaped. Stupid Pollyanna was too dim to even realize she'd been in training to be a whore. The other one had been bringing her along slowly. All that time wasted. Didn't matter now. No need to remember. Yes, yes, all was well now.

Mother would be so pleased. She would never make him take those pills again. When he did things wrong, that's when Mother made him take those pills. But this was going to work perfectly. He would prove he didn't need them anymore. She always said it was a secret. The pills were a filthy secret. She was ashamed of him when he needed the pills. Now they could get rid of them forever. She liked it when he made a complicated plan look easy. She would be so proud of him this time. She would call him her smart little man again. No, no, Mother's smart little man doesn't need any nasty pill to make him smart.

All it took was three wireless transmitters, two wireless monitors with microphones and voila! Done! Well, a convenient location helped, too. But that was to be expected when an Angel guided him. Easy, so easy. The method to control those men couldn't be simpler. A few little tablets in the water cistern under the house and they would sleep like babies. Unsuspecting buffoons.

The island made it effortless to drug them. Everyone caught rainwater off the roof and stored it in a cistern under the house. The filter system could not remove the drug. Bottled water was hard to come by out here so there was little danger they wouldn't drink the water from the faucet in one form or other. On a hot tropical island, you needed to drink a lot. Perfect.

Ah, there was the Angel! He watched her walk through a room as he had been doing since he arrived. So beautiful. The graceful sway of her perfect body soothed him. How lovely she would look after it was over. Yes, yes, she was perfect.

I'm coming for you, darling, just a few more hours to wait. I'm coming, sweet Angel. He knew she heard his thoughts. That's how they communicated these days. She was so like Mother. Sometimes he heard her calling to him at night. Such a good Angel.

By late afternoon, Tammy was climbing the walls in boredom. The guys didn't want them to go outside. It was impossible to secure the entire beach and gardens. Miguel made an art of ignoring Tammy, so Kathryn took on the task of amusing her.

They played cards for hours. Every time Rem moved through the room, he dropped a kiss on her head, her cheek and her lips. His hands never failed to trail over interesting terrain. One time his hand wandered under the table. It swept up her thigh to push into her shorts and thrust a single digit right up her wet cunt. His finger inserted to his knuckle as he kissed her and finger-fucked her briefly. Her cunt gushed hotly, clamping down on the unexpected intruder. She had no control as her hips jerked in response. Pulling away, he sauntered out of the room sucking his finger loudly like a lollipop.

"For heavens sake! Get a room!" Tammy demanded at his not so stealthy play.

"I've got a room, brat!" Rem turned to shoot her an unrepentant glance. "But someone showed up and barged in. So deal with it." He laughed and continued on his way. The sibling grousing was an old routine that helped add some normality to the situation.

Kathryn laughed and pretended to be embarrassed. She wasn't and he knew it. She liked him caressing her, touching her. It felt right. Even in front of people. Perhaps only around these people who were their family. It didn't matter, or it mattered more. It wasn't an exhibitionist issue as much as it was an irresistible pull between them. Her previous life gave her a lack of modesty that wasn't exactly immoral as it was a comfort with her own skin. Now that there was no need to hide it, she relaxed into herself. This was the real Kathryn, the adult who accepted herself and her life with all its facets. Rem gave her the confidence and safety to give up the concealing clothes. She'd discovered she liked the sexy wardrobe he'd bought her. Liked it a lot. He encouraged it outrageously, eating her up with his appreciation of her physical form.

It made her aware of his claim on her every second. His possessiveness was exciting, tender and a little raunchy, but mostly it was solid. His attention and obvious desire for her on every level though new and fragile, was also elemental in its completeness. There were no doubts for her. He'd made his intentions very clear, both with her and about the possibility of a baby. She was safe emotionally and physically. It flowed over her and she glowed with it. Kathryn was almost afraid to think about it. The fulfillment of every fantasy ever conceived was a scary concept to grasp.

* * * * *

Charlie and Blaster buzzed the house before they landed. Rem and Miguel had both been patrolling the house and veranda all day, certain danger was close. It hung in the air like a malevolent spirit. Both men felt the prickle of watching eyes with that peculiar sensitivity acquired in combat.

They'd been in touch with Gray several times. However, the conversations were brief and frustrating, adding nothing new.

Charlie and Blaster bounced in, apparently fresh as daisies after their quarter mile hike from the airstrip. Both of them made a point of kissing the girls hello for the entertainment value of watching Rem and Miguel scowl.

Blaster whistled low and long at the new Kathryn, clothed in shorts and tiny tank top.

"Wow, baby! Finally decided to let the butterfly out, did you?" He laughed as he picked her up and planted a smacking kiss on her lips. Laughing at his antics, Kat smacked his shoulder playfully.

"Put me down, you big lug," she demanded. She didn't get put down.

Charlie plucked her out of Blaster's arms. Turning her to face him, he grinned and took his time scanning the new Kathryn hanging two feet off the ground in his powerful hold.

"Damn, woman. Why'd you go and take up with ugly, old Rem?" he whined mournfully. He was just pulling her close for a kiss when two strong hands snatched her away from him.

Rem gathered her close. He wrapped her legs around his waist and her arms around his neck, sat her on his hip again and frowned at the two grinning fools in front of him.

"Mine!" he stated defiantly. "Find your own woman to maul, you sorry bastards."

Kathryn nuzzled his neck and kissed his cheek as he glared at the laughing bunch. Grunting his satisfaction with her attention, he turned to the kitchen and strode in with her wrapped around him like a barnacle again. She couldn't stop the grin at his possessive grumbles as he grabbed sandwich makings from the fridge and set them out. Everyone else followed to gather around the kitchen table and eat supper. Rem just barely let her have her own chair. His was pulled up close and one of her legs hooked over his thigh while his arm rested around her back.

After the light supper was done, Rem put on a pot of coffee. Over coffee, the patrol plan was hammered out and they agreed to wait until tomorrow to make a decision on their next move. Hopefully, Gray would uncover the tango by then. That's the last thing anyone remembered.

Chapter Nine

** හ**

Gray stabbed numbers out fiercely. Flying at thirty thousand feet with Jackson piloting, the mobile communications operations plane winged its way south at top speed. Gray hadn't been able to reach even one of the four men on the island. He had every beeper, cell phone and computer terminal ringing, dinging or vibrating. Nothing.

After thirty minutes of no response on the ground, Gray called Jackson and they'd gotten their asses mobile. Nobody went dark and silent this long without notice unless they were in deep shit. Four highly trained specialists do not get in deep shit this side of a full-scale assault.

* * * * *

In the villa, Miguel lifted his pounding head off the table and tried to focus. Everything seemed fuzzy and far away. Even Tammy's screeching sounded tinny and distant. Miguel grabbed his head and squeezed his eyes shut.

Rem grunted as the needles stabbing into his brain roused him. Damn, Tammy was still yelling. Lifting his head, it felt like he was lifting a ton of bricks. Goodness, did that girl never shut up? As he looked around with slightly unfocused eyes, Rem felt shards of ice slide through his veins. The room around him came into focus.

Around the table, only Miguel stirred. Blaster and Charlie were slumped over and obviously unconscious. Kathryn and Tammy weren't there. But he could hear Tammy! His eyes zeroed in on the center of the table. There sat a small monitor, Tammy's hysterical voice streamed out of it.

Rem also realized that every phone and beeper was going off. He snatched up his cell phone and grunted into it as his eyes traveled the room frantically.

Gray yelled into his ear, "What the hell is happening?"

"Drugged! Women gone. Incoming audio, possibly visual," Rem barked into the phone.

Miguel's chair crashed backwards as he too registered where Tammy's voice came from. Rem flipped the ON switch below the screen.

It opened a little window into hell. There, in a dimly lit space were Kathryn and Tammy. Circling them numerous candles flickered, illuminating a ghastly nightmare. Kathryn stood on her tiptoes. Her hands manacled together over her head with sadistic metal cuffs already biting into torn flesh. A thick chain stretched up out of view over her head. Her feet were cuffed to the floor with the same biting metal, spread wide apart. Nearly suspended, the chain above Kathryn pulled her up harshly to her toes. She was naked.

Similarly restrained, though not so severely stretched out, Tammy hung facing Kathryn fully clothed.

Charlie and Blaster groggily sat up as the phone fell from Rem's nerveless fingers. He stared into the screen and roared his pain.

The situation crystallized at first glance for Charlie and Blaster. Both of them ignored the sledgehammers that pounded away at their brains with the compartmental discipline of combat-trained responses. They scrambled with various handheld devices. In record time, they had them flicked on and plugged into the back of the monitor. Blaster grabbed Rem's cell phone and spoke low and fast. They had Gray linked on the transmission in less than three seconds.

A masked face appeared in the screen, close enough to the camera to block most of the women. He wore a black leather hood that laced up in the back. It covered everything to make his features totally indistinguishable except for eye color.

"Ah, the useless muscle for brains woke up," a digitized voice crackled out of the speaker. "Good of you to join us. I'm sure Kathryn here is happy we can finally begin." The voice guffawed in manic laughter as he turned to stride over to Kathryn. As he moved away from the camera, what he held in his leather-gloved hand became visible. A vicious Spanish quirt. Its double falls of supple leather strips swayed obscenely as he neared her. He wore military fatigue pants that were shoved into high combat boots laced to mid-shin and a black T-shirt. The handle of a sidearm could be seen protruding from his waistband.

The team had all agreed that the setup caller Marco had to be involved. Since the voice on the phone was distorted when he called Kathryn they weren't sure if his boss was part of it or not. Looking at the figure on the screen, they all knew he had been. This was not Marco. His height and body mass were all wrong, but it matched the other suspect perfectly. How involved Marco was wasn't clear now. He presented an unknown.

"Nooooo!" Rem bellowed. "You touch her and I'll reach in through your nose to remove your nuts. Oh, God, NO! Get away from her!" he screamed as the hooded figure circled Kathryn.

"Listen to your lover's screams, my disgusting bitch," the mechanical voice crooned. "He pleasures me so. You will scream even louder, though. Oh, yes, you will raise the roof with your pitiful cries." The hooded man smoothed a hand down her neck, down, down, until he cupped a full breast. Lifting its weight, he looked into the camera and laughed. Rem's threats poured out of the microphone. The hooded man closed his hand and squeezed cruelly. Kathryn gritted her teeth but didn't make a sound.

"Oh, yessss," maniacal man hissed. "A quiet one." His hand slid down pale flesh to her exposed cunt. Gloved fingers closed and squeezed hard again with a rough, quick clench and unclench motion. Kathryn jerked, but still not even a gasp escaped her. Rem's litany of how many ways he'd kill the man picked up.

Tammy cried continually as she begged the man to leave Kathryn alone. She promised anything if he would just let them go. Everyone ignored her.

Suddenly there was silence from the monitor. The hooded man turned to look at his screen. Rem's back was to the camera, his body moved in quick, jerky movements. The man in the dungeon could not see what he was doing. It didn't matter. They would not find him. He turned back to his prize. He would soon have all their attention again. Of that, he was certain.

In the kitchen, Blaster had just grabbed Rem by the neck and shoved a handheld PC in his face. On screen, Gray signed fast.

"Have transmission. Am tracking. It's local to you. Bounced maybe three times." Gray shot the info at Rem. "Kat signed with fingers while man turned away. Did you see it?"

"No. You?" Rem flashed back.

"2 D 3 in A. S. Sign. Clue?" Gray asked in sign. They weren't talking out loud because of the obvious mic in the room. Also, Gray needed to keep Rem's back to the monitor. He couldn't even imagine how many ways he'd lose his mind if that was Prin.

Miguel, Charlie and Blaster grimly watched both the monitor and the sign conversation.

Suddenly a scream tore through the monitor. It was Tammy. Rem jerked around in time to see the second blow land on Kathryn's white flesh. The man was whipping her tender breasts. Angry, red welts already visible rose on milky-white skin. Two vicious marks from the double-tongued Spanish quirt glowed across each breast. Kathryn's body wrenched under the heavy blows but still not a sound issued from her mouth.

Rem fell to his knees in pain, unable to even cry out. Information, the situation, his utter failure to protect her, her complete vulnerability to the sick, fucking bastard, it all destroyed him. Nothing on earth had prepared him for this. He could take pain. He could endure torture, but watching it inflicted on Kathryn ripped out a fundamental piece of him.

"Shut it OFF!" Gray shouted in desperation.

The hooded man jerked his attention to the monitor. "You shut it off and she dies." He smiled cruelly behind his mask. "If I don't see that bastard's face in front of this screen, I'll disembowel her where she stands." Laughing arrogantly again the man turned back to Kathryn. Certain he'd secured his audience.

He moved behind her and reached around to stroke both hands down her torso. "Do you know what happens when you pull the intestines out of a woman through a very small hole?" His gloved fingers glided up and down her trembling belly. "It takes her hours to die. Almost a day." He traced the red marks across her breasts with the handle of the quirt. "These are just little love taps compared to that."

Looking back up at the screen the man frowned. "Your little boyfriend's too squeamish for this?" Rem was now standing alone in front of the monitor. His entire body clenched, as were the hands at his sides, no one else visible around him. "I promise you, it's going to be a delicious show. Perhaps they went for snacks?" The Observer wasn't concerned. There was too much to do. No need to worry about an idiot more or less.

Rem forced his face into immobility. The only thing he had to offer Kathryn was his strength. He'd stand there with her and give her the one thing that could pass between them. His absolute guarantee she would never be alone again. She had to believe in him and in his protection. If he couldn't come for her, he'd send a malevolent force the likes of which this earth feared to face.

The man stepped back and brought the quirt down twice more in quick succession. Burning red stripes appeared across Kathryn's soft stomach and then across the velvety, tender flesh of her pubic mound and hips. Her body convulsed as much as possible. The cuffs cut into wrists and ankles viciously. Rem's body jerked, mirroring hers. Neither of them made a sound.

Tammy screamed and thrashed in her restraints. The man turned to her in disgust. "Be quiet, Angel! I haven't the time to deal with you now, wait your turn!" he admonished sternly.

Tammy paled and began begging and pleading again. Telling him anything she could think of. He frowned darkly at her. She was not obeying. Her mouth spewed out atrocious things. Mother would have to wash it out with soap. For now though, he must help her learn to obey.

The man went for the item he needed, stepping out of the camera view.

This time Rem saw Kathryn's fingers move in quick flashes. She signed 2 D 3 over and over. He answered her with a simple statement. "They come," in American Standard Sign language.

Rem figured if she was signing, the man was not watching. He looked up quickly to check the progress of the other men in the room. They stood well back behind the monitor out of range for both mic and vid cam.

Rem's eyes burned with a demon's own, venomous threat as he watched them prep, fast and silent. All three men already had dark flight suits zipped low on lean hips. They wouldn't pull on the Kevlar-reinforced upper halves 'til Go time. They efficiently buckled up and strapped on utility belts and specially modified thigh holsters. Handguns were checked and water added to the baffles of sound suppressers. Ambidextrous safeties softly hissed on and off both sides of the Heckler & Koch USP9SD pistols to check ease of action. Every weapon strapped onto their bodies blended into the matte background of the flight suits. The dull, black finish on both guns and blades gave the weapons themselves an even more sinister look.

Deadly knives and throwing stars were checked and stashed for effortless access. Everything that could be strapped on was. The larger, more lethal toys were all stored on the plane. There they would pull up a fake floor and finish the lock and load ritual.

Each man stuffed a charcoal gray mask into his belt. Its color perfectly matched the flight suits. Not too black for a bright night, but dark enough to melt into the deepest shadows. When the lightweight hoods were pulled on, everything was covered. They could easily breathe and talk through the space-age fabric, so even nose and mouth were obscured. They became faceless night wraiths. Seen only with heat sensors, and even then, the suits deflected most of their body's heat emissions. Dark angels of death armed with almost every weapon known to man. The duel-vision headgear worn over the head masks would give them the look of aliens with three glowing green eyes when activated. For most of the population, they were from another planet. A bleak place where they were hunters and every unknown — presumed prey.

During the bastard's threats, Gray and Miguel figured out Kathryn's sign — 2 D was Daryl's Doll House obviously. The 3 stumped them until Gray checked for a third Doll House. They knew there were two in the US. One in Atlanta, one in Miami. Could there be a third? Sure enough, there was one set to open in three months in Belize City. Its location was just a twenty-minute air hop from the island.

They would be out of there in less than two minutes. Jeep to airstrip and flight prep at least nine minutes. In the air, twenty minutes. Time to site should be ten to fifteen minutes. Depending on resistance and location layout, the firefight, less than five minutes. Fifty minutes total. Fifty minutes he, Kathryn and Tammy had to survive this.

Rem was tied to the villa's kitchen by the sick bastard's demands. The others assured him in sign they would get her. Gray and Jackson had already landed in Belize City. They'd been nearly over it when the transmission tracked-out to right there. Kathryn telling them exactly where to look helped greatly. Now they were nailing down the fastest route from the airport and the building floor plans for possible access.

He would know on the live feed as soon as they had her. The unit knew Kathryn bought them time with her silence. The man's promises to make her scream told them he would work at it until she did. Precious, excruciating minutes, purchased with her blood and spirit. They wouldn't waste one of them. Too many times to count Rem had trusted them with his own life. This time, he trusted them with his world.

* * * * *

Gray swiftly decided no outside help. Local cops would get in the way. Their unit functioned on a highly specialized level as a killing force. This mission came with intense motivation. No one asked what the takedown protocol was. Anyone who gave a damn wasn't welcome. The grim-faced warriors could each have done this solo with this level of incentive. It was sheer insanity to show them the torture of their own, their women. The target was hard. Extreme prejudice a given.

Gray made one call just before Jackson touched down in Belize City.

"Bill, this is Gray," he barked into the phone. "Yeah, it's been a while. I need two clean vehicles, dark windows at the private plane hanger in fifteen minutes."

"It'll cost you," Bill warned him around a yawn.

"Charge anything you want. Park them and walk away. Don't look back," Gray's voice dropped dangerously on the warning.

"Christ, man! If this is something I don't want to know about, call someone else! You can't involve State in this shit!" Bill yelled back at Gray. The seriousness of the situation suddenly came into focus for Bill as his sleepy brain processed Gray's clipped directions.

"Bill! Do it now!" Gray snarled at him. "American blood is on the floor. It's a woman and she's buying us time with it. We don't have the fucking time for anyone else."

"Damn, I've never known you to work with a woman," Bill marveled.

"Not an operative. A wife." Hideous menace lashed out in Gray's tone as he said that.

"Shit in a blender! This is gonna be messy," Bill whispered in shock. "Need anything else?"

"No. The vehicles will be there in the morning. Don't worry. We'll clean up after ourselves." Gray hung up abruptly.

"That's what I was afraid of," Bill mumbled to himself as he pulled on his pants and hurriedly left his embassy bedroom.

* * * * *

Grimly Miguel nodded at Rem and the three men slipped out. The clock was ticking.

The hooded man returned to the picture frame. He stood behind Tammy with a large ball gag.

"You must learn to obey, Angel. I will help you all I can. But Mother requires obedience!" he warned her and forced the rubber ball into her mouth. He quickly strapped it behind her head tightly.

"Now you will be quiet." Tammy thrashed and screamed behind her gag. The man shook his head. "Okay, Angel. I'll give you the attention you crave," he conceded. "But only for a moment. This is to help you understand. You must obey."

Coming around to her front, he quickly unsnapped her shorts and jerked the zipper down. Tammy froze, her eyes wide and terrified. The man swiftly grabbed both sides of her shorts and ripped them in two. The two halves slid down her legs, leaving Tammy in a g-string.

"So you've taken up her wicked clothing! Only bad girls wear this shit!" The hooded man grabbed the flimsy thing and ripped it off her body as he screamed at her. "You must be punished!" Furious at her, the man's hand cracked loudly on Tammy's ass, spanking her hard and fast. He yelled over and over again that only bad girls wear that shit. She would not be a bad girl again! He beat her in openhanded girlish abandon. Landing blows all over her body in a chaotic way. He seemed to be losing his tenuous hold on reality as he rained down blows on Tammy.

Kathryn laughed softly. "Giving up so soon, Jonathan?" she taunted, leaving him in no doubt that she knew who he was despite the hood. "You can't get a squeak out of me, so you're going for the screamer?" She tsked softly and laughed again. "What a lazy disappointment you turned out to be. Has it always been this way for you? Beating on tied-up women. What? Did Mommy whip you with a switch and you secretly liked it?"

Her taunting worked. The man turned to her jerkily, leaving Tammy. Rem felt bile rise in his throat. Swallowing hard, he steeled himself for the abuse that would fall on Kathryn.

He knew she'd had to do it. She couldn't let Tammy take it anymore just to give herself a break. She wasn't made that way and her generous heart would not let her. Pain, concentrated pain, it really could kill you to watch people you love enduring it. He wouldn't let it in right now. If she suffered it without a break, so would he.

The Observer—Jonathan—backhanded Kathryn across the face. Blood poured down from her split lip. "Don't you ever mention Mother's name! You filthy piece of whoring shit," he screamed at her.

Breathing harshly, Jonathan stepped back and turned away from the women. He paced somewhere out of Rem's sight, but Rem could hear a low mumbling as he talked to himself. This guy had taken a header out the "Reality Door" a while ago, probably why he didn't know with whom he was dealing. It explained a lot about his lack of concern when the other men disappeared from view. At least he wasted time being demented. Every minute he kept away from the women was a minute closer to the end of this fucking nightmare, a moment stolen from pain. Living from moment to moment was the only way to survive this.

Jonathan came back after about five minutes and turned toward the screen. Having an audience was very gratifying, he decided. "A mouthy little bitch. Street trash from the start, you know. Came in all marked up and filthy. I knew she was hopeless. Already used up," he commented to Rem as if commiserating with him.

"Well, we know what to do about that, don't we?" Jonathan walked behind Kathryn again and studied her ass. He glanced up over Kathryn's shoulder at Rem. "Lovely ass, don't you think? Just right for a fine whipping. Big and creamy, every lovely mark shows up so nicely." His hands caressed the round globes gently, leather slid over flesh in a whisper touch. "I've always enjoyed looking at a smooth ass. We can see our work so well on the smooth ones."

Suddenly his arm jerked as he plunged a leather-coated finger deep into her asshole with enough force to breach clenched muscles painfully. Kathryn's head jerked forward on a gasp.

"Ahhh, never took it up the ass, have you, bitch?" Looking at Rem, he tsked softly just as Kathryn had. "And I thought all you muscle-bound types liked it that way. You're disappointing me, muscle man." Jonathan pulled his finger out slowly. "Well, we really must correct that immediately. What's a good ass whipping without a nice big plug up your butt?" He hooked his chin over Kathryn's shoulder, pressing down cruelly to increase the strain on her distended joints.

"And here," he continued reaching around her with one hand. Two fingers spread her pussy lips wide open. His other hand came up under her and two thick, gloved fingers forced their way up her cunt. Sawing in and out brutally as he laughed softly. "This juicy hole needs to be stuffed full. Ohh, nice and tight! Not been fucking her regularly?" he questioned Rem snidely. "Or you just have such a tiny dick it can't do the job?"

The hand holding her cunt open came up off her. He brought it down hard directly over her clit. Striking her cunt repeatedly while he dry-fucked her with his fingers. Jonathan laughed and giggled as Kathryn's face contorted in pain. "Oh, yess, that's it, bitch. You like that don't you?" he taunted. "Show him how much you like it! Look at her juicy cunt all puffed up and pretty red now. See how she takes a finger-fuck, bastard?" He laughed.

"Enough fun for you, whore. Time for your toys." Jonathan pulled his fingers out of her and moved out of the picture again. He returned immediately with a large ass plug. It was cone-shaped at the top, expanded to at least two inches with a half-inch indention to hold it in. It culminated with a wide flat disk at the end. Holding it up in front of her face Jonathan grinned evilly behind his mask again. "No lube, just all you."

Kathryn's face twisted into a sneer. "Damn, you are a pathetic failure at this, aren't you? Is that what it takes for you to get a woman to scream? What are you? One of those losers Mommy didn't like? Is she telling you how worthless you are right now? Don't you hear her laughing at you? Weak little girly boys have to use props to get things done."

Rem sucked in air. Oh, God! She'd gone too far! He could feel it. Fear like nothing that'd come before sliced through him. Burning, cutting, ripping blades of fear whirled through his system.

Jonathan turned slowly away from both Kathryn and Rem. He stood there a moment, shaking his head and moving in little jerks. Again, he spent several minutes talking quietly with himself. It became apparent he thought he was conversing with his mother. The shattered mind he was displaying induced no sympathy. His insanity was dangerous and vicious. Jonathan moved out of the picture and came back with a bottle of water. He'd calmed down and seemed to be holding onto his sneering persona with difficulty. He took a long drink from the bottle and looked at Rem.

"Bottled water might have helped you tonight. How's your head? Feeling better, are we?" Jonathan asked snidely.

"Actually, it's pounding like a hammer. What did you use?" Rem breathed a desperate sigh of relief. If he could keep him talking it'd give Kathryn a break. Use up more precious minutes.

"Ah, that would be giving away our little secrets, can't tell. But you have to admit it is a brilliant plan. How many were there? Four of you muscle-bound idiots? And here I am with the women. There you are, by your lonesome," Jonathan crowed in manic delight.

Rem no long worried that Jonathan would perceive the absence of the other men as a threat. He was lost in his world of superiority and godlike power. This dementia allowed no room for deductive reasoning on the level of reality. It totally engulfed him in the world he'd created in his mind.

"Yes, it is a brilliant plan. I can't figure out how you did it. How did you drug us?" Rem's deep voice rumbled as he tried to sound admiring. "Never seen it done so well, and that's saying something."

Jonathan's ego warmed to his subject. "It was so simple. The water cistern, stupid. It's so tiresome, consistently outsmarting you people. I'd like a challenge someday. Even with only two days, well, really one day to plan, look where we are. Victor and Loser. No challenge whatsoever. Pleasant as it is to chat," Jonathan continued, "I seldom have the opportunity to enjoy my plan with someone. Don't think I don't realize you're trying to distract me, pathetic, mental midget that you are. I see right through you. It doesn't matter how long this takes, imbecile, it will end the same. The only question is how long can she live through it? We have all the time in the world. But why wait?"

"The live feed is brilliant. How did you manage that?" Rem tried to recapture Jonathan's attention with more ego stroking. "I've never seen anything like it. You should be teaching this stuff. There are a lot of people who'd pay top dollar to learn from a professional like you." Rem was desperate. If he could only keep the deranged bastard's attention a little longer he'd say anything, do anything.

But Jonathan couldn't be distracted as he turned back to faced Kathryn. "Mother really doesn't like you. Neither do I. We think it's time you started paying for your sins. But now we don't care if you scream or not. When you feel ready, you will beg me to jam this plug up your virgin ass. Only when this is in you, will you be released. Only then will you be sent to the place you deserve."

He lifted the quirt high and brought it down harshly across her breasts. "Your sins are known." Another lash to the undersides of her breasts. "Your Judgment has come." He marked her ribs this time. "You soiled perfection." Her armpits each received harsh blows. "You do not deserve the mercy we show you." He wrapped the wicked duel strips of flexible leather around her hips and butt.

Chapter Ten

හ

Outside, fast and silent, dark ghosts moved in. Two melted into the tropical night—headed for the rear of the long warehouse-style building. Three soundless gray shadows moved around the front. Jackson stopped to hang back in deep cover with the monitor. He would let them know if the situation turned critical inside and they needed to give up stealth for speed. Gray and Miguel moved forward to the edge of the asphalt.

It was a difficult approach. Huge, lighted parking lots surrounded three sides of the building making any approach totally exposed. The backside did have dumpsters and service entrances with ramps. All handy for cover, but only when next to them. There were three vehicles parked close to the front door. No cover there. Add to that the unknowns—the expertise of the forces guarding it, unknown, weapons unknown and with the need for total stealth paramount, this little field trip became interesting.

Gray and Miguel crouched down to survey the parking lot and building. They were at an angle, far enough away to see three corners. There appeared to be one guy stationed at each corner of the building. The guards were neither alert nor actively patrolling. A good indication this bunch was locals, hired on for a short-term job. Mostly they were out of sight of each other and didn't appear particularly concerned about checking in on their buddies.

Miguel smiled in a chilling fashion as he lifted the Tango-51 sniper rifle to his shoulder to sight the three targets. The sniper rapidly adjusted his scope and sighted again. Crosshairs were double-checked and locked. That would leave one guy at the back corner for the other two specialists.

Glancing at Gray, Miguel nodded. Gray clicked his throat-voice radio once and received a single click back in his ear bud. Everyone was in place. Everyone had the target marked and sighted.

"Go!" Gray commanded softly into the radio.

A whispered pop from Miguel's rifle and the guard at the rear corner slumped against the side of the building. The man appeared to be resting. Another soft pop and the guy closest to them slid down the wall slowly. The dead guard accommodated them by not making a sound as his body crumpled to the ground. Gray was already moving as the third man fell over silently. Gray sprinted low and fast to the furthest body at the front of the building, leaving the nearest one for Miguel. They swiftly dragged them around the corners away from the front door.

There were tall rows of window panels down the length of the building. They were the type where lower sections opened out at a slant. Only one on each side of the front was open, probably to create a cross breeze for the reception area. The rest were closed and painted from the inside so no one could see in or out.

The unit knew the interior was cavernous. The front was the club. It had a relatively small, walled-off reception area that the open windows led to. The rest would be the bar and stage. The back had been partitioned off for offices and a dressing room, behind that were twelve private playrooms.

The doors at front and back would be guarded since they'd bothered with guards outside. Gray pulled out the optic cable. A handy little tool to see under doors and in open windows without sticking a head into someone's line of fire.

Crouched below the open window, Gray lifted the optic to the corner. Four more rough types sat around a table playing cards and drinking beer at the other end of the lobby area. Gray almost laughed. They weren't guarding either the door in or the door to the club. The only light was directly over their heads and would restrict their vision, leaving the rest of the room in dark shadow for them. Obviously, this was a fluff job as far as they were concerned. Even their weapons were strewn about out of reach. Gray handed the optic viewer to Miguel.

Miguel shook his head over the easy kill zone these guys made of themselves. He then nodded to Gray when he signed they would enter here. They hoisted up and over the sill like two pieces of the night slithering in. Silent as mist they moved low and slow until all four men were easy targets. Miguel pulled out three throwing-stars and signaled Gray to take the man with his back to them.

Miguel didn't limit himself to guns. Utilizing anything that moved through the air to a target, he rated A1 on every known scale. The throwing stars Miguel carried could slice through a neck to the backbone with frontal entry and proper throw style. Gray would get the other man with the long, wicked hunting knife he had holstered between his own shoulder blades.

Swift and silent the deadly dark blades did their work. Four bodies slumped over the table with stunned expressions on their faces. Back to back in classic defensive style, Miguel's restless eyes scanned the three entrances to the reception area as Gray slid the optic under the interior door. The viewer panned the huge room. At the back of the space, center stage, they found the target beating Kathryn in manic oblivion.

* * * * *

As Jonathan continued with his demented litany, Kathryn lifted her head and looked directly into Rem's eyes on the screen. His face was cut in harsh lines. The strong jaw locked, cheekbones starkly outlined under taunt flesh. His straight nose pronounced as pain carved deep grooves beside grim lips. His eyes blazed into hers and he felt it. She drew his soul from him and sheltered in it. Kathryn wrapped it around herself and gathered the strength he offered. She was silent.

Every ounce of Rem's being reached for her and she took it. He felt her give her consciousness into his keeping, simply surrender all that she was to her faith in him.

Her face became still as her eyes fixed on his even though her body jerked with each blow. The knowledge that she protected her sanity by shutting this event out of her consciousness bloomed in Rem's mind. The ability to do that was rare. Usually found in survivors of prison camps and such. The Special Forces tried to train it, but it was never fully known if it could be done until the need for it occurred. Kathryn could do it. He saw it happen and knew in his heart that she'd done it before. He tucked the knowledge away. No time to think of why she knew how to do this. Right now, he had to give her the focal point required to maintain the disconnection.

It seemed as though eternity passed between them. The ages came and went. Time became a fluid river rushing around them, but not touching as she submerged herself in him.

Thankfully, Jonathan was too far gone and didn't have the strength to break her skin with his clumsy, flailing blows. He was sinking fast into a demented state of total incoherence. Nevertheless, every lash rained down on Kathryn cut Rem to the bone. His body burned with pain. He counted silently in his head. Each blow would be repaid and he needed a count.

* * * * *

A sudden bright flash and loud bang blinded the camera and Jonathan as the front door burst open. He dropped the quirt and spun on his heel to stare in disbelief at the large men at the far side of the room. It was a long vault of a room and they were rushing toward him. Jonathan thought one thing and one thing only. They could not have Tammy back.

Jonathan yanked a gun from his waistband, dropped to one knee and aimed at Tammy's heart. A long body leapt through the air. Miguel dropped his sniper rifle and slapped two hands to his sidearm in midair. At such a short range, the rifle would rip right through the mark and might hit Kathryn behind him. Arching through the air, seemingly suspended in front of Tammy, Miguel's pistol was rock-steady in his outstretched arms. Two shots blazed from Miguel's handgun in such quick succession that the sound blurred into one bang.

The shots entered both of Jonathan's shoulder joints a split second after Jonathan pulled his trigger. Red blossomed across Miguel's biceps as his body crashed to the floor. Jonathan screamed and was thrown onto his back as the double hits shattered his shoulder ball joints. He immediately lost all use of his arms and hands.

Miguel's choice of target was a message to anyone else who might be in the room. They were not kill shots in the normal sense. They were more malicious than that. The shots were calculated to cripple and painfully bleed out a mark. The unit was aware they hadn't accounted for the Marco individual. The level of his participation in this was still a question. If he had been in the room or lurking somewhere around, the sadistic kill method was meant as a warning and a promise. As an ex-Army Ranger, he was not really a challenge, but certainly trained enough to be a threat. He would recognize that the shots were perfect hits, not an accident.

Then everything happened at once. Gray stepped in front of Kathryn and wrapped silver covering around her. It was a space-age material that could fold into a five-inch square, yet cover a man when unfolded. The back door to the stage burst open as Blaster and Charlie barreled through.

Blaster dropped to search Jonathan's now unconscious body for keys while Charlie remained on guard for any straggler defense force. Gray barked at Blaster to hurry.

Jackson, the EMT among them, gave up cover as soon as shots were fired. Entering he went straight to Miguel and quickly assessed damage. Miguel insisted he check on Kathryn and let him get Tammy down. It was a flesh wound, hardly worth the time.

Blaster found the keys and quickly unlocked Kathryn. Gray caught her crumpling body. Jackson bent over her a few seconds to test bones and gently massaged her shoulders. She did scream then as the pain of returning circulation racked her, but it was a good scream. The fact she made a sound at all meant she knew she was safe. Rem felt tears stream down his face.

Jackson carefully wrapped Kathryn's bleeding wrists and ankles while barking instructions at Charlie who was now binding Miguel's arm. Blaster took Tammy down and wrapped a silver cover around her hips. Gently he unfastened the gag and flung it across the room. She immediately knelt at Miguel's side to investigate his wound. Finally, she was silent and let the men work around her.

Everyone tried to ignore the motionless body on the floor. Jonathan wasn't dead yet, but his unattended wounds were bleeding out quickly. Even if he could have survived the wounds, he'd never have use of his arms again. Because the women kept glancing at his unconscious, mangled carcass nervously, Charlie grabbed a tablecloth and draped it over the body.

Charlie sliced a look back at Gray as he lifted his pistol over Jonathan. Gray gave him a curt nod and made sure he was directly in Kathryn's line of vision. Jackson subtly shifted to cut off Tammy's view while Charlie fired one last shot. The soft pop through the sound suppresser on the HK USP9 pistol could almost have been unnoticed if everyone in the room hadn't flinched at the final solution to Jonathan's problems. No one noticed Gray's head jerk up at the shot.

Suddenly every part of Gray switched on. There was something here he couldn't see, but felt with the deep part of himself that walked the universe. It was as if there'd been a movement he saw in peripheral vision, but nothing was there when he turned and looked directly. A chill swept over Gray. This type of knowledge was more dangerous than anything they'd faced so far. Icy silver-blue eyes swept the room and each person in it. It evaded him, but he was certain they were not done with the malevolent spirit Jonathan had embodied.

Gray picked up Kathryn as he turned to the screen and Rem with a sharp look. "Stay there. Charlie will fly her back to you. Little over an hour and she's in your arms. Get sane by then. She'll need you."

"Wait!" Kathryn gasped. "Rem, Marco went back to the island to pick up Jonathan's computers from the fishing village. Jonathan was going to call him when he was done with us. He's waiting in a room at the inn."

Remington's jaw clenched. "Baby, you know I have to get him?" he stated carefully, both hands framed the monitor as if he could touch her. "You know he was completely involved in this, don't you?" The grim lines of his face showed his concern for her feelings, yet firm resolve to clean every threat to her off the planet.

Kathryn smiled tenderly into the screen. "Honey, I've had a hard night and I'm tired. Please *take out* the trash before I get home. Okay?" Her choice of phrase lifted all restraint.

Rem laughed softly and caressed her precious face on the screen. "Consider it done, sweetheart. I'll be at the airstrip."

Gray strode out of the room carrying Kathryn with Charlie at his side and barked back at Blaster. "Take it down. I want the dirt to burn. No evidence, no remains." Gray's jaw clenched as he tried to shake the dark feeling they were not done here. It didn't add up in a logical way, but he could still feel it, almost taste it. Total destruction of the property might be the answer—he hoped it was trapped here and would find its end within the violent surrounds it had created. The ritual arrangement of the candles was a nagging reminder that things might have been occurring here that were not confined to this time and place.

"No problem, boss. As soon as the injured are out, it's gone." Blaster chuckled down at Miguel who still sat on the floor. "Think you can limp out of here with one good arm, hotshot?"

"Shut up, Blaster," Miguel growled. "Help Tammy and get my rifle."

"I'm fine," Tammy murmured. "Let's go." She slipped her arm around Miguel as he rose off the floor in a fluid motion that belied any injury. Shocked at the slender arm around his waist, Miguel glanced down and realized she was trying to help him. Miguel leaned a little weight on Tammy and let her lead him out. It was Tammy who reached down to sling the sniper rifle over her shoulder with practiced ease. Miguel frowned at her natural, smooth handling of the lethal gun.

"You probably shattered your scope when you dropped it," Tammy commented quietly. "It's an expensive one, too. Sorry about that."

"You know about scopes, little girl?" Miguel questioned. The "little girl" name became an endearment as a hint of his Latin accent purred through his voice. Molten golden eyes caressed the top of her bent head as she led him across the parking lot.

"Yeah." Tammy gave him a sideways glance. "I know a bit about them."

Miguel felt a shiver ripple down his spine. It had nothing to do with the cool breeze. Tammy's subdued attitude worried him. Her apparent ease with high-powered weapons terrified the shit out of him. Rem had some *splainin'* to do. Briefly, his jaw clenched as he bit back any further response. It wasn't the time. But there would be time. Very soon. He'd make sure of it.

* * * * *

Charlie set the plane down soft as a feather landing on a pillow. Wrapped in a blanket in back of the plane, Kathryn appreciated the effort. Even turning her head was a painful exercise. Every joint and muscle, every tendon and ligament had been stretched or twisted beyond endurance. The beating hadn't helped either. She barely hung onto consciousness as every bump and jiggle shot intense pain through something. But she needed to see Rem. Although she knew he could handle an unsuspecting Marco, she needed to actually see him to be sure.

Charlie swung the door open and lowered the steps. Rem bound up them, shot past him with a grunt and headed straight for Kathryn. Dropping to his knees beside her, he reverently framed her face with gentle hands. "I love you, Kathryn," he breathed into her sleepy eyes.

All she could manage was a weak smile back at him. Jackson had given her a painkiller to help her endure the traveling. Now, finally, she let it overcome her in deep rest. Rem kissed her closed eyelids reverently and was grateful she'd be oblivious for the rough trip back to the villa.

He lifted her tenderly and carried his precious cargo to the Jeep. Charlie grinned at him, but didn't comment on the tears streaming down Rem's harsh face. A man had a right to some emotions in a situation like this.

"I need some R&R," Charlie stated as he drove them to the villa. "That little nap the bastard gave us didn't do me a bit of good."

Rem laughed at him. Charlie could ride his adrenaline-high from the recent takedown to China and back. He didn't need sleep. He was assigned to hang around and make sure Rem and Kathryn would handle this. If Kathryn had injures they didn't know about or slipped into a coma, they needed to get stateside in a hurry. Or, if Rem couldn't deal with it, someone else would be nearby. No man left behind. They would watch over both of them until everyone was convinced this was over.

"Where's Tammy?" Rem questioned.

"Insisted on going with Miguel to Miami, Miguel liked that idea. He did the wounded act for her benefit convincingly so she'd go with them. Don't worry. Gray and Miguel will make sure she gets all the help she needs," Charlie assured him.

Miguel was an amazing actor when he wanted to be. The only reason he'd put on the pitiful act was to convince Tammy to come with him. That way he could be sure she got over the trauma of the last few hours. He'd see she received counseling support if she needed it. It also released Rem to concentrate on Kathryn's needs.

Rem smiled. "Anyone babysitting them?"

"Yeah. Gray said something about Miguel doing his convalescence with Prin and him at their place. Tammy will have a sweet female around if she needs her. Don't worry. Baby Sister is being looked after. She's even going to think it's all her idea to go with Miguel.

"What about the water at the house?" Charlie questioned.

"The house has a well, also," Rem answered. "Most houses here don't so the bastard didn't know about it. I switched over and left all the faucets open to flush the pipes. I'll have a company come in to drain and clean the cistern in a few days."

They were back at the villa now. Rem carried Kathryn straight to his room. He called back to Charlie over his shoulder. "There's a test kit on the kitchen counter. If the shit is washed out, shut off the faucets, will ya? I'll see you tomorrow."

Rem laid Kathryn down gently on his bed. Quickly, he retrieved several wet washcloths from the bathroom and cleaned her sleeping form. Carefully, every bit of blood and dirt was removed. Then he rubbed liniment into each muscle and joint to ease the pain. He paid special attention to shoulders and hip joints. Her hair was braided carefully so if she moved in her sleep it wouldn't pull.

Finally able to crawl in beside her, Rem was afraid to pull her into his arms. It might hurt her innumerable bruises. If she hadn't been asleep, the silk sheet would irritate her abused skin. He lay there and watched her sleep as the sun climbed over the horizon. He needed sleep. She needed him at full capacity when she woke up. Rem closed his eyes and willed himself into a light, battlefield type of sleep. Never fully unconscious, always marginally aware of any movement she might make. It would probably be a very long time before he could stop guarding her every second.

Kathryn's tortured moans woke him. Her body jerked and twitched through the nightmare.

"Oh, baby, don't. Please don't," Rem begged as he kissed her face tenderly. "Don't go there with him. I'm here, baby.

You'll never be alone again. Come back to me. Be here with me." His gentle pleas woke her.

Tired eyes opened to his worried face. Kathryn moaned softly at the effort as she smiled. "My hero," she whispered softly. "Always with you."

His lips touched hers gently, glazing across her face with butterfly kisses.

"Bathroom, please. Can't move," Kathryn mumbled.

"It's okay. I've got you. I'm afraid this will hurt, baby. Take another pain pill before we try this." Rem reached to the nightstand for the pill and bottle of water.

Kathryn swallowed gratefully and let him fuss over her a few more minutes.

"Got to go now, Rem," she muttered, but didn't bother to open her eyes. Rem scooped her up—he had to lock his jaw as she sucked in a deep breath through the pain. They strode into the bathroom and he sat her on the toilet. Rem knelt to hold her up and she laid her head on his shoulder, still not opening her eyes. It was a good thing. It cost him too much to watch her struggle with the pain to do such a simple task. Her silent endurance tore new places in his heart. His face was a mirror of her struggle and he knew he couldn't hide it.

"Do you want to go back to bed, baby?" Rem asked when she finished. "We could take a quick shower if you want." He knew he'd cleaned her thoroughly last night. Yet a need to wash off the disgusting experience would be heavy in her mind. The tub was out because of the deep lacerations in her ankles and wrists. She couldn't manage a shower on her own, but he'd stay in the shower with her for hours if that was what she needed to feel clean.

Kathryn turned her face up to him and tried to smile again. "You washed me last night, didn't you?"

"Yes. From head to toes," Rem confirmed fiercely. "There's not a scrap of his filth on you, honey. But you need to feel clean. You need to experience it for yourself. I understand that. You won't have to do anything but sit on the stool, I'll wash every inch of you as many times as you like."

"It's okay, Rem. It's okay because I know you took care of it." She caressed his worried face once with her hand. "Take me back to bed, please."

That's when he knew he had her. She'd really given him all of herself, her trust and her faith. She'd gifted him with her very being. If he said a thing was done, it was done.

The gift of her trust sent slow, embracing warmth curling through him. It lit dark corners of doubt and fear and gave him some small peace. In the back of his mind, he'd been afraid. Afraid this experience would drive her from him. Make her see him as a reminder. Perhaps be twisted in some way since he witnessed everything with her. With one phrase, she released him from that fear. She took the hideous event and made it something they would live through together. She bent it to bind them in ways only survivors could understand. Trust was her most precious gift, one he knew meant more than any love words could possibly convey.

Rem kissed her forehead and carried her back to bed. "I need to rub some more of this stuff on you." He held up the liniment oil. "And we have to change your bandages. All right, baby? That pain pill kicked in yet?"

"Be gentle with me. I'm spun glass, you know," Kathryn whispered.

Rem barked out a laugh at her gentle ribbing. Humor from her was a miracle. Humor meant her mind would deal with this. Humor meant this amazing woman wanted and accepted him for who he was and what he brought to the relationship. Oh, god, he loved her sharp tongue.

Two days later Rem carried Kathryn into the den where Charlie was about to fall off the couch laughing.

Kathryn could walk just fine. Rem couldn't put her down. She let him carry her all he wanted. The thing between them had its roots in touching, holding. Both of them needed it, but she suspected he needed it more.

He still felt his failure to protect her deep in his soul. The truth was, knowing the facts and accepting them were two different things for him. Intellectually he knew it was not his fault. He couldn't know every possible method someone might use to get to a target. All the training in the world could not prepare a man for absolutely every eventuality. Yet it had happened while he guarded her, which would mark him for a very long time.

She knew he had nightmares about it. Kathryn's nightmares ended that first night. Rem healed her in ways that went beyond this one event. Horrible and ugly as it was, he and the unit coming for Tammy and herself put something back in place for Kathryn. It freed her to trust, to believe in impossible dreams again. It wiped out a lifetime and replaced it with this magnificent man. He didn't fully realize the extent of her recovery yet. He would eventually.

She'd accepted the betrayal of Jonathan and Marcos for the ugly thing it was. Over the years her exposure to Tammy's family had shown her what real caring was. It had been a slow process she hadn't even been aware of until the moment she realized who was under the mask of her kidnapper. Then the truth had been stunningly clear. Every action of those two was revealed in glaring relief. Her impoverished soul had seen them as men they'd never been. Each kindness they'd shown her was simply a method of binding her to them as a victim.

They'd know exactly what they were doing and preyed on her needy ignorance. What they'd offered her had not been real affection or acceptance. Now she saw their supposed kindness as the ugly use of a young woman. That realization might have been even more damaging if it hadn't come at a moment when she'd accepted the iron-clad certainty that Rem would come for her. The unit was an extension of himself. She understood the bond between these men clearly. She saw it more clearly than most women could.

She knew he needed to care for her, tend her. Somehow make up for the fact that it had ever happened to her. Being big about letting him fuss over her was a sacrifice Kathryn felt willing to make. She laughed and kidded him often, but not when it counted. Not when the pain leapt fresh and harsh in his eyes. With time, as the marks faded from her skin under his gentle care, he would gain the strength to accept that it had been out of his control.

She hoped it wouldn't take too long for Rem to forgive himself. But until then, if he needed to carry her, he could. Letting her out of his sight hadn't even been considered yet. It would come in time. Her big warrior would get over it.

"What the hell?" Rem questioned Charlie.

Charlie couldn't talk so he just pointed at the TV screen. CNN was on and they were doing a story on the mysterious disappearance of a prominent strip club owner. Kathryn frowned while Rem started grinning.

The story told how the club owner mysteriously disappeared on the same night both of his American clubs burned to the ground. No one was injured at either site. The cops could find no evidence of arson except for the fact both clubs burned at exactly the same time. These disturbing events were being attributed to a shadowy mob figure known only as Sweetheart. Sweetheart was an associate of the club owner and a frequent customer in both the Miami and Atlanta clubs. On the condition of anonymity, sources have confirmed that the club owner agreed to testify against Sweetheart in a highly secretive State Department investigation.

"What? Who's Sweetheart and how did he get involved?" Kathryn demanded.

Rem sat down on the couch and tucked her in beside him. "It's a long story. But here's the short version. A couple years ago Miguel and I were on a deep-cover mission in Miami. We came upon an overturned school bus in a canal. We got all the kids out, but by the time we finished, the press had shown up. Miguel, an amazing mimic, went into his Tony The Mobster impression to protect our cover. All I had to do was stick my gun in the front of my pants and act like muscle. Even called him 'boss' a couple times in sentences that involved, 'You want I should break da camera, boss?'

"He convinced the reporter not to take pictures and that he didn't need anyone to know about his good deed. He did it in a heavy Jersey accent with a lot of nose rubbing and hand twitching. It was the funniest thing I ever saw. The reporter bought it and wrote up this glowing article about the bad guys with hearts of gold. Made superhuman heroes out of us. The AP picked it up and the story went global.

"The mob didn't deny it because it made them look so good. Made romantic figures of them again. The State Department couldn't admit they had no idea who the heavy hitter was. Or even where he was. So Sweetheart was born. Miguel only uses him when we have to. It's damn dangerous to tiptoe between those two organizations.

"This time it's perfect again. The mob will neither confirm nor deny the guy because he made them look superhuman again. It puts an elegant twist on their kind of muscle. No bodies lying about, but a really powerful visual of what happens when you go against them. Blaster must have had a party doing this one. The State Department can't admit they know nothing about this guy because they'd look stupid. So, there you have it. All nice and tidy."

"Good Lord," Kathryn grinned. "You guys are scary. How many times has the news been your cover story? And if you do it, don't a lot of others? Shit!" she breathed as the enormity of what she said dawned on her.

Rem and Charlie grinned at her. "It's why we do what we do, darlin'. Not everyone has to know what's going on out there. Just some of us."

Epilogue

෩

Two days before Christmas Rem took Kathryn back to the ranch. In the three weeks at the island, most of her bruises had faded. The lacerations on her wrists and ankles were only thin lines, which were healing nicely. His folks insisted they return for Christmas. They were deeply shocked at the events since they'd been away and needed to see their children and Kathryn for themselves. It was a parent's response that could not be denied.

Shortly after they returned, Rem's father cornered him on the other side of the kitchen from the women. "I take it the story your mother and I heard was the abbreviated version?" Robert Morgan questioned his son seriously.

"Yeah. The details are something Kathryn will have to tell you if she wants to." Rem rubbed his neck and glanced quickly across the kitchen to where Kathryn and his mother chatted at the table. He still struggled with being able to let her out of his sight.

"Is she going to be all right, son? Is there anything more we can do?" Robert pressed.

Rem smiled. "Dad, if I could think of another thing to do for her. I'd do it. I think she's going to smack me if I make one more suggestion. Actually, out of the three of us she's dealt with it better than anyone."

"That was my next question. I know how Tammy is, mostly because Miguel gave us a call last night. But how are you?" Robert wanted to know.

"I'll get there," Rem murmured as his eyes moved back to Kathryn. "What did Miguel say?"

"He's worried about Tammy. Says she needs time to work this out and wanted to assure us she wouldn't be alone. He's bringing her down tomorrow. Miguel said she's changed. He wanted us to be aware of it. He was concerned because the questions people naturally want to ask her seem to drive her into some sort of shell." Both men sighed. "She blames herself for all of it. He's afraid she's let it affect her in ways that might not be healthy. He wanted us to know he hasn't been able to get her into counseling yet. She's refused. It's his number one priority though. But she has to want it, too."

Just then Kathryn looked up and smiled at Rem. Immediately he moved to sit beside her, his big body almost curved around her as he draped an arm around the back of her chair. "Honey, do you need a rest?" Rem asked as he nuzzled her ear.

"Good grief, Rem. I'm not an invalid," Kathryn complained and laughed. "Almost as good as new. Besides, it's Christmas. We've got shopping to do." Both men groaned as the women laughed.

"If you don't want to take me, I'm sure your mother and I will do fine," Kathryn offered.

"No, no, no. I'll take you. But tomorrow after a good night's sleep," Rem insisted.

"Oh, so it's like that, is it? This rock on my finger gives you the right to regulate every minute of my life?" Kathryn asked in mock seriousness.

Rem leaned over and pulled her more fully against him with an arm around her waist. His mouth swooped down to meet hers forcefully. Her lips opened at his insistence and his tongue plunged deep. His wicked invasion intimately stroked sensitive tissue as he sucked her tongue into his mouth. He kissed her until she melted into him and wrapped her arms around his neck. He kissed her deeply until she forgot their audience, their surroundings, everything but the pulsing passion rising from his touch. Rem pulled back and grinned into her bemused face.

"No. That's what gives me the right," his gravely voice asserted.

"Beast!" Kathryn glanced up at his parents and blushed as she pulled away from him and tried to sit in her own seat. Rem lifted her easily to sit her across his lap in a familiar gesture for them. Both parents smiled.

"Perhaps he's right, dear," Rem's mother agreed gently. "You can make him spend all day in the mall tomorrow." The sly smile she shared with Kathryn spoke of female bonding well underway.

"You're such a help, Mom," Rem groaned.

* * * * *

Early Christmas morning Rem felt Kathryn slip out of bed. He opened one eye and noted the sun was just about to peek over the horizon and the closed bathroom door. Both eyes open now, he frowned darkly at the closed door and waited.

Yesterday's workout at the mall should have been included in Special Forces training. He wasn't sure they had anything close to approximating the endurance required to do one day of Christmas shopping with your lover. It was too damn early to be up after that marathon! Kathryn was fully recovered, no question after the way she drove him yesterday.

The closed door irritated him. He liked it much better when he had a good excuse to keep an eye on her at all times. Logically he knew she was fine. Emotionally he needed to physically see her. Of course, it was almost exactly four weeks since the party where this all started. He supposed it was about time she should want some privacy. He just couldn't bring himself to even pretend he didn't mind.

Finally, she emerged and smiled sleepily at him as she crawled back into bed.

"You all right, honey?" Rem asked and cuddled her back into his side.

"Fine," she mumbled into his chest and closed her eyes.

They lay there quietly as he caressed her back with an arm around her and stared up at the ceiling. Just having her out of his sight that long disturbed him enough to bring him fully awake.

"Merry Christmas, Rem." Kathryn smiled, as she realized exactly why he wasn't sleeping.

"Merry Christmas, love." Rem kissed the top of her head.

"You know I love you?" Kathryn rested her chin on her hand over his heart as she looked up into his handsome face.

Rem smiled down into her serious little face. "Yeah, but it's nice every time you say it."

She laughed softly and added, "Not letting me out of your sight yesterday made it really hard to get you a present."

"I've got what I want, honey. You, 24/7. Can't think of anything else I need," Rem murmured.

"Well, I still do have something for you." Kathryn grinned slyly.

Rem's brows climbed his forehead. "Oh, yeah? That look makes me wonder if it's a good thing."

"That depends on you." Kathryn dropped a kiss on his chest, which elicited a growl from Rem. His hands went from lazy caresses to sensual exploration.

"Afraid to tell me?" his voice dropped low as he gently turned them both so he leaned over her gloriously naked body. His hands glided over her breasts to pluck up her nipples. He had a deep fascination with those tempting mounds. His fingers circled the stiffened tips and stroked them as they stood up for him.

"Not afraid...you're no help, though. Who can think when you do that?" Kathryn moaned as his mouth enveloped a pouting peak, suckling hard. Her back arched off the bed for him and he slid an arm under her to keep her just like that. All perked up and presented for his pleasure. Her nipple popped out of his mouth as Rem grinned into her passion-glazed eyes.

"Am I starting something we can't finish?" Rem asked.

"Huh?" Kathryn was too dazed to care what he said.

"You were in the bathroom a long time. It's been about four weeks. I just thought, you know, period, no sex?" Rem questioned.

"Ah. Oh, no. Well, eight and a half months from now I probably won't want to. But now it's fine." Kathryn gasped as her hands glided down his body.

Rem froze. The grin faded from his face as he stared at her. "Eight and, ah, half months? Eight and a half months?" His voice rose as he repeated the phrase. "What? Are you sure?"

Kathryn laughed at his consternation. "Yeah, yelling isn't going to change it, Rem."

Rem sprang out of the bed and landed on his feet beside it. You'd think she'd burned him. As the full implications of her statement rolled over him, panic edged his voice. "Are you okay? Do you need anything? Are you sure?"

Giggling up at the nearly frantic, magnificently naked man, Kathryn pointed to the bathroom. "Go look for yourself. The test is beside the sink."

Rem whirled and rushed into the bathroom. Kathryn lay there and waited a full five minutes before he emerged again. She couldn't help laughing at the dazed, beaming face that reappeared.

"As I said, Merry Christmas, darling." She smiled up into his wondering eyes as he stood over her again. He just stood there and gazed down at her in astonishment.

"This can't be that much of a surprise, Rem. We talked about it. Remember?" Kathryn gently reminded him.

Rem sank to his knees by the bed as his hands moved reverently over her face. He leaned down and kissed her. "Merry Christmas, my love," he whispered as he pressed his cheek to hers. "Thank you, thank you, thank you... What the... Oh, God! I think I'm going to be sick." Again, he jumped up and rushed to the bathroom. The man who came out a few minutes later was pale.

This time Kathryn was out of bed and met him halfway across the room. She slipped an arm around his waist and led him to the bed. She carefully sat him down on the edge. "Are you all right, Rem? What's wrong? Are you sick? Did you eat something bad yesterday?" Her concerned questions almost matched his earlier tone.

Rem pulled her between his legs as she stood in front of him. His big hand tenderly spread across her lower tummy to span her from hipbone to hipbone. In slow motion, he bent forward and rested his cheek against her abdomen. Kathryn combed her fingers through his hair in an attempt to soothe him.

"Baby, I'm fine. Well, sort of. Sorry about that. Won't happen again. How do you feel?" he mumbled into her stomach.

"Better than you, apparently. Are you okay with this? I mean. When we talked about it at the island I thought…well, I thought you would be happy," Kathryn trailed off sadly.

Rem's head shot up as he realized she thought he was sick because he didn't want the baby. He grabbed her shoulders and held her firmly so they looked directly into each other's eyes.

"Kathryn, I love you more than life. I want this baby more than that. It terrifies me. It terrifies me as a man because I didn't protect you. I couldn't live with it if I somehow could not protect our child." He lifted a finger to her lips as she started to interject. She subsided and he continued.

"I know, honey. I know it's something I have to get over. There's nothing I want more than you and the sweet angel tucked under your heart, Kathryn. Don't ever doubt it." He folded her into his arms and held her gently. "I love you, Kathryn. I need you. Those things will never change. I wish I knew how to thank you for the best Christmas present a man could have.

"But do me a favor," Rem continued seriously. "Try not to laugh at me too much and don't tell the guys. It looks like I'm one of those guys who'll have the morning sickness with you." He dashed off to the bathroom again while she sank down on the bed laughing.

"You'd better feel up to finishing what you started, big boy," Kathryn called after him. "Somebody got me all hot and bothered in here. Cravings are very important to pregnant women! We can't control them, you know. My silence is contingent on sexual satisfaction at the moment."

On the island Rem hadn't made love to her for a week after the event. When Kathryn finally had enough of that, she'd attacked him. Aggressively pushing him to assert his dominance again. Forcing him to see those horrid hours had no bearing on their life. He'd laughed at her afterward, shaking his head. Both of them knew they needed to get back to being who they were. If it changed them, they were giving Jonathan power, even from the grave.

As Rem stepped back in the bedroom he was confronted by the sight of Kathryn lying on the bed, her legs spread wide, both hands between them. Rem crawled up the bed from the bottom, his eyes trained on the pink cunt her slender fingers were investigating. He stretched out between her legs on his stomach, resting his chin on the heel of his palm about six inches from the fascinating show.

Just looking at her like this filled his soul to overflowing. Loving her fed him in ways mysterious and intense, simple and direct. She saw in him the man he hoped he was. Then she gave him herself so fully she stole his breath with her splendor.

Before him lay a moaning wanton who pleasured herself in wicked abandon. Exposing her most intimate self to him fearlessly. He could barely keep from drooling as her fingers held flushed cunt lips open for the delicate explorations of the other hand. His eyes feasted on the lovely vision she presented as two fingers slipped inside her. He could see her body clench down on those digits as they stroked in and out. It was too much, he needed her taste.

Dragging his tongue down her inner thigh he licked his way to her dripping cunt. Licking around the fingers slicing in and out until she pulled them out and held them for him to suckle. He slurped them into his mouth, sucking avidly. His tongue pressed between them to gather every drop of her. Done with her fingers, his face sank down to the source of his delight. She held herself open for him.

He worshiped her. There was no other word for the reverence with which he paid homage to each precious pink fold. Then as his tongue entered her depths, his eyes closed and a low rumbling purr vibrated up his chest. He wasn't even aware of it as his tongue plunged into her. The purr sent an unexpected tremor through Kathryn's body, jerking her pelvis into his face.

Rem responded by sliding his hands under her ass and held her pressed into his face as the purring became louder interspersed with low growls. He ate his cunt avidly now with animal intensity. This was his—his woman, his cunt, his world. They'd almost been taken from him. In this moment as the reality of having placed his seed within his woman broke over him, something dark and elemental emerged from the depths of his soul.

It was the pure deadly warrior. The one he'd held under control for so long. That part of him he'd tried to "civilize" over. There would be no holding back anymore. Gray called it his animal spirit and had once told him it was the Florida Panther. Rem knew the world Gray walked was sometimes unexplainable, but he'd never experienced it. Now the powerful beast washed over him and he understood it. This part of him that was forever feral and wild would guard his woman, his child. This was the part of him that had known exactly who and what the threat was, from the beginning. Long ago the beast within had claimed her as his mate. It had been willing to kill at every turn. It would kill now if anything threatened the sacred circle of his family. Fear and doubt faded away as he welcomed the beast into his entire being.

Accepting that part of him was a necessity now. There was too much to lose. The snarling big cat within would never allow a threat in his territory to remain unanswered. Releasing the beast to guard and protect at all times ensured his family's protection in ways the civilized man could never do. He accepted that his mate might not like it all the time, but it was no longer negotiable. Her safety and the safety of their children came first.

Children? Rem stilled on the inside and listened with his entire being. He could clearly feel Kathryn's spirit winding around his, but there was more — faint, flickering, two distinct others with them. One female and hesitant while the other only slightly stronger seemed to shield his sister. Male. Son and daughter. Knowledge and welcome flooded his soul. The big purring beast within acknowledged and accepted them in simple joy. Assuring the small ones there was nothing to harm them, ever. The knowing could not be said in words, but could not be denied in spirit. It simply was.

Finally he understood the change that had come over Gray after he'd claimed Prin. The man merged with the raw power of the predator was the only way they could face the world at they knew it. Fierce warriors who'd seen exactly what the world dished out had no other option for handling the intense emotions associated with a family.

Kathryn's body shuddered under his mouth as she came with mewing moans. Rem smiled into his sweet kitten's cunt and kept drinking her. She'd start begging soon and he'd give her what she wanted. But this time something was different.

As her moaning turned to pleas for him to enter her, he deftly flipped her over. Guiding her knees up, he spread her wide while ensuring her tender abdomen was not crushed in any way. He pressed the head of his cock to her opening. One hand held her hip while the other snaked around her to spread over her flat belly and hold his children. Baring his teeth in a snarl of satisfaction he pushed into her tight channel slowly, forcing them both to feel every inch of his invasion as his body claimed her.

With unhurried, careful purpose he pulled out and repeated the process. Balanced on his knees behind her, he allowed none of his body weight to rest on her as he fucked his woman and cradled her precious gift in his hand. Kathryn begged, pleaded with him for more, harder, faster. Her only answer was the low purring growl as he continued to torture her with the steady, deep thrust of his body. His hand on her hip held her under him giving her no option but to accept the pleasure. It restrained her attempts to thrust back on him.

It went on and on, pushing her higher and higher. Kathryn surrendered to his relentless caress with a sobbing gasp. Each steady invasion drove her slowly and insidiously past the point of reason. Flooding her entire body with an elemental fire that gathered strength and intensity like nothing she'd ever felt before. Tears streamed out of her eyes as the pleasure teetered on the edge of pain. He held her there, demanding she fly higher than she'd ever gone before. Finally she screamed out her release as her body shuddering into soul-wrenching release.

His body pulled back and slammed into her hard, a single time, as he joined her at the edge of the universe. His roar of completion thundered around the room while powerful jets of seed emptied into her body. Both their trembling bodies glistened with sweat in the early morning sunlight as he sank to the bed beside her collapsed form. His hand was still spanning her belly between her and the mattress.

Kathryn rolled over beside him and stared up at the ceiling in slightly stunned shock. The long intensity of their lovemaking overwhelmed her. His arm was now beneath her, curved around her waist and again his palm rested across her lower abdomen. In gentle, almost undetectable moves he caressed her as they both regained the ability to breathe normally. Slowly becoming aware of the soothing petting she glanced at him.

His eyes were closed and there an almost imperceptible smile on his lips. She realized she'd never seen him look so completely relaxed. Certainly not since the kidnapping and never before that she could remember.

"Rem, what are you doing?" she asked as his fingers started tracing patterns around her navel.

"Playing with the children," he murmured softly.

"Children? I'm having a baby, it's usually called the child," she corrected mildly as she analyzed the subtle change, which seemed to have come over him.

Rem chuckled and heavy-lidded eyes opened to gaze down at her. He rolled over on his side so his head rested on the palm of the hand that had been wrapped around her while the other hand continued the finger-play on her lower belly.

He smiled at her then leaned down to place a gentle kiss on either side of her navel. Rising back to look in her face his grin was huge.

"You can wait for the sonogram, little mommy, but you'd better be thinking up two names," he assured her as shock spread across her face.

"Twins?" she breathed as her eyes rounded. "How can you possibly know that? That's just mean, Rem." Her tone changed to scolding. "What if there's not? Then we'll be disappointed." Her hand covered his over her belly, stilling it. He swiftly switched with her and pressed her hand gently into her abdomen.

"Say hello to your son and daughter, little mommy." His purring chuckle was undeterred by her scolding. "And if you don't believe me, I'll take you over to visit Winter Eagle this afternoon. Gray's grandfather will tell you the same thing."

Kathryn's mouth opened in that stunned "O". She knew about Gray's grandfather. Knew he saw things in ways most did not understand. Rem's certainty and his willingness to back up his knowledge with the Seer convinced her. Along with the indefinable change in him that spoke of unshakable confidence.

Rem swooped down to claim the expression, which had always jolted him intimately, but he still couldn't help laughing into her mouth. The kiss was a playful eating at each other as Kathryn realized an even bigger shock. Her Knight in Shining Armor was back. The change in him was complete. For her, all the silly, little girl dreams were true. He would give them to her on a gilded platter if she let him and keep digging into her soul 'til he found each and every wish she'd ever had.

Tears were streaming down her face when he lifted his head. "What?" he demanded as panic flooded his system at the sight. "Are you hurt? Is something wrong?" His hand hovered over her abdomen, his entire body tightened and almost vibrated with volatile emotion.

Smiling at him through the tears she caressed his cheek. "No, Sweet Prince," Kathryn murmured. "This is liquid joy. Pregnant women cry all the time. Get used to it."

Rem searched her face a moment longer then suddenly relaxed, he buried his face in the pillow beside her head and groaned like a wounded animal. "You are going to kill me with this, aren't you?" he moaned pitifully.

Before she could answer his head jerked up, he jackknifed off the bed and dashed into the bathroom, cursing like the hardened combat veteran he was the whole way. Kathryn watched this display in consternation until she heard the retching. Rolling onto her stomach she buried her head in the pillow to muffle her peals of laughter as Rem suffered another bout of morning sickness for her.

It was Christmas Morning in every way possible.

Enjoy An Excerpt From
JAMIE'S CHERUB

Copyright © GAIL FAULKNER, 2005.

All Rights Reserved, Ellora's Cave Publishing, Inc.

✥

Jamie MacKelvin ambled into the lovely old colonial church and glanced around. It was the right address, but there was only one live body visible and she was dangerously perched atop a tall ladder at the front. The ceiling wasn't vaulted as high as some of the more modern structures but, still, it was too high for the little human up there with no one holding her ladder. As he silently moved down the aisle, his appreciation grew for the enticing cherub industriously hanging filmy stuff up above the altar. There was a heavy scent of lemon wood soap wafting off the rows of pews, blinding his sense of smell for a few seconds before he neared her.

She was ridiculously high to be leaning over like that. He would have frowned if the position hadn't given him a look at the sweetest ass he'd ever seen. It was plump and round and, well, something about it required he squeeze it. Then she twisted to grab another do-dad from the tray on top of the ladder and he froze. As much from fear any distraction would startle her as from the heart-stopping view she now gave him. In that bent and twisted position, her waist disappeared and she was all tits and ass.

Saints preserve us! Her breasts were all the ass was and more. Much more. The heavy, round globes strained her tank top and threatened to spill out as she grabbed her item and swung back around. Didn't the little daredevil realize how dangerous it was to swing that much weight around up there? The ladder shifted and he used his inherent speed to silently race up the aisle to grab it. She leaned over toward the wall once more and continued her task.

In the dash to the ladder the beast within inhaled deeply and knowledge exploded through his body. Mate! His unbelieving eyes widened in shock as he dragged in more air. Her passionflower scent was a full-bodied aroma that wrapped its heady fragrance around him with mouth-watering temptation. It kicked him in the groin as it unfolded into the long-searched-for promise.

His hands closed over the ladder rails and he felt every molecule of his body expand. The urge to howl was barely bitten back as he looked up at the only female who could complete him. Searching for her had taken almost four human lifetimes. Finding her here unexpectedly rocked him to the pit of the dark wolf he was. The astonishing fact that she was endangering her life atop this ladder enraged him. She was the most precious female on Earth! Didn't she know she had no business taking her luscious self up on such a dangerous thing as a tall ladder?

From below, the visual she presented was lush curves and an indistinct face. However, her scent was all the identification he needed, the woman was his in every way that mattered. A priceless gift he'd treasure until he died. There atop that ladder stood every wish and hopeless daydream a lone wolf could ever have.

Containing the whirlwind of emotion she ignited in him, he cleared his throat to get her attention in the most civilized way he could manage right now. She jerked as he'd expected and would have tipped the whole thing over if he'd not been holding it.

"Oh!" Her breath whooshed out as she looked down at him and clutched the top of the ladder for balance.

The tall man below her with shoulder-length, rippling black hair should have looked effeminate with his deep blue eyes and perfectly sculpted features. Long black lashes could be seen even from a distance as he gazed up at her. Emma almost felt dizzy as she gazed into the clear blue eyes those lashes framed. The stunning eyes were part of a face whose strong features were stamped with rugged male beauty. His square chin was tilted up showing her the corded neck and a tuft of black hair curling out of his casual shirt. From her angle, all she could see was his face and impossibly wide shoulders. But it was enough to send a little shiver of appreciation through her loins.

"What in the name of—" he was forced to pause as her beautiful face registered for the first time "—ah, what are you doing up there?" he demanded, muscles flexing to control impending catastrophe.

It wasn't really a strain for him, the power thundering through his body at that moment could have lifted a Mack Truck. Mate! His body surged with heat, need and overwhelming strength. She triggered every one of his primal instincts, producing a dizzying rush of adrenaline. Pressed against his belt buckle was the part of him that insisted it needed her most. He'd not been this hard in public since he was a pup.

"Hello," she beamed at him with a radiant smile. "I'm just finishing up here. You must be looking for Jack MacKelvin."

Cheerful green eyes twinkled in an angel's face, framing her expression was a mass of sable hair held back in a haphazard ponytail. Loose curls escaped the confines of her hair band, surrounding slightly flushed cheeks. A pert little nose sat above the most edible set of lips he'd ever seen. 'Course it didn't really matter what she looked like to a wolf. It was simply another thing to drive him insane at this point.

"All the guys are already out back. The groom's dinner is going to be a bar-b-que so they're doing the pit. Just through there—" she pointed to the left " —and out the back door."

He stared at her blankly, absorbing her into his world. The wild rush of possessive anger he'd felt over his mate being perched atop a wobbly ladder seemed to fall out the back of his brain as he looked up at the adorable goddess.

Her figure was full and the most hedonistic, sexy thing he'd ever seen. There wasn't an inch of her that wouldn't be a pleasure to squeeze, lick or pet. She'd melt into a male like thick cream flows over hard chocolate. Oh, Jesus, thinking about her and cream was a mistake. His body clenched even tighter as he floundered through that thought.

"How'd you know who I was looking for?" he asked dumbly, mostly to keep her talking while he absorbed her scent and analyzed it. She was human, fully human. That was a shock, but immediately dismissed as unimportant next to the fact he'd found his mate. Nothing mattered when weighed against that.

"You're big, beautiful and male. You've got to be one of the groom's men. As I said, they are all right through there." She pointed again, her fingers flicking to move him in the right direction.

Emma could appreciate all of the beautiful male below her, but he seemed a bit dense. What did she expect when he was a poster child for the "Mr. Wet My Panties" club? She had far too much to do to worry about Lost and Handsome's inability to figure out direction.

"Yes, ma'am. I won't be going through there until you're off this ladder." He responded to her shooing motion. Tightening his grip on the ladder, he braced his legs as she turned again to pick up another pretty piece to attach to the arrangement over the altar.

"Don't mind me," she called down as she worked swiftly. "This is almost done. Go on and have some fun." *Yep, dense, she mused to herself.*

"Certainly. As soon as you're done." Jamie responded, recognizing she wasn't about to come down. Little angel had no idea he'd never be leaving her again.

From

⚜Cerrídwen Press⚜

Enjoy An Excerpt From
BLACKWIND: SEAN AND BRONWYN
Book 1 in a two-book series

Copyright © CHARLOTTE BOYETT-COMPO, 2005.

All Rights Reserved, Ellora's Cave Publishing, Inc.

He was sitting at the lunch counter when Bronnie entered. He did not look at her as she took the seat beside him. "We'll have trouble with your mother and father," he said, poking his straw up and down in his Cherry Coke.

Bronnie nodded. "You may be right."

"I know I am and you know it, too."

She swiveled her stool to face him. "How does that make you feel, Sean?"

He turned his gaze fully upon her. "It doesn't matter. I'm used to people telling me what I can and can't do. What I can and can't have."

"What is it you want?"

He smiled. "To be with you."

Bronwyn blushed and ducked her head. "I want to be with you, too."

"We'll be together one day, Bronnie. I swear."

She looked at his unsmiling face. "Do you believe in destiny?"

He leaned his arms against the counter. "I believe what is meant to be will be."

"So you think you and I were meant to meet?"

"As surely as the wind blows, a *ghrá mo chroí*."

Bronnie grinned. "That's Gaelic."

"Aye. Do you know what it means?"

"*Chroí* means heart," she replied, proud of her knowledge.

"*Ghrá* means love," he said softly. "The phrase is 'love of my heart'."

Her eyes widened. "'Love of my heart.'"

"As you will always be," he said, holding her gaze.

She folded her hands in her lap. "I love you, too."

He looked down the counter and his eyes narrowed. "Hey!" he called out. "You have a customer down here. You think you can tear yourself away from lover boy long enough to take her order?"

The waitress turned away from the uniformed Air Force serviceman with whom she was flirting. "Hold your water, sonny. I'm coming!"

"Did you hear me?" Bronnie asked, a little embarrassed by his rudeness to the waitress, but exhilarated by his show of authority. She was not prepared for his answer.

"I have loved you from the moment I saw you. You are mine, Bronwyn McGregor."

A chill went through Bronnie, she shivered. "You think so, do you?"

"You understood that long ago." He glanced at her. "Didn't you tell your mother so?"

"Soul mates," she agreed, liking the sound of the words. "Destined to be together." She didn't question how he knew what she had told her mother, even though another chill traveled down her spine.

He reached out to cup her right cheek. "Never fear me, Bronnie. For as long as we draw breath, I will do everything in my power to keep you safe."

"What can I getcha?" the woman behind the counter asked as she sidled up. Popping her gum, she pulled the order pad from the pocket of her apron.

"A Cherry Coke to go," Sean answered for Bronnie. He wasn't looking at the waitress, but through the front window of the variety store.

"Is my mama staring at us?" Bronnie asked.

"If looks could kill, I'd be a pile of ashes," he said, and turned so he faced the back of the counter.

"Daddy will no doubt have a talk with me tonight," she sighed.

"About the unacceptable company you won't be allowed to keep."

"I don't care what they say, Sean," she said fiercely. "If we have to hide our love, then—"

The waitress came back with Bronnie's drink. "You got a real anxious boyfriend here, sweetie," she said. "He 'bout wore a hole through the glass lookin' for you." She leaned forward, propping her elbows on the counter and affording Sean a good look down the front of her white uniform. "'Course if I had a boy as cute as this one a'waitin' on me, I'd make sure I hurried up to get to 'im." She flicked her tongue across lips.

"Get out of my face," Sean sneered.

"Care to try a woman instead of a little girl, handsome?" the waitress cooed.

Sean glared at the woman, but she just winked at him, laughed and headed back to her serviceman.

"That's what my mama calls a brazen woman, I guess," Bronnie said, her face flaming. She took a long sip of her Cherry Coke.

"That is what your mama would call a whore," Sean countered, digging into the pocket of his jeans for money to pay for Bronnie's drink. He slapped the coins on the counter.

Bronnie didn't reply. She sat there sipping her Coke, her eyes glued to the ice in the cup.

"If I gave you a token of my love for you, would you wear it?" he asked.

Bronnie was stunned, completely unprepared for the question. She stared at him. "Are you serious?"

"Aye, I'm serious, woman."

She turned to look at the nearby jewelry counter where several rows of friendship rings twinkled in the glass case.

"Not one of those," he said irritably. "This."

She looked down at his outstretched palm. Nestled there was an octagonal silver disk, its edges braided with intricately intertwined Celtic knotwork. At the top of the pendant was a trinity triangle—three triangles interlaced into one. Below that were symbols that looked familiar to her.

"It's called a Claddagh," he told her. "This is a very special Celtic wedding amulet."

She cocked her head. "I think my granny has a ring with these symbols on it."

"She most likely does. But this one is one of a kind. It belonged to my grandmother. Her husband was a silversmith and he made it for her for their Joining day."

"What do the symbols mean?" She reached out to trace the engraved hands, heart and crown on the charm.

"Will you accept it?"

She looked into his eyes, her finger still on the charm lying in his palm. "Yes."

"And all that it means?"

"Which is?"

"Put your trust in me, Bronwyn. And know I will never do anything to harm you."

She took a deep, quivering breath. "All right. Yes, I will accept it and all that it means."

"The amulet is silver, for that is the metal of purity to designate love in its purest form. The intertwined knotwork around the edges represents eternity, the linking of our lives through the ages. It was placed there to remind the one who wears it that the love of he who gave it would never end. The unbroken lines of the Trinity Knot triangle symbolize spiritual growth, eternal life and never-ending love. It also symbolizes the Father, Son and Holy Ghost. Celts believe all life is reincarnated, that we are continually re-born after we leave this world. If you love a woman in this life, you will love her in the next."

He took her wrist, turned it, and placed the amulet in her palm. He closed her fingers around it.

"I have bared my heart to you, Bronwyn Fionna McGregor. From my hand into yours do I place it, crowned with my eternal love and devotion." He squeezed her fingers. "Wear my heart close to yours and we will never be apart, for where my heart goes, so will I." Bringing her hand to his lips, he kissed it. "Let love and friendship reign," he whispered.

erridwen, the Celtic Goddess of wisdom, was the muse who brought inspiration to storytellers and those in the creative arts. Cerridwen Press encompasses the best and most innovative stories in all genres of today's fiction. Visit our site and discover the newest titles by talented authors who still get inspired - much like the ancient storytellers did, once upon a time.

Cerridwen Press

www.cerridwenpress.com

Why an electronic book?

We live in the Information Age—an exciting time in the history of human civilization, in which technology rules supreme and continues to progress in leaps and bounds every minute of every day. For a multitude of reasons, more and more avid literary fans are opting to purchase e-books instead of paper books. The question from those not yet initiated into the world of electronic reading is simply: *Why?*

1. *Price.* An electronic title at Ellora's Cave Publishing and Cerridwen Press runs anywhere from 40% to 75% less than the cover price of the exact same title in paperback format. Why? Basic mathematics and cost. It is less expensive to publish an e-book (no paper and printing, no warehousing and shipping) than it is to publish a paperback, so the savings are passed along to the consumer.

2. *Space.* Running out of room in your house for your books? That is one worry you will never have with electronic books. For a low one-time cost, you can purchase a handheld device specifically designed for e-reading. Many e-readers have large, convenient screens for viewing. Better yet, hundreds of titles can be stored within your new library—on a single microchip. There are a variety of e-readers from different manufacturers. You can also read e-books on your PC or laptop computer. (Please note that Ellora's Cave does not endorse any specific brands. You can check our websites at www.ellorascave.com or

www.cerridwenpress.com for information we make available to new consumers.)

3. *Mobility.* Because your new e-library consists of only a microchip within a small, easily transportable e-reader, your entire cache of books can be taken with you wherever you go.

4. *Personal Viewing Preferences.* Are the words you are currently reading too small? Too large? Too… ANNOYING? Paperback books cannot be modified according to personal preferences, but e-books can.

5. *Instant Gratification.* Is it the middle of the night and all the bookstores near you are closed? Are you tired of waiting days, sometimes weeks, for bookstores to ship the novels you bought? Ellora's Cave Publishing sells instantaneous downloads twenty-four hours a day, seven days a week, every day of the year. Our webstore is never closed. Our e-book delivery system is 100% automated, meaning your order is filled as soon as you pay for it.

Those are a few of the top reasons why electronic books are replacing paperbacks for many avid readers.

As always, Ellora's Cave and Cerridwen Press welcome your questions and comments. We invite you to email us at Comments@ellorascave.com or write to us directly at Ellora's Cave Publishing Inc., 1056 Home Avenue, Akron, OH 44310-3502.

THE
⚲ ELLORA'S CAVE ⚲
LIBRARY

Stay up to date with Ellora's Cave Titles in
Print with our Quarterly Catalog.

TO RECIEVE A CATALOG,
SEND AN EMAIL WITH YOUR NAME
AND MAILING ADDRESS TO:

CATALOG@ELLORASCAVE.COM
OR SEND A LETTER OR POSTCARD
WITH YOUR MAILING ADDRESS TO:

CATALOG REQUEST
c/o ELLORA'S CAVE PUBLISHING, INC.
1056 HOME AVENUE
AKRON, OHIO 44310-3502

Got Sex?

Share it with the world or just make a BOLD statement in the bedroom with an Ellora's Cave Got Sex? T-shirt.

got sex?

we do.
ELLORA'S CAVE
Romantica Publishing
www.ellorascave.com

$14.99

The world's largest e-publisher of Erotic Romance.

ELLORA'S CAVE PUBLISHING, INC.
⚿ WWW.ELLORASCAVE.COM ⚿

Discover for yourself why readers can't get enough of the multiple award-winning publisher

Ellora's Cave.

Whether you prefer e-books or paperbacks,

be sure to visit EC on the web at
www.ellorascave.com

for an erotic reading experience that will leave you breathless.